WANTING JUNE

CINDY SIMON

Black Rose Writing

www.blackrosewriting.com

ISBN: 978-1-61296-021-0

PUBLISHED BY BLACK ROSE WRITING

www.blackrosewriting.com

Printed in the United States of America

Wanting June is printed in Cambria

In memory of my mother, Ruth Libert Haley

ACKNOWLEDGMENTS

I am grateful to my mother, Ruth Libert Haley and my father, Albert James Haley who made writing this book possible.

I want to thank Black Rose Writing and Reagan Rothe for publishing my story and their assistance in the process of birthing it to the world.

Thanks to my very good friends Jane, Carolyn, and Claudia for their never waning cheerleading, love and interest.

And a very special heartfelt thanks to my family, Stu, Matt and Bonnie, for their countless hours of editing, listening, supporting and encouraging me every day to keep writing and to keep dreaming!

"Calculating selfishness is the annihilation of self."
—Anton Chekhov

CHAPTER ONE

Kenneth Patrick walked up the three worn wooden steps as if his legs were filled with concrete. Someone was playing the saxophone. Had he left the radio on? He clenched his fists against his thighs and willed the tall pines surrounding his white clapboard house to confide. A few top branches swayed in the soft breeze. It could be a neighbor.

His skin itched. The woolen cloak that was his past was heavy today. Kenneth touched the flask in his jacket pocket. Ten years ago today, June disappeared. He had no choice but to do the same, landing here on Cape Breton Island, in Nova Scotia, Canada.

Kenneth squeezed his blue eyes shut. His wife's thick wavy auburn hair bounced as she did her silly cha-cha dance. Kenneth wanted to put a hand on one of June's round hips to bring her closer but his front door swung open and the jazzy saxophone sounds of Lester Young's "Lady Be Good" made his eyes fly open. He inhaled as though he were diving into deep water. He stumbled over a loose floorboard, reached out a hand to grip the porch railing and the flask of scotch in his jacket pocket banged against his ribs. He swiped at a few of his black and grey curls as they fell across his forehead.

His mother's words returned like a knocking inside of his head, *'It is all about choices Kenny,'* and he staggered through the doorway.

"Still moving like a drunken tortoise." Jazz Martin pounded his back.

"I don't recall sending you an invitation." Kenneth's breath danced in his chest.

"Quite a hole you've dug." Jazz laughed.

"Not deep enough apparently," Kenneth said. He felt sarcasm

ooze through each word as though the letters were porous. Kenneth backed into his kitchen and turned around. He knew why Jazz had come. He took a long swallow from the flask of scotch and then shoved it back into his jacket pocket. The volleyball game with June as the ball had begun *again*.

"You remember?" Jazz grinned like a cat drunk from a bowl of milk. Kenneth groped for the nearest chair as a strong gust of memories threatened to knock down his lanky frame. He shut his blue eyes and immediately the dark red blotch shaped like an island on the carpet appeared before him. The phone cord, a coiled snake around June's body and the receiver was just out of reach of her right hand, which was mashed up against the massive mirrored dresser. Her hair was matted with the same island of burgundy.

"Who took her?" Jazz pummeled him. Kenneth squeezed his eyes tighter.

He had needed a minute. He didn't know someone was in the house. Or that they were waiting. Or that they must have been timing everything? In the bathroom, he had splashed water over and over, until his face was a puddle. He had buried his burning skin into her towel and inhaled. He knew all these moments like the back of his hand. Glancing into the mirror he had seen with sudden clarity the years of secrets, the coercing, and the dangerous triangles he and June had woven. First with Jazz and the experimental work he pushed on them, then with Genieve, June's sister. Her incessant jealous scheming had included introducing Tom to June. Tom had kidnapped June, holding her hostage in some remote Asian village as the prelude to years of threats. Tom had needed June to remain under his control for the work or for his own purposes? Kenneth realized the answer to both meant the same thing.

Kenneth left the bathroom and went back to her. It was like falling from a great height. His breath stuck like a gob of phlegm in the back of his throat. June was gone! An island-shaped blood stain and twisted phone cord lay where only moments ago June had been.

He coughed. Jazz whacked him on the back and the last conversation he had had with June swarmed like a disturbed nest of hornets.

"I have to finish what I started with Jazz," June said. She put one hand on the front doorknob. Kenneth grabbed her arm and tried to pull her into him. Her hand slid off the doorknob but she leaned away from him.

"The risks are," he said. Kenneth shook his head. "Think of the kids." His voice dropped to the floor. "Think of us."

She turned her face to meet his, her eyes were like how he imagined a shark's, black and life-less. She raised her chin a notch. A gesture of defiance their daughter had learned. "You convinced me to do the work with Tom and Jazz, remember?" He stepped back and folded his hands across his chest. She went back to the door.

"Yes, at first, June, listen to me. It's not worth it," he pleaded.

"It has always been worth it to me, don't you see that Kenneth?" Tears slid down her cheeks with each word.

"No I see you choosing Jazz and the work over your family." Over me, he wanted to add but didn't. He knew it wouldn't matter.

"You were the one who infected Jazz with that awful virus. He's spent years searching for a cure. You ignored the warnings about Tom." Her voluminous auburn hair bounced as she spoke.

"His lies," he said. He watched her back as it rose and fell with each breath she took. After a long moment she spoke. Her voice was dull with a deep pain he recognized.

"Are you going to deny your affair with my sister too?" He felt himself shrink into the sandy tiled floor beneath his feet.

"Genieve is far from blameless," he said. "I'm sorry." He delivered the words into the long silence that had followed as he reached for her. "I love you. Let's leave this mess behind us, June." He gripped her soft skin. "Let's start over somewhere, far away, together." Tears glistened in her long dark eyelashes. She shook her head and a shower of cold air clung to his skin long after she closed the door behind her. A few days later she was a red stain island on their bedroom carpet. Kenneth was forced to leave his life in Maryland and disappear just as she had.

"You know we have to clean up this old mess Kenny and I have come up with the perfect plan," Jazz said. He reached into Kenneth's pocket. He unscrewed the cap on the flask of scotch. Kenneth stared into the small opening like it was a portal. The amber liquid, his friend for a long time, beckoned. Jazz brought the bottle closer and Kenneth could smell the scotch but he became distracted by Jazz's large hand wrapped around his old friend.

"Penny wants the truth. So I've decided she will marry Brian in a sort of repeat of you and June, a generational saga." Jazz chuckled. Kenneth swung his body around. The flask tumbled to the ground. Kenneth felt his skin prickle with tiny shards of the glass bottle though it had not shattered *yet*. The unbroken bottle became a muddy river by his feet.

"My daughter will never agree to an arranged marriage!"

"We all have to pay our dues," Jazz said.

"Over my dead body," Kenneth said. He clenched his teeth.

"A fine possibility," Jazz said. He laughed. His cold arrogance pushed all the oxygen out of the room and Kenneth collapsed into an old broken wooden dining room chair.

"What choices, mom?" he whispered.

CHAPTER TWO

"You need the truth as much as Penny does," Jazz said. He gestured across the room to where there was a couch with a variety of cushions and two moss green chairs that looked like they were permanently inhabited by ghosts. Jazz's arm swung around to the old table and mismatched chairs where Kenneth remained sitting.

"I am running out of time." Jazz hooked his fingers in the belt loops of his dark jeans.

"You cannot bribe my daughter, because you're sick with guilt and regrets over the work you imposed." Kenneth held up his palm. "Does this young man Penny has to marry owe you?" Jazz shrugged. Kenneth stabbed the air with his index finger. "You failed June and nothing can ever change that Jazz!"

"The same is true for you Kenny and I disagree. We can change it," Jazz said.

"She is lost," Kenneth shouted.

"It's been ten years today," Jazz said.

"I am well aware of the significance of today! June was lost long before," Kenneth added.

"All the more reason to find her," Jazz said.

"What's the point now?"

"Ever heard of 'the truth will set you free'?" Jazz asked. Kenneth walked to the other side of the room. He looked out the window at the massive evergreen trees.

"I loved her," he said, "You don't know the meaning of the word."

"Debatable, don't you recall who she chose in the end?" Jazz said.

"And on whose conscience her fate rests," Kenneth said. He

felt like a pitcher at a baseball game throwing the next fast ball.

"That would be Tom and Genieve and this small exercise of mine will prove this if you will agree to cooperate," Jazz said. "However if you don't have any desire to clear your name for your kid's sakes than you are more of a coward than I imagined, and know this Kenneth, I will proceed based on your daughter's wishes!" Kenneth felt on fire. Jazz ran a hand through his graying thick blond hair.

"Is that a threat?" he asked. Penny had always had questions he couldn't answer but to believe that she would willingly align with this man? Talk about ridiculous and dangerous.

The stench of this old mess had bothered him for a long while. It affected his relationships with his other two sons, Greg and Sam. He fingered the bottle that had made it back into his pocket and tapped the fingers of his other hand on his thigh.

"Remember Kenny," Jazz murmured near his right ear. "Someone was waiting for you." He paused for a moment. "The day June left *you*." Kenneth felt the knife in his heart twist. A shadow, a figure in the doorway when he swung back around after returning to find June missing, was it an unknown or Genieve? Tom? Or Jazz? This had tortured him for ten years.

Kenneth spun around. A wave of dizziness assaulted him. His stomach heaved. He ran to the kitchen sink, flung his black professor-like glasses aside and splashed cold water over his unshaven face. Leaning his tall, long limbed frame back against the counter he took several deep breaths.

"It's rotting inside you Kenny. Penny suffers with questions about her mother and she called me seeking answers," Jazz said. He looked tall in his small kitchen. Kenneth bowed his head.

"June wanted your help, later on that same day. Remember what you told me? You were drunk but I am sure you said she called and cried out 'help' before the line went dead. This was after she had vanished, right?" Jazz drilled the scene back through him like a nail boring into his soul. "Convince Penny to marry Brian. Her life, her future depends on it, Kenneth!" Kenneth felt the words slap him.

What was it that Pema Chodron, the wise Buddhist monk who

was practically his neighbor, said? 'Only to the extent that we expose ourselves over and over to annihilation can that which is indestructible be found in us.' Kenneth flew to the row of tall file cabinets that lined the wall behind his dilapidated couch. He yanked open one file drawer then another and another. He grabbed the contents. Notes from the experiments that were supposed to save lives, not destroy them, scattered everywhere. His blue eyes ignited with fury. He stabbed the air with his whole hand.

"The work was about control." His breath was as loud as a thunderstorm. "You performed unspeakable acts!"

"You did them too," Jazz said. His voice was filled with a quiet conviction.

"You will not involve my children!"

"Have you forgotten Kenny? They are not all yours." Jazz chuckled. Kenneth strode out the door. Jazz's laughter followed like fists showering his body in a fight. The familiar island gray sky and tall pines created a tunnel enclosing him.

"Manipulating people with substances in order to see how far they'd go," he murmured. The tunnel of trees nodded with the breeze.

Kenneth wandered toward a large rock. He held his face in his palms. He had to resume playing Jazz's games, with Penny now? Drops of water lightly massaged his skin and he looked up to watch the rain fall. He shivered. His soggy clothes clung to his skin. He walked back to his house.

The place felt empty but he searched the rooms. The phone rang before he finished.

His mother's words echoed in his mind as he strode back to the kitchen, 'Seize the moments Kenneth, they're all you have.' He picked up the receiver.

"Hello," he said.

"Jazz has put a plan in motion." Genieve's sing-song voice ran along his spine like a screechy piece of chalk on a blackboard. "Keep a close watch on my niece. She's the target."

"So I've heard," Kenneth said. "Can we meet?"

"Maybe, I'll be in touch and I'll handle Tom," Genieve said.

"No, wait," he said. The phone line went dead. "That has never worked." Kenneth sighed. Nothing has changed. Why would he think it had, just because ten years has passed? But to use Penny, to allow her to end up like June, was unthinkable. He hadn't seen Penny in years, or his two sons, Greg and Sam. Footsteps, he flinched as a slow triumphant smile spread like butter across Jazz's features.

"Well, well you and Genieve are still together. I can't say I am surprised. It does explain your reluctance to uncover the truth and why you have chosen to live like a recluse," Jazz boomed. Kenneth balled up his fists.

"Go ahead Kenny give me your best shot!" Jazz smiled. Kenneth narrowed his blue-grey eyes and clenched his fists harder against his thighs. "Do you recall how I was adopted? Mom died while I was in fifth grade. Dad's physical and emotional health went south. I lived at my best friend Milman O'Mackery's house, Brian's father by the way. Mil and I grew up using plants for medicines, examining cells. We were going to become research doctors, Kenny. But Mil well, he couldn't dream with me. He settled for a wife and two sons, John and Brian, a myriad of jobs, and so I have to help him out whenever I can."

"What has this got to do with," Kenneth said.

"John fell apart while working for me and that didn't sit well with Mil, Ruth his wife, or Brian. Marrying Penny would be a good thing for their family too, another tool to fix another mess brought about by these triangles that June wove," Jazz explained.

"Your brand of twisted thinking makes little sense to the rest of the world Jazz," Kenneth said.

"Mil helped me discover what happened to my mother. He found letters, photos and notes."

"So?"

"How else can we understand our mistakes?" Jazz asked him. He gestured at the mess of file folders and notes Kenneth had flung earlier. "You have to realize by now that June had an agenda."

"She struggled to overcome an ugly past. A past filled with people who were successful at making her feel stupid and worthless. You drew her in with your promises of fame and fortune."

"You too, Kenny," Jazz said.

"She became a guinea pig in your passion for fame and money," Kenneth explained.

"One of my best, if not the top one," Jazz said.

"You're sick," Kenneth sneered.

"Yes and that is your fault and that is why time is of the essence. Brian understands this."

"All the more reason Penny cannot marry him! You will not damage this next generation just because," Kenneth said.

"Shut up!" Jazz cut in, booming like a loud speaker. "Your naïveté is far from charming. You pine away up here in the woods, examining every inch of those days with a den full of files, trying in your useless, passive manner to fix things."

"You pushed June to go further and further. You played June and Genieve against one another!" Kenneth shouted. "Go away Jazz. Find another way to make peace with *your* mistakes. You are not going to use my daughter or Milman's son!" Kenneth said.

Jazz locked eyes with him. A slow smile spread across his face. "Genieve uses you."

"Get out!" Kenneth yelled.

"Life is about cycles Kenneth! This marriage will happen." Jazz turned to go. "Oh, and the true paternity of Greg, Sam and Penny will emerge. The truth hurts, Kenny, as you well know when June chose me and the work over you, time and time again!" Kenneth turned the shade of an apple.

"I am the agent of truth and change. You have never been able to deny that one!" Jazz laughed harder.

"Sam is mine, and there is no proof about the others." Kenneth rasped. Jazz shrugged and walked to his rental car. Kenneth closed the front door and another one of his mother's expressions came to mind, 'Sometimes you have to step back into the mess before you can be clean.' But *mom*, he looked up at the ceiling and whispered.

"What if it's an endless world of messes that I can't ever seem to extricate myself from?" He shuddered. It was too late. He had to fight Jazz and this time he had to win.

CHAPTER THREE

Penny bounced from one untied sneakered foot to the other. The chocolate chips, the chocolate covered fudge creams, or the fancier Milano cookies? She clutched her younger brother Sam's extra large sweatshirt jacket in one hand to cover her pajamas. With her other hand, she pushed a tendril of her long curly brown hair that had escaped her pony tail off of her cheek.

"Personally, my late night favorites are these," he said. His voice sounded like sand under her shoes. The tall man with thick wavy blond hair pointed to gourmet strawberry cream cookies with a jelly icing. Penny dropped the package of chocolate chip cookies she was holding. He smiled and put them back on the shelf and handed her the strawberry creams.

"They don't contain caffeine." His turquoise eyes were like magnets to her moss green ones. "But they are sensual." Beautiful white teeth gleamed as he extended his hand.

"Brian O'Mackery," he said. Penny stared at his long fingers. "You are not only a late-night cookie-craver like me; you're a Three Stooges fan too?" Penny bunched up Sam's jacket with a tight fist.

"No thanks." She shoved the cookies back onto the shelf. He laughed. Heat crept up her average, curvy five foot five frame, as though someone was slowly lighting her on fire. She backed away but he followed and touched her arm. His forearm was muscular and a light sprinkling of blond hair tickled her exposed wrist. She turned and he dropped his arm. She watched him ruffle his hair as if he were unsure of something.

"Well here." He pushed a package of chocolate shortbread cookies into her ribcage. "Chocolate is good for you. It activates a part of the brain linked to serotonin. So it relaxes and makes you feel good." He flashed what must be his trademark grin. It was contagious. Penny's lips turned up of their own accord and she ran.

"I'll see you soon Penny Patrick," Brian called. This only made her run faster. She rounded the corner and power-walked down the next aisle, wondering why she was such a lunatic magnet. Her eyes darted around as she made her way down another aisle. He seemed to have vanished. Good! Remi and Dana, her two closest friends, would tell her to go with the flow! No! That's what her mom did.

Ten years ago was the last time she saw her mother and she had no idea what had happened. Except that June had become too caught up in giving herself away to other people, men especially and not in good ways and now she was gone and that would never happen to Penny. Or at least she had made that vow. Recently she made another one. That is, to finally learn the truth about her mother, all of it, despite what her brother's, Sam and Greg, warned. They wanted to keep their fears locked away and their anger at June fresh. She wanted to throw open the dusty old windows and pay claim to her worst fears and let her resentments fly out the door!

She contacted the one man she knew would make it happen. One of her mother's addictions, and the man her father blamed for everything, Jazz Martin. She hadn't seen her father much since he moved to Nova Scotia, Canada. She didn't know if her mother was alive, in hiding, dead, in an institution, or alive and well. Penny was determined to carve out a very different life than her mother and her father but how could she get on with it if she was standing on a foundation made out of thin air? Floating in this land of lies, denial and half-truths made her anxious. Always doubting herself, always wondering what had happened to her mom, she lived like a panther in too small a cage, pacing, circling, looking for a way out but trapped by the zookeepers. So aligning herself with the *enemy* was her only option.

Penny went back through the store and grabbed a few baking items, lemon, yeast, and plain yogurt. Baking always soothed her and through the years she had come up with many unique and quite tasty creations, judging by how her brothers and friends shoveled it into their mouths! She stuck them into her basket and headed for the checkout line.

"Allow me," Brian said. As if on cue in a movie, he stepped behind her and started unloading her basket.

"Why?" Penny moaned but kept her back to him.

"You don't like when people try and help you," he said.

"You are not people," she hissed. "Go away!"

"Wow, that's a first. I've been called lots of things but never," he said.

"Please leave me alone," she interrupted. Her voice grew louder.

"You gave up on store bought stuff, huh?" Brian said. She could almost feel his words poke her in the ribs, like her brothers did when they teased her. "Didn't you contact Jazz Martin?"

The world slowed and everything tilted. She stared at Brian. She was aware her cashier was talking to a sympathetic coworker about her boyfriend's infidelities.

"He has an interesting plan for us, Penny. Listen, I am curious though, is baking interesting concoctions a hobby of yours?" Brian stepped closer. "What sort of things do you enjoy making from scratch? My mother often baked breads, rolls and sometimes cakes from fresh whole ingredients. I miss that since I've been on my own."

Her mind twirled like a boat caught in the current. Her basket tumbled and the cashier made a grab for it. "Thanks," Penny mumbled. The woman started scanning her items. Penny pulled her wallet out of her small stuffed purse just as Brian swiped his credit card and paid for everything! He placed the items in plastic bags and took her elbow, ushering her out of the store.

"Let me go, please." She tried wriggling free of his grasp.

"I will in just a second. I need to explain the plan you signed up for." Admiration flowed through his words. Penny opened her mouth.

"Brian O'Mackery," he said. He extended his hand. Penny

groaned and reached out to take her bag of groceries. Her untied shoelace caught in the crack of the curb. She screamed as she tumbled to the ground. Brian caught her. Penny jerked away and slammed her head into his chin. Brian grunted. She tried to twist free but he pinned her against him. She felt the warmth and strength of his body

"You are making a scene," he murmured.

"It's my only hope. That and my brothers' fierce revenge," she cried.

"Sam and Greg," Brian said. He tightened his grip. A few customers trickled out of the store and stared at them.

"My wife tripped. I've got it covered, thanks!" Brian grinned and hugged her to his wide chest.

"He's trying to kidnap me! He – he stalked me!" Penny yelled.

"She needs her medication and she'll be okay. Thanks for your concern," Brian said. He smiled and spoke in a firm voice. "We'll be home soon sweetheart. Just calm down and let me get that shoelace." Brian bent over her. "You called Jazz remember?"

"I didn't know his plan included being stalked in the grocery store!" She wanted to cry. She was turning into mom.

"Okay your shoe is free," Brian said. He helped her to her feet. "Jazz – I have a proposition for you. Sorry if I have scared you tonight. Wil warns me about saying too much at once. Are you okay?"

"No!" she brushed her clothes off and walked toward her silver Subaru. The sight of it brought a slight caress to her tense shoulders.

"My buddy, Wil, and I have been friends since kindergarten. We played every sport you could name," Brian said. Penny yanked her keys out of her pocket. She rolled her neck from side to side. It had been a long day of counseling work at the crisis center. Right now she felt like she needed a crisis counselor of her own! Brian followed at her heels like an eager puppy dog.

"Mostly I was better, but occasionally he beat me," Brian said. "We dated some of the same women; he's an accountant, recently married too. Hey wait up! Don't you care about the proposition?"

"What proposition? You're rambling on about Willy. You're weird and I'm tired. Just tell Jazz I'm not interested in this part of his game."

"It's not a game to me," Brian said.

"Look Mr. Brian Macabee," she stopped near her car. They stood under a street light. "I don't know who you really are," Brian interrupted.

"Brian O'Mackery, and that's important for you to get right by the way," he said.

"Fine, whatever." She pressed the button to unlock her car. The familiar beep greeted her like an old friend.

"Don't you care about locating your mother and her sister Genieve and about deciphering what the experiments really did to the people we both love?" Brian's voice deepened with each accusation. Penny gripped the keys so hard they tore into the skin of her palm. A loud blaring noise, made her jerk forward. She dropped her keys. Headlights blinded her. Brian lunged toward her. Some teenage boys laughed and slalomed out of the parking lot. He hugged her to his chest. Her head reached his collar bone.

"All I wanted were a few groceries," she said. Penny wiped her eyes and leaned into his hug. He wrapped around her like a warm fuzzy blanket. He smelled like the pine forests of Maine.

"It was Uncle's idea to catch you off guard, in a daily-life-routine type setting. I am sorry," he murmured. His warm lips brushed her hair. "But on the flip side it was good I was here to save you, twice now!" There was that handsome, contagious grin again. She sighed.

Tears leaked out of the corners of her eyes. "Jazz Martin is the reason my mother became messed up." Brian picked up her keys and held them out to her.

"Jazz is dying, and the answers you want may die with him," Brian's eyes turned silver-gray and glowed in the moonlight, like a wolf's.

Penny was quiet as she looked down at her sneakered feet. She kicked at the ground, took a deep breath and scanned the star-filled sky. "Mom jumped into schemes concocted by Jazz, dad and Genieve." She stepped back her green eyes were hard, cold jade. "I vowed never to live like she did!"

"No of course not," Brian said. He stepped closer. "But Jazz is going ahead with his plans no matter what. Better that you have me as an ally, Penny. I know Jazz well and I need a way to get out from under his control!" he pleaded. "We can help each other."

"How can I trust anything you say? I just met you and not under very trust-inspiring circumstances. Plus you work for Jazz," she said.

"Like I said, you don't really have a choice," he said.

"You're saying Jazz is God?" she demanded.

"Pretty much, but together we can change that and we can have fun," he said. He flashed the grin for a second then looked serious. "Look," he said. He held up a palm, "I want to put Jazz in his rightful place, don't you?" She watched as a bolt of anger flashed across his face. "I detest the vile ways he attempts to control people and how way too often he succeeds."

She felt a genuine determination come through, but for what? 'Take the plunge,' the voices of her friends echoed in her head. 'What are you thinking?' That would be her brothers' angry words. But she was the youngest and didn't have the memories they did. Of course Sam and Greg said that was a blessing and wanted her to keep it that way, always her protectors.

"Brian," she said. A wave of pain washed over her like a cold burst of Maine ocean spray splashing up onto a rock. She wrapped her arms around her midsection. Brian fell to one knee. He grabbed one of her icy hands. That now seemed one of the warmest spots in her body. Moon light and stars gleamed down on her like she was an actress on stage.

Brian grinned. His eyes became the color of a Bermuda ocean.

"Brian, wh—at," she said.

Brian's grin widened. "Marry me!"

CHAPTER FOUR

It was Friday. Penny turned on her computer and sorted through the pile of writing projects on top of her beige file cabinet. She yawned, feeling the heaviness of working long shifts at the crisis center as a therapeutic counselor the last four days. She liked helping people set goals and regain hope but today she could let out the breath she'd been holding all week. Standing by her office window, she watched the top branches of a huge oak tree wave at her.

What was she going to do about Brian's marriage proposal? It felt as if a deranged stranger had offered her a puppy. She had sped home from the grocery store last night like a NASCAR driver. She wore a hole in the carpet of her bedroom with her restlessness. Why did she have to marry someone to find mom?

The spring-grass colored walls of her small office were dotted with wisdom. She read Erika Jong's, 'If you don't risk anything, you risk even more!' And, 'I am open to all the lessons my fear brings me.' This was from a yoga class she took a few years ago. She swiveled her desk chair away from her computer. Two tall black swivel chairs and a small table her brother Sam had made in shop class in junior high school sat opposite to her. A prayer plant that needed transplanting and a fern, along with rocks from the Wells and Kennebunk, Maine beaches adorned the table. She smiled. Her two shelves crammed with books and notebooks resembled her father's hair when he nervously scratched his head. She traced a finger over the huge world map that covered the far wall, finding India, where she knew her mother was held captive for weeks by a man named Tom Mott.

Her two brothers Greg, a doctor, and Sam, a private investigator of sorts will fight this marriage plan of Jazz's every step of the way. Nancy, Greg's wife, a holistic practitioner, specializing in massage, Reiki, and acupressure, would support her. But after two years of trying, she was pregnant and she was only two and a half months along, and that meant Penny could not introduce any stress into her life right now.

She returned to the blank computer screen and scrolled back to last week's chapter. Soon her hands were flying over the keys. The phone rang and Penny rolled her neck from side to side. She checked the clock. Two hours had flown by. She didn't recognize the number. The phone continued to ring. Her hand hovered over it for a moment then she picked it up.

"Do NOT make the wrong choice," said the garbled voice. Click.

"What is that? Working with Jazz? Marrying Brian? Doing nothing forever?"

She made herself a cup of tea and returned to the computer. She switched her focus to a piece she was working on about a local ceramic artist. She needed to submit it soon to the local paper's Sunday art section editor. An hour and a half later she stretched her shoulders and neck, did the dishes, put in a load of laundry and called her brother, Sam.

"Listen and don't interrupt," Penny commanded. She could hear Sam clicking keys on the computer. "Are you working on a case?"

"Yeah, hang on and let me finish this one thing." Sam specialized in helping the police solve difficult cases, not just locally, but across the country. He sometimes involved himself in FBI matters or took on private jobs for concerned – and often wealthy – individuals. His cases included missing children, discovering proof of affairs in divorce cases, and even some murder and drug investigations.

"Shoot!" Sam said.

"Something happened," she exhaled.

"That's life, and often a reason people call each other," Sam joked.

"I sort of met this guy at the grocery store."

"Not really my style but go on," Sam said.

"He proposed to me!" The words tumbled out of her mouth like a kid who hated a food he just tried.

"Talk about a fast mover! You'll have to break it down for me sis, aisle by aisle," he laughed.

"Sam! I called you for support," she snapped.

"Was it during one of your late night baking runs, Penny? I've warned you about the loonies!"

"He was sent by Jazz Martin," she said.

"What?" Sam shouted. He was angry now.

"He knew names and stuff about mom, Aunt Genieve and dad."

"Penny," Sam said. He sounded like a kindergarten teacher scolding a student.

"He's Jazz Martin's adopted nephew. This is Jazz's plan. Plus Brian hopes to extricate himself out from under his Uncle's powerful thumb."

"Jesus Penny," Sam shouted. "You don't *have* to work with anybody!"

"Well I can't find anything out on my own. I've been trying to do that for the past few years!"

"So you agreed to a plan Jazz Martin concocted? An arranged marriage," he said. He spit the words out like they were rotten.

"I haven't agreed to anything." She paused. "At least not yet, I haven't."

"Start from the beginning," Sam snapped.

"I called Jazz Martin a few months ago. I told him I wanted his help learning about our family's past. He said that my call was perfect timing. He promised to be in touch soon and then Brian showed up at the grocery and proposed!" She felt as if she were sliding down a pole on her way to fight a fire.

"Stay put, I'll be there in fifteen minutes, okay?" Sam said. Penny paced back and forth in her living room after she hung up. Her Labrador-retriever-German shepherd mutt yawned. He was stretched out in a sun spot near the window. When she looked at him, he wagged his long tail. His chocolate brown eyes were only half open. She bent over and scratched his ears and he gave her a loud snort-y sigh.

"Let's walk," she said. Henry came back to life. His tail thumped to the beat of a fast rock n' roll song. She leashed him. The mild air and sunshine felt good. "I need to call Remi," she murmured. Remi was her best friend of ten years. They met as sophomores in high school. Penny smiled, picturing Remi's advice.

"Go for it! It is what you have been asking for, for so long!" Penny never went wrong listening to Remi.

Penny checked her cell phone. Twenty minutes had passed. She turned around.

"Hey," she said. Penny greeted Sam as she walked up the driveway. He leaned against the side of his navy blue truck while Henry danced like a toddler.

Sam pulled her into a tight hug, enveloping her from his six foot three frame. "Hey, I called Greg." His thick black hair hung down over his gray eyes.

"Wolf," she laughed. She had thought that of Brian a few nights ago. Is this what I need two wolf-looking men in my life?

"Yes, I need a haircut and a shave, I know," Sam laughed. He looped an arm around her shoulders as he petted Henry. "What's up boy? Hungry, Henry?" Penny laughed. "Hey, baking is your stress reliever," Sam said. His gray eyes sparkled.

"Yeah and eating is yours," she teased.

"I might as well indulge while I can," he said. Sam patted his flat, taut belly. "Besides at twenty-seven, I still have lots of growing to do." He smiled and pointed to his heart and then flexed his developed biceps. Penny rolled her eyes and they went inside.

"Greg thinks it's a set up," Sam said. He slid a whole slice of her blueberry chocolate crumb cake into his wide open mouth.

"You eat like a crocodile," she laughed.

"You're getting in bed with much worse if you say yes to this ridiculous proposal Penny."

"I am not getting into bed with anybody!"

"Yet, but marriage involves more than cake and a ring!" Sam

swallowed his third piece of cake.

"You better make sure you have one enormous cake at your wedding Sam!" she said.

"The truth is not all it's cracked up to be." Sam took another slice of cake.

"I am tired of not knowing!" Penny said.

"So you are willing to marry a guy you know nothing about, except that he is intricately involved with Jazz Martin? The man, in case you forgot, who systematically destroyed our parents and countless others with his so called curative experiments!" She shrugged. What was the point of arguing?

"You said yes?" Sam demanded. Again she said nothing. Sam balled up his napkin and shoved it into his pants pocket. "I will dig up what I can on this guy, what was his name?" Sam's anger rumbled beneath his concession like a mild earthquake.

"Brian O'Mackery," she murmured.

"I hope you're keeping your last name!" He rubbed the top of her head vigorously and then he placed a loud kiss on her forehead. "Keep safe, love you," he said.

"Wow thanks for all the support!" she said to the closed front door. "And for eating almost a whole cake," she yelled at the door. Henry's tail thumped against the floor.

Penny returned to writing. Her fingers rested on the keyboard unmoving while the cloud of June hung over her. Wanting to know her mother was a magnet leading her to what? Answers she'd be better off not knowing? Danger she should avoid? Fear of June clung to Penny's skin like a wet towel. How could she be free if she couldn't understand her mother's choices? June wanted something illusive, searching for it in relationships and work. She chose work that was unethical and people who used her. Penny picked up an empty shell next to the computer. Her eyes flooded.

The door bell rang. She sucked in her breath and wiped her eyes. Fear was false evidence appearing real, remember? Henry never believed that when she hauled the vacuum out of the closet. He grew frantic, moving in circles, barking and running away. Penny smoothed her thick hair. Henry's fur bunched up on his back while he barked.

"How's it going?" the gravelly voice said. She couldn't see the face behind the enormous bouquet of exotic wild flowers. Bright reds, oranges and yellows combined with a sweet honey-like aroma wafted toward her. "We need to set a date, Pen," Brian said. He walked in, pushed the flowers into her hand and picked up a small pirate figurine she had on a side table in the living room. "Pirate-lover, aye, matey," he laughed. "You are full of surprises!" Brian strode to the fireplace and touched a family photo. A vise grip settled around her stomach.

Brian flashed a spectacular dimpled-grin at her. "Nice place, your brother's help you get it?" She nodded. He put an arm around her shoulders. "Hey, Wil thinks my proposal in the grocery store parking lot left a lot to be desired."

"The know-it-all best friend since birth." She took the bouquet into her kitchen.

"Don't insult Wil." Brian sounded like a scolded puppy. "Been writing today?" He came up close behind her. Penny trimmed the stems and fit the bouquet into two large vases. She set one bouquet onto the kitchen table and took the other one out to her living room window ledge.

Brian grabbed her hand and pulled her toward the brown couch in the living room. He shoved aside the multiple maroon colored pillows and yanked her down next to him. "You need adventure!" Penny scooted away. He was way too charming and attractive. He fogged up her brain and it made her feel inside out.

"Part of this proposal involves money. Jazz is loaded from years of rich people funding experimental work."

"I don't." She ran her teeth over her front lip.

"You could write more and work less hours at the crisis clinic," he said.

"Why do I know more about Wil than the man I am supposed to marry yesterday?"

Brian wrapped an arm around her shoulders. "A little mystery is good for the soul, haven't you heard?" She was a jack rabbit. Across the room in one second, she folded her arms across her chest.

"Look I'll fill you in on my life. I promise." She rolled her eyes. "Most important is my protection from uncle and heck if the grocery store parking lot mishaps were any indication you need a rescuer in your daily life!" In three steps he was next to her and he kissed her softly on her cheek. His lips were electric.

"I'm starving and nothing is ever solved on an empty stomach. Let's set a date for our nuptials over a hearty meal okay?"

"Men and food," she said. She raised her fingers to her cheek. It was still tingling from his kiss. He looked amused. A headache formed and she rubbed her forehead.

"How about that veggie place in town?" he asked. "It has this one sandwich, they pile it high with this mixture of sprouts, carrots, tomatoes, cucumbers, three kinds of cheeses and it's layered with this special kind of sauce that's a mixture of spicy and sweet." Brian winked at her.

"Go eat!" She threw open the front door.

"Not without you." He didn't budge from his spot.

"I'm not hungry for romance, adventure, money, the truth or food!" she shouted.

"Why doth the lady protest so very much?" His grin was wicked. "Penny, you are hungry for answers, and for change. Your life will not be complete until you know. You can't move forward, or feel whole until you face all the skeletons that haunt you."

"So you're a shrink?" She could have said mind-reader!

"It has been my own experience. Jazz robbed my family too. I tried to fight him. I lost credibility financially, in my relationships, and I became sick with a lot of weird uncomfortable symptoms. I realized he was infecting me. He must have put it in my sports drinks. Jazz found a hundred means of toying with me. I was evicted, lost my car. It took me several *years* to recover. My father, Milman had similar issues. My brother, John had it even worse but that's a story for another time. My mother, Ruth detests Jazz."

"So you resigned yourself to the role of his puppet?"

"Only to gain what is necessary." Brian looked her straight in the eye, "The end of Jazz's power over my family, for good.

Together we can beat him, quicker and with more cleverness."

"Games again and you're crazy," Penny said. A small smile played across her face.

"You're intrigued," he said. He cupped her chin with two long fingers. "He's going to give you $10,000 up front if you agree to the marriage, and more after we spend a few weeks together and then announce our engagement."

"He's bribing me while trying to make our marriage seem legitimate?" she laughed.

"Let's go eat," he said. "I want to tell you about the life I made for myself, apart from Jazz."

"Like?" She watched her neighbor across the street struggled to put her stroller into her trunk. She must be about to run errands with her sweet little baby daughter. Penny swiveled her dark forest colored eyes back to meet his earnest and pleading silver ones.

"I have a degree in history. I do research, teach and I am trying to write a book."

"Interesting," she said. Is he for real?

"No one in my family understands. I recognized a kindred spirit when Jazz told me about you," Brian said. If he was a wolf what did that make her?

"You set things in motion when you contacted Jazz," he said. Henry stood next to Brian, resting his head against Brian's thigh. "Dogs are very wise." Brian patted his head.

"Traitor," Penny hissed. Henry's tail slowed its wagging. Brian stared through her. Penny dropped her eyes to the floor. Brian laughed.

"What's with the name?" he asked.

"Henry Wadsworth Longfellow, Mom loved the classics." She tied her sneakers. "Okay, one meal, Brian. That's all I am agreeing to right now." They got into his black SUV. A few minutes later, they pulled up into the parking lot of "Vi's All Veg Bistro."

"It's all about revenge for them Penny, but for us." Brian touched her arm before they walked into the restaurant. "It means finally having control." His lips curved but his eyes remained serious.

"Control and revenge are Jazz's weapons," she mumbled.

"He doesn't own the patent," Brian threw over his shoulder as they made their way inside.

"He holds all the cards, Brian. It's the same thing," she said. "And I thought we were supposed to be better than their games!" He took her hand after they slid into a booth.

"We are and we have more of the cards than you might believe. Agree to marry me and I'll gladly show you."

The waitress brought two tall glasses of ice water with lemon slices and Brian placed their order. Penny took a sip and tried to sort out the real meaning of his words.

CHAPTER FIVE

Kenneth sat on a bench near the ocean. He finished his five mile morning walk. His mother's advice, 'Those with the biggest teeth are the loudest cowards', was like the tide flowing toward him. Shivering, he put his sweatshirt back on.

Kenneth squinted at the massive facility high up on the cliffs on the other side of the inlet. It stared back at him. He clutched the photo of June. She was smiling up at him as he held her close against his side. Kenneth pulled out a small flask from his jacket pocket and took a sip. Off to one side he could see the little ocean village that he lived just outside of. Today it was bustling with activity. Fishermen pulled boats in from morning jaunts filled with their bounty.

Like a curious spectacle the imposing structure across the inlet drew him back and the dense fog of Jazz Martin descended. A light rain mixed with the salty wetness on his face as he stuffed a cold hand into a front pocket of his jeans and pulled out his cell phone.

"I am leaving today. When can I see you?" he asked.

"I have to juggle a few things," she said.

"Genieve, I need your help," he said.

"I know," she said.

"Is Tom with you?" he asked. He took a hearty swallow of scotch.

"Spend time with Jazz. Learn more about his plan," she said. Her words were hurried. He watched the fisherman unload their boats.

"I have to go Kenneth."

The foamy cold water cascaded over his heart. Jiggling his right leg, the icy tentacles continued slithering through his chest.

He bent over and held his head in his hands. Rain hit the leaves of the enormous trees like glass shattering. His life splintered into tiny shards of moments until he could hold onto only a tiny speck of hope, and he had survived this way with June for a while. June had had practice when she was a young child and dealing with her mother's abuse. Like the time her mother had put a rat in her bed while she slept. June had said that she awoke to it nibbling on the skin of her face.

Kenneth returned to the cottage and made lunch. A tomato and cheese sandwich on pumpernickel bread. His eyes grew heavy while reading and he fell asleep. The ringing of his phone startled him. He ran a hand through his curls and rubbed his eyes. It was five-thirty.

"Hello," he rasped.

"Dad, you don't sound too well?"

"I was sleeping," Kenneth said. Sam cleared his throat. "Yes I know Penny's supposed to marry Jazz's adopted nephew, Brian O'Mackery."

"Okay, well, I haven't been able to find out much about Brian yet except he has a degree in history, writes and teaches some. But mostly he does hinky *jobs* for Jazz." Kenneth savagely scratched at his gray curls as Sam spoke. He leaned back against the couch and closed his eyes.

Kenneth sighed into the phone. "We can't allow Penny to,"

"Be used for bait to find out who took mom away."

"Yes, I am flying back, Sam." There was a long pause. "I know it has been a while," Kenneth murmured. Sam was silent. "Can I stay with you?"

"Uh, yeah, I guess so," Sam said. A long pause followed. "I'll see you soon dad."

"Okay." Kenneth grabbed his coat off the hook and slammed the front door. A half hour later Kenneth blinked as he walked into the dimly lit bar. He nodded to the old bartender.

"Hey," called Quincy.

"Scotch, straight up, and leave the bottle, Quince, thanks," Kenneth said.

"Is everything okay?" Quincy asked as he set the glass and bottle in front of Kenneth.

"Daughter's getting married," Kenneth mumbled. He downed his first of many shots.

"Let me guess, you don't like the guy?" Quincy asked. He nodded to another customer who was signaling him from the back of the bar.

"Long story, can't talk about it right now Quince," Kenneth said. He grabbed his glass and bottle and went to the familiar dark corner of the place. The music of Charlie "Bird" Parker floated to him. He was a genius of the 'bop' movement, and an incredible saxophonist. Or so Jazz had informed him, along with stories of how his mother became a guinea pig, like June for the sake of science. And tales of two-timing June which of course led Kenneth to comfort her and soon they were married and June was pregnant with Greg. Kenneth poured another shot of scotch. His life became a soap opera. He had escaped. He had had no other choice since June disappeared with her blood on his hands ten years ago.

Kenneth closed his eyes and leaned back against the booth, allowing Jazz's voice to burn like smoldering ash in his ear.

"One time June and I ended up in the ladies room," Jazz laughed. "I won't go into details." His laugh sounded like a sink that was turned on after years of neglect. "In the palm of my hand, Kenny." He cupped his right hand. "All of them are guinea pigs in whatever ways I say! Controlling others does require creativity, Ken. People pay big money. So think of it like this. We are fulfilling the needs of many businesses, families and individuals while lining our pockets quite nicely." Jazz's laughter went on for an eternity.

Jazz cloaked evil in a beautiful fur coat. Kenneth pushed the memories aside and stood up, a little unsteadily. He thanked Quince and paid his bill. He walked home, inhaling the fresh evening air. Kenneth made a quick stop at the local market.

He arrived home and made a ham and cheese omelet. He took a bowl of vanilla ice cream with maple syrup drizzled on top into his den. Opening up the last file, his notes took him back to after Greg was born. Kenneth discovered June's journals and learned that the baby was Jazz's.

'What you choose to avoid rips you to shreds,' his mother's words echoed. Greg turned three and June left for weeks of intense work on one of Jazz's projects. Kenneth dove into the deep end of the pool, working like a fiend on any project, including many Jazz tossed his way. Genieve was everywhere, helping out at work and watching Greg.

June returned. Her notes spoke of being a subject for Jazz and Dr. Marty Mapman's latest experimental work concerning controlling addiction from a psychology perspective. She wrote about living in a lab for weeks. Her moods shifted like lightning. Nights held a fierce passion that was not unpleasant. Soon they were celebrating Sam's conception. June gave up her work with Jazz. She took up piano lessons and taught dance classes at the local YMCA. She had taken extensive dance lessons as a child. It brought her peace in an often ugly upbringing. Sam was born without complications.

Kenneth folded his arms under his head as he lay awake in bed the next morning. Sometime during the night he had gotten up to get a drink of water and use the bathroom and found his way to his bedroom. It was nine-thirty. Kenneth slid the music of Thelonious Monk into his stereo. He was an innovative pianist from the nineteen sixties. Kenneth returned to the den with a plate of scrambled eggs and toast and a steaming hot mug of hazelnut coffee. He opened his file drawers. He needed to make plane reservations but that could wait another few minutes.

When Sam was three, Jazz offered them a trip to Asia. Kenneth was told he would study how addictions took hold and led to immune system problems. June occupied herself by teaching dance classes, taking piano, and making the rounds to the constant parties. Greg attended elementary school in India and Sam went a few afternoons a week to an American woman's home where she ran a preschool.

Tom Mott was a very attractive and cunning associate of Dr.

Marty Mapman's. June entrusted Mortle, a young Indian man Jazz must have paid, to escort her over to Tom. Kenneth surmised from her journaling that she had grown bored. It was a chance for her to resume the old addiction work with Jazz. The servants and his boys complained one evening that they hadn't seen her in weeks. He called Genieve. She believed Tom was holding June captive, forcing her to do the experimental work around the clock in a remote village in India.

He rinsed his dishes and made plane reservations. He had to keep Tom far away from Penny. Tom's obsessive needs were like quick sand to those around him. Genieve was living proof! Tom used her to try and satiate his loss of June.

Kenneth hauled out his big black suitcase from the closet. It was dusty. He coughed. Genieve had kept Tom away but was her power slipping? She loved Penny. Sometimes though, love was not enough.

C H A P T E R SIX

Penny was dripping. She grabbed her towel and ran for the ringing phone. It was Sunday. Her lunch with Brian at Vi's All Veg Bistro on Friday had been nice. He was funny. Her soup and sandwich were delicious. Today he was taking her out for a boat ride.

"Hello!"

"Marry Brian!" The line went dead. She let the water drain out of her tub and sat down on the edge. Henry stretched and yawned, and plopped down near her wet feet. He licked the water off of her toes. It tickled and she smiled a little and patted his head.

"I guess that's the right choice, Hen?" The phone rang again. She studied the caller id. She exhaled like Henry before he sleeps at night and picked up the receiver.

"Hey Pen," Dana said.

"Hey."

"What's wrong," Dana asked. They had been close friends for several years now. They met at the crisis center. Dana knew when Penny was upset about something and she was always ready to listen. Penny made a sound like she had something caught in her throat.

"I'm trying to take a bath and eat breakfast and the phone keeps ringing! What's up with you?"

"Penny, what's wrong?" Dana pressed.

"I was proposed to!" Penny blurted.

"What? Who – Mark at work? Or that guy you were dating a few months ago, what was his name? John no, Jake, I forget, tell me!"

"I will if you shut up for a second!" Penny laughed. "It isn't anybody you know."

"What, how did that happen?" Dana asked.

"It's," Penny said. She hesitated but she had opened up the can of worms because she needed to talk about it. "It's this guy from my past – that I – well our families were connected and so we've hooked up through this mutual adopted uncle. It's a long story. What's new with you?"

"Penny this sounds weird, and not at all like you," Dana said. Penny was glad she had ignored her attempt to change the subject.

"What do you mean?" Penny asked. Though she knew full well what Dana meant.

"You plan things for a long time. You're logical and practical, not whimsical and spontaneous, no offense!" Dana laughed. Penny heard her friend's discomfort.

"Thanks, I think. I haven't agreed to anything yet. My brothers are dead set against it." Penny vigorously rubbed her towel over the remainder of her wet body. "Maybe it's time for me to loosen up and say yes to adventure and spontaneity. I have been missing out on things. You've told me so plenty Dana."

"Okay, true enough but," Dana said. She drew the last word out, sounding full of doubt.

"Listen, I can't really talk about it right now."

"Okay. I know I interrupted your bath and morning routine."

"It's okay," Penny said. "We're going out for a boat ride today."

"Cool. Is this guy cute, nice, smart, and funny?"

"Yes," Penny chuckled.

"Does he love you and you him?"

"I thought I said I didn't want to talk about it!" Penny pulled on clothes and brushed her hair, put on mascara and lipstick; she was practiced at multi-tasking while on the phone. She added a bit of green eye shadow to match her pine tree-colored top.

"Yeah okay, sorry again. I should let you go. Listen I was wondering if we could trade shifts. I can't work next Wednesday morning, so if you could come in early for me then I could cover your early shift on Thursday?" Dana asked. Her voice grew distant.

"Sure yeah, that should be fine."

"Thanks, I'll let the powers that be know and pencil it in on the schedule," Dana said.

"I know, you don't understand me right now, and I wish I could tell you more. The truth is I don't really know much. It is a long story, going back to my mom. So please, Dana be patient with me. I will need to lean on you and Remi, trust me."

"Okay," Dana said. There was a slight caress to her voice.

"I need to find out some things. I have wanted to for a long time and now it seems I have a chance to go for it. Brian is fun, smart, handsome and nice and he is trying to make some big changes of his own. It's complicated." Penny sighed. "We had a nice lunch over the weekend. He makes me laugh and he rescues me when I fall!"

"Okay, I sort of get it, I think," Dana laughed. "You have my support of course Pens, keep me posted."

Penny threw back her head, feeling the 'merry little breezes', dance across her skin. The 'merry little breezes' were a favorite childhood story character. Her father had loved to read to her from books where nature came alive. Sweet and tangy sensations of the luscious raspberries she was eating, curled her tongue. It felt wonderful to be out on the water. Spring is the season of beginnings, of possibilities. She turned to Brian. He was watching her.

"You're beautiful, Penny," he said.

"Thanks," she said, looking at the shimmering wavy water. She reached for some more raspberries. "So far our dates involve excellent food," she smiled.

"Healthy and tasty," Brian agreed. Penny filled her mouth with crackers, salmon spread and seafood salad. "Tell me something about your childhood," he said.

"Fourth grade was my injury year," she said. "I sprained my knee when a mean fat girl fell on me during a game of 'sardines.'"

"Sounds fishy," Brian joked. Penny laughed.

"And just before a major piano concert," she said. Penny hesitated, wondering which version to tell. She opted for the truth. "My mother closed the car door on my thumb. Though she said I caught it in the door. Basically, she didn't even notice. She was stoned on pills, probably that Jazz prescribed."

"Ouch," he said. "I mean that on all accounts."

"Yeah, I couldn't play too well." Her words came quickly. "Later that year, I woke up one morning to a blood soaked pillow."

"This isn't a feminine story is it?" Brian busied himself with locating container lids and cleaning up their spread. Penny laughed.

"No, it's still nauseating though. I picked at a scab and broke a blood vessel on the outside of my nose."

"Wow! Always the achiever," he teased.

"It was embarrassing. I had to wear this patch with a silver rock in it – silver nitrate I think – over the cut the doctor cauterized. Dad took me to have it done. What about you?" she asked.

"My injury year was seventh grade. I had so many falls, fights, and mishaps that year," he shook his head. "I had black eyes, bloody noses, skinned knees, elbows and forehead. I sprained my ankle twice and cracked a rib!"

"Sports?" she asked. Penny popped another heavenly hazelnut chocolate truffle into her mouth.

"Mostly that, and a few fights, with the rest due to clumsiness —that awkward age when your body and mind are not in sync yet," he said.

The rest of the afternoon went by quickly for Penny. They talked about the beauty of nature, what they had liked in school, and friendships they now had. Brian dropped her at home. She thanked him for the flowers he had stopped and bought her on the ride home.

"I had fun." She looked up at the stars.

"Do you know the constellations?" He put his hands on her shoulders. Penny shrugged. "See those three over there? That is Orion's belt." He whispered in her ear. It was like a feather moving up and down her spine. He gently stroked strands of her thick hair so they lay behind her ear. The hair on her arms, the back of her neck, and the top of her head, stood at attention. "The group over there." He kissed her neck. "That is the Pleiades and the bright star flickering that looks kind of reddish? That's Mars." He wrapped his long muscular arms with the soft golden hairs around her waist. She fell into a warm bath. He smelled like the stars, spicy and fresh. His slight beard scratched against her cheek and his lips painted little kisses all over her neck.

"See you soon." He caressed her with his words. She shivered and wrapped her arms around her middle when he moved away and smiled. He waved as he sauntered toward his car. She went inside, rubbing her cheek as she shut the front door and walked up the stairs to her bedroom.

The next three weeks were a blur. He took her to the movies and dancing. He was a fabulous dancer! They cooked together and took long walks, roaming through old bookstores and sipping French raspberry sodas. Drinks thick with cream, flavored syrup and seltzer, and it became a new favorite warm weather treat. They biked, hiked, played tennis and went for runs together. She forgot about why they were together. They shared so many interests. She ignored her brother's warnings. She heard her father was due into town soon. He had made plans but had decided to do some traveling of his own first before arriving.

One day, Brian announced that Jazz Martin was back. They had to meet with him to discuss their engagement party. The bubble she had been living in burst. They were at the park eating a picnic lunch. Brian launched into some family history.

"My brother John failed at his marriage and then rehab. I gave up. I love him." His eyes were glued to the ground. "I just had to learn detachment. It was hard to watch him go down. I thought." Brian stopped and looked up at a sky made of huge snow colored cotton balls mixed with blue. Penny put a hand over his and Brian's fingers encircled hers. His eyes seemed to match the patterns of the sky. "I prayed a lot. It worked. He found help, eventually. Jazz funded everything." The clouds in Brian's eyes turned stormy grey. "Of course he was the original cause of John's problems."

"Why didn't he help my mom into a recovery program?" Penny stood up with her fists clenched. Brian rose.

"How do you know he didn't try?" She spun around and faced him, ready to argue.

"I am only saying, Penny, that John wanted to face his problems."

"And that my mother didn't?" she said. The truth of his words hit her. Her heart sank to her feet. Brian didn't say anything. He tugged her hand and they walked toward the small bubbly stream. That only a few moments ago they could only hear.

"Tell me about your dad."

"While mom drank more and took pills that Jazz said she needed to for the experiments to work, so she could become famous, dad worked. Then he drank. She disappeared. Until one day she was gone. Dad couldn't explain it because he was drunk. Affairs ran the gambit, and included my mother's sister, Genieve and a bad boy named Tom that Aunt Genieve coveted. The happy ending involved dad running away to an island in Nova Scotia Canada where he chooses to hide, obsess and drink his guilt away."

"Sorry." Brian stood next to her. Her pained and moist green eyes locked with his soft sea blue. He reached for her hand and squeezed it.

"I—" she said. Tears crammed her eyes like an over-filled sock drawer. "I can't believe she's dead!" Her chin went up as it quivered. Her mother's gesture of strength and Brian squeezed her hand again.

"Maybe she isn't," he said.

"Jazz turned people into addicts! That was his experimental work, wasn't it?"

"That's possible," he said. He looked thoughtful for a few moments. "We will find out for sure." His blue-gray eyes were like a new sprout in a spring garden as they locked with her despair. "I'm sorry."

They reached her front door. "Who funded the research?" she asked.

"Jazz employs scientists and doctors, like Dr. Marty Mapman who invest their time and money and powerful rich folks contract him."

"Why would anyone choose to participate?" She slung out the question like a sailor throwing an unwanted pile overboard. Trying hard to keep the tears at bay she fiddled with her keys.

"Power, control, fame," he said. Brian leaned down and kissed her forehead. She closed her eyes. His lips were soft and warm like fresh baked bread straight from the oven.

"No not the doctors or rich people. Why did my mother let them?" Her throat tightened.

"Use her?" he asked. She nodded. The faucet in her eyes gained momentum. "Jazz and Tom convinced her of the importance of the work. At least that's why my brother John did it." Penny shook her head. "I know it sounds pathetic." She put a hand over her mouth and looked away. Everything blurred. Her eyes were puddles of pain.

Brian laid a hand on her back, "Speaking of the devil, Jazz is taking us to dinner tonight to plan the engagement party." Brian hugged her. She cried into his chest. He sighed against her hair. "We'll find out what happened to June, okay?" She nodded into his shirt. "I care about you Penny. I am NOT like him."

"Time will tell." Penny's voice was muted. He released her and bent to kiss her cheek, lingering and finding her mouth. She dove in, feeling lovely tingling sensations float through her watery limbs.

"Despite everything Henry, I really like him!" She told her mutt a few minutes later.

CHAPTER SEVEN

"Remi, I need your help, desperately!" Penny wailed into the phone.

"Calm down girl. That's Rem's specialty," her best friend said.

"We have to plan my engagement party tonight at some fancy shmancy restaurant." Penny had filled Remi in on things, a few days ago. "I feel like I am living inside of a tornado."

"Do the under the arm pad thing," Remi advised.

"What?" Penny sniffled.

"In case you start sweating like a pig," she announced. Penny moaned.

"What if I vomit? We are probably going to some exotic Indian restaurant," Penny added.

"Well the underarm pads won't help with that too much. Take a breath," Remi said. "Try and hold on until you can make it to the bathroom!"

"I am seriously in over my head here. I really like Brian!" Penny fell back on her bed, feeling the softness of her mother's old quilt. Scraps of material all sewn together in beautiful patterns of greens and blues not by her mother, but her mother had wrapped her worries, her hopes inside of it. Penny had had it re-sewn in places where it had unraveled. She should have someone stitch her up! Maybe by unraveling her mother's story she would discover the necessary threads?

"Penny, honey," Remi interrupted. "Are you there?"

"Yes, sorry, what were you saying?"

"Listen to me sweetie, you are going to get through this and it'll be worth it to put the screws to Jazz. Brian is here to help you. It doesn't mean you have to marry him, but if it's meant to be, well then, let things unfold, don't fight it too, too much, okay?" Remi said.

"Thanks for nothing," Penny mumbled.

"Just remember to breathe, look deeply into his sexy eyes and drink a lot of water."

"Oh great advice, I'll need a brown paper bag while I jog to the ladies room," Penny giggled. Remi joined her and they couldn't stop laughing.

"Stop or I'll wet my pants right now!" Remi choked out. "I've been on this new diet and I have to drink eight glasses of water a day. I always need to pee!" They laughed harder.

Penny hung up and curled up in a ball. She ran her fingers up and down her mother's quilt. The doorbell rang and Penny was shot out of a cannon.

"Remi, help me!" She breathed in and out through her nose. Henry barked his head off and wagged his tail like she had just arrived home.

"Traitor, again," she said. Henry's whole body wriggled with joy as she raced down the steps holding her robe tightly about her.

"Hey, come in. Sorry I am not quite ready!" She called over her shoulder as she ran back up to her bedroom. She flung open her closet door and ten minutes later she descended the stairs. Brian whistled and came to give her a hand with the last few steps. The emerald green skirt came to just above her knees and a button down v-necked, collared top of the same color did bring out Penny's eye color.

"I am not too good at walking in these things." She pointed at her high heels.

"Me either," Brian replied. She laughed and bent to give Henry instructions.

"Be good. Mommy will hopefully be home in one piece, in a little while."

"That color looks spectacular on you Penny. Jazz will be so dazzled he'll forget whatever tricks he has up his sleeves for us tonight."

"Fat chance of that happening," Penny murmured. Brian laughed. He stepped closer.

"Gardenias!" he exclaimed. She smiled and smoothed her thick waves.

"Thanks." She eyed his dress pants and crisp gray button-down shirt. They got into his car and before she knew it they were pulling up in front of the "Bombay Grill."

Brian sat close to her and intercepted questions from Jazz. The food was beautiful and very colorful. She nibbled, thought of Remi and smiled. Jazz's intense steel blue eyes focused on her. A torpedo about to hit its target, Jazz smiled at her.

She felt the glint of the dagger in his eye and knew it could pierce her heart. Penny looked down at the thick white tablecloth. He laughed as she traced the patterns of swirls in the cloth.

"You must miss your mother every day?" he said. She raised her chin. Jazz chuckled. "You are just like her, you know?" He leaned back in his chair and took a long sip of wine.

"Hardly," she snapped.

"Let's dance." Jazz offered her his hand. She looked at Brian then back to Jazz. "Contrary to global rumors, I don't bite." Jazz took her by the elbow and led her out onto the dance floor.

"I don't know how to dance to Indian music." Her breath came in puffs. Maybe she needed that brown paper bag!

"Fake it! Show strength my dear, and a sense of adventure, like your mother." He took hold of her one hand and wrapped the other around her waist. She tensed and moved awkwardly as he forced her to move in rhythm to the exotic music.

"My nephew and I digressed to outside matters my dear, and I apologize; you must have felt ignored." He smiled and again Penny felt the glint of his eye, a needle pricking her skin.

"So what do you remember?" Jazz held her tight. His lips close to her ear as he spun her around the dance floor. For a second Penny had a flash of a picture of her mother. She was yelling and crying. Jazz was there and so was her father.

"About what," she asked. She caught sight of Brian sitting at the table alone with his head resting on his chin. He looked unhappy. Right back at you, she thought miserably. Why is Jazz the one asking the questions? Because for now I am his pawn, the ugly thought surfaced like a monster from the black lagoon. She almost laughed at her morose mind. She knew she must play along but she hated every minute spent in this man's company.

"Well you tell me my dear, and may I add you are a marvelous dancer, taking after your mother, hmmm?" He mumbled into her ear. She stiffened. "Somehow, I am certain it wasn't handed down from that man you call your father."

She stumbled. He leaned forward and whispered in her ear again. "You are playing way too far out of your league my dear, if you decide to partner up with Brian and take me on! Shall I remind you of what happens to those who cross me?"

"My turn," Brian said, tapping Jazz on the shoulder. Jazz stepped back and opened his arms, nodding at Brian. Then he leaned in near Penny's left ear. Penny felt her head begin to throb as Jazz's words seemed to penetrate right into the center of her brain.

"Are you ready to experience everything your mother chose?" Jazz whispered.

"What was that about?" Brian demanded.

Penny rubbed her forehead. "I need to use the lady's room." She walked away. Penny splashed cold water on her face and reached into her purse for her cell phone that had begun to vibrate.

"Hey how's it going?" Sam asked her.

"I hate that man with every fiber in my being." She exploded into the phone. No one better come into this restroom any time soon.

"Good so you're done with this whole thing! I am glad you finally see the light about Brian O'Mackery," Sam said.

"Sam! I'm talking about Jazz Martin, not Brian!" she cried.

"Oh for God's sake Penny, stop all this nonsense. They are two peas in a pod. Brian works for Jazz, have you forgotten all this simply because he's tall, blond and well built?"

"Idiot!" She stuffed her phone back into her purse and ignored it when it vibrated a few seconds later. Fine! She could do this on her own. She didn't need her brother's insults or closed-mindedness.

Penny sighed as she made her way toward their table. Jazz was leaning in close to Brian and talking up a storm. The look of agitation on Brian's face said he had had it as much as she. Or was Brian a great actor?

"What can you tell me about your desire for children?" Jazz smiled and stood up to pull her chair out for her.

"How many are you ordering?" Penny threw back. "And for what purposes?" she asked. Her sudden anger made her body hum like a bee. Bring it on, old man she thought. Thanks Sam. Jazz threw back his head and roared with laughter. Brian scowled and Penny remained standing, opening and closing her fists.

"Leave us to figure out kids when we are into our marriage by at least a few minutes, Uncle," Brian retorted. He stood up. Jazz's lips twitched. Penny pushed her chair against the table. Brian copied her.

"Where are you off to? We are not finished yet. Young people today always seem to be in an all-fire hurry. Though I suppose I used to be that way. I hear Kenneth made it into town late yesterday after his sudden unplanned little vacation time. Probably panting after your Aunt Genieve, like he has for many years even before June disappeared, but to no avail I am willing to bet. She is otherwise occupied with one of your mother's rejected lovers. What do you hear from Tom, my dear?"

The room spun. She had joined the Mad Hatter's tea party in Alice in Wonderland! Was Kenneth working for Jazz? Aunt Genieve was with Tom Mott? He was the one who kidnapped mom in India!

"Better call Wil tonight," Brian muttered. Penny glared at him. Anger surged up through her like lava in a volcano.

"Oh now dear, put a lid on it. I am not telling you anything you don't already know! When is Tom arriving with Genieve, in time for the engagement party perhaps?" Jazz thought she was stupid!

"We haven't set a date yet!" she screamed. Heads turned and a waiter ran over.

"Is everything all right?" the waiter asked. Brian jumped up.

"Sure, sure, wedding jitters is all," Jazz said. The waiter nodded, keeping an eye on Penny and slowly backed up before turning around.

"Hey I don't want to leave here without another dance – how about it Pen?" Penny shook her head no, but Brian dragged her out onto the dance floor before she could protest. He held her close. His arms tightened around her and he whispered.

"You're only like your mom in the good ways." He murmured against her hair. "We'll figure out what Tom and Genieve are up to, okay? And whatever role your dad is playing. Obviously Jazz has jealousy issues with your mom and Tom and," he said.

"Shut up Brian. You can't fix any of this or change what he thinks!" Her voice squeaked. He hugged her closer. His lean muscular strength pushed against her wooden body.

"Jazz loves to incite people. Don't allow him to control you."

"But he does," she said. Each word etched in despair.

"Your mom lost herself in Tom and Jazz's lies. You won't." Brian tilted her chin up. His determination penetrated her anxiety. Puddles of sadness made it hard to keep looking at him.

"I watched it with my brother John, remember? Never again, I promise." He kissed her ever so softly. She wanted to sink into the hope and comfort he offered but wasn't that just what June had done? Brian was charming and alluring. She had to keep her guard up. He kissed her hair then the corners of her eyes as they leaked confusion.

His lips touched hers. Her thoughts dissolved like honey in a warm cup of tea. The song ended. Brian smiled and touched her cheek. They held hands and turned back to their table. Penny's heart dropped to the floor. A cold chill swept through her. Jazz was grinning like a Cheshire cat that had swallowed the canary!

CHAPTER EIGHT

Kenneth sat in Sam's kitchen sipping his second cup of black coffee and tapping his foot along to the beat of the music. He thought of the jazz concerts at the outdoor theatre on Cape Breton Island in the spring and summer. He could never imagine moving his feet as those Scottish men and women did. Watching an old oak tree wave to him outside Sam's kitchen window he had pangs of homesickness, for the woodsy path that took him along the cliffs that were close to his home. Cape Breton was filled with hundreds of lakes and rivers, dense forests and trails that led to hidden waterfalls. Kenneth's favorite spots were along the rugged cliffs. Some days he imagined plunging down into the sea going deeper and deeper. Icy water cooling the hot shame of the mistakes he had made with June.

Once after a concert, there was a loud rustling and a great horned owl took flight. 'It is better to fly high, spreading your wings as far as they can go, than to twitter along the ground all scrunched up like a turtle.' Another of his mother's sayings flew into his mind while his eyes searched the woods for the owl.

"Morning dad," Sam said. Kenneth jumped. Sam poured a cup of coffee and a bowl of cereal as Kenneth nodded with his rounded shoulders. He drew his bushy gray eyebrows together into a bird's nest.

"Where were we?" Sam asked. They had been up late talking about the past.

"Tom was abusive. I could see the evidence."

"You mean physically?" Sam asked.

"Yes and emotionally. She said Tom laced the vodka she grew to love with something." Ingredients Jazz perfected to study addiction. Drugs, a mixture of them, concocted to activate the pleasure center of the brain. He downed the last of his coffee, wishing it were his beloved scotch.

"He thought he could gain control over her body and her mind," Kenneth said. 'The tiniest aspects of a person can flood us, leaving a sinkhole behind when they move on.' Yes, mom I know.

"Do you know how she escaped Tom when he had her in that village for weeks and weeks?" Kenneth asked. Sam shook his head, no.

"A boy named Jabby helped her leave one night when Tom was out getting supplies. They traveled for days and days in the open desert. Jabby found herbs and bits of plants to help June grow stronger and less sick. They were remedies he had heard of from the shaman of his village. Plus, she stole what Tom called the 'immune enhancers,' which assisted in recovery from the addictions. Some were being tested for tissue engineering using molecules that promote new blood vessel growth or even organs or hydro gels that could regenerate bone. We dabbled in some gene therapy that could correct abnormal cells that became unable to receive inhibitory or healing messages so that these cells could actually learn to stop their own destructive growth, thus helping the body to heal itself from abnormal cancer growth, or even viral and bacterial infections," Kenneth sighed. "I digress, sorry." Sam shrugged. He is bored, Kenneth thought.

"Anyhow, as they reached the city a group of hooded men with knives tried to stop them. They beat up Jabby. June stabbed one of them with a needle she had confiscated from Tom's supplies. In her journal she said Tom sent them."

"Mom escaped," Sam stated the obvious.

"She passed out and someone brought her home while I was at work. The servants bathed her, fed her and tended to her cuts. She was asleep when I arrived home."

"Who brought her home?" Sam asked. Kenneth shrugged, stood up and stretched.

"How did she become involved with Tom?" Sam brought his dishes to the sink. Kenneth did the same.

"It had to have been Jazz on both accounts, though he denies it," Kenneth said.

"Maybe Aunt Genieve," Sam threw in.

"I've considered that possibility," Kenneth said.

"Dad, where did you travel before coming here?"

"You think I was with Genieve?" Kenneth locked eyes with Sam. He would make a good poker player.

"You and Genieve keep up," Sam said.

"She's with Tom." Disgust lined Kenneth's words. "Think whatever you want. You all do anyway but she was there when June wasn't. She helped raise all of you when June chose other pursuits. She—"

"She hated mom. She hooked up with Jazz and Tom and you to stick it to mom! Aunt Genieve could have been the one with mom the day she disappeared." Sam pummeled him. Kenneth slumped into the nearest chair.

"No, Jazz had to be the one. I will prove it finally," Kenneth said. His voice was low. It held the hardness in his heart. "He laced my scotch with his concoctions of drugs. I panicked and drank it after I found June gone. I ran around the house and fell down the stairs, banged my head and passed out. He was there. He carted her away and now he's trying to snare Penny."

"You don't know anything dad. You were drunk as usual. You blame Tom or Jazz or Aunt Genieve. Mom chose to get mixed up in Jazz's experiments. She was lost. You never had a chance. Go back to Nova Scotia. Greg and I will take care of Penny," Sam shouted.

"You hate me." Kenneth slouched further down into the chair, "Understandably. I have not been much of a father but I have another chance here, Sam. We need to stick together and expose Jazz and free our family from his grip."

"You never answered my earlier questions," Sam accused.

"I took a few days to try and find Genieve and Tom. I wasn't successful so I went in search of Dr. Marty Mapman."

"One of the doctors who works for Jazz," Sam said. Kenneth nodded. He ran a hand through his grey curls. "Did you find him?" Kenneth shook his head, no. There was a long silence.

"I have made a lot of mistakes." Kenneth's jaw muscles felt as though he had chewed his way through a pile of rocks. "I love your mother, Sam, I always have and I always will. The problem is she allowed some sick individuals to convince her to do things."

"I need to go for a run. I'll be back," Sam interrupted. Kenneth heard his quick steps on the stairs. A few moments later Kenneth heard the front door open. "See you in an hour or so, dad."

"I may be out," Kenneth called. He heard the click of the front door. He assumed Sam heard him. He brushed his teeth and stepped outside to check if he needed a jacket. He wanted the element of surprise. So he hadn't told anyone of his plans. It would be a long walk but he was used to that from living on the island.

He set out at a moderate pace. He had researched the directions before his trip. He glanced down at the map he had constructed. It didn't appear to be too complicated. He walked briskly now, noticing the scraggly lower branches of the tall pine trees. They were ugly. He swatted at the black flies that swarmed around his head.

The feather-like limbs of the balsams seemed to point the way. He breathed in the cool spring air. He hoped she would welcome him. The white peeling barks of the birch trees made the blue sky appear more vibrant.

An hour and a half later he walked up her long driveway, glancing at the flower pots she had yet to fill. He knocked on the door.

Penny had decided to make it a quiet day after her night with Jazz and Brian. She went to church in the morning and afterward took a long walk with Henry. She came home to "noodle" – a phrase she picked up from an Oprah show. A famous guest, whom she couldn't recall, had shared this idea in the 'Remembering Your Spirit' segment of the show.

Penny meandered around her own home like a nosy stranger, letting her spirit speak. Henry came running into the room. Penny stroked his furry neck. Henry wagged his tail and they both stretched out onto the couch. Penny pushed her journal onto the end table. Henry rested his snout on her outstretched thigh. His chocolate brown eyes gazed curiously up at Penny. She scratched his ears. His head popped up and he jumped off the couch. He barked just as someone knocked on her door.

"Dad?" She couldn't believe her eyes.

"Yes." He breathed in the sight of June. "You are beautiful." His eyes watered. He cleared his throat. "May I come in?" Penny nodded and opened the door wider.

"Could I trouble you for a glass of water?" he asked. Penny's legs were made of cooked spaghetti noodles. She wobbled to her kitchen sink and brought back a glass of water.

"You have a lovely home, Penny." He watched her studying him. "I frighten you," he said. A wave of sadness curled around his chest making it hard to breathe.

"Look I'll get right to the point of my unannounced visit. I don't want you working with Jazz or marrying his adopted nephew!"

"I am not working with Jazz Martin!"

"What would you call it then?" Kenneth demanded. Penny stood up.

"You can't just waltz in here after years of hiding in Canada and order me around dad!"

"I realize I haven't been there for you very much, in a long while, maybe," he exhaled. "Maybe ever," he added in a soft voice. "However that is no reason to sign on to one of Jazz's schemes! Why didn't you come to me first?"

Penny opened her mouth but nothing came out. She went to sit down on the edge of her couch but miscalculated, banged her hip, tripped and awkwardly plopped onto one of the cushions. Tears sprang to her eyes.

"Jazz is trying to gain power and control over you, Penny," Kenneth said.

"He already has," she said.

"No!" Kenneth shouted.

"Only he can give me the answers I have wanted," Penny cried.

"This is dangerous. There's no need to rush into some bogus marriage because the great Jazz Martin deems it to be the means of finding June! You can't trust any of his promises."

"Oh like I can trust yours?" Her words were like lemon juice being squeezed into his eyes.

"Jazz Martin is not the only one involved. I am pretty sure of that. Get yourself out while you still can unless...you are already indebted to him in some fashion?"

"No." Ice framed her answer.

"He's a user Penny."

"Then tell me, why does he want us married? And who else is involved?"

He couldn't answer her first question. Not because he didn't suspect the answer but because she couldn't know, at least not yet. He thought for a moment about what he could say. "I don't really know why he concocted this marriage idea. He loves to wield his power. His thinking is warped. He probably is hoping to attract Tom Mott, your Aunt Genieve and his doctor, Marty Mapman."

"Attract them?" she asked.

"He—Jazz started out with biological experimentation, you know stuff having to do with viruses mainly. Then he used people – human guinea pigs! He garnered all sorts of money, from shady businesses to rich private individuals with extreme agendas who, like him, sought control. He created sicknesses in people, through addiction. Tom, Genieve and Marty were involved in this work but have since scattered. I don't want you involved!"

"You and mom performed that work too, didn't you?" she accused.

"Yes we worked for Jazz and were his subjects."

"You're afraid that I can't say no, that I am weak like mom!" Kenneth looked away. She was vulnerable just like June had been. Penny shoved her hands into the pockets of her jeans.

"Where is she right now?"

"I can't," he exhaled.

"NO!" she shouted. "You mean you won't! Do you remember that night ten years ago?" Penny's heart danced around in her chest like someone wildly abandoning themselves to some crazed musical beat.

"I scared you," Kenneth whispered.

Penny couldn't breathe that night or right now. She paced like she was in a marathon. "You purged all the tales of mom's descent into addiction hell. You said she wouldn't be coming back and that you had to go too. Sam and Greg would look after me. I had to accept this and not cause trouble. It wasn't safe. I'd end up messed up like her or worse. Well, I did what you ordered and I've been scared long enough. I am going through with whatever I have to, to learn the truth." Penny rubbed the tears on her cheeks.

"Penny," Kenneth whispered. He couldn't remember much of that night with Penny. He had been pretty drunk.

"It's like a piece of me is missing dad and I need to retrieve it. I can't move forward or feel safe or know who I am!" Penny cried. "I hate the secrets and the lies!"

Kenneth released a long held breath. Penny continued. "You've just been waiting for Jazz to die haven't you?"

Kenneth hung his head. His body was slumped in the shape of the letter c. He felt like a coward. His misery threatened to swallow him. "I – I, need to face things." His voice cracked. "I am sorry."

Penny sucked in air in little puffs. A thick silence filled the air.

CHAPTER NINE

It was Monday. Penny jiggled her keys. There it is the key to her office.

"Hey Pen," said Dana. Penny smiled at her closest friend next to Remi. "How was your weekend? Is there any hot news to report?"

"Brian and I went out to dinner and met his busybody uncle and my long lost maybe dad showed up at my doorstep full of orders and remorse."

"Sounds like you need to talk, sweetie," Dana said. Penny shrugged as she flicked on the overhead light in her office and dropped her purse in her bottom desk drawer.

Kenneth had left after he admitted he had spent years waiting for Jazz to die! Penny had sat on the couch a long while, feeling exhausted. Waves of sadness washed over her like an ocean before a storm. She wrote in her journal, cried and walked Henry. She wished the day would end.

"I'm okay. How about you, still single and loving it? Or are you back to your desperately-seeking-husband-and-nearly-too-old-to-have-a-baby phase?" Penny teased.

"Okay, I'll bite." Dana grinned and plopped down in one of the beige upholstered office chairs off to the side of Penny's desk. Their boss walked in.

"Either of you care to administer to the many waiting clients?" Angela mocked. As bosses go, Penny couldn't complain, she had had much worse. Angela tended toward sarcasm and eccentricity but was fair and generally non-moody.

"Sure," replied Penny first. "What's up?"

"Well, a Mr. Maranino needs assignment to an area shelter. He requires the usual food vouchers to the diner, general health assessment and intake interview."

"Got it," Penny said. Why does she feel the need to review things that I know by heart five times over? Nodding to Dana, Penny left in search of Mr. Maranino.

He was not hard to spot. His clothes were tattered. His beard was scraggly and his hair looked like it had been dipped in bacon grease. Penny wondered if her mother might have ended up in a place like this looking like Mr. Maranino. She flinched. Fat, opaque worms were skydiving off of his head. She stopped moving and looked down. The white worms were dancing near her shoes.

"Mr. Maranino," Penny said. She cleared her throat. "I'll be right back." Penny scooted through the door and down the hallway. Breathless, she bumped into Angela as she was coming out of Dan's office, after no doubt giving him her morning wake-up call too.

"What's wrong?" Angela asked.

"I think Mr. Maranino may have slight problem qualifying for any home right now."

"Why?"

"He really needs Dan and Ron's makeover! He either has a bad case of monster-size head lice, or some other big, white, ugly, deformed bug has taken up residence all over his scalp."

"Probably maggots," Angela remarked. "Okay, let's assemble our best cleaning crew! Thanks Penny, we will see to his immediate care but could you do up the paperwork and see if any slots are available at any of the local shelters for later when he is ready?" Penny nodded and headed to the central offices to find the necessary phone numbers and papers. She hoped her next client was not teeming with quite as much life!

Her day progressed fairly routinely. Although that meant taking a call from a woman recently raped during an evening of too much partying. She had trusted the wrong man to take care of her. What if she were doing the exact same thing?

She left work ten hours later. Kicking off her shoes as soon as she walked in the door to her home, she poured a tall glass of water and plunked in several ice cubes. Her answering machine winked its red eye at her. She let Henry out. He began barking up a storm. She ran to the back door to call him in before her neighbors called the dog-catcher! The door bell rang.

"Hey," Brian said. Penny sighed.

"What are you doing here Brian? It's late and I'm exhausted from work." Henry nuzzled Brian's hand and she glared at her four-legged best friend.

"I was worried about you," he said. He reached for her hand as they stood in her foyer.

"You thought Jazz or one of his evildoers had kidnapped me?" She laughed. He turned the color of the maggots in Mr. Maranino's hair.

"I'm okay," she said. "I've had a few busy days. Sorry I haven't called you back but listen, I was just about to turn in." As if on cue she yawned.

"You don't look okay," Brian replied. She shrugged.

"I was worried about you Penny. I care a lot about you." He hesitated. "Do you want to talk?"

Penny didn't say anything. She rolled her neck from side to side. Suddenly she felt tense and agitated. "I probably won't sleep much anyhow. I have peach cobbler," she said. He laughed.

"Sam came to see me," Brian shared as Penny cut him a piece of the cobbler. "He'll beat me up and throw away my remains if I harm one hair on that lovely head of yours," Brian said. He had a deadpan look on his handsome features. Penny laughed.

"Here you go." She handed him a large helping of the cobbler. She sat down at the kitchen table with a small piece and he joined her. She took a bite. Brian took a few quick swallows from the glass of water she had poured him.

"Kenneth apparently feels the same. They think I am in imminent and horrible danger from your Uncle and his latest plan to turn me into a guinea pig." She watched Brian as his eyebrows shot up.

"Wow," he said. His gaze locked with hers.

She took another bite. "Tell me about Jazz's life?" she asked. Brian's sea gray eyes bore into her.

"This was really good." He pushed back his empty plate. She noticed the muscle in Brian's jaw twitched. "Who wants to know about Jazz's life, you or Kenneth?"

"Me. Why does it matter though?"

"Jazz doesn't think too highly of Kenneth. Here let me help." He joined her at the sink and stuck his fingers into the soapy water and began washing dishes with her. One minute Brian seemed on her side and then the next he was defensive and clearly on Jazz's side of things.

"You clear the table and I'll fill the dishwasher," he explained. Henry had been stretched out on his side but he lifted his head and stared at Penny, sticking his snout high up in the air, he sniffed. His tail thumped on the linoleum and then his head flopped back down and his tail grew quiet. Penny looked at Brian as she put dirty silverware into the dishwasher.

"Want to take a walk into town or go down by the river?" he asked.

"I want to understand the man."

"It can't be done."

"I want to try!" she said.

"Why doesn't that surprise me? Okay, here's what I know. His mom died suddenly—she became sick on one of their world travels. His parents were either both medical research scientists or maybe one was an actual doctor. Or one might have been a biologist. Or wait, his dad was the scientist and his mom was a clinical social worker or psychiatric nurse." He frowned. "Don't quote me on any of that."

"How could I? I don't care about *that* stuff. Focus, Brian! So his mom died suddenly?" Penny prodded.

"Yes. And while she was sick, his dad tried to save her with all sorts of experimental stuff that he had researched and used before, or so my dad suspects."

"So Jazz is following in his parents, or at least in his dad's, footsteps?"

Brian shrugged. "How about that walk Penny, a question-free one though. Whaddya say Hen, are you up for a walk?" Henry grunted and raised himself up. Brian laughed and scratched him behind his ears.

"What was the research about?"

"Unusual infections, viruses and the immune system, I think."
"And his mom got one?"

"Something went wrong with her immune system in some rare fluke type of way. Jazz's father was beside himself. When she died, he totally lost it. He ended up blaming himself for her death."

"He was to blame though, wasn't he?" Penny pressed.

"Probably," Brian headed for the closet where she kept the leash. Penny followed.

"Okay here's the tale. Jazz witnessed his father's breakdown and then only a few months later, his dad died. Without much known close family around and because he and my dad were such pals, he came to live with dad. Eventually, my grandparents made it official, adopting him within a few years. I think Jazz was in junior high school by that time." Brian yawned.

What if Jazz was responsible for both of his parent's death? Maybe he was experimenting with the viruses on his parents? Penny's mind was like a Mexican jumping bean. Penny copied his yawn.

"I don't feel like walking now." She would ask Sam to investigate Jazz's family. Henry wedged himself between them and panted.

"Sorry bud, she said no."

Penny laughed and stroked Henry's back. Brian drew close and looked at her lips. She stepped back. He put his hands on her upper arms and lowered his head, kissing her.

"Speaking of Milman, my father that is, he and I are not real close either." He kissed her forehead and then he pulled her in close for a hug. She was stiff as a board at first but it felt nice, like being wrapped up in a warm blanket. She relaxed a little.

"Maybe this whole thing will bring about several good things. Like me and you getting closer, your dad and you finally talking in an honest way, us growing closer to our fathers." He smiled. "The possibilities are limitless and there are reasons for our union,

Penny."

"Does everything I say, or do go back to Jazz?"

"No, hey thanks for a tasty snack." He hurried out the door.

"What's next?" she asked.

"Planning our engagement party," Brian said. He turned back to her. "Jazz is working on it but he asked in the meantime if we could join him for a game of tennis, or a day of sailing or hiking?"

"For a dying man, he sure likes exercise."

"That's Jazz. He cannot sit still for one moment," Brian said.

"Hiking sounds good," Penny said. They made plans for Saturday. She waved to him as he drove away. Henry stood looking out the door with her.

"Oh sorry, do you need to go out again?" She let him out and poured another glass of water.

As she changed into her pajamas, Henry jumped up on the bed. He scratched at the covers and curled around and around until he made a kind of nest. Penny plopped down beside him. He reached his snout up close to her as she rubbed her face against his head. He licked her ear as she petted his head. She got up and went to the bathroom to brush her teeth.

She smoothed the pillow case and stretched out. She flipped onto her right side and squeezed her eyes shut. Every muscle in her body felt like strings on a violin. She turned over, breathed deeply and drifted off. Her mother's face appeared. Brian was smiling. Kenneth and Jazz stuck each other with long needles. She sat up and hugged herself. She ran her fingers along the different quilt squares as she settled back down. Penny drew the covers up to her chin and squeezed her eyes shut. Sleep crept toward her again like Henry when he was stalking a squirrel.

Images of her mother jabbed at the fringes of her mind as if June was instant messaging her. Penny pulled the covers up over her head and burrowed deeper.

CHAPTER TEN

They hiked on an open path along the ocean, high up among the cliffs. Trees and woodsy terrain alternated with miles of visible green ocean vistas. The weather cooperated, providing a day of sparkling sunshine and enormous, puffy, white clouds amidst azure blue skies. Penny sucked in the fresh air.

"Did you ever confirm whether Kenneth is your real father, my dear?" Jazz threw out the first fast ball and Penny choked. She coughed and banged on her chest. Brian grabbed Jazz's arm.

"It's not as if the thought hasn't occurred to you before, my dear," Jazz said. Penny glared at Brian.

"Relax my dear, he can't compete." Jazz winked at her and then stared at Brian. "Who would guess that I was adopted?" Jazz chuckled.

"I am not adopted," Penny snapped. Brian stepped around the tree root Penny had just climbed over as the three walked in a row.

"What about your two brothers, who is their father?" Jazz asked. Penny stiffened. The ocean and trees dimmed. She put a hand to her aching side and her foot caught. Brian jumped forward. She swatted his hand away but Brian squeezed her elbow, hard.

"Danger lurks in the nooks and crannies of life," Jazz chuckled. "Biology must be a concern." Birds chirped. Leaves rustled. The ocean though now hidden from their view could be heard. Waves crashed against rocks. Brian stepped between her and Jazz and Jazz laughed. Penny wiped her face as it grew wet from her eyes that couldn't stop leaking. Brian offered her his hand. She hesitated but took it.

They hiked for a while in silence. The ocean became visible.

Waves sprayed white fountains of foam in the air. Suddenly, Jazz put a hand to his chest and began massaging.

"Just need to catch my breath." He sat down on a rock and dug a hand into one of his pockets. "Excuse me," he said as he fished out three pills from two bottles. He put them into his mouth and then drank from a water bottle he had been carrying in his backpack. He kept his eyes closed for a few minutes. Penny's eyes darted over to Brian. Their eyes met and Penny saw confusion. Jazz rolled his neck from side to side and let out an enormous breath as if he were a whale.

"Perhaps my father is right here," her voice was soft. Her eyes stared without blinking into Jazz's darkening blue ones. For a moment Penny thought she saw pain, maybe even guilt. She couldn't be sure.

"Your mother was," Jazz said. He smiled. "A beautiful, alluring woman and terribly vulnerable to manipulation, do you share that with her, Penny?" An oven turned on in Penny's face and she walked down the trail, ready to scream. She went quite a distance, ignoring Brian's calls until he was beside her, panting.

"Hey, wait up!" She stopped. Are you hungry?" Brian unzipped his backpack and drew out various containers and bags of food. She glanced around.

"Where's Jazz?" she asked. Brian spread a large checkered table cloth on a rock. She watched him arrange mixtures of foods. He put Brie, colorful vegetables, salmon dip, sweet, yeasty smelling soft bread and cool refreshing cider on the makeshift rock-table. He put out his hands in a gesture of invitation. She didn't move.

"Uncle is on his phone somewhere back there in the woods," Brian explained.

"His phone works up here?" Brian shrugged. She drank a cup of cider. She looked out over the expanse of ocean and rocks. Bursts of spray wet her face.

Suddenly they could hear Jazz. "Yeah, and I want him followed! I want to know every move that two-timing bastard makes! And get back to me, fast!" There was a pause. "Hey it's me, where are you? Okay listen, here's what I need."

"Brian, we are his pawns." She stood up. Brian nodded. She inhaled. "The ocean reminds me of death."

"What," he said.

"You know, of what's most important."

"Is that the black Irish side of you?" He grinned.

"What do you think is most important?"

He exhaled. "I knew I wouldn't get off the proverbial hook. Not death, I feel it when I am training, pushing my body to its limits."

"Precisely, it is about death!" she exclaimed.

"I think way too many people live on autopilot. You have to work at finding meaning, and in ways that match who you are, but it is worth it."

"So in a way it always comes back to death," she said. He shook his head.

"Do you think acceptance only comes in tiny increments over time?" Penny asked.   Wisps of hair blew around her face and he touched one.

"Sometimes," he said. He was slow to answer.

She pulled away. "I want to understand June's life. Why can't people just tell me what I want to know?" She kicked at some loose stones near her one sneakered foot.

"Maybe they don't have the answers," he said. "You think it will help you to know how to live your life?" he asked. He looped his arm around her shoulders.

"Yes." Her voice was hoarse with an ocean of unshed tears. "I think people prefer secrets and lies to the truth. Mom warned me not to ever trust anyone or anything, she'd say, 'Life sucks you in to an enormous pit, swallowing you, trapping you and killing you!'"

"Wow, your death view of life makes sense now." Brian scratched his head.

"Her eyes were like that of a shark's; empty, like death. Driving with her was a nightmare. She careened wildly, her head close to the steering wheel, gripping it, slouching low; her face barely made it above. I yawned five hundred times. I couldn't find enough oxygen."

Brian held her close against his side. "You don't have to accept her choices or her bleak, angry-at-the-world, advice. Feel angry at her for abandoning you, and your family." Brian paused.

"I hope you misbehaved plenty on my account?" Jazz laughed as she and Brian jumped apart. "Ready to plan that engagement shindig as we dig into that nice meal Brian prepared?"

After they ate they walked down the hills in silence. June danced before Penny; laughing with Jazz in their old living room, fighting with Kenneth at night. Their voices carried through the walls into her aching heart, making an ocean of tears soak her pillow. She was drunk, angry, silly and strange, Penny thought.

Penny tripped and slid. She screamed. Her feet flew out from under her. The ground was muddy from recent spring rains. Brian was beside her. Her body thumped into his. He danced.

"Thanks," Penny whispered. Brian grinned and kissed her. Penny squirmed out of his embrace and strode ahead. Jazz laughed and it echoed. Penny balled up her fists. He probably planted the tree roots in her path to make her appear weak, dependent. They arrived at the parking lot.

"Why don't we set the engagement party for three weeks from now? That would keep it on a Saturday. I'll start letting folks know with formal invitations." Jazz patted Brian's back and touched her cheek and then he was off in a spray of gravel and dirt. The car was soon a speck in the distance. Penny kicked at the loose gravel and then she turned to Brian who stood leaning against the passenger side door of his black SUV.

Penny growled. "I hate that man." She stomped to the car.

"Me too," Brian said. He laughed. "You are cute when you're mad though," Brian tried to take her hand. She glared at him. "Don't hit me, Penny please, I bruise easy." He laughed but turned to her with a sober expression as he started the car. "He wants to hurt you, or better yet make you hurt yourself. He hopes you'll lose control and do stupid things."

Like my mother did, she realized as she yanked the seat belt over her and then jerked her body so that it faced the car door and folded her arms across her chest.

"Why am I agreeing to his cockamamie plan?" Her face grew hot and red. "I will bring him down if it is the very last thing I do on this earth!"

"He's not going to win this time." Brian drove down the mountain.

"He's despicable!" She hated herself in this moment.

"It's a rush, the money and the power." Brian blushed. "I admit it, but I am over it. I see how he hones in on people's vulnerable points. He's made it his life's work. I think that's really what the experiments are about." Brian sighed and squeezed her hand. "I believe your mother was one of the few that he lost."

"You think he killed her?" Penny knew he could be right.

"I am not sure, but I think she managed to elude him in one form or another." Penny looked at Brian's profile as he drove. What was he saying? She turned to stare out the window. Trees flew by and soon more buildings came into view.

"Do you know if Kenneth is my real dad?" she asked, still keeping her head turned toward her window.

"No," he said. She watched as his fingers tightened around the steering wheel. She turned to face him. He sighed.

"I think Kenneth is not your biological father."

"Why?"

"Jazz is throwing it in your face for a reason."

"Who is?" she whispered. Please don't let it be Jazz, she prayed.

"I don't know," Brian said. They drove the remainder of the ride in silence. When he dropped her off, Brian merely held her hand through the window, bidding her goodbye and promising to call tomorrow.

Today hadn't been a total waste. She had gained a tiny bit of progress toward some truth, though it was about her father and not her mother. That still meant something. She headed straight for the phone to call Sam. This had to be the type of thing he could research.

CHAPTER ELEVEN

June had made Kenneth promise that he would not let any harm come to Penny. What had Jazz said to her about his plan for Penny? His mother had said, 'Our greatest teachers are those whom we despise and idolize.' He supposed he had learned about power from Jazz. Or should he say powerlessness? It was horribly humbling and frustrating.

He gestured for another scotch. The bartender slid it toward him. Kenneth glanced around the dark, dingy place and homesickness for Quincy's bar in Canada squeezed his heart. He sipped his drink and checked his watch, another twenty minutes had passed. He flipped open his cell phone, no messages or missed calls. Kenneth paid his bill. The bright sunshine hurt his eyes. Genieve wasn't going to call. His mother would remind him that, 'Not only can love blind us, but it has the power to make us do things we spend the rest of our lives regretting.'

He drove the rental car to the old neighborhood and parked across the street. A fish out of water flopped around in his stomach.

"You infected Jazz and you left me in that hut with Tom!" June's words echoed. Kenneth leaned his forehead against the steering wheel and gripped the seat underneath him.

"It's too late." Aaron, his colleague at the lab had said when Kenneth had tried to discover a way out from under Jazz's control for both he and June. "There are clinics to prove it! Let her go and run far, far away from here Kenneth," Aaron said.

Kenneth cried out and slammed the car door. The street was deserted. He walked toward the old house where he and June and the kids had lived for many years after returning from their Asia trip – the same trip in which June's escapade into the remote village with Tom Mott and her subsequent narrow escape had occurred. He tried to quell the images and voices in his head but they grew more and more insistent.

"I love him Kenneth! I always have," she said.

"You love me!" he shouted. The tears streaming down her face said it all.

A scream of rage erupted through the muscles of his body. Sam and Greg were wrestling in the yard. Penny was playing with her paper dolls on the porch. June was on the phone again with Jazz. Kenneth dragged the rake across the lawn pulling the decaying leaves into piles.

Ten years ago he came home from work. June lay on the floor of their bedroom. A small red spot was on the carpet near her head. A bottom drawer of her large dresser was slightly open. Had she fallen and hit her head after having too much to drink? Clothes were strewn all over their unmade queen-sized bed. A jar of lotion was open on her dresser along with what he thought must be eye shadow. It was a purple powdery substance with a small brush next to it.

"June," he said. The phone cord was tangled around part of her body. He touched her throat. She was warm and still had a pulse.

He stood on the front lawn. The bushes were overgrown. The grass needed mowing. His face felt hot with the memories. How many times had he imagined discovering her hurt and unconscious? No amount of worrying could help fix someone and yet he had spent so many, many years trying.

He stumbled out of the bedroom and into the bathroom. He needed to think. He tried to clear his head with icy tap water. It was only for a few minutes. He considered running for help to a neighbor maybe? He couldn't involve the police, not yet. Too many lies and secrets might be exposed. Or he could run far away like Aaron had suggested a few days ago in the lab. No, he couldn't leave her like this. He went back to their bedroom. She was gone!

He squinted. Shadows formed around the dark looming house as the sun set. He shivered.

Someone had laughed. The room spun. June's blood on the lavender carpet and the long curly phone cord taunted him. He raced around the rooms checking under beds, yanking the shower curtain back. CeCe, their poodle, barked and trotted with him. An open bottle of scotch on the kitchen counter was a magnet. He was thirsty. It must have been tainted. He'd gripped the railing that lined the staircase and forced his legs to move. He was on a carnival ride, the giant twirling teacup one.

Kenneth inhaled and coughed. He stood on the porch. His hand rested on the tarnished, gold-colored front doorknob. He had to wait for Penny. She was skiing and wouldn't be home for several more hours. How could he tell her June was gone? That he hadn't been able to save her mother?

His back ached. CeCe licked his face. Had he fallen or was he was pushed down the long winding stairs? He lay at the bottom of the stairs. He smelled the scotch. The carpet was wet. He saw the open bottle by his feet. He heard whispering his name and June's? Jazz, Tom, Genieve or Marty, or was there someone he hadn't thought of? He should have stayed with June. He should have called for help right away. Instead he fell down the stairs.

"June," he whispered. "I need you." He turned the knob.

The phone rang. He gripped the stair railing. A soft voice thick with tears whispered, 'Help!' June? Genieve?

"Hey, what the hell do you think you're doing?" A sharp male voice shouted. Kenneth swung around. He squinted into the beaming headlights. Panic swept through him as though he were struck by lightning. He twisted and turned the doorknob. It wouldn't open! He wrapped his two hands around it and yanked up and down on the knob.

"June, baby, I'm coming!" he shouted. Tears poured down his face.

"Help," she cried. The line went dead.

"Hey mister," he said. The large burly man put a hand on his arm and squeezed. "Get away from my house."

It's, it's not," Kenneth cried. "I live, lived here, my wife, she's – she was in trouble."

"Okay, sir, look, you need to calm down. I live here now. I've got my kids in the car," the man pointed to the car in the driveway. Kenneth blinked as the headlights held him in the spotlight. He looked at the man and stepped away.

"I," he said. Kenneth backed away further.

"You need help. You want me to call someone for you? Maybe you shouldn't drive!" The man called out as Kenneth hurried back to his car.

"June." Kenneth repeated her name over and over in his mind. He wrung his hands. He leaned against the car door and gripped his key with two hands. His stomach hurt. He sat down in the car. The man hurried his children into the house. The door shut. Kenneth flinched. His key wouldn't fit into the ignition. He tried again. The car started up and he sped down the street. He squealed around the corner and a car honked. He swerved and drove faster until he came upon the convenience store he remembered. He screeched into the parking lot. He leaned his head back against the seat and closed his eyes. The rest of the day after June had disappeared tumbled through his mind.

As the effects of the scotch began to wear off, he swallowed some Tylenol and Advil and limped out to his car. He hurried to the lab, making his way to the back entrance. He heard two voices. The hammering inside his head along with the growing stiffness he felt throughout his body distracted him. He stopped and caught his breath. The two voices became louder. His head was full of wads of fuzzy cotton balls.

"Why isn't he answering his pager? It's been over an hour."

"They are on route. It takes a while to get there. He's probably waiting until she's there to let us know."

"Come on let's get this part done and get out of here. He won't be out too much longer."

Too late, I'm here; he thought and almost laughed aloud. Kenneth watched as two figures, a man and a woman made their way into his office. The door shut and he stood up. He looked back down from where he had come and then back to his closed office door. He checked his watch and thought of Penny. He needed to get home soon. June had made him promise to be there for her today and always, and to never let any harm come to her, ever.

He clenched and unclenched his fists as he stared at the closed door. He turned abruptly and sprinted as best he could down the hall. When he reached the double doors he slammed the pinky-finger end of his balled up fist into the red emergency button. Then as glaring lights flashed and the deafening sounds of the siren pierced the air, he ran outside. His head spun back and forth. He raced to some shrubbery that edged the property, to where he thought he might have a perfect view.

He was sweating. He wiped his brow and squatted. A wave of nausea and dizziness assaulted him. He fought to keep his balance. He leaned awkwardly into the bushes. He shot a hand out to steady himself. His legs ached and his head throbbed. Twigs and small branches from the bush scratched his face. It stung and he inhaled sharply, just as two figures scurried out of the back of the building. The same exit he had come through minutes before. The man ran for a car parked nearby. The woman stood still with one hand above her eyes. She had long blond hair. June's hair was auburn and Genieve's this month was black as midnight. But they both wore wigs on occasion. Who is the man she's with? He should know. He blinked and tried to think but the fuzzy cotton balls clogged his synapses.

The woman was searching for something or someone, maybe him. It could be Cathy, the plastic surgeon's wife who was furious with June. She had blond hair, didn't she? He tried to remember. Had June had an affair with the surgeon? June had met with him a few times. He did some work for Jazz. Cathy had become interested in Jazz's work or more likely he had drawn her in, like a spider to his web.

He heard the sirens over the emergency building ones. The police were on their way. The woman jumped in a car and it sped off through a back alley. Kenneth jumped up. He ran like a drunk toward his car. The sirens were loud. There wasn't much time. He jogged back to the lab and pulled at the locked door. He went back to the bushes. Police cars arrived and his heart sank. Bright lights shined on him.

"Hey you, stop where you are, raise your hands in the air." The policeman shouted at Kenneth.

Kenneth swiveled his body left then right. He held a hand over most of his eyes.

"N—no—no you don't understand." He pointed in the direction of the alley.

"Keep your hands above your head sir!" Two officers were joined by two more police who raised their guns and pointed them at Kenneth. Several other police cars arrived along with an ambulance and fire truck. Some were wearing protective gear and ran around to the front of the building.

Kenneth rubbed his eyes. He went into the convenience store and bought a bottle of whiskey and took it to the car. His cell phone rang.

"Yeah," he said.

"Kenneth." Her low raspy voice felt like a caress. He felt her long fingernails reach through the phone to scrape his heart.

"I was remembering the day June left me, tell me was it you and Tom who took June away?" He took a long swallow of the amber liquid. The wild fish in his stomach quieted.

"She left you many times Kenneth," she said. "And no, it wasn't us. I don't know who took her away."

"Why can't you come here, Genieve?"

"I will soon," she said.

"I need your help. Penny's in danger. I promised June." He drank. She was silent. "Remember," he slurred. "I was blamed for three vials of the missing retroviruses. June's disappearance fell on me and the data we collected without the consent forms. The experiments we did on human subjects with the drugs, the pills Jazz had formulated to see how addictive they could be!" Kenneth said.

"Kenneth you need to sober up. Penny needs your help." Genieve said. She hung up.

"I have spent ten years in exile for nothing," he mumbled. He drank more whiskey. He put his cell phone on the seat beside him.

The police had questioned him at length. They confiscated piles of notes, he had made about the experiments involving the testing of various addictive substances and their effects on the immune system, brain function and psychological health. Jazz had ordered him to keep copious records. Kenneth thought he had locked them away in places only he could find.

He had been set up so he could be sent away. No charges were ever filed. Penny cried when he and a police officer told her June was gone, perhaps dead. They couldn't be sure. It would be investigated. But in the meantime she would be under Sam and Greg's care. He had to go away. More police searched his home, taking bottles of scotch with them, and samples from the blood stains they found upstairs. They dusted for fingerprints and found his, Genieve's, Jazz's, Tom's, Cathy's, all of the kid's, June's, it was pointless!

Penny couldn't look Kenneth in the eye. Greg arrived late that night and he and Sam took Penny away. He saw his kids only in brief intervals over the next few weeks of the investigation. Then he disappeared, traveling for months and finally ending up in Nova Scotia, Canada and eventually settling on Cape Breton Island

His mother's words echoed, 'A bit of clarity Kenneth, here and there, that's all life can show in a moment, so grab it, but for goodness sake, learn to put it to good use or it's worth nothing!'

"Why can't I ever seem to heed your teachings?" He looked up. The investigators stopped calling. Tom and Genieve went overseas. Jazz retreated to a remote lab in Alaska. Kenneth existed in Canada. The kids ignored him.

Yet they all stayed connected through sporadic phone calls and visits because of their collective need for June. She lived in all their worlds. Was she dead? Where was she? Who was she with? No one admitted anything.

"Ten years and now Penny has to get married, a new Jazz Martin experiment?" he slurred. "Why? Is it time for a reunion?" Kenneth closed his eyes. June? No it was Genieve and she was smiling, touching his cheek. Why couldn't he tell them apart?

Kisses...in the kitchen, he forced his eyes open. Genieve helped with the kids while June was off working with Jazz. Genieve encouraged June to go. Jazz needed her as a subject. Why didn't Kenneth stop it? Genieve was convincing. It had been so easy to let her decide. He turned to the scotch she and Jazz provided. It helped way too much.

'Life is about circles, Kenny. Everything turns in on itself eventually,' his mama had said. Kenneth rubbed his face. Everything became blurred. The scotch and Jazz's tricks, Genieve and June, the rightness of his work and Kenneth couldn't think. So he acted upon what was right in front of him the most. The scotch and Genieve and the triangles grew bigger, existing everywhere he turned, secrets flourished and answers remained elusive.

He started the car and drove slowly out of the parking lot, gripping the steering wheel as though it were the last rock to hold onto on a high cliff.

CHAPTER TWELVE

It was Sunday. Penny had met Sam and Greg for lunch at the town bakery, high up on a hill overlooking a lake.

"I can't believe the engagement party is less than two weeks from now!" she moaned. She nibbled at the assortment of veggies that fell out of her smoked turkey wrap. It was a gorgeous day. An azure blue sky above her and a light breeze that tickled her bare arms and ruffled her hair as it hung loose around her shoulders.

"Too bad dad couldn't join us today," Greg said. He rubbed a hand across Penny's back. Sam was worried about Kenneth. He was drinking heavily, disappearing for hours, sometimes days and then sleeping for long periods of time.

"I've hardly been able to catch up with him," Sam said.

"There they are," Jazz announced, grinning as he came up and stood over Penny. Brian was by his side, like a puppet.

"This is a private lunch," Sam snapped.

Jazz laughed. "No worries we already ate. Do they have mocha lattes in there?" He pointed to the small white house that was the bakery. No one answered him. Jazz shrugged and started to walk over to it when he halted mid-stride and gripped his chest. A look of pain and confusion passed over his face. He stumbled. Brian had one leg inside the picnic table spot next to Penny. He hopped and bolted over to Jazz.

"Come sit down." Brian led him back to the picnic table.

"Pills, right front poc—cket," Jazz said. His words were garbled. Brian stuck his hand into Jazz's pocket in search of pills.

"Where is the pain coming from Jazz?" Greg asked.

"No—no, no doctor is Marty. Call him Bri." Jazz huffed. His hand shook as he brought it to his chest. His face scrunched up. "Oooohhhh," Jazz moaned.

"I've got them!" Brian pulled out a small vial that was half-filled with tiny, round, white pills.

"I don't have my bag with me. I didn't drive." He squatted next to Jazz. "We should call an ambulance. What are your symptoms?" Greg had his cell phone out. Brian shook out three pills per Jazz's instructions. Jazz opened his mouth and Brian placed them on his tongue.

"No ambulance," Jazz said. He swatted Greg's phone out of his hand. "Sick, long time, lab accident, Kenneth and June's fault." Jazz's voice was hoarse with pain.

A man and woman from a nearby picnic table walked over. "Is everything okay here?"

"Fine thanks." Sam nodded. "He's old. It's nothing we haven't dealt with before!" The couple looked from Jazz to Sam and then to Penny. She smiled and thanked them. They walked away craning their necks to check on the situation as they headed toward the parking lot.

Jazz smiled a little.

"Nice show," Sam said. Greg stood up.

"He's not faking it," Brian said. Penny thought he sounded uncertain.

"Such loyalty," Sam said. Penny heard the sarcasm.

"Now," Jazz said. He breathed hard as though having run a marathon. "Boys, thanks for," he said. Jazz paused. He patted Greg's hand. Penny jumped. She knew her face must look horror-stricken.

"Uncle, not now," Brian interrupted.

"On with the show," Sam said. He waved his arms like a conductor.

"Sam," Greg scolded. "Jazz I think you should be examined."

"It happened before June plastered herself all over Kenneth, her second choice since she realized I'd never marry her." Jazz smiled. He suddenly appeared fine. Penny's jaw dropped. Brian stuck his hands in his pockets and turned to look at the lake.

"Bastard," Sam spit out. He walked toward the parking lot.

"Biology can be ugly," Greg said.

"Sorry," Penny muttered. She came to stand by Greg.

"Yes it can." Jazz laughed. "He's Kenneth's," Jazz said. He pointed to where Sam stood beside a tall, old oak tree. "June's sexual habits make it difficult to know about your paternity my dear," Jazz said.

"Shut up!" Greg clenched his fists and moved toward Jazz. Brian interceded.

"Time to go find Marty for a check-up and a rest, Uncle," Brian said. He turned to Penny. "I'd like to take you over to meet Wil?"

"I don't know Brian," she said. Penny held up a hand. "Why did you come over here? How did you know we were here? What did you want?" She hurled the questions like a pitcher trying for a strike out.

"My dear, I am always aware of your activities." He grinned at her. A snake coiled around her stomach. "I had hoped to catch up with Kenneth," Jazz continued.

"He's not here." Sam stood next to Penny and spoke in a low menacing tone.

"What sort of drugs do you ingest?" Greg asked.

"None of your business doc unless you care to join our work team," Jazz said.

"No thank-you," Greg retorted.

"Let's go Uncle, Kenneth isn't here and I believe you've overstayed any welcome you may have had," Brian said.

"He's never welcome," Sam growled.

"Let's get some ice cream," Greg said to his two siblings. Penny and Sam nodded. There was an ice cream stand right next to the bakery and the three of them walked over to it. They decided on splitting two kinds of milkshakes, one peach vanilla and one extreme chocolate, at Penny's request. They walked together admiring the flowers. Then they sat down again at another picnic bench.

"Do you both think he's faking his heart condition?" Penny asked, handing the chocolate shake to Greg. Brian and Jazz must have left. She didn't see Brian's black SUV in the parking lot.

"Yup," Sam said. He spun his straw around. He looked angry.

"I hate him," Penny groaned. "I'm glad he's not my father. Sorry Greggie," she added.

"Don't be so sure, sis," Sam said.

"You found out something?" Penny had asked him to look into it after the hike.

"Not yet, but you can't rule it out," Sam said. "Do you guys know I tried mom's purple and pink pills? The one's she kept in the Sucret lozenge containers by her bed." Greg held up a hand and was about to speak, when Sam continued over him. "Nothing much happened, other than feeling a little hyper or sleepy depending on which ones I took. I think mom was gullible to the power of suggestion. She wanted somebody or something but never what she had at any given moment."

"What do you mean?" Penny asked.

"Well, much as I hate to admit it, Jazz is right. Mom wanted Kenneth to save her from Jazz I guess at least some of the time, like when she was pregnant with Greg and knew Jazz would never marry her, as he admitted. Then she was drawn back to him when she kept agreeing to be a test subject for his experimental work. Then she met Tom overseas and later Kathy's husband, some neighbor cosmetic surgeon guy, I forget his name." He glanced at Greg but he only shrugged. "All I am saying is Jazz has a point about her habits."

"You're awfully quiet." Penny murmured to Greg after sucking down about half of the extreme chocolate milkshake and pushing the remainder toward Sam.

"I hate that he is technically my father," Greg said. Penny linked her arm through his thick hairy one. She put her head on his big shoulder.

"Sorry," she murmured for the second time. Greg sighed. "You'll be a very different father than Jazz or Kenneth, Greggie."

"Thanks," he said. No one said anything for a while. The brothers finished the milkshakes and tossed them into the trash can. Greg said he had to go check back in at the hospital. Sam sat with Penny under a large tree and they tried to piece all they were learning together.

Brian arrived an hour later and waved her over to his car. Sam warned her not to go but she didn't listen and they headed to Wil's house. Sam had glared at Brian and told her to be careful.

"What is this?" she asked referring to the music.

"Sorry. Jazz was listening to Earl Father Hines to soothe himself – classic Jazz." Brian switched the music to classic rock. "He swallowed more pills in the car. Then he pulled out two small vials of substances he created with Marty Mapman's help." He held up a hand. "Now before you bombard me with questions, Marty is his personal physician and a prominent medical researcher on Jazz's payroll for years, okay?" Penny nodded as Brian finished explaining.

"What exactly are in these 'secret vials?'" she asked.

"Chemical mixtures they concocted based on Marty's work with enzymes and viruses that may live in arterial walls. He explained he's leaning more and more on Marty and his curative substances. He kept calling Marty over and over on the ride home."

"Sam thinks he's faking," Penny said.

"I know you do too," Brian said. "I have my own doubts, but I have to play along Penny, so bare with me no matter how it might seem. I am on your team, okay?"

"I guess." She turned her head to look at the neighborhood they had just entered. Modest-sized homes painted earth colors, nothing too special, she thought. The big trees were nice.

Brian paused as he pulled into Wil's driveway. The house was dark and there were several large green garbage bags piled up by the side of the house. He frowned.

"What's wrong?" Penny prompted.

"I'm not sure." Brian looked worried as they walked up to Wil's front door. She felt nervous as they rang the bell to Wil's house. Brian seemed anxious too.

"Hey – oh man, did I catch you at a bad time?" Brian asked as Wil opened the door, dressed only in his boxer's. His hair stuck out in wild disarray. "Penny this is Wil!" Wil rubbed his face and eyes and yawned.

"Oh hey nice to meet you, come in! Deedee—my wife, is away with some girlfriends for a few days and I was just resting." He opened the door wider and they stepped in. Brian gasped. Penny put a hand up to her mouth, trying to hide a smile.

"Wow," Brian said as his eyes traveled the room. Old food boxes and wrappers, piles of clothes and papers were strewn everywhere. "This place is a junk heap."

"I'll whip it into shape before she comes back. I have been working crazy hours. Pull up a seat." Wil shoved a heap of clothes onto the floor.

"I think I'll stand a while, maybe until Deedee gets back." Brian turned to Penny and mouthed an apology to her. "I have to admit I was pretty worried when we pulled up to the house. I thought maybe some tragedy had struck."

"Like what?" Wil seemed genuinely baffled.

"Like someone died, and maybe they did after all." Brian scrunched up his face in a disgusted look. "What's that?" Brian pointed to an open carton as he held his nose. "It looks like somebody's brain."

"No foul play to worry about! That's your Uncle's department," Wil said. "It was egg foo young I never got around to finishing. Want me to heat it up for you?" Wil grinned.

"Sure, look, do you want some help cleaning up?" Brian asked.

"What did you come over for?" Wil asked, sitting down on the floor and yawning so wide, Penny thought he could swallow a tennis ball.

"Support, however I think you need it more than we do. Jazz put on one of his 'I am dying one minute and fine the next shows.'" Brian swung his arm around. "This is grounds for divorce." Wil scratched his dirty hair and laughed. "Are there any empty trash bags left?" He eyed the twenty full bags that appeared to be lining the living room wall.

"You sure you're okay? Deedee hasn't run off on you has she?" The three of them filled and lugged bags of trash out back.

"Sorry, I'm not making a very good first impression, am I?" Wil laughed. "And I am sorry about Jazz and his antics. He is a jerk of the n-th degree!"

"There's the wisdom Brian raves about." Penny laughed a little.

"She thought you were some sort of Zen Buddhist master!" Brian chuckled. "I think this might have taken care of that idea, huh, Pen?"

"Images can be deceiving. I am learning a lot about that right now," Penny said.

"Not where I am concerned." Brian murmured close to her ear. Their eyes caught and remained steady for a few moments. Penny dropped her gaze first. They went back inside after hauling several large trash bags out the front door. They washed up and made some coffee.

"So when is the big day gonna be?" Wil asked as they sat on the now cleaner couches and chairs in the living room.

"We are now less than two weeks until the engagement party. It's not next Saturday but the one after. I want the truth about my mother's life and an answer to what really happened to her ten years ago," Penny blurted.

"In the meantime she has to marry me. A feat she dreads," Brian said.

"He's not so bad." Wil smiled at her.

"I told you the date of the engagement party Wil. You better have put it on your calendar!" Brian said with irritation.

"Don't worry, I am the Zen master remember." Wil chuckled.

"Why do I have to agree to participate in Jazz's plan to find my mother?" she snapped.

"Life is a series of hoops we have to jump through," Wil said.

"Profound," Brian said. Penny could hear the hurt in his voice.

"It's not like you love me Brian. You're hoop-jumping too for your own reasons," she said.

"Hey you two want to help me indulge in a last hurrah of take out junk food before Deedee returns?"

"Sure," Brian agreed. He kept looking at her with such soulful eyes. Quit it! She wanted to holler at him. They ordered an extra large pizza with everything on it.

"Aw watch out, we just cleaned this place up," Brian said. He watched Wil teeter a loaded slice towards his mouth and a few toppings fell to the floor. The fifteen toppings they had agreed upon looked ready to slide every which way. Wil laughed and moved his mouth back and forth catching most of the meat and veggies. The rest managed to slip off onto his shirt, which already had remnants of the last few days of late night snacks.

"Seriously," Wil said. "I think you two have something going on. Just because it began under very odd and quite arguably ugly circumstances, you should see it through. Deedee and I met while arguing over the last box of Christmas lights at Wal-Mart and just look at how we turned out!"

"Yeah, just look." Penny glanced around at the chaos. Brian shot her a look but Wil threw back his head and laughed.

CHAPTER THIRTEEN

The phone rang. Penny was headed to the park to meet Sam. They ran together a few mornings a week if their schedules permitted. It was Wednesday and her first client at the crisis center wasn't due to meet with her until ten. It was seven-thirty and she would have time for a nice run and shower before she met with her client.

"Hello," she said with tentativeness. She had not recognized the number on her caller id.

"Get ready to participate in an experiment, dear. It's time." Click.

She couldn't identify the voice. It sounded mechanical. She glanced at the clock. She was going to be late.

They hugged as soon as they met. "You look tired," Penny said to her brother Sam. The sun was shining. The air was cooler and dry. Summer seemed to be whizzing by. Penny yawned and stretched. She sniffed the sweetness of honeysuckle blooming nearby. The clear blue sky felt like it stretched on forever and the leaves on a nearby huge maple had begun just a tiny, tiny bit to sing their song of color. She decided to focus on the beauty in the world not these stupid phone calls, or Jazz's plan!

"Don't worry, it's a good thing. My business is growing lately."

"Sorry I interrupted you." Her voice caught.

"Uh oh, the flood gates are about to open!" Sam grinned at her and looped an arm around her shoulders. "Let's walk," Sam said, holding her arm as he directed her to a path.

"I want to know about dad and your research and are you dating anyone lately, Sam?" she prompted. Sam moved quickly. She huffed and puffed trying to keep up.

"Move!" He commanded all of sudden.

"Sorry I am being nosey on that last front especially." He grabbed her arm and propelled her to move faster. "What happened to warming up first?" Penny couldn't keep the whine out of her voice.

"Sis put those legs into a higher gear!"

"What is your big all-fire hurry," she snorted. "Had too many late night fast food runs?" So much for noticing nature, she could barely breathe right now.

"Shush, just follow me!" he said. They circled around the park and outside to a street close to the water and ducked through an alley. They emerged in a residential neighborhood. Sam spun around. He was concentrating.

"Sam." She breathed hard. "Wha – what is it?"

"We're being followed! Penny, please move it!"

"I have a cramp and it is getting worse!" She held her side and bent over while she continued to run. She gulped air in, in short gasps.

"I thought you exercised regularly."

"Shut up! I didn't call you so you could drag me out for some marathon! Tell me first about your research. I need a distraction." She panted.

"Dad is still up to the same old, same old. Drinking, disappearing, and sleeping. No girlfriend or dating right now, I don't have time so there's that for your nosiness. Most of my research is private and confidential Pens, you know that." He motioned for them to begin jogging. "Sorry about how you had to grow up pretty much without mom and dad." He jogged in place while she stretched and took long slow breaths. "Dad was way too obsessed with work, listen, are you sure you want to know the identity of your biological dad?"

"Why wouldn't I?" She glanced around. Who was following them? Someone they knew or was it the phone caller?

Sam was quiet for a few minutes. They jogged side by side. "It might be hard to find out if it was one of June's fleeting lovers."

"Sam, who is following us," she whispered. He shrugged. His face was stitched tightly together.

"You hate mom," Penny said after a while.

"Sometimes," Sam said. His voice was soft. Penny felt a wave of love for her brother. They ran through the residential streets. A suburban neighborhood straight out of a Spielberg movie!

"I had another call this morning." She told him.

"That could be who is calling you," he said.

"Who, mom," Penny asked. She was glad that she had confided to him about the anonymous calls that had begun as hang-ups a few months ago and now had progressed to one-line commands.

"Maybe," he said.

"Yeah or it could be whomever my father is, or Jazz, or it could be Aunt Genieve!" She threw her hands up into the air.

"Or Brian playing with you," he said. "What did the caller say today?"

"That I am about to become a subject in an experiment!" Sam picked up the pace.

"You already are with this phony baloney marriage. Maybe you should move in with me for a while Pen," Sam suggested.

Penny laughed. "No thanks, the stress of that might kill me!"

"Ha ha, it might be better than the alternative," he said. She saw the loving worry in his dark eyes.

"You have mom's eyes," she blurted. He didn't say anything but she had the feeling he took it as a compliment.

"I have been taking care of myself for many years now and have done just fine as you can see! I have no intention of becoming a victim of some addiction experiments like mom did."

"Greg and I have always been there for you." He was hurt.

"Of course, I didn't mean—" she started. He interrupted.

"It's different now with this whole engagement mess you've agreed to with Brian," he said. "I learned some more about Tom Mott. He took mom and others to remote villages in India to run all sorts of experiments on them, way beyond even what dad and Jazz did. Tom spent years trying to lure mom back with phone calls and letters, even visiting her a few times."

"Did she succumb? Where is he now? Is he a part of Jazz's plan?"

"I can't be sure," he said. "I think he and Aunt Genieve got hitched a few years after dad moved to Cape Breton Island. Tom has to harbor ill will toward mom, Jazz, and Kenneth."

"Because he didn't get his way?" she asked.

"He didn't win," Sam said.

"Boy games," she remarked. Sam grimaced. "Could he be my father?" Penny gasped as the awful thought ran through her.

"Who knows? Anything is possible," Sam commented.

"Aunt Gen would know," she said. "Sam I have always wondered about her. She hated mom the most. Do you think she killed mom?" Sam spun around and jogged backwards.

"There's no proof of any killing, Penny."

"There's no proof she's alive. Why else would she stay completely away from us for ten years now?" Sam shrugged. "Does anyone know where Aunt Genieve is now, if she's even alive? SAM!" Penny shouted as she tried to keep up with Sam's increased pace.

"Let's get out of here," he said. He slowed so he could run next to her. They were back in the park and she felt Sam's edginess return. "You do know that Aunt Genieve and dad had an affair for years? I suspect they still carry on!"

"This is crazy! Or it'll make me that way," she cried.

"You see why I have had no interest in dredging all this up? Mom, Genieve, Jazz and Kenneth, and Tom, all screwed around while experimenting with drugs and some weird intense psychotherapy and it eventually caught up with all of them. End of stupid story." He was bitter.

"Genieve and mom overdosed on sex and drugs?" The words flew out of her mouth. She was appalled and she giggled. Sam cracked a wide grin.

"Why do you keep saying everyone is dead?" Sam said a few moments later. They wound their way back through the park.

"I told you!" she shouted.

"Because they're not in our daily lives!" he said. "Greg thinks, and a few of my contacts agree, there were biomedical and psychological components involving the immune system and emotional centers in the brain involving personality."

"Like a sex change operation only involving personality changes not gender?" She clarified her thoughts aloud. Hysterical laughter threatened along with a sense of horror. Her side hurt again. "Can we stop running?"

He shrugged. "I need more time."

"Isn't that kind of thing totally unethical, not to mention illegal?" she asked. He put his arm around her shoulders and squeezed her close to him protectively.

"Yes, but Jazz seemed to be working for some very powerful folks with hoards of money. Money won out over ethics," Sam said. They walked in silence for a time. Penny looked up at the clear blue sky that held a few enormous puffy white clouds, her favorites normally. But she barely noticed.

"What if it is mom?" She blew out her breath and rolled her shoulders. She grabbed Sam's upper arm. "What if she's the one calling me?"

"So now she's not dead but is threatening you? Why Penny, why would she do that?" He squinted at her. "Is there something you're not telling me?"

"Look they sell freshly squeezed lemonade." She pointed to a small stand across the grassy area where they were walking.

"Penny," Sam scolded. He saw through her poor attempt at avoiding his question.

"These calls are not exactly threatening. They're more like telling me what I should do or what could happen. She was worried about me. She made dad promise to take good care of me."

"Another promise broken by him," Sam said. "That's totally wishful thinking Pen."

"She doesn't want me to do this marriage thing with Brian. She's afraid of what might happen to me or maybe she's being made to call me. Or this whole scheme of Jazz's is forcing her to face her past— and come back!"

"Oh Pens, so now you think Jazz or Tom or someone held her captive for ten years?" He wrapped an arm around her. She pushed away from him and took a dollar and few coins out of her pocket.

"A small please," she told the vendor. "Want a sip?" She pushed the cup at Sam.

"Penny," he said. Sam took a sip.

"It's good, huh?" she asked. He nodded.

"Forget the lemonade, look you can't dream like this. Mom's gone. She's not facing anything ever! She's not coming back, no way!" he said. There was vehemence in his tone.

"Gone how? You mean she ran away and chose to avoid us because she started a whole new life and forgot about us? You can't possibly have proof of that, Sam!"

"Tell me when you get another call, okay?" he said after a long pause.

"Okay," Penny sighed. "You don't have to believe me right now. I would just like it if you would open up your heart and mind to the possibilities I am suggesting, okay?"

"What the hell would that be? She's dead. No, wait she's being held captive in someone's dungeon of torture. She's calling to direct your life from afar. Oh no wait she has a whole new identity and family!"

"Fine I am crazy! Just stop it!"

"I will if you'll stop being so stubbornly set on marrying Brian," he raised his voice.

"It's a chance to put Jazz in his place." She smiled through trembling lips.

"You mean use the guy's own plan against him?" Sam's disbelief was smeared across his face like a thick coat of make-up.

"It's possible, remember Sammy, open mind!" She waved her index finger at him. "You are failing already!"

"Between you and me, I highly doubt Brian's the one to outdo Jazz." He held up a hand. "You're marrying Brian to put the screws to Jazz even though you were the one who contacted him and agreed to *his plan* which turned out to be marrying his adopted nephew?"

She laughed. "Crazy again, I hear you loud and clear, Sam!"

They walked in silence a while.

"Mom and dad's lives were crazy but we can make very different choices, Penny" he said.

"Precisely why I called Jazz," she said. Sam shook his head as though trying to fling a bug off of his scalp. He irritated her.

"Race ya?" Sam announced and they ran hard. Eventually Penny gripped her side.

"You always win!" she said, coming to a stop. "I have to do this Sam. Are you with me?" He nodded and rubbed the top of her head. She put up with it.

"What choice do I have?" Sam put his fist up to her chin. She ducked. He laughed and put his arm around her neck. "Promise me you'll be careful," he whispered in her ear. His voice sounded full of emotion.

"Of course," Penny said. She leaned against his hard chest.

"Let me have the answering machine if you haven't erased anything. I'll get you a new one, okay? The timing of the calls may be important Pen." He hugged her. "It's going to be all right. I am glad you told me. I am going to let Greg know which means Nance will know too."

Penny bobbed her head up and down against his chest. A small sob escaped.

"Go ahead it's an old shirt." He laughed and rubbed her head with his knuckles. "Listen, bone up on the workouts so you can keep up with me next time." Penny elbowed him in the ribs.

"Ouch," he moaned. "Meet me tomorrow for breakfast if you have time before work?"

"I'll check and call you." She wiped her wet eyes.

"I'll cook those chocolate chip and blueberry pancakes you turned me on to," he said. She nodded.

Penny watched Sam retrace their steps. She hoped he found clues about who might have been following them. Penny let out a big breath as she drove home. She put some music on and began to hum along to an old Alan Jackson country tune, 'Little Bitty'. Penny drove slowly, drying her still moist face. She looked around. The grass was such a Kelly green. It had been a good summer for rain. She put down her car window all the way. Her hair blew wildly in the cool breeze. She thought of the 'The Merry Little Breezes', characters from a childhood nature story, her father must have read over and over to her. She smiled as tears collected in the corners of her eyes. She twirled a bushy curl of hair in her fingers and fidgeted with the radio.

She called Brian when she pulled up at a stop sign. She got his voice mail so she hung up without leaving a message. Penny turned up the music and drove the remaining distance home. She sat down on her couch and watched Henry eying her lovingly from his spot on the ground. Then she punched in Brian's number once more.

CHAPTER FOURTEEN

"Hey, I am glad you called and wanted to get together tonight." Brian told Penny as they sat together in her living room that evening. She had worked a long shift at the crisis center after her run with Sam in the morning. She wondered what Brian's daytime routine included but she had more important questions to ask him first.

"I'm glad you weren't busy."

"Nah, just doing my nightly weight lifting routine," he said.

"I wanted to ask you something," she said.

"Yeah me too, but you go first," he added.

Penny sat across from him in a high-backed chair, a find her brother Greg took credit for, having gone to some garage sale in an old wealthy neighborhood. She crossed her legs and cleared her throat. The chair was comfortable. It was a beautiful hunter green made with a soft velvety fabric. She leaned back. The color suited her living room, which was made up of earthy tones.

Brian laughed.

"What?" she asked him.

"That monstrosity of a chair," he said laughing again. "Where in the world did you find such a relic?"

"Hey watch it. Greg found it for me. I love this thing." She stroked the upholstered arm.

"It's a great-grandma chair."

She laughed. "Whatever."

Suddenly Henry growled then he began barking. He ran around to the side door of the house, the door that was in the kitchen. A loud noise followed.

"What was that?" Penny jumped up.

"You stay here. I'll go and see."

"No way," she said. "We are not living in the middle ages Brian."

"How did I know you were going to say that?" he asked. He ran toward the kitchen. Henry was barking furiously.

Her large jade plant lay on its side. Dirt was all over the floor. Brian ran out through the open door into the back yard. Henry barked for a moment in the doorway then he trotted over and nosed Penny on the arm and stuck his wet snout up at her face.

"I'm okay, good boy," Penny reassured. Henry turned and ran outside to where Brian was striding around the yard. Penny followed her mutt.

"You see anything?" she asked. Brian shook his head.

"Are you okay?" he asked. She shrugged and went back inside. Brian followed and whistled for Henry to come. Reluctantly and with a few more low barks and growls, with the fur on his back standing at attention, Henry trotted in with them. He went right to Penny again and sniffed and nosed her hand. She petted him and sat down at the kitchen table as Brian closed and locked the door.

"Do you keep it bolted?"

"At night, yes," she said. "Maybe it is the guys from the park today or whoever is making those phone calls—I should call Sam."

"What are you talking about?" Brian snapped. He pulled a chair out, angling it to face her, turned it around and straddled it. Penny stood up and walked over to the sink.

"Tell me Penny." Brian came to her and put a hand on her shoulder.

"Some guys were following Sam and me as we ran in the park earlier." She narrowed her eyes and brought them up to meet his. "And I've been getting these calls, with advice about marrying you or forewarning about upcoming experiments."

"You think it's Uncle Jazz?" he asked.

"Maybe," she said. "What do you think they wanted?"

"I don't know. Is anything missing?" he asked.

"I'm not sure." She glanced around her kitchen. Everything looked in order, however once again looks could be deceiving.

"Someone may be trying to scare you," he said.

"Or kidnap me!" Her voice cracked.

"In order to involve you in the experiments?" he asked.

"Yes they want to turn me into June or prove I am just like her!"

"Why did you want me to come over?" Brian asked.

"I wanted to know more about the work Jazz orchestrated." She grabbed the broom out of the bathroom closet and swept the plant dirt into a pile.

"He's obsessed with wanting to understand 'body failures,' from a psychological-emotional perspective. I thought we had discussed all this before?"

"I thought he studied addiction," Penny demanded. He wants to turn me into an addict like mom and dad. She wished she could sweep Jazz Martin out of their lives forever!

"Penny, listen to me." He placed one hand on the broom. She stopped sweeping.

"Ask Jazz where my money is please." She let go of the broom. "And make sure he knows he will not turn me into an addict." She walked toward her front door. It was time for him to go. She was tired and this night was not turning out the way she wanted.

He sighed. "I will. You don't trust me." He caught up to her and reached for her hand as they stood facing each other.

"Nope, not as far as I could throw you," she said. He laughed.

"But you do like me." He drew her into his arms for a bear hug. He smelled strong and comforting, if there were such aromas. He released her and went down on one knee as he dug a hand into one pocket. She sucked in her breath as he removed a box from his pocket and handed it to her. She looked at the box and slowly shifted her eyes downward to his as he knelt before her. Her heart sped up.

"Marry me Penny Patrick!" he pronounced. A huge grin spread across his handsome features. "This is why I came over tonight!"

"We both keep repeating ourselves." Her legs felt as wobbly as her voice.

"Open it," he ordered. She lifted the lid of the small box and fingered the square diamond set in a gold band.

"It is beautiful." Her heart was skipping beats. Electricity like before a summer storm swirled around her. He spun her around, grinning so much she couldn't help but respond with one of her own. They slow danced and he dipped her. Her world was turning upside down and she was giddy. He kissed her and she plunged into deep cool water. He took the ring out of the box and slid it on her finger and he kissed her hand. She sunk into his chest, as though it were a most comfortable bed.

"Brian, I," she said. Penny pulled away.

"I know you don't trust me," he finished. She looked down at the floor, with two fingers he pulled her chin up. His silver eyes gleamed with an intensity that made the hair on her arms stand up. "I admit I have foibles but we have chemistry Penny, lots in common and if it isn't love yet, it is getting close, don't you agree?"

"What sort of foibles?" she asked.

"Putting you in danger is not one of them." He stroked her cheek. His lips twitched. A smile erupted. "I forget the toilet seat *sometimes*. I like to stay up late and watch stupid TV. I am not big on cleaning bathrooms. Sorry, lots of bathroom issues I guess." He frowned.

"Okay." She smiled despite her fear. "I meant other things."

"Like am I in cahoots with your dad or running my own scheme against your family?" She frowned. How could he guess Sam's theories?

"Sam can think up a number of scenarios I'm sure and of course he has a much longer history with you than I ever will have. I am not plotting anything with anyone or by myself. You would see through me Penny."

"Maybe, maybe not," she said. Her words were tossed in like a missing ingredient in a recipe. He shrugged.

"Time will tell then," he said. She was surprised at his confidence. "Now tell me your quirks. A man has a right to know what he's getting himself into for the rest of his life!" She twirled the ring around her finger.

He flexed his arm muscle. "I can take it." Her eyes twinkled as she met his. He winked at her then he squeezed her hands as he held them between his two large ones. "You leave the toilet seat up too? Or is it something much worse?" He elbowed her ribs. She attempted to slide away. He swung an arm around her waist.

"I am grumpy in the mornings."

"Every single morning?" he asked.

"Brian this is irrelevant," she said. He was irritating. "It is late." She stood next to the front door.

"Come on, spill it. Don't be shy," he said. "I am not leaving until I know all of your defects!" He planted his feet in the middle of the hallway like a tree with deep roots.

"I am not a morning person. Just ask either one of my brothers. I tend to run late. My brothers remind me of that one ad nauseum." She sighed. "I sleep with stuffed animals and I enjoy lentils and marinated artichokes for dinner."

He scowled, "That last one I am concerned about and the stuffed animals could become a problem." He winked.

"Brian, this is stupid." She put a hand on her front door knob. "Someone just broke into my house." She ran a hand through the top of her thick hair. "The last thing I feel like doing is playing silly meaningless games." She twisted her body around to face him and held up her left hand, wiggling the ring finger. "This is pretend, remember?"

"Not for me anymore, it isn't." His eyes darkened to the color of storm clouds. They bore into her like a deep ocean oil rig. "Jazz is taking care of the engagement party. Be prepared for a fancy shin-dig." He kissed her cheek. "I have fallen in love with you Penny. I want to marry you. I will make this work, I promise."

Long after Brian left Penny kept leaning against the front door. Brian's declarations echoed. She stared at the diamond ring on her finger. It blurred then she blinked and it winked at her as a shaft of moonlight sparkled through her window.

CHAPTER FIFTEEN

Kenneth slept it off for a few days in a seedy downtown motel. He didn't want the kids to see him like this. He didn't want to be found after his trip back down memory lane for the umpteenth time. Since on this occasion he had tried to break into the old house where he and June had raised three kids.

He had to pull himself together and confront Jazz, put an end to this cockamamie plan once and for all. He would not be Jazz Martin's puppet again and his kids would not be sucked into any plan of his either. Later he would come to regret that he had not gone to see Penny first.

Kenneth parked the boat of a rental car and stretched his long tired limbs. Leave it to Jazz, he thought, to rent an ostentatious house, even for a short time! He walked up the long brick path and knocked on the door. He waited and knocked again. He could hear music, the sounds of Coleman Hawkin's saxophone and the song, 'Body and Soul' playing. He called Jazz's cell phone and peeked in the living room window. The house looked dark inside. He turned the front door knob. Locked! He checked the living room windows. Nope, the house was sealed up as if it were winter.

Kenneth tortured his curls until he looked like he had electrocuted himself. He heard the crunching of gravel. A car pulled up beside his rental one and a tall blond athletic man exited. Kenneth squinted. He was young and handsome.

"Hello," Kenneth said.

"What are you doing?" the man asked.

"I'm Kenneth Patrick. I am here to visit with Jazz Martin. Are you a friend or colleague?"

"I'm his nephew Brian O'Mackery." He put out his right hand to shake Kenneth's. He had a strong grip. "You are Penny's fa—

father," Brian stammered.

"The marriage is not going to happen." Kenneth walked back to the front door.

"She accepted my ring last night." Brian caught up to him. They stared at one another. Brian's eyes shone as brightly as the sun above. "I love her."

"Not possible," Kenneth said. He lined each word with granite. He gestured to the front door. "Do you have a key? Jazz is not answering my calls or when I knock."

"No but I can probably get in through the back," Brian said. They both strode around the side of the house to the back door. He began jimmying the lock.

"One of your talents I suppose?" Kenneth didn't try to conceal the disapproval in his voice as he watched Brian break in. "Is it really your intention to outwit Jazz?"

"I imagine Jazz has taught you an illegal thing or two," Brian retorted. "As to your question," Brian flung back. "Yes and couldn't the same be said of you?"

Kenneth didn't care to respond. He shoved past Brian into the cool dark house.

"Uncle," Brian called. They came in through the kitchen. It stank like rotting garbage. Stacks of unwashed dishes and trash littered the counters and sink. "He and Wil must use the same cleaning crew!" Brian mumbled. He hurried through the rooms on the first floor, calling out to Jazz.

"Jazz," Kenneth added. Brian took the stairs two at a time. Kenneth came up slower behind him. A rustling sound, he and Brian stared at one another.

"Up here," Jazz squeaked.

"Where," Brian said. He raced to each doorway and peered in, fumbling with light switches until he came to the last bedroom at the end of the long hallway.

"Bathroom," Jazz answered. Brian and Kenneth came to a halt at the same time. Jazz had shrunk. Laying between the toilet and sink, curled up into the fetal position, he was disintegrating.

"Uncle, what happened?" Brian asked, touching his brow.

"You're warm."

"Sick, heart, stomach," Jazz croaked.

"How long have you been laying here? Did you take your pills? Let me get help." Brian stood up and pulled his phone out of his pocket.

"A while, need to call Marty," Jazz whispered. He tugged feebly on Brian's pant leg. "Don't appreciate you keeping company with him." Jazz pointed a shaky finger at Kenneth.

"He's my future father-in-law," Brian said. Kenneth watched him scan his phone contact list. Kenneth assumed he was going to call Marty.

"Aaaaah," Jazz screamed. He gripped his abdomen, writhing like a freshly dug up worm.

"Uncle you need to see a real doctor! I am calling an ambulance." Brian dialed the emergency number.

"Marty isn't a real doctor?" Kenneth asked.

"Call Marty," Jazz said. He kicked at Brian's legs.

"Not in my book," Brian shouted. He moved lithely out of Jazz's range. "You need an ambulance," Brian hissed.

"Have you got any of the old anti-dote on you, Kenneth?" Jazz rasped. Kenneth shifted his position so he could take a better look at Jazz's face and shook his head.

"What have you done to yourself Jazz?"

"You're in as bad a shape as me Kenny." Jazz made a choking sound. Was he trying to laugh?

"I am not the one that needs help right now," Kenneth said. He felt a strong urge to pounce on Jazz and pummel him with his fists. He wanted to drag the last bit of life out of him to honor June and protect Penny.

A 911 operator was speaking. "State the nature of the emergency sir! Sir, are you there? Sir," said the stern voice. Kenneth reached over and took the phone out of Brian's hand.

"You can't." Brian tried to grab his phone back as Kenneth ended the call.

"Do you have any of the anti-dote Kenneth?" Jazz propelled his body at Kenneth. His arms flapped like an owl hoarding its prey. Kenneth stepped sideways.

He stabbed the air with his index finger. "Get out of Penny's life! Tom and Genieve will show up without all of these games."

"No! It's too late," Jazz squeaked. Kenneth's face tightened up like a clenched fist. He was like a lit stick of dynamite. He jumped on top of Jazz's tightly curled body and growled like a wild animal. Jazz screamed.

"I'm calling the shots," Kenneth said. "You're finished."

"Never," Jazz yelled. The two men rolled around on the tiled bathroom floor until Brian wrapped his arms around Kenneth.

Kenneth elbowed Brian hard in the stomach. Brian grunted and fell to the ground. Kenneth brought his hands up to Jazz's throat.

"It's over," Kenneth said. He grunted and tightened his grip around Jazz's throat.

"Hey," Penny said. She spoke into the phone the morning after Brian gave her the ring.

"What's up sweet girl?" Remi was so comforting.

"I cannot believe it."

"What? You're pregnant?"

"NO! Bite your tongue Rem!"

"Ouch!"

"What?"

"I bit my tongue like you said," Remi said. Penny laughed, already relieved. She took a deep breath.

"Okay spill it sweetie," Remi demanded.

"Sam thinks Brian and dad, at least I think he may be a dad to one of us, probably Sammy, may be working together!" She had called Sam first this morning. He was not happy that she had accepted the ring! She hadn't been able to tell him about the break in which had been the main reason for her call.

"Okay, so Brian's working for Kenneth not Jazz? I guess it's a small world and all that jazz – oops, poor choice of words! So what's the deal with the dad issue?"

"Rem listen please, I need you to be serious. That means much more than a handshake and a cup of coffee for goodness sake and the dad thing is like a game of musical chairs."

"Oookay, on the other thing, who is Sam's inside source that has proof of all this?" Remi declared.

"No one of course, he hates Brian he thinks he's been plotting maybe about—about – mom since – she since – *that day she disappeared*!"

"Why are you whispering? Is someone there? Are you being followed again?" Remi asked. Penny was so glad she could confide anything to her friend.

"No, no I'm at home, though I am not safe here either." Penny went on to explain the break in.

"Okay, listen, this is not good. Someone's either trying to whig you out even more than you already are. Or scare you away from learning the truth about June. Or they mean serious business and you better find some reliable protection." She heaved a long sigh when Penny kept silent.

"Brian was a kid back when your mom disappeared, like you, a teenybopper, oh honey, listen – oh boy, I see it now. Sam has you marrying a deadly spy for goodness sake's! You never should believe your brother's overactive imagination and give into his overbearing protectiveness and yet somehow you do, time and time again," Remi stated.

"So I should take Brian's word over my brother's?"

"NOT. You might not be able to trust either one of them right now."

Her throat filled up. "He gave me a beautiful ring!"

"Sam did?"

"No!" Penny shouted. She was crying now.

"Just kidding, honey, my blond moments come fast and furious now that I am headed toward that frightening old age marker---thirty!" Penny laughed. "Is it a big one?" Remi asked.

"Rem," she scolded. She dried her tears.

"I was talking about the ring he gave you. At least I thought we were!"

"Remi, you're bad. We are not doing that though I am attracted to him. The ring is large!"

"Maybe he really doesn't know a lot of Jazz's plans or about the 'real' work he does," Remi said.

"Maybe," Penny drew the word out as though it were a rubber band being stretched for flight.

"Listen, you knew going in this was all a game. Practice some detachment. Have you ever looked into a twelve-step program? You're childhood makes you a perfect candidate. It might help you put some of your mom's demons to rest, better than all this crazy roundabout truth seeking." Remi softened her tone at the end.

"I wish you were here with me Rem."

Remi sighed. "Look, why don't you come here? We can talk and laugh and eat LOTS of chocolate. I'll help you bake crazy concoctions."

"I can't but you'll be here soon for the engagement party right?"

"Of course, wouldn't miss the fakery for the world," Remi laughed. Penny thanked her and agreed to be careful. She dried her tear-streaked face only to have the phone start ringing again.

"Hello?"

"Hey, sis," Sam's deep voice greeted her.

"Hey," she said slowly.

"I want you to be safe. You should stay with either Greg or me," he said.

"Sam," Penny admonished.

"Okay, never mind, you're a big kid, I know."

"Try adult," she corrected.

"Listen, dad is probably headed to see you soon and lecture you about this marriage farce," Sam reported.

"Where's he been?" she asked.

"Drying out at some hotel downtown," he said.

"Great," she said.

"Yeah, hey have you had any more of those phone calls?"

"No, okay thanks for the warning about your dad coming over," she sniped. "Maybe he'll let me know how he and Brian are working together.

"It's just a theory, sis. No need to get your panties in a twist. Come over later, okay? Oh hey, that's my other line and I think it might be Greg. I'll see you soon, okay? Be careful." Sam hung up.

Penny headed upstairs to work on her book. It was Friday. Her writing day, usually her favorite day of the week but she felt frazzled. Remi had helped her but it was wearing off. She might find a way to incorporate some of what was happening into her story.

"I'll take you out a little later Henry, okay?" She told her mutt as he sat by the door with his head cocked and a questioning look in his milk chocolate colored eyes. She worked for a while until she heard Henry barking. She saved the pages she had written. It had flowed out of her today like a waterfall! She jogged down the stairs.

"No one is there Hen but you need to walk don't you? I do too I guess; let's go." Her mutt cocked his head at her words. He stretched. She hooked on his leash. They stepped outside. Henry sniffed the air and wagged his tail. Penny walked to the park, rolling her shoulder muscles which felt as stiff as a piece of wood. It would be dark soon. The days were slowly becoming shorter as the summer drew toward its close.

As she walked, the hairs on her neck prickled and her stomach tightened. Penny looked around and felt for the cell phone in her pocket. Henry trotted then stopped. His large head moved back and forth, surveying everything. Low growling noises escaped his clenched snout.

"What's the matter?" she whispered to Henry. She stood on the outskirts of the small park. Trees lined the sides. A little girl noticed them and came running over from the playground equipment.

"Does he bite?" the girl asked.

"No," Penny said. Henry dutifully wagged his tail and lowered his head. He sniffed her hand.

"What's his name? How old is he? We have a puppy again. Our old dog just died a few months ago. Her name was Sammy. We named our new dog Georgie." A woman walked over with a baby in her arms.

"Mommy doesn't he look like Sammy?"

"Honey, let's leave the poor lady to her walk. Sorry," she said. She looked up at Penny as she bent down close to her small daughter.

"It's okay," Penny replied.

"He's cute. Georgie is brown and black and smaller. Sammy looked like your dog."

"Honey let's go. Sorry again to bother you." The mother pulled her daughter back in the direction of the playground equipment. Penny turned around. Two men stepped on either side of her. One held something out to Henry.

He patted Henry's head as Henry emitted a low growl while gobbling up the item in the taller man's hand.

"What did you feed him?" Penny shouted.

"Penny Patrick we have business."

"No thanks. What did you give my dog?" Her heart was hammering out of her chest. She felt sick. Where were the mom and the little girl? The park was deserted.

"Love your mutt, do ya?" The shorter hairier man whispered close to her ear. "If you scream or make any kind of fuss, dear old Henry dies!" Penny stared down at Henry who was growling but wobbling like a drunk. A sob caught in her throat like a piece of carrot.

They hustled her toward a van on the other side of the park. One walked behind her and had something hard shoved up against her back. It hurt. Was it a gun?

"NO I can't! I am meeting my brothers. They're expecting me in a few minutes. They'll – they'll know – I am missing," she said. Henry was barely able to walk. One of the men stuck a muzzle on him and picked him up and shoved him in the waiting van. Penny hesitated. She looked to the van where Henry was then she backed away and tried to run.

"Help, Help, please!" She sobbed and hit the ground. Her legs were made of jello. She pushed herself up. The tall man looped his beefy arm around her midsection. The other shoved something at her face. She smacked at their hands but the foul smelling cloth against her nose and mouth made her feel woozy. She coughed and stumbled and they shoved her into the back of the van.

"He—he—lp," she whispered. She felt a furry lump brush the side of her face. She jerked away then she heard a familiar snarl and then a whine.

"Hen," she said. Penny reached out for him just as she pitched backward and hit her head on the car door handle. "Ouch," she slurred. The van took off like a ride at an amusement park. Penny's limbs felt as light as air. Henry snored while she floated among the clouds.

CHAPTER SIXTEEN

Penny's eyes were glued shut! Her right hand was stuck and so was her left. She concentrated on her breath like she had learned in a meditation class. She squeezed her eyes until they moistened. Stay calm! She raised her head, opening her sticky eyes slowly. Her wrists were strapped to the table she was laying on. IVs were attached to her right arm and leg and her ankles were strapped to the table too.

A light brown liquid dripped from the IV bag on a stand with wheels, into the tubing attached to a vein in her right arm. Dizziness flattened her to the table.

"The experiment," she said. Penny breathed like she was running a race. She wiggled like a snake and a gooey wetness oozed from around the back of her head onto her face and neck.

She prayed to the water stained ceiling above her. It'll be okay. Sam will find us, she thought.

"Henry?" Beeping sounds from a machine with lines and pictures to her left caught her eye as she lifted her head again to search for her mutt. She moaned like a wounded animal.

"Thanks Jazz and mom." A polluted river of regret swam up her tight chest into the back of her throat.

"Help me." Her pine green eyes pleaded with the warped ceiling. She exhaled and closed her eyes, garnering strength. She heard music from India? There was chanting. It was soft whispering and a beautiful, familiar sound! Henry was snoring. She twisted, cried and laughed. Henry was sprawled not too far away on the ground, sleeping.

"HENRY!" She called and then again, more sharply. "HENRY, COME!" He didn't budge. The words playing in the background seemed to formulate like a mantra inside her brain, *Feels good.*

Tingling sensations coursed through her, like surges of adrenaline. Every nerve ending throughout her body felt electrified.

Sam was right! Brian is in on it. It was all an ugly plot to addict her like June, to continue the work for generations and she walked right into it, agreeing to everything! Horrified, Penny twisted, using all the strength she could muster. Don't panic! She yelled until her voice grew hoarse. She cried until she whimpered with exhaustion. She twisted her neck to look around. A few of the sticky things had popped off. She inhaled to ward off the nausea. Sweat dampened her hair. Something pinched her leg. She curled sideways and pain shot through her lower leg. A needle was poking her skin. She rocked back and forth until it fell away. She could do this. She was on a roll. She moved like fish out of water.

Giddy with success, bubbles of laughter erupted from her chest like a water fountain and she giggled until, tears poured down her cheeks. She curled to one side and her eyelids which were now made of bricks closed. She dozed off.

Kenneth heard Brian shouting as if from a long dark tunnel.

"Stop it! You are going to kill him!" He released his fingers from around Jazz's neck. Brian shoved him. "Get out!"

Kenneth backed out of the bathroom and into the bedroom. Jazz grimaced as he rubbed his neck and coughed. He glared at Kenneth and Kenneth kept his gaze steady. Brian fussed over Jazz like he was a helpless baby. Disgust washed over Kenneth as he watched the two of them.

"Call Marty Mapman." Jazz croaked like a frog. Brian ordered an ambulance. Jazz groaned with displeasure. Kenneth backed up to the doorway between the bedroom and hallway. He caught Jazz's sky blue eyes just as he winked! A knife twisted in Kenneth's gut. He narrowed his eyes and Jazz winked again. There was no mistaking it this time! He would kill him! No one would stop him. Kenneth strode forward, fists clenched, fueled by a rage he had not been able quell in over a decade!

The wail of the ambulance stopped him in his tracks. He would not go to prison for this man! He had to help the kids, especially Penny. He jogged down the stairs and out into the late afternoon sunshine. He gunned the car down the long driveway and as he drove down the neighboring streets, the ambulance screamed by him.

A short while later Kenneth stood outside Sam's door, listening to the loud voices from within the house. He held his fist up but doubted he would be heard. Suddenly the door swung open. Sam yelled over his shoulder.

"I've tried her all afternoon. Where could she have gone?" Sam shouted. Kenneth lowered his hand.

"You pissed her off when you accused Brian of being in cahoots with dad," Greg countered.

"I made amends! I thought all was copasetic!" Sam shouted. He spun to face Kenneth. The storm cloud on Sam's dark handsome face became violent.

"Calm down, Sam, she's probably with Brian. Aren't they in the throes of engagement party plans? They're probably with Jazz," Greg said.

"No she is not with either of them," Kenneth said. He stepped into the hallway.

"Nice of you to make an appearance," Sam scowled.

"She's been unreachable," Greg said. He came out of the kitchen, wiping his hands on a small red towel. Greg nodded at Kenneth and Kenneth returned the gesture.

"She's not with Brian. He's with Jazz, who collapsed at his rental home, sick with some old bug, and is now at the hospital," Kenneth said, "You don't look so hot." Kenneth studied Greg's face.

"He works too hard and suffers with more and more headaches." Sam folded his hands across his chest.

"Ever tried some of the alternative healers?" Kenneth asked Greg.

"No thanks," Greg replied. "You want some coffee?" They all moved into the kitchen. Greg poured them all mugs of steaming hot blackness.

"Thanks." Kenneth dipped his nose close to the swirling hot steam rising from his cup. "Smells like hazelnut," he said. A small smile crept across his lined face. It felt strange as though his features were made of stone. Greg curved his lips and nodded.

"We haven't been able to get a hold of Penny since yesterday," Sam said.

"We had breakfast with her yesterday," Greg added. "She went to work and then went home we think. She's not at work today. She doesn't answer her cell phone." Kenneth nodded and took a long swallow of the strong black coffee.

"This is good. I tried to get Jazz to call off this whole charade but Brian wouldn't allow it. It shouldn't be long before he's gone though. He seems pretty sick," Kenneth murmured. "I almost finished him off a little while ago but again Brian interfered.

"You tried to kill Jazz?" Sam threw back his head and laughed from his heart.

"I told you I was not successful!" Kenneth scowled at Sam. "As usual," he said. He wanted to pound his fist into his chest.

"At least you tried," Sam said.

"Penny's in way over her head." His skin prickled with brambles of agitation. He stood up and sat down. His mind was cloudy. He blinked. The grittiness in his eyes made it hard to see.

"She has been followed, threatened and coerced!"

"I know she's in trouble Sam! Why the hell do you think I'm here?"

"Maybe to help all of us deal with *your* past?" Sam sneered.

"Have anything stronger? I need to lace this with something!" Kenneth blurted as he stood up again, fists clenched. He stretched his neck by putting each ear back and forth, toward a shoulder.

"No," Sam snapped. "Save that for later."

"Fine, what's *your* plan?" Kenneth shot out his words like they were cannons.

"We have to focus on finding Penny," Greg said. He rubbed the base of his neck and rolled his head from side to side. "I need to check in at the hospital and with Nance. Dad, you know we are," Greg said. He inhaled sharply and released a long breath. "Expecting?"

"Expecting?" Kenneth repeated. A wave of exhaustion hit and he yawned. Sam grabbed the empty mugs and slammed them into the sink. Kenneth jumped.

"Nance is pregnant and due in a little less than seven months now," Greg said.

"I am happy for you both," Kenneth tried to smile but his lips were made of cement. He ran a hand through his grey curls and stood up. Greg reached for his cell phone and left the room. Sam shoved the mugs into his dishwasher. Kenneth scratched his messy curls.

"Was your plan to off Jazz today?" Sam's words felt like lemon juice squeezed in his eyes.

"No, but opportunity knocked," Kenneth proclaimed. "Look, let me buy you both dinner and we can figure out what's going on with Penny." While Sam went to check with Greg in the other room, Kenneth let his heart sink to the floor. He knew he should have gone to see Penny first. He felt the urgency but he ignored it in his quest to confront Jazz, which once again proved pointless! He washed up in Sam's downstairs bathroom. They would find Penny. She would be all right. He would stop Jazz's plan before it was too late. He had to, he had promised June!

Sam, Greg and Kenneth knocked on Penny's door on their way to eat. They called her cell phone repeatedly and her voice mail came on each time. They sat outdoors while eating turkey and pastrami subs; a family favorite, from a local deli that allows the patrons to create their own combo sandwiches. They had loaded theirs with coleslaw and Thousand Island dressing.

"Where is Aunt Genieve?" Sam asked.

"Stuck in Asia somewhere with her husband Tom Mott," Kenneth announced.

"As far as you know," Sam stated. "She or they could be here in town."

"I didn't realize she married Tom," Greg commented.

Kenneth nodded first at Sam with reluctance and then at Greg. They ate in silence for a time.

"This might sound crazy but are my headaches in any way related to your work?" Greg asked.

"You think you were experimented on?" Sam's head shot up. Kenneth kept his head down as if studying something interesting on his plate. "Answer him," Sam demanded.

"There's a lot you don't understand," Kenneth blurted. He put down what was left of his sub and pushed it away from him. Greg rubbed his forehead and put his half-eaten sandwich back on his plate and shoved it aside as well. He stood up.

"Did you experiment on me?" Greg demanded. "That is a pretty straight-forward inquiry!"

"NO! I personally did not, but you know I am not your father in the technical sense," Kenneth shouted. He stood up to face Greg. "Jazz took liberties with all that he considered his and I think," Kenneth said. He paused and he dropped his voice to a soft, resigned murmur. "He used you like he did many others. He'd come up with ideas or someone would offer him financing or have some new substance they were looking to test and he would grab subjects."

"Did he ever bother with consent forms?" Sam asked. Kenneth snorted in response.

"But what was the point? It's not like he was ever close to curing any diseases or discovering new medicines," Greg asked.

"That's not how he looks at the work," Kenneth replied.

"So he just did stuff for the sport of it and for the money?" Sam yelled.

"Pretty much," Kenneth agreed.

"I remember being with him sometimes in a lab," Greg said slowly. He scratched his head.

"You never told me this." Sam was angry.

"I barely remember anything Sam," Greg said.

"Look, I can make some suggestions about the headaches if you would like, and try and explain more about the kinds of work Jazz did, not that I know all the ins and outs of it like you both seem to think. However, right now what is most important is finding your sister."

"And learning Jazz's real plan," Sam added.

"And making our own plan to eliminate that bastard," Greg added. "I don't care if he is my father!" Kenneth smiled at Greg and nodded with vigor. Sam interrupted.

"Already failed at that." He pointed to Kenneth.

"There are always more than one means of skinning a cat,"

Kenneth said.

"True." Sam's grin was slow to form.

All three cleaned up their trash and agreed to pay a visit to Brian and Jazz at the hospital.

They arrived at the hospital a short while later. Greg headed off to check on a few of his patients, promising to meet up with them later. Sam walked up to the information desk. The woman looked busy, but when she looked up briefly he asked about Jazz Martin's whereabouts. The woman looked him up and down. She pushed her frameless glasses back up her long nose and shrugged.

"He was supposed to arrive by ambulance and be examined within our cardiac care wing." She returned her attention to the paperwork in front of her. Sam cleared his throat and asked for clarification.

"He never made it," she informed.

"What happened?" Kenneth asked. She shrugged and looked at her computer screen.

"They never arrived here," she said.

"So the ambulance crashed? Or did he die?" Sam leaned forward, clearly agitated.

"I have no idea sir. You'd have to take up your concerns through the rescue service directly. We are only responsible for the patients after they arrive on our premises."

"Don't you have a way to track things?" Sam was incredulous.

"Sir, like I said, the rescue service is in charge until arrival." She had lowered her glasses to stare at him, a serious but bored look on her face.

"I don't understand. How can an ambulance not make it?" Sam turned to Kenneth. Kenneth leaned over the woman's desk.

"Is there anyone at this hospital we could question a bit more, Ms, uh, Ms. Calhoun?" Kenneth read her name tag. She had busied herself once more with files and papers that seemed to be scattered haphazardly over the long desk in front of where she stood with her head bowed.

"If you would be so kind as to help us out, it is a long and complicated story," Kenneth began.

"It always is, sir," she interrupted.

"Yes, well, my daughter is missing and the man in the ambulance, Jazz Martin may be responsible," Kenneth explained. Sam interrupted.

"Yeah before my sister dies because of one of his experiments!" Sam snapped.

"Okay look, I really don't have time for this. They never reported in. We know they were dispatched to help this – this –"

"Jazz Martin," Kenneth supplied.

"Yes, but that is all we know." She waved a hand dismissively.

"This is ridiculous," Sam griped.

"Sir, I have done all I can." She directed her comments toward Kenneth, ignoring Sam completely. "Perhaps you need to contact the police at this point. Please I am going to have to ask you to leave. I need to help other people." She indicated two people who were lined up behind them.

"Can I help you?" She smiled at the woman behind Sam. They moved off to the side awkwardly and stood for a moment. Then Ms. Calhoun made a swift exit through a door on the other side of the desk after speaking to the woman behind them.

They tried for a few more minutes with a doctor who wandered through and a nurse who appeared but no one was helpful. They referred them to the police.

"This is insane!" Sam yelled.

"I agree but Sam you have to stay calm." Kenneth warned. People were staring at them and nurses were scowling in their direction. "It's late. We should get some sleep. Let's go."

They paged Greg. He said he would look into it for them. He was busy with patients this evening. He'd let them know by the morning. Kenneth tried Jazz's cell phone, and Sam tried Penny's again. They both didn't have any luck. Kenneth convinced a very reluctant Sam to drive them back to his house for some sleep.

"Fine but first thing in the morning we find Brian," Sam announced. He sped down the dark streets. Sam looked up where Brian lived as soon as they were home. It had been a long day. Kenneth was exhausted. He didn't bother changing clothes and was asleep in seconds after finding his way to Sam's guest room.

CHAPTER SEVENTEEN

The next morning Penny awoke with the sole purpose of escape on her mind. She was not her mother and she would prove it to everyone! She gave another tug of her left arm and leg. The restraints loosened. Her skin throbbed where the IV had been. She flexed her wrist and fingers until they were free. She did the same with her ankle and left leg. Sweat trickled down the sides of her face while a fierce determination filled her every pore.

She cried out as she yanked the remaining wires from her upper neck. The machine bleeped as she rolled off the table and fell to the ground on her hands and knees. Everything ached but she froze and listened. No one was coming. Someone sneezed. She jerked her head up. Another sneeze, she laughed. It was Henry!

"Hey buddy. Are you awake?" Penny heard his tail thumping against the floor. "Good boy! Listen, we need to get out of this medical dungeon. Can you help me?"

Henry's tail wagged again and he hoisted his body up as though he were old. He stumbled like he was drunk. "Henry, wait!" she commanded. "No!" She pointed to the pool of wet sticky stuff. "Move!" she commanded. Henry sidestepped it, wobbling his way to where she sat on her heels, gathering her strength and glancing around the sparse room. The strange whispery music had stopped.

Henry stuck his nose up into the air and sniffed then sneezed and sneezed again. He barked. A weak sound and Penny wanted to cry.

"Shhhh, it's okay." Penny's head pounded to the beat of a drum. She cocked her head to listen. Nope, no one's coming. She stifled a yawn. How nice it would be to lay her head down and doze but she forced her eyes to examine the dark empty room.

Except for the table she had been tied down to and the machine with all the wires and beeping noises, the wide, long room had one other small table, a tall wide cabinet and a window!

"After I rest a little bit more we'll break out of here, Henry." Penny curled up on the floor in the fetal position. In a few moments she was asleep. Henry settled close to her, growling as he snored.

"Shhhh," she murmured. She drifted off once more.

The tall figure watched Penny and Henry while sipping a concoction of milk, honey, spices, coffee, a shot of chocolate liqueur, and a quarter teaspoon of vanilla extract. The last ingredient was a tribute to June. She had had a musky vanilla scent.

The small camera in the upper right corner of the room provided all the information necessary to stay informed. A few branches of a huge tree outside scraped the glass of a nearby window as the wind picked up. The figure grinned.

"Good, a storm." The figure drained the chai drink, savoring the spices while waiting for Penny's rescuers to arrive on the scene.

They banged on the door and shouted! The sun was still climbing the sky.

"Okay, okay," Brian said. He opened his front door as he ran a hand through his hair. He blinked and yawned. What is he doing asleep at this hour? Kenneth thought.

"Don't you have a steady job?" Kenneth asked.

"Sure, that would be doing Jazz's dirty work like kidnapping my sister!"

"That's a little harsh even for you Sam," Brian said. He flopped down on his long brown couch. Sam opened closets and cabinets as he spoke.

"Where the hell is my sister?" he demanded.

"Where is Jazz?" Kenneth scanned the room. He traced a finger along the pad by Brian's cell phone.

"I have not stashed either of them in any of my closets, cabinets, shelves or tub! Thanks for all the trust, guys." Brian stood up with his hands on his hips. "What is this about?" He looked at Kenneth. "You're the one who tried to kill Jazz yesterday!"

"Penny is gone! Is that your plan to seclude her away somewhere secret so you can force this marriage to happen?" Sam shouted, stepping up to Brian and wrapping his fist around his t-shirt and pulling it up close to Brian's chin. "You're probably drugging her too, addicting her to the work? Because that's what it is always about isn't it? The damn work," Sam screamed in Brian's face. To Brian's credit he looked aghast with anguish and shock, Kenneth thought.

"Wha – what do you mean, gone? I—you can search the house, neither Jazz nor Penny, or anyone else for that matter is here!" Brian looked and sounded very small, Kenneth thought. Sam let go of his shirt. Kenneth went to the sink and came back with a glass of water for Sam. Sam shook his head, no. Kenneth shrugged and drank the water. Brian stood in the middle of the living room like a statue. Kenneth found the coffee maker and hunted for a new filter and coffee while Brian slowly sat down on a stool next to the breakfast bar across the counter from where Kenneth was making coffee. Sam strode back into the kitchen like a taunted hornet.

Kenneth heard him banging doors and drawers, muttering obscenities as he searched Brian's home.

"We have been trying to call you," Sam accused. "We have been up all night long and there's no sign of her!" Kenneth had slept like a baby.

"He has no idea what we are talking about Sam," Kenneth stated. "Isn't that rather obvious?"

"It's all an act, just like with Jazz," Sam responded.

"You don't have to talk as if I'm not here!" Brian interjected. Then he reached for his cell phone and turned it on. He saw all the missed calls. "Sorry," Brian mumbled. "I—it was all too much. I, I saw them load uncle into the ambulance and I tried to follow but they were going too fast. He—he never made it to the hospital."

"We know," Kenneth said.

"I tried to find out what happened but gave up after a while. I guess, I fell asleep, I turned off my phone. I," Brian said.

"Save it. Just tell us where Jazz is holding my sister!" Sam was agitated.

"I'll try my father, Milman, maybe he knows something," Brian said.

"You got anything to eat in this place?" Sam grunted as he walked around picking up photos and knickknacks, opening up more cabinets and drawers of Brian's.

"Some things never change," Kenneth said. He watched Sam hunt for food.

"I can see that," Brian said. His voice had a twinge of cynicism. "Sure yeah, no problem, help yourself to whatever is in the fridge! I'm sure you will anyways." Brian left the room to make the call to his father, Milman just as Sam's phone rang.

"Yeah," Sam barked into his cell phone. Kenneth watched as Sam's face turned red with emotion.

"Penny?" he shouted. "What, can you say that again? Penny!" He shoved the phone back into his pocket. "It was her phone," Sam explained. Instantly it rang again. Sam yanked and the phone flew out of his hand and across the room. He lunged for it, stumbling, catching himself on the arm of a forest green recliner and answering breathless.

"Hello," he said. His face collapsed like an old man in grief. "It's Greg." He spoke for a few minutes and then hung up. "Nothing, the ambulance carrying Jazz seems to have disappeared into thin air."

"I think I have an idea where Penny might be," Brian said as he walked back into the room. He had thrown a pair of jeans and a fresh t-shirt on. Kenneth sloshed coffee into a tall stainless steel cup and twisted on the lid. He needed something much stronger to survive this circus! However he had to keep his wits about him. So his special flask would have to wait until later.

"Let's go then," Sam announced and ushered them all outside.

–

Penny staggered under the burden of pulling Henry along. Her legs wobbled as Henry lurched, his legs as unsteady as hers. She sat down and looked across the large room, from where she had come to where she now sat and sighed.

"Oh Hen this is crazy." She patted his head as it rested on her thigh. She sighed again and glanced at the door nearby. Then she grabbed the door handle. It didn't budge. She squinted in the partial darkness and looked around. She thought she could make out another exit across the space in one corner. A small window was on one side as well. What was her best option for escape?

She sat down again and Henry fell onto her lap once more too. Something pushed uncomfortably on her leg. She shifted.

"Oh Hen, we are saved!" She pulled out her cell phone, praying it was charged enough to work. There was only one bar line left on it. It must have been on for a while and she didn't even know it. She noticed she had messages but she ignored that for now. She wanted to save what charge she had.

"People must be looking for us Henry." His ears perked up. She punched the programmed number for her brother Sam.

"Sam! Get off the phone," she cried. Penny tried Greg and Brian. Their phones were off! She clutched the cell phone above her head. *No!* Henry began licking her other hand. Tears slid down her face as Henry nuzzled her arm. She ran her hand along his back and wiped the wetness from her face. She tried all three numbers again. No luck!

"Sam will rescue us soon," she said. Penny patted Henry's big paw. "I should probably try and figure out what all this stuff means." She looked at the bleeping machine. Why wasn't anyone checking on her? The thought made her nervous. She put a hand to her belly. Empty gnawing brought a wave of nausea. A noise and Henry growled. She ran to the table, hoisted herself up and signaled for Henry to be quiet. He positioned his muscular frame in front of the table as if he was her shield. It could be Brian, and her eyes filled up and the tears ran down her cheeks. She could never trust him now. The sounds grew closer, male voices. Panic seized her. The table shook. Henry growled and she watched his thick black fur gather on his upper back as he let out a low bark.

The figure watching her from upstairs grinned. The fun was about to begin!

Penny frantically punched numbers into her cell phone. Her brother Sam shouted at her to speak up. She could only whisper. Henry lunged at the door as the handle moved back and forth. Penny let go and her phone clattered to the floor. She yelped and rolled over. She fell off the table and slid down into blackness, hearing Henry's bark echoing from a long dark tunnel.

"She must have turned her cell off," Sam muttered. He combed his long fingers repeatedly through his thick black hair. They drove outside the city limits to a few old abandoned buildings Brian had suggested. Milman thought they would find Penny at one of them. Jazz had used them for experiments some time ago.

Kenneth rode with Sam. Greg was at the hospital working. Brian decided to search for Jazz since he might know Penny's whereabouts.

"Any luck?" Brian asked. He had called Sam.

"No, your ideas were a waste of time and we can't afford that right now," Sam snapped.

"Jazz is still missing. My father is investigating that and I'm trying to locate Jazz's physician Dr. Marty Mapman."

"Great, super, wonderful," Sam said. "None of those jerks matter. We need to find my sister."

"I'm sorry," Brian mumbled.

"Save it. Her life may be at stake. It is time to fess up!"

Brian exhaled into the receiver. "I can understand your suspicions," he said. "Let me keep trying to find out all that I can. In the meantime you should spend some time quizzing your father!"

Sam threw the phone onto the passenger seat and pulled the car over into a shopping store parking lot.

"Sam," Kenneth started. He wanted to help his son but he didn't know what to say. They were back in town. He tried to think. "What did her message say again?"

"That it was a large room with a table and some medical equipment," Sam snapped. He ran a hand over his face. "She's lost and afraid and we're sitting here in a parking lot having no idea what to do!" He slammed his fist down and leaned his head back into the headrest just as his phone played 'Rosalita' by Bruce Springsteen.

"Yeah?" he yelled. "Okay yeah, I am on it!" He gunned it. Kenneth held onto the side of the passenger door for dear life. The wheels squealed as he drove.

"Where are we going?" Kenneth asked.

"Bobby, my detective friend, gave me a lead. I need to talk to Greg," Sam said, fumbling with his cell phone as he sped around street corners.

"Let me talk to him and you drive, please Sam," Kenneth implored. Sam reluctantly handed over his cell phone.

"We are on our way," Kenneth told Greg. "Oh what did you find out?" Kenneth asked. He then said to Sam. "Greg spoke with a nurse about Jazz."

"Put the phone on speaker," Sam said.

"Uh hang on, Greg. How do I do that?"

"There's a button on the side of the phone," Sam said exasperatedly.

"Okay," Kenneth struggled for a minute but found it. "Go ahead Greg."

"The rumor is he had his own private doctor called, I'm assuming that would be Dr. Marty Mapman and that he was taken to a clinic for special treatment," Greg informed him. "One of the paramedics called in eventually. He didn't want to get into trouble and apparently he's dating one of Aileen's, that's my nurse confidant, friends down in admissions, so it should be a fairly reliable rumor, if such a thing exists." Greg laughed. It was a short brittle sound. "Before you ask I don't know the name of the clinic but she thinks it isn't too far out of town. I still have some work to do with one patient who's having some complications from his surgery. I'll be in touch soon."

"We need to find Marty Mapman and this clinic," Sam said.

"Call Brian and have him reach his father," Kenneth suggested. "Or rather you tell me the number and I'll call while you slow down and get us to Penny in one piece!"

"What are you doing?" Kenneth asked Brian a few moments later.

"I am sitting behind my massive desk staring out at my slight view of the river. The trees are beginning to change color, what's up?" Brian sighed.

"Why aren't you trying to find Jazz? Or how about Penny, or why aren't you talking to Milman about which clinic your precious uncle is hiding himself?" Kenneth huffed and Brian interrupted.

"What's the point Kenneth? Everyone has lost trust and faith in me if they ever had it in the first place. This whole plan of Jazz's is a mess which means Penny will never marry me and I am stuck under his thumb so here I sit trying to work at my real job which is teaching history and writing a book one day like Penny hopes to do by the way. Instead though all I can do is push papers around and pray Penny is okay." Brian sighed into the phone again.

"Make yourself useful. We all have our problems. Look at how I have been and continue to be blamed for every bad thing that happened to June. Things that your uncle or Tom did! Don't quit now. Where will that leave you? In an even worse predicament, trust me! Call Milman and try and locate Marty Mapman."

"Hang on I have another call I think it's Jazz," Brian said.

Kenneth told Sam and they waited. "This is bogus," Sam said as he drove and Kenneth held the phone to his ear waiting on Brian.

"Marty saved him again," Brian said. His voice sounded flat, almost lifeless when he came back on the line with Kenneth.

"Of course he did, what's new?" Kenneth said. "What was that?" He heard crashing noises. Brian was breathing heavy.

"I trashed my office." Brian huffed into the phone.

"You should have let me strangle him when I had the chance!"

Kenneth swore into the phone. Brian laughed. It was the sound of a dry cough.

"Killing is not a good option for anyone," Brian stated.

"I am not sure anymore about that. Look, he won't win much longer. Marty must be running out of options. There are only so many powerful drugs," Kenneth interrupted. Why am I helping this young man? Kenneth scratched his curls. Brian is a decent sort and he and Penny discovered something special amidst this ugly circus. June wants Penny to be happy and loved so he must try to find the good within Brian, for now at least.

"Did he claim to know anything about Penny?" Kenneth asked.

"Nope, look I am going to pick up Wil, and meet you, tell me the address again of where you think Penny is?" Brian asked. Kenneth hesitated but in the end gave it to him. Sam glared at him.

After another long half hour of tense, silent driving, they pulled into a parking lot next to a faded yellow, weather-beaten looking house. Brian and Wil drove up next to them before they had even had a chance to get out of the car.

"Let's go," Sam called out. "You sure made it here fast." Sam glared at Brian and Wil.

"I care a lot about your sister despite every evil thing you think, Sam," Brian said.

"Boys, boys," Wil said. He placed himself between the two of them as they walked toward the old yellow farm house.

"Careful," Kenneth reminded. He took out a flask he brought along at the last minute in his jacket pocket. He took a long swallow. He had a feeling Tom Mott was here. He needed fortification before that confrontation!

Sam ran up to the door, ahead of everyone. The porch steps creaked under his weight and the screen door nearly fell off as he yanked it open. Brian and Wil locked eyes before following Sam inside.

It smells like a hospital, Kenneth thought and hurried after Sam as he sped down the dark corridor toward the back of the house where a set of double doors with a lock on it appeared.

CHAPTER EIGHTEEN

No one had come! Penny waited on all fours beside the table. Henry stood beside her emitting low growls. The door handle stopped moving. Penny sat back on her heels and stroked Henry. After a few minutes she tried calling Sam. He must be talking to someone. She turned toward the small window toward the back of the room.

A noise, coming from outside! She swiped at the wetness on her face. Henry wagged his tail and yelped. The door handle shook. Henry's tail wagged slowly then stopped. He cocked his head at the door. Could it be her brother? Henry wobbled and slid. Penny's legs felt like cooked noodles.

"Penny?" Henry barked at the voice coming through the door.

"Penny, it's me, Brian!" Henry scooted toward the door, wagging his tail. Penny hissed at him.

"Wait!" she called. Penny waved a hand for Henry to hide with her, but he ignored her.

"Penny!" Brian rattled the door over and over. Then she heard Sam's voice.

"Penny! Penny, are you okay? Stay back. You're the one who got her into this mess," Sam said. Penny smiled.

"I have a right to be here. I want to see if she's okay!" Brian said. Penny started across the room. Henry wagged his tail harder. Suddenly the door burst open. A herd of people rushed toward her. Brian and Sam were first and Wil and Kenneth lagged just behind them.

"You okay? Never mind that was a bad question," Brian said. Her whole body shook in answer. Fresh tears fell like a dam that had burst. Sam ran to her. Brian scooped her up in his arms and he buried his face into her neck as he cradled her against him.

"I'm so sorry Penny. I am so very sorry. You have to believe I had nothing to do with whatever this horror is, okay? Please." He pulled back to look her in the eyes until Sam shoved him. Brian let her down and glanced around the room. Sam looped an arm around her shoulders.

"Can you walk, sis?" Sam asked. Kenneth was studying the machines and tubes near the table where she had been strapped in. Brian and Wil joined him.

"They drugged me Sam, and Henry too. Henry!" she called. "Where is he?"

"He's right over there by the door." Sam pointed. She nodded and wiped more tears away. "Who drugged you? Where – when, Penny, tell me," Sam demanded.

"I—I don't know who obviously, I was at the park and this little girl was talking to Henry and then her mom came over. They disappeared and two men rushed over to me and gave Henry something to eat that made him sleepy and they put this smelly cloth over my mouth, shoved me into a van and I passed out and woke up here. I was hooked up to all that stuff." She pointed back to the table. "Tubes were in my arms and legs and I yanked them out and I tried to escape and call all of you but the connection was bad and I fell off the table and hit my head when I heard footsteps. I was so sleepy and Henry couldn't walk." Sobs rose like a wave cresting and swallowed up her voice. Sam held her close against his side and she buried her head into his shoulder.

"Can we go home?" She hiccupped. Brian and Wil walked over.

"I can take her home," Brian said. "If you want to stay and check things out with Kenneth," Brian reached up to stroke Penny's disheveled hair, back from her face. She saw his blue eyes were dark and pained as they searched hers.

"No, I'll take her and come back," Sam said. He tightened his arm around Penny.

"It looks like the same stuff they used on June," Kenneth said. He walked over to them. "But to be sure I've taken some samples. I will see what I can do to get it tested in a lab."

"What is it? What did they put in my body?" Hysteria rose up inside of Penny. Whatever was in her veins was flowing through her right now!

"I am not sure Penny. Half the time Jazz, Tom and Marty used placebos. It was a lot about mind games, honey. Don't let Jazz or any of this make you feel crazy okay? Choose to believe you're okay and you'll remain unaffected." Kenneth spoke calmly and firmly, staring intently into Penny's eyes. She took a deep shuddering breath and her tears stopped. She nodded. Kenneth reached to hug her.

"It's probably a variety of sedatives—barbiturates, tranquilizers, maybe some alcohol and herbal tinctures, designed to relax you and create pleasant floating sensations?" Kenneth explained. Penny nodded and wiped at the new waterfall cascading down her cheeks.

"Maybe Greg can have it tested at the hospital," Wil interjected.

"Can we leave this place please?" Penny couldn't keep the quaver out of her voice. "It's creepy." She took measured steps toward Henry who sat by the open door watching them.

"I'll take you home right now. Come on Wil. We can figure all this out later," Brian said. He took Penny's hand. She glanced at Sam. He was looking at Kenneth who was back examining the table and machines.

"You can check in with Sam. I'll call Greg and he can examine you while I find the clinic Jazz is recuperating in," Brian said. Then in one fluid motion he scooped her once more into his arms and carried her outside.

"Wait!" Sam protested but Penny was exhausted.

"I'll call you as soon as I'm home," she said. Brian whisked her outside to the car where Wil already had the back door open. Wil patted her arm as Brian helped her settle into the back seat.

"Get Henry into the car, Wil," Brian directed.

"We'll get him to a vet, don't worry. He'll be okay Penny," Brian said. Tears filled her eyes like running water in a bathtub.

"Why me, you know I am not a dog person, Bri," Wil whined. As if in agreement Henry let out a big bark. Wil called over his shoulder to them. "He doesn't like me. Come on pooch. Come," Wil whistled. Henry growled and limped, growled and limped. All of a sudden he yelped.

Penny pushed off the back seat and into Brian's arm. He held it across the door like a gate.

"What's the matter?" Wil turned and hurried back to the dog. Henry held his front paw up and sat down in the parking lot. He whined. Wil knelt down.

"I need to go help him Brian." Penny watched with concern

"No you don't. Wil can manage just fine."

"Oh right I forgot he's the Zen master!" She grimaced.

"He has his limitations like all of us Penny." Brian's gaze was serious and full of pain.

"You hurt your paw, boy?" She could hear Wil prompting Henry in the parking lot.

"Limitations and deception are two very different things, Brian." She stared straight back at him.

Henry growled at Wil and bared his teeth. Wil scooted back.

"Okay, okay, no need to get your feathers in an uproar, er fur, whatever. Come on. It's only a little further to the car."

"Oh Wil, hate to cut your little tete-a-tete short but we do have more important things then your bonding time with Henry!" Brian was impatient.

"Hey I'm trying here, but you gave me a tough assignment," Wil said. Finally they approached the car. Henry limped and slipped clumsily but made it into the seat and on top of Penny.

Henry plopped his entire body onto hers. She laughed a little through her tears and hugged Henry closer to her, if that were possible.

"You okay?" Brian reached in to shift Henry but suddenly withdrew his hands as Henry started barking fiercely. Penny stroked his back and murmured soothingly to him and he lowered his bark a few decibels.

"Just get us home!" Penny shouted. Brian nodded.

"Sorry, I am so very sorry Penny and I know you won't believe me when I tell you I had nothing to do with this nor did I know this was part of the plan!" Brian pleaded with her as he drove slowly out of the parking lot.

Wil grunted and turned to look at Penny. Penny opened her mouth to explain how she could never believe in his innocence when suddenly they heard Sam. He was running out of the building and shouting something. A police car pulled up beside Brian's car, tires squealing as the squad car came to an abrupt stop. The policeman and Sam charged toward Brian's side of the car.

"Hold it!" The men shouted at Brian and Wil. Brian stopped the car and jumped out.

"We just rescued her, sir." Brian pointed inside his car but when the policeman leveled his gun at him, he shot both his arms into the air above his head.

"Hey he's telling the truth!" Wil leaped out of the car. Penny rolled onto her side in the back seat and moaned. Henry barked as if he had cornered an animal in his yard. Gunfire was about to erupt! Hadn't she experienced enough danger?

The tall figure grinned. "Sam's got 'em now with his police buddies." The small upstairs window afforded a great view. "Penny must be dying in the back seat of her lover's car."

"Brian is not her lover! Why did you involve her? And why the hell are the police here?" Kenneth did not try to hide his irritation. He was winded from climbing up the steep back staircase just before the police arrived. He had pushed open an old wooden door to find his familiar nemesis.

"Oh they'll be lovers soon enough. And don't worry Kenny, Penny is fine for now. However Genieve and I have a plan for the family, since Jazz has created the perfect opening for implementing it. The timing couldn't be better."

"You are NOT addicting Penny like you did June," Kenneth said.

"You better get back down there. You might actually be needed. You should make sure no one gets shot at this point in the game." He urged.

"We are not playing a game. People's lives are at stake! Look, I want to know what exactly you gave Penny if anything," Kenneth demanded.

"Have it analyzed. That should prove futile." Laughter erupted from the tall man as if he were a child at Christmas. Kenneth watched Sam and Brian arguing as Penny slumped further down in the back seat. Wil tried to pull Brian back toward the car. The policeman kept his gun cocked at Brian.

"Let's try and work together, hmm, Ken?" Tom Mott turned and winked at him.

"Where's Genieve," Kenneth hissed.

"It would become a whole lot more interesting if the policeman would just shoot him already!" Kenneth cringed at Tom's harsh laughter.

"Perhaps if you were the target," Kenneth interjected. Tom spun from the window to stare at him.

"Ha ha Kenny, you always did possess a wry sense of humor. Too bad you have very few other talents. No! Actually I believe Brian seems to be a decent guy and though I don't care for the idea of the marriage scenario of revenge that Jazz Martin has devised in his sickened state, Penny seems to favor him," Tom said.

"How the hell would you know?" Kenneth snapped.

"Oh I know plenty Kenny." His grin was fierce like an over confident rich CEO, Kenneth thought with disgust.

"Maybe, maybe not," Kenneth replied. He stared into Tom's coal black eyes. "June didn't pick you. You kidnapped and harassed her for years, all for naught, Tommy! Except to lead you to this ugly place of your own sick and twisted ideas of revenge, like drugging Penny! Genieve won't have your back. She and I promised June that Penny would never be harmed from old past grievances. You will never get your way Tom!" Kenneth walked out of the room.

"She's going down, Kenneth like June and there's nothing you can do to stop me you weak beaten down worm!"

Kenneth spun back. He saw fury and a haughty look that made his skin crawl. He clenched his fists. "Over my dead body."

"That might just be part of the plan, Kenny." Tom laughed. It was the sound of a hyena crossed with a snake. Kenneth reared up like an animal poised to fight. He mustered all of his power.

"That will be your fate this time around, not mine," Kenneth said. He walked out into the bright sunshine looking twenty years older from just the last few minutes with Tom.

CHAPTER NINETEEN

"Uncle Jazz, uncle Jazz, can you hear me?" Brian said. They were standing outside by several cement benches. The ocean was less than a mile away. Penny scowled. Why had she tagged along with Brian to this meeting with Jazz at the Harbor Inn? She should have gone straight home to rest and called Greg over to fully examine her. But no, she felt guilty, because Brian had been held at gunpoint because of her suspicions. Sam's cop friends were loyal and Sam hated Brian. He was convinced that Brian was a part of her kidnapping! Did she believe Sam or Brian's clueless puppet act?

Jazz opened his eyes. "I was thinking about Marty's amazing cures that keep me going despite what Ken—oh never mind." He narrowed his eyes at Penny. Penny sighed. This could be her chance to question Jazz. Brian had informed her of the ambulance fiasco. Another attack of his mysterious illness and once again an amazing recovery!

"What happened to you, my dear? You look terrible." Brian jumped in. Penny sunk down onto the hard rough bench. She inhaled the salty air.

"Uncle, she was kidnapped and drugged!"

"What?" Jazz squinted at her. "I—I didn't know." Jazz tapped his forehead. "Tom Mott," he groaned.

Flames of a roaring fire licked Penny's body and black spots speckled her view. She was on the giant spinning tea pot ride at the amusement park.

"Penny?" Brian called from miles away. She swayed and slumped against Brian's side. His long muscular arms wrapped around her torso. She was in a cocoon.

"I should have brought you straight home to Greg." Brian's

voice was thick with concern.

"Go then," Jazz said. He was in the ocean waves. Penny fought the black swirling water, threatening to suck her down, down, down inside. "My driver's here. I 'm tired. I'll talk with you later!"

"No, ans-answers," Penny mumbled. Brian squeezed her against his chest.

"Later," he said.

"No, no—w," she cried.

"You need to let Greg examine you and rest until this stuff passes through you, whatever it is!" Brian carried her back to his car. He called Greg and left an urgent message.

Penny lay still as Greg examined her head and leg, took blood and checked her pupils.

"What's the prognosis doc?" she joked.

"I don't know. You really should let me take you into the hospital so I can run a battery of tests, Penny." He sighed. "Did you tell me all of your symptoms?"

"I am not going to the hospital!" she cried. Greg patted her arm.

"I know, I know, it's just hard to figure it out from here, like this." He pointed to his small medical bag and the supplies he had added that were now spread out on her coffee table. "Symptoms," he prompted.

"I am dizzy. My leg and head ache. I feel sore all over but maybe that's from my fall. And I feel like I was run over by a big, heavy, sharp object if that makes any sense."

"How do you mean that?" Greg asked. His eyebrows bunched up together. It made her smile. "What," he asked.

"Nothing, I don't know. I feel prickly – like my skin is vibrating or something – it's not a bad feeling though, it's strange. I feel foggy too," she added. Greg took additional blood as the day wore on and he administered antibiotics and vitamins with a few injections. He left when her eyelids filled with cement.

Henry was being taken care of. The vet had stopped by at Sam's pleading. The extra payment had helped. He was given some kind of strong tranquilizer, but she would report more fully after a complete examination and some blood work.

Penny moved to pet him but only met air. Sleep was a kaleidoscope of men grabbing her, the little girl at the park, the IV's, and Sam and Brian fighting. An incessant ringing pulled her slowly back, the doorbell! She groaned. Hours had passed. She felt like she had spent the day skiing. She could barely move she was so sore.

She hobbled to the door like an old football player after a game. It was late. It could be Kenneth again. He had come when she was groggy. One of her brothers must have provided him with a key to her house. She had vague images of him instructing her to drink and eat things and swallow a pill or two. He murmured stuff about mom and Jazz. She shook her head and winced. Greg gave her a shot that helped with concussions. When would it begin to work? And why am I alone? Panic enveloped her like an ill-fitted glove. Kidnappers, the threatening phone callers, the guys who broke in or who followed us at the park, her hand shook against the knob.

"Penny," he said. She heaved a sigh of relief.

"Sam?" she asked.

"Hi," he said. Sam fanned the hair back from his face and gently kissed her cheek. He shifted his weight from one foot to the other.

"You smell like fresh air and a bit of lime."

"I showered and shaved." He kept his eyes glued to the floor.

Her stomach cramped. Nausea rose up like lava inside of a volcano. She made it to the toilet and lay down on the cool tile of the floor and closed her eyes. Her insides boiled like sauce left on the stove too long.

"Hey, it's okay." Sam squatted beside her. "Did Greg and dad help?"

"Yes," she grunted. "Go!" She pushed him back. He didn't budge, "Sam I'm going to puke!" Sam rubbed her back as she threw up. She washed up and Sam helped her back to the living room couch. She vibrated like a cell phone on a table and Sam wound his arms around her. She lay back down onto the couch and the doorbell rang again.

"Relax. Maybe now you'll feel better." He spread the afghan she kept on the side of her couch over her.

"You are not welcome here." Sam shouted at the door.

"Is that the best you've got? Where are your police buddies, Sam?"

"They could be here in seconds. Don't push me!"

"Sam!" Penny admonished from her prone position on the couch.

"Penny! It's me, Brian. Will you please tell your overprotective brother to allow your fiancé to check in?" Brian asked.

"Brian," Penny said. She exhaled like a whale with its blowhole.

"I want to take care of you." His gray eyes were soft and moist as he stood over her. Sam snorted.

"That's my job. You're fired as if you were ever hired in the first place!" Sam said. His words were like a barbed wire fence.

"I'm so sorry Penny." Brian traced a finger around the black circles under her eyes and across her pale cheeks.

"She looks like death warmed over." Sam said.

"Thanks," Penny said. "Look I appreciate all the concern. I do. But all I – I really want to do is take a bath right now," she declared. She steadied herself on the couch arm as she stood up. Brian and Sam both rushed to assist her.

"Sit. We'll get the tub going." Brian eyed Sam.

"Go ahead I'm not leaving you alone with her!" Sam said. Brian jogged upstairs. Sam helped her pick out fresh clothes and hovered nearby while she undressed and flung a robe around her bare body.

"I can take it from here, please. I'll let you know when I need help again, okay?" She shut the bathroom door and sank into the warm water. They both stood outside the door asking often if she needed anything, and if she was okay.

A short while later, they were in her living room eating leftover soup that Nance had brought over late last night. Penny sipped some chamomile tea and Brian brought her a large glass of water.

"Greg said to be careful about staying hydrated," Brian said.

"Thanks," she said. Her strength and clarity returned in increments as she ate. Henry lay by her feet, having been returned to her while she was in the bathtub. He tried to keep a close eye on things but his eyelids kept fluttering shut. He snored loudly.

Penny pushed away her bowl and glass and leaned into the couch cushions. Brian came back over to her and kneeled close, reaching for her hand. Sam stood close behind Brian.

"I'm sorry. I know uncle does bad things for," he said. His stormy sea-colored eyes were like the motion of a broom sweeping inside of her. "For control I guess."

"You think?" Sam squeezed the sarcasm out as if he were icing a cake.

"What if someone is setting him up?" Penny suggested. Brian held her hand as she closed her eyes for a brief moment. She felt so weak.

"Set uncle up?" Brian echoed.

"Why, is the goal to eliminate him once and for all?" Sam added.

"It could be the same people who are following me and calling me, and breaking into my house." Penny yawned.

"You don't believe Jazz and Brian are doing those things?"

"No," she answered. Penny yawned again. "That just doesn't make sense to me."

"Thanks," Brian said.

"Maybe but Penny, enough, you need to rest." Sam swooped in and carried her upstairs to her bedroom. He tucked her in and kneeled beside the bed. Henry jumped up and pressed his long strong body up against her side. So that when he stretched out they were nearly the same length. He sighed and put his snout on her belly. Penny smiled a little and petted his head. She rubbed her brick-laden eyes.

"Let me figure things out for a while Penny," Sam said.

"With my help," Brian added. He stood in the doorway. Sam stiffened like a block of wood. Penny patted his hand.

"Test him," she whispered. "It'll make us all feel better." She smiled a little again. "Oh and Sam can you call work for me? I don't even know my schedule for this week."

"Okay, but you're not going back to work until you are stronger," Sam said. He turned to leave. She held onto his hand.

"Thanks," she whispered to Sam. Brian spoke.

"I understand if you two want to check me out further," he said. "I am going to double my efforts, Penny to regain your trust and that includes you too, Sam." They went downstairs. She could hear them arguing over the dishes.

Penny awoke the next morning and stumbled to the bathroom then fell into her bed for another long nap. When she awoke, the sun was high in the sky and she stretched her body top to bottom. Hearing Henry bark, she rose and let him out. Feeling hungry, she grabbed some bread and a banana and then headed back upstairs. She took a long hot shower. She inspected her body's injured spots. She had a dull ache in the back of her head and her leg was sore where the IV had been but she felt a lot better.

After she got dressed she headed down to the kitchen for something more to eat and hit the play button on her answering machine. She listened to Dana's messages about work. She examined her calendar with a frown. She hit the stop button and phoned the clinic. She munched on some raspberry yogurt and a hunk of havarti-dill cheese. Her appetite was returning. She explained her ill health as a horrible stomach bug and agreed to a few extra unpopular shifts to make-up her time. She would start the day after tomorrow, and fill in over the weekend. Sam must have forgotten to call. Well, he had a lot on his mind. She listened to the rest of her messages. She pushed her food away when her face grew hot.

"Enjoy your first in a series of *treatments*." A raspy robotic sounding voice mimicked. "You wanted to know what happened to your lovely alluring mother." Click! Henry scratched to come in and there was a knock on her front door.

–

Tom lowered himself into the diner booth table opposite Kenneth. He grinned at the young, pretty waitress.

"I'll take the number four, thanks," he said. Kenneth frowned.

"I was here yesterday," Tom explained. "What's up?"

"I think we should stop right now. He's dying. It won't be long now," Kenneth said. He reached for his coffee but then set it down without taking a sip. His hand shook. Tom smiled.

"Maybe you need a dose or two. Want me to set it up?"

"No thanks. I have mostly kicked such habits," Kenneth responded. He had the sudden urge to race back to his Nova Scotia, Canadian home as fast as possible.

"Does that explain the prolonged exile? Or was it my marriage to Genieve, your second true love?" Tom chuckled. "Or perhaps it was the fact that you were responsible for June's, uh, what should I call it? Not quite demise, but close enough." He laughed. Kenneth gripped his mug so hard he thought it might shatter into a million fragments.

"Look, Kenny, there's no sense wimping out now. Haven't you done your share of that most of your whole life?" Tom said. Kenneth slammed down his coffee, spilling it. He stood up and sat back down as Tom waved a hand around the restaurant.

"Take your stupid pot shots at me Tom. You and Jazz are quite good at that but this is about Penny!" Kenneth hissed. "Please leave Genieve alone. She should be allowed to make her own choices but then again you have never granted such rights to any woman or any person in your life for that matter!"

Their orders arrived and Kenneth picked at his food. Tom wolfed down his entire plate of eggs, home fries, bacon and pancakes. Kenneth looked away. He is a disgusting, self-righteous pig!

"You want to be the hero, how sweet." Tom spoke as though Kenneth were five years old. "Doesn't your mother have some version of an old dog never can learn new tricks, Kenny?"

"If you're so clever why do you have to kidnap women and

drug them?" Kenneth snapped.

"It's about the work Kenneth, nothing else!" Tom sounded irritated. Heads turned, staring with curiosity. Tom shoveled forkfuls of banana cream pie into his mouth. Kenneth imagined the whip cream as poison Tom was inhaling.

"No it's about you, Jazz, and Marty using drugs and mind games to find power over others'," Kenneth said.

"Don't pretend for one second to know my intentions Kenneth. You aren't even privy to your own!" Tom's voice was like chalk scraping across a blackboard.

Later that evening, Brian and Penny sat waiting at the Indian restaurant. "I hope this was a good idea," Brian said. When Penny remained silent he continued his fretting. "I shouldn't have let you talk me into this."

"You didn't. I started this whole search-for-the-truth thing," Penny said.

"We are not going to find out anything. He has a way of manipulating things." Brian stopped. Jazz smiled as he approached the table and eased himself into the throne like chair.

"I am glad you're feeling well enough to attend our meeting tonight Penny. I am sorry again about your slight mishap. I had nothing whatsoever to do with it. I was sick with my own issues. I believe the same villain is after us both. So we must carry on and figure out who exactly is behind all this misfortune and put to rest the long unanswered questions about who turned out the final light in your mother's life. Now, where are we with the plans for this glamorous engagement shindig?"

Penny reached for her water. Her heart raced and her hand shook as she held the glass of water.

"Now Penny, my dear, your beloved mother was not a coward!" Jazz wagged his finger at her.

Penny's hand shot up. Her water glass sailed across the table and flooded Brian's lap. He jumped up and began mopping at his soaked pants with his large white cloth napkin. Penny's mouth opened and closed. She shivered, like she had just stepped out of the pool on a cold day. Brian dropped his napkin and came to her side. Jazz dipped his Naan bread in the spicy cold yogurt sauce.

"You know, you both seem to have acquired the pre-wedding jitters. Relax. You obviously have fallen in love. That is wonderful. I thought that might happen. I hoped for it actually. Now listen you two have not inquired into my recent health problems," he scolded. "Sit down, sit down, you're obviously too weak to support yourself, my dear!" Jazz took a sip of his water. "And may I remind you, you were the one who initiated this whole process. So you need to keep calm through the expected ups and downs of this journey. It is life, you know and I should know considering the roller coaster ride I have had." Jazz dipped more Naan bread into the chilled yogurt and smacked his lips in appreciation.

"Eat and you'll feel worlds better. Indian food has many healing herbs, you know?" Jazz coaxed while Penny slumped back down into her chair. Brian scooted close and reached for her hand. She pulled away.

"Remember there are no mistakes, only opportunities my dear. Now I am hungry for some of that wonderful aromatic basmati rice." He signaled and instantly a waiter appeared. Jazz ordered. "Indian food is a wonderful tonic for digestive upset and nerves as I was saying earlier, hmmm?"

"You want to know what happened to June." He paused and took a sip of water. "I assume that has not evaporated in your dive into self-pity?" The accusation hung in the air as the first course arrived. Penny had to admit it smelled and tasted good—she took tentative small bites at first, it was delicious. They started with vegetable Samosas and dipped them alternately in cucumber yogurt sauce or mango chutney as more food arrived. Brian opted for the sizzling, spicy, bright red shrimp shish kebab. Penny went for an eggplant potato item, while both tried the basmati rice and chapatti bread. Penny found herself filling her mouth with the enjoyable spices and exotic tastes. Jazz requested another Indian beer and filled his large plate again.

"The food is magic." He smiled. "Try to remember learning about the past and your mother may come in all sorts of experiences. Now the engagement party is set for next weekend.

I've got a lovely hotel in mind, gorgeous tiny lights and greenery, flowers to add to the beautiful elegant décor and it should involve a sit down dinner – with a seafood main course, or we could do this, and go with India cuisine?" He coughed.

"Either one is fine, uncle," Brian intervened. Penny nodded. Jazz coughed again and again. Grasping the table he coughed deeply then he gulped his water. He reached into his shirt pocket and quickly swallowed several colored pills.

"The wedding ceremony will follow, in say, four to six weeks?" He paused for a moment and waved his hands around. "Penny you must find a suitable gown and arrange for any travel plans for extraneous family members. Don't worry about any expenses. It is my treat!"

"Shall I invite my mother, aunt Genieve and my father—who is he by the way?" Penny tossed her words into the air as if they were confetti. A small giggle tickled the back of her throat and once she started she couldn't seem to stop. The sheer madness of it all! Why pretend any longer? Jazz laughed with her and patted her arm. She bent over the table unable to stop laughing.

"Penny," Brian said. He sounded like he was standing on the edge of a cliff.

"I am crazy! This nightmare has spun out of control." Her breath felt like a stick shift car with an uncoordinated driver.

"Yes," Jazz agreed. Penny glanced around the restaurant. People stared back at her.

"Penny, let's go," Brian whispered. He shot his uncle a hard look. Jazz laughed.

"So much like your mother." Jazz winked at her then smiled at Brian. "They love to be the center of attention and cause scenes!" Brian lurched out of his seat. Penny knocked her chair over, standing up abruptly. Two waiters rushed over.

"Is everything okay?" one asked.

"She's overwrought, it runs in the family, this sort of hysteria," Jazz explained. "I had thought." He shook his head. "You would be the stronger one of the two, but perhaps I was wrong? The apple never falls far from the tree, I suppose."

Brian stuck his face right up close to Jazz's. "Shut up!" The waiter startled. Another righted Penny's chair.

"Maybe you should leave?" The other waiter quietly advised. "Your, your conversation is not really conducive to the atmosphere we try to maintain at our facility," he explained. As he spoke the room spun and black crinkles appeared in Penny's line of sight.

"Hey, Pen, are you all right?" Brian's voice came from inside a tunnel. His lips were moving. Brian leaped and caught her.

"Oh my, she's not pregnant already is she Bri, ole fellow?"

"You are despicable." Brian growled like Henry did when he felt threatened. The waiters and now the owner squatted down beside Penny and asked.

"Shall I call 911?"

Jazz answered. "Not necessary. She has a habit of outbursts and fainting spells. "Probably early pregnancy dizziness." He lowered his voice conspiratorially and gave them his credit card.

Brian held her close. "Sorry, I made a horrible, ugly mistake, *again*, Penny."

"Can you take me home now?" she murmured. "I try to be tough but it never works," she wailed.

"Me either," Brian said. His soft whisper in her left ear felt like a feather.

"Because you both are attempting to play way out of your league," Jazz scolded. "See you next Saturday!" Jazz left. Penny's tears fell like a sudden rainstorm. Penny wished desperately for a hole to swallow her up.

"Uncle is a pig, don't listen to his mind-game crap, this is his specialty," Brian said. This is why my mother and brother hate him and my father has his problems with him too."

She was grateful for Brian's constant chatter but she knew with a horrible certainty she was just like her mother. Jazz was weakening her. She was participating in the same experiments, sucked into Jazz's world, becoming vulnerable like her mother, trusting and open, hoping to prove things that were better left alone. Sobs ripped through her as though she were in labor while she stumbled into Brian's black SUV. He scooted over and held her tight. Her sniffles were muted because her face was smashed against his broad chest. She cried harder as one thought kept hammering at her heart. What am I doing trusting Brian?

The figure crouched behind Penny's bushes and cursed. The hours crept by.

"Henry. Come, Heeeeennnnrrrryyy," the man said. Presumably a neighbor watching Penny's beloved mutt, whistled a few times, as he squinted into the darkness.

The figure bent lower into the bushes. There was a thump and jingle, a door opened and closed and it was silent again. The tall dark silhouette rose and snuck around to the front of the house. This had been pointless. Perhaps it was too soon for another round? Plus, isn't patience supposed to be a virtue? The figure let out with a chuckle. It was the sound of a ghost full of old grudges.

CHAPTER TWENTY

Penny took her time in the morning. Her shift at the clinic didn't begin until noon. After showering she threw some fruit and cheese and a piece of homemade chocolate blueberry crunch zucchini bread into her lunch bag, she whistled for Henry and they took a brief walk. She kept a hand in her pocket on her cell phone and spun her head in all directions, monitoring her surroundings every second. Henry seemed especially alert too. Plus her neighbor had thought he had seen someone lurking around her house last night! When would this nightmare end when she married Brian? He was good at catching her just before she tripped or fainted but that did not mean she could trust him let alone really marry him!

Maybe the point was to disappear like her mother did? She held her breath through most of the walk, exhaling like a whale when she left Henry inside. Penny secured all of her windows and doors before leaving for work.

Dana greeted her as she walked into the office she shared with another counselor who worked the days she didn't.

"Hey, how are you feeling'?" Dana asked. Worry laced her sing-song voice.

"So-so," Penny admitted. "What's on for today?" She reached for a tea bag and mug.

"That bad, huh," Dana said. She put her arms out and Penny stepped into them. "Oh honey, hang in there. She pulled away and looked Penny straight in the eye. "Are you up for this today?" Dana swung an arm around the office. Penny's eyes filled up. She stepped back and shrugged. She bobbed her tea bag up and down, up and down, sloshing some of the hot water over the side of the mug.

"You look trashed." Dana didn't get to finish. Their boss walked in smiling and nodding to each.

"Ah, my two prize counselors hard at work, am I interrupting?"

"Nope," Dana muttered.

"Good to see you Penny." Angela ignored Dana. "Must have been some hellish bug?" The stones that were composing Penny's face cracked.

"She's falling in love with someone from her past. It was set-up and it's moving along fast!   In fact, you'll be receiving an invitation to her engagement party, that's next Saturday, right Penny?" Dana babbled as if injected with truth serum. Penny's jaw hung open. Angela coughed. "I mean this is all on top of being sick with that bad flu bug thing, whatever it was," Dana stammered and blushed. "Sorry," she murmured. Penny couldn't seem to close her mouth.

Angela laughed. "Oh, so it's only half physical?" she asked. Angela used quotation marks. "The rest is of the heart."

"Yes and no, Angela, it's really complicated, and honestly has nothing to do with work so I have no idea what possessed Dana to tell you my personal business!" Anger opened the door for Penny's voice.

"Well, it is good for me to know about my employees. Honestly dear, I have been concerned about your absences here. Listen, love is usually complex, especially if it's linked into our past and others become involved, so let things unfold naturally, now on to work ladies."

"Thanks," Penny said. Angela patted Penny's arm and smiled, though her eyes were full of questions.

"Schedules are in the box ladies. So let's get going." She exited with a wave and headed into Dennis's office. Penny heard her heels clicking on the linoleum floor as she and Dana walked to where their schedules were posted.

"So what's the latest on our friend Michael?" Angela asked Dennis. Penny vaguely recognized the name. She bent close to Dana's ear.

"I trusted you Dana! How could you?" Penny hissed like a snake ready to attack its prey.

"I'm sorry. I had diarrhea of the mouth. Angela's been pretty mad about all the shifts you've missed. We can't afford to lose you and there's no harm done. She'll be getting an invitation soon to the engagement party and you know Angela, she would have asked you a million and one questions."

Penny reluctantly agreed. She carried her tea over to the microwave and heated it up again. The clinic sizzled with hopeful energy. Phones rang for the abused women's shelter, women who sought a safe place for themselves and their children, and were on the cusp of forging a new way of life. Phone lines lit up for the crisis hotline and walk-ins straggled through the doors looking for meal vouchers, job search assistance or information on places to sleep, off the streets for a night or two. Some came in for a "wash down" to eliminate the dirt and bugs that had come to live on their bodies. Many walk-ins came in for counseling because of a recent severe crisis. Ordinary people tossed into a raging river, were at their wits end and availed themselves of the county's free services. People could also make appointments and visit with a counselor for up to 12 weeks for only a nominal fee. Often, those who used the facility gave back something when they found jobs and turned their lives around. It had been perhaps the only safe place they had ever known and a gateway to a whole new existence that might have otherwise been impossible.

Dana came and stood by Penny. "Please tell me you're not mad at me and why does Angela always call them 'our friend'?" Dana whispered.

"You know why," Penny said. She was still angry at Dana, but she tried to make the feelings subside. She didn't have the energy to get through her day here much less hold a grudge.

"Yes, she tries hard to make all of this." She waved a hand around. "Seem like a, a homestead," Dana said. They laughed. Dana gave her hand a squeeze. Dana mouthed back 'sorry' and her friend's eyes were filled with tears. Penny hesitated then mouthed back, 'it's okay'.

A few minutes later, Penny sat with her first client of the day. It was a new woman with two small children. The baby toddled over to Penny's desk and proceeded to reach for everything while the mother spoke. The three year old sat in the corner of the room on the floor and emptied the contents of a bag she had been carrying. Crayons of all shapes and sizes, probably forty of them if Penny had had to guess, spilled out and rolled along the floor. The girl opened a coloring book and began ripping pages out of it.

"I don't know the father," the mother said.

CRASH! The paper clip holder on the desk went down and spilled onto the floor. Next the pencil and pen holder and its contents, teetered and with one further swipe it smashed against the tiled floor. Penny took deep slow breaths.

"I just need some help you know? I can't keep doing this much longer. I can barely get up in the mornings. I heard this place can help, you know?" She was not yet 20 years old. She lowered her head and wiped her eyes and nose. A sob escaped and in an instant her two children were by her side. She lifted the baby onto her lap and the three year old stood by her mother, patted her arm and then laid her head onto her mother's shoulder.

"You came to the right place Anne. We can help. I know it must have taken a lot of courage to come here," Penny reassured. The woman sniffled. "That and my last change for bus fare."

Penny cleared her throat and squeezed the woman's hand. "Anne, let me tell you some of the things we can help you with and then there are some we can't. Then you and I can figure out what would most benefit you right now. Okay?"

The woman nodded and Penny went on to lend help as best as she could. Dana poked her head in and together they chuckled as they squatted and cleaned up the piles of office supplies littering Penny's floor.

Her next two appointments she had been working with for several weeks, in fact they both had come in the same week. The two families were both jobless. They were living off and on with people they knew, on the streets or in their cars. Shame permeated their body language though each expressed it in different ways.

Penny was once again reminded to never take anything for granted. The one family was eager and receptive and the mother in particular was trying hard with her three children to keep them happy and as unaffected as possible.

With the other family, Penny struggled immensely. They were terse with her and she felt as though any help she provided was never enough. The parents argued incessantly about everything and the two children seemed to take their cue from them. Penny gritted her teeth when she saw their names on her roster, sometimes hoping fervently they would move onto somewhere else. Then, feeling guilty, she'd will herself to be extra compassionate and resourceful when they arrived, only to be gritting her teeth ten minutes into the hour and half session.

By the time they could break for a late afternoon lunch, she and Dana were tired. Besides their regulars they had each seen several unscheduled walk-ins and handled a few crisis calls and now as they ate, they attempted to catch up on the volumes of paperwork. A lot of record keeping was necessary, however tedious.

"What's your evening look like?" Penny shrugged. "I haven't looked yet! I am afraid to," she said. Penny laughed as she ate her fruit, cheese and bread. She felt better. Maybe the distraction of work was good. It felt like the first time in a while where Jazz, Brian, mom, and dad hadn't dominated her thoughts.

"Well check, because I thought maybe we could zip out for a cuppa somewhere together?" Dana asked.

"Yeah sure," Penny said. "If I have enough of a break and we are covered."

Dana nodded. "I want to hear more details about your life if you will still share them with me after my debacle with Angela earlier?"

"Yes, even though it's been nice to forget about all of it for a while. Oh, I forgot I need to put a call in to Sam soon, I promised."

"Mr. Over Protective. You are lucky. I wish I had a sibling like that."

"It's not always what it's cracked up to be! Are you and your sister on the outs again?" Penny asked.

"Yup, what else is new?"

"Sorry," Penny said.

"Yeah me too," Dana added.

They returned to work. After a while, she took a break and called Sam and then Greg. Sam was trying to fit in some of his own work. He was helping a private detective with a big case and the police with some research that would help them on a homicide. His jobs were frequently interesting to hear about when he could let her know and not violate confidentiality or compromise safety. However, Penny couldn't focus on much else outside of her world so she hadn't asked him for details about his work.

Greg was out for the afternoon with Nance somewhere Sam reported, and she was glad. They needed time away. Her late afternoon was long, but she and Dana did get out for an hour. They had a dinner of soup and homemade mini loaves of bread at a nearby favorite coffee shop. Penny slurped down one of her favorite drinks; a decaf mocha latte heavy on the chocolate. She loved a good French vanilla soda or a fruity, creamy smoothie but that was for a different season.

"So you really are going to marry this guy that you hardly know? Is there some secret you are not telling me?" She dropped her voice and leaned across the table. "Like about how you were kidnapped and drugged?"

"Wha-what, where did you hear that," Penny stammered.

"You were talking to your brother earlier," Dana blushed. "Sorry I couldn't help but overhear a little bit."

"You were eavesdropping," Penny accused. A flash of anger whipped across her face like a sudden bolt of lightning.

"How else is a good friend supposed to find out her good friend's news when her good friend doesn't open up?" Dana said. She was hurt. "You can confide in me Pens. I am not usually such a blabber mouth, I promise," Dana's eyes watered.

"It's complicated," Penny muttered. Her voice was soft. She

swallowed hard, her throat made a gulping noise. "Brian, he – he is nice, handsome, smart, funny and definitely charming. And his uncle probably knows most of what happened to mom since he was the cause of most of her problems." She hesitated, her eyes moved around the restaurant but she only saw Jazz's gloating face. "Someone is trying to scare me." She inhaled and let her breath out in slow increments as though she was afraid of losing it.

Dana's eyes widened and she swiped at the wetness that rolled down from each eye. "Were you kidnapped so Jazz could run experiments on you? What kind of experiments and why? How did you escape? Why marriage, I don't get it?" Dana asked. Penny explained as best she could what had happened to her and how Sam, Wil and Brian had found her.

"The marriage thing I guess is so people from my mom and dad's past come out of hiding. I hope to find out the identity of my real dad, since it seems Kenneth is not my biological father. He's Sam's while Jazz is Greg's father," Penny said. Dana's eyes stayed wide and she kept opening and closing her mouth, wanting to interrupt Penny suspected, but controlling herself. "Like I said, it's complicated and everyday it only grows more so." Penny sighed deeply.

"It sounds like this is becoming dangerous. You could become an addict!" Dana leaned across the table. Penny sat back against the booth.

"I don't really know what they gave me. It may have only been a mixture of placebos and tranquilizer-type drugs, or at least that's what Greg and Kenneth said. Greg's trying to run tests on the samples Kenneth took from that old farmhouse I was taken to," Penny said.

"How do you know you can trust Brian?" Dana squeezed Penny's hand. Penny had been folding and refolding her napkin. She pushed away her tea. Her stomach lurched and she put a hand to her lips as if she might be sick.

"I don't. Let's change the subject. I can't talk about any of it anymore. It makes me feel sick, literally."

"You do look green around the edges." Dana smiled at her

with a face full of compassion.

"Tell me about – is it Ben?" Penny sniffled.

"You're sure you want to hear about my problems with everything you have going on, Penny?" Penny nodded vigorously. "Uh well, long story, but maybe good." She leaned across their table and lowered her voice. "He's changing." She looked around then back at Penny. "And for real this time," Dana whispered

"Are you sure?" Penny put another bit of butter on her warm, soft, yeasty-smelling bread and pulled pieces off one by one, laying them on top of one another.

"No, hey are you going to eat that divine bread or play with it?"

"Go ahead," Penny said and pushed the bread toward her friend. "So how has he changed?"

Dana made a face. "You decimated it!"

"I was testing its 'pile-ability,'" she laughed.

"Ben is more serious."

"He's always been serious about you, Dana," Penny blurted.

"I know, but I see now how devoted he is to his mom and sisters. The gun thing is still there but he's toned down the obsession about watching every sport known to man."

"Lots of guys have that. What's the gun thing again?"

"Well he's an ex-cop but he still likes to carry his gun *everywhere* and he pulls it out sometimes, talks about how important having his gun is to him and then sometimes he kind of fingers it, almost lovingly." She wrinkled her nose. "He well he— I've witnessed his temper and it scares me." Penny nodded and she watched Dana devour the bread as she spoke.

"It is obvious you care for him and this gun thing, well, like you said, he is an ex- cop and he's probably seen a lot of stuff. Has he ever been abusive in any way with his temper?"

"No."

"Lots of guys love sports and it could be a good thing that he is so close to his family."

"I don't know, it's just he gets real intense and moody and then he rubs or touches his gun. He is possessive of those he loves. He questions me a lot sometimes about where I've been, who I've talked with and it feels smothering and overprotective."

"Sam can be like that with me," Penny said.

"It's not like I have lots of other choices to pick from." Dana threw away her garbage and they rose to leave.

"That is not a reason to stick with this guy. Look, I can't believe I am saying this, but take it slow. There's no need in your case to rush things, okay?" Penny said. Dana nodded. "Maybe talk to him about how his temper, his gun, and about how all of his intense questioning un-nerves you and see how he reacts. It's always good to be honest."

"Yeah just what I was thinking," Dana laughed. "Listen to your own advice!" They repeated this last line in unison.

Returning to the clinic, Penny allowed the last of the evening rush to sweep away all her thoughts. Then in the middle of one of her appointments Penny had to excuse herself. She ran to the bathroom. Tears suddenly, uncontrollably streamed down her face. The client had reminded her of her mother somehow, not in her appearance but her demeanor, her problems with addiction and estrangement from her children.

She splashed water on her face over and over again though careful not to smudge her mascara and stared into the mirror. She used several paper towels to dab at the wetness. A powerful desire for her mother overcame her. She flung herself into a stall and sobbed. She wished her mother had allowed her to help her. Why hadn't she confided in Penny? She missed that and now, now that she was older, she wished for the chance to be friends with her mother, despite all the mistakes. Penny prayed with all her heart for the opportunity to talk with her mother about anything!

She wiped her eyes and face as best she could and resumed her duties until finally she could leave. By the time Penny arrived home at nearly 10:30 PM, she was exhausted. She greeted her exuberant mutt.

"Oh Henry I am so glad to be home again. "You okay boy?" She laughed as he lunged at her, trying to plant kisses on her face. After he calmed down a bit, and she let him out, Penny slugged down two glasses of water. Her machine flashed with four messages. It was a new machine that Sam had provided her with after he confiscated the old one. She hesitated a moment then pressed the long black button and smiled. Remi exclaimed over the engagement party coming so soon. Of course she'd find a way to be there no matter what. Her father was next.

"I wanted to see how you're feeling? Call me soon." He started to leave his number but seemed to change his mind. He mumbled something then hung up. Penny frowned. Next was a hang up. Then she heard Brian's voice.

"Hi, just called to ask you to promise me one thing?" Crackling noises grew louder. His voice was garbled. "I want you"—crackle, "to promise me," pause, "that you'll," he kept drawing out his words. "That you'll," static interrupted and Penny put her ear close. She heard voices arguing maybe, then Brian's soft whisper, "n---l."

The machine clicked off with the time. Penny punched the button again and listened but it wasn't any better. Then she tried again and it gave her one more message she must have missed earlier because it was after the old messages of Dana and work.

"Can't wait to meet up with you at the party," the distorted voice said. Penny slammed her fingers down onto the machine. Henry trotted over and nudged her hand with his cool wet black nose that now wore a smear of brown dirt above his nostrils. Penny jumped and then laughed. Henry wagged his tail furiously. His ears went back against his head.

"Sorry boy, it's okay. You've been digging again. I could open a miniature golf course in your honor Hen!" She patted his large head. "It's been a long, long day Hen. You ready to retire to the upper reaches?" She laughed at her use of the old expression her dad would say before going to bed at night. She opened the back door, glanced around nervously while Henry performed his nightly duties and shut and locked it up as soon as Henry ran back inside.

Penny sat at her desk the next morning on what was her favorite day of the week – Friday. Her day to write! She had to work tomorrow morning in order to make up the missed hours. Oh well, it wouldn't be that bad.

She typed a little then looked out the window at the sparrows and finches hopping around the yard under her birdfeeder. The trees were still mostly green with just a hint of a crown of yellow or red. The computer screen in front of her displayed a collage of smiling puppies. She sighed and scooted her chair back, reaching for her blueberry tea. She inhaled and smiled. Happiness! She pulled her chair up to the computer and reread the words. Her hands began to move until her fingers were flying across the keys.

Wil and Brian were out for a long run that afternoon. Kenneth walked briskly behind.

"I have got to focus on the party otherwise my greatest fears will be realized by my own stupidity," Brian said.

"Well, that happens often enough in life doesn't it buddy?" Wil huffed as they ran through the hills.

"I feel like a teenager," Brian said He pushed his body harder as Wil and Kenneth struggled to keep up.

After another several miles they both fell down, exhausted, in the clearing they had found as they began slowing their pace. Wil rolled over, looking at his friend.

"I can't believe the old man kept up with us," Wil whispered.

"I walk a lot," Kenneth snapped.

"I am not doing this again. My legs are going to give out." Wil said.

"Sorry man." Brian breathed like the choppy waters of the sea.

"Since you have been involved in this thing with her, you are a bear! You need to be with her. Show her your love the manly way!" Wil scolded. Brian threw Wil a look. Kenneth grunted his disapproval.

"But don't be a total jerkoid like Marv, what was his name?"

"Wilmern," Wil said. He wiped the sweat off his face and onto his shirt as he sat up. He laughed.

"With a name like that what could a lady expect?" They

laughed and Brian pulled his tired friend up.

"So go clean up, find her and seduce her like you never have any woman before, pull out all your charming stops. Just leave the details out please, whenever we meet again!" Wil pleaded in a whisper.

"Boys please, Penny is my daughter!"

Brian grinned. "It would be enjoyable"

"Yes, it usually is." Wil laughed and threw his friend down on the ground. They wrestled and laughed. Kenneth rolled his eyes and a small smile played across his lips. Greg and Sam used to wrestle around. Is it possible Brian really loves Penny? Is he as decent as he appears?

A short while later, Brian was showered and dressed, and Kenneth his new shadow, was beside him as they drove to Penny's house. He drove fast and missed the stop sign. A loud horn honked and he jumped. His car jerked and he came to an abrupt stop midway through the intersection.

"Watch out! Is this how you drive my daughter around?" Kenneth admonished as the car Brian narrowly missed sped by and the man hung his head out the window cursing at Brian as he drove on by.

"Sorry!" Brian called. "I'm about to get married."

"No excuses! And it's a farce, need I remind you," Kenneth snapped. Kenneth had to find a way to put a stop to Tom before he destroyed Penny, but how? Genieve had made herself inaccessible, another question to which he had no answer. Jazz was on the way out at least that was clear.

"I am falling in love with her, sir." Brian interrupted Kenneth's whirling thoughts. They stared hard at one another.

"Yes I heard you with Wil. Time will tell. Keep your eyes on the road!" Kenneth growled. "And you're enmeshed in Jazz's web. That is not real love. Your Uncle does not know the meaning of the word unless it applies to self and power."

"I agree about Jazz but not about my feelings for Penny. They are real even if our romance began under auspicious circumstances. Couldn't that be said of you and June, sir?" Brian asked. Kenneth said nothing.

"This is our chance to outsmart him. I need answers about my family too. He used my brother and my father like he did all of you," Brian explained. Kenneth studied Brian's handsome profile. 'Actions are like a heavy downpour, Kenny' his mother would say, 'while words are the soft raindrops.'

They pulled up in front of Penny's house. Her car was not in the driveway but her front door was open and they could see a shadowy figure pass through her living room.

CHAPTER TWENTY ONE

Brian and Kenneth raced up to Penny's doorway. Brian shouted first, "Penny!" Kenneth bolted inside. Henry threw back his big black head and barked. His fur bunched up on his back as he kept barking. A tall man tried to shush him.

"Henry, it's okay," he said.

"Where's Penny? Who are you?" Brian asked.

"Oh hey, are you the handsome fiancé? Nice to meet you I'm Din, Penny's handy neighbor. I watch over Henry when she works her long shifts at the crisis center," Din shook Brian's hand and patted Henry's head.

"Brian O'Mackery, nice to meet you too and this is Penny's father, Kenneth," Brian said. Kenneth shook Din's hand.

"Penny's still at work, I believe for a while yet. Are you two going to wait here for her?" Din asked. Kenneth glanced at Brian and they both shook their heads, no.

"Okay well I will see you both at the engagement shindig next week?" Din said as he and Brian walked outside.

"Drop me off at Sam's," Kenneth said. Brian nodded and they drove in silence to Sam's house. "You're going back to wait for her, aren't you?" Kenneth asked as he opened the door to get out of the car. Brian nodded. Kenneth frowned. He knew what Brian wanted. He hoped Penny resisted. He slammed the door and strode up to Sam's front door. But after Brian pulled away Kenneth switched direction, deciding to take a long walk to try and clear his mind of the picture of Brian and Penny together.

A few days later, Penny sipped champagne at her engagement

party as bolts of electricity coursed through her veins. She rolled her neck from side to side but it didn't help right her world which was tilted at an odd angle. What am I doing? What am I doing, reverberated inside her head like a drum.

"Hey," Greg said. He pulled her to him in a shoulder-to-shoulder hug. Penny trembled.

"Marriage of any type is scary," he whispered. "Your version defies all logic."

"Yeah, I can't seem to stop crying." Penny sniffled. "I feel exhausted and off-kilter."

"Sounds normal Penny, given the circumstances. It may take a while for whatever they loaded you up with to leave your system. Keep hydrating, mostly with water, okay? And Pen, don't underestimate how much stress you have been under." He hugged her to his side again.

"I need a plumber." She dabbed her eyes. Greg smiled.

"Brian is smitten," he said.

"With Jazz's plan or me," Penny said.

"I think he is a good guy with decent intentions who managed to get caught in some very ugly stuff. It happens."

"You make it sound accidental. Brian agreed to work for Jazz for years, Greg. You and Sam sure disagree." Penny rolled her eyes.

"Things aren't always as they seem on the outside Penny or even because people tell us a version doesn't mean there isn't more to it and life don't always come to us in nice, neat packages. Sometimes you have to brush off the debris and excavate."

"You believe in this marriage?"

"I want you to find happiness. Look at Nance and I, we took the leap a few years back. I was," he said. Greg put a hand to each side of his face. "I was incredibly nervous and the trust issues were enormous given our childhood."

"I remember." She thought of his terrible what-iffing on his wedding day. He broke six dishes at the rehearsal dinner and spilled red wine on two older ladies!

"I know your situation is different." He scratched his head. "However my gut keeps telling me Brian really cares for you and though he chose to remain caught up in his uncle's web his love for you is not an act."

"Glad you can be so trusting and sure." Penny laced her words with disbelief. "Did the lab analyze the stuff Kenneth brought back and what about my blood tests?"

"Nothing unusual showed up Pen, just some traces of common barbiturates," Greg said. Penny nodded. Why was she disappointed?

Brian danced over to her, laughing, and he took hold of Penny's hand and twirled her around.

"Hey beautiful," he said. His smile was as wide as the Gulf of Mexico. "How are you feeling?" He kissed her ear with tenderness.

"Okay." He pulled away and gave her a lustful once over which took her back to a few nights ago.

He stopped by just as she snuggled under the covers trying to get warm and comfortable. It was turning colder at night as fall was really settling in. She heard her doorbell ring and she decided to ignore it. Henry barked.

"I am not getting up!" Henry cocked his head and continued barking. His tail wagged as if she had been away for a week! He jumped off the bed and ran down the stairs. His barking was high pitched now.

"Okay fine Henry, you open the door, since you seem so eager to have company! It is after eleven at night! Normal people don't come over now and have you forgotten our ride in that van to that creepy place with machines and drugs? Go to sleep!" She grumbled and pulled the covers up over her head. The bell rang for the fourth time and Henry barked louder if that were possible. She flung the covers back and wrapped her thick red robe belt around her waist and slid her feet into slippers.

She looked through the peephole and saw a man's chest. "Who is it?!" She waited.

"Brian. Sorry I know it's late, I must have missed you when you arrived home from work. I was waiting but I grew hungry and tired so I went home but I couldn't sleep so I came back and I saw your bedroom light on." She flung open the door.

"Brian you are going to wake everyone up with your yammering!" She put her hands on her hips.

"There's something important I need," he murmured. "To do," he said. His eyes were soft as he bent to kiss her cheek. "Sorry." He touched her long thick waves of hair. "You are a vision Penny." His eyes shone. He cleared his throat. She hesitated and opened the door a little bit more. Brian walked in, took off his coat and sat on the living room couch.

"Kenneth and I tried to come by earlier but you were out. We grew worried when we thought we saw a man in your house but it was Din?" Penny nodded. "And he explained how he takes care of Henry. I needed to make sure you arrived home safely and that you're okay?"

She put a hand to her chest, "I am fine!" She went back to the front door.

"Hey did you get my message?" he asked. Her right hand squeezed the front door knob and she turned around to face him.

"It was garbled." She sighed. "Brian." She spun back to the door and opened it, letting in a blast of cold fall air and she shivered. "You can see I am fine. You're important thing will have to wait. It's late and I'm tired."

"Come sit with me Penny and close the door. It's cold!" He patted a spot on the couch beside him and brought out a small box from his pants pocket. His blue eyes sparkled like sunshine on a lake. Her legs were cooked noodles. She shut the door and sank onto the couch next to him. He lifted the lid of the box.

A beautiful turquoise and silver bracelet lay against black velvet. Her heart thumped like an unhappy bull at a rodeo.

"There's more." He kissed her. Fiery waves of desire replaced her blood. She closed her eyes and gripped the arm of the couch.

"Penny," he said. He touched her knee and like a reflex her eyes flew open. He was down on one knee. Her wooden lips twitched while he slowly raised the small lid of another box. His warm mouth, sweet like a baked caramel apple massaged hers. His eyes were ocean waves, smoothing her rocky heart into sand.

"It doesn't matter how life works. It's what we do with it that counts." He raised her left hand to his mouth. "I love you." He slid the rectangular diamond studded with sapphires onto her engagement finger and strung kisses around her mouth and jaw line lighting her up like a Christmas tree. A hurricane whipped her senses.

"Hey," he said. He stroked her cheek.

"What?" she jumped. Her eyes popped open like a jack-in-the-box.

"Help me up please." He groaned.

"What?"

"Too much hard running with Wil, my knees or at least I hope it is only my knees. My insides feel squeezed into a knot." He groaned again.

"Yeah," she murmured. "Now you know how I feel everyday!"

"I might be stuck in your living room for the duration of my life!" He moaned.

"What's the difference? That was your plan from the start."

"Penny, please help me!"

"Stop with the drama." She snorted. He held out his right hand. She grasped his forearm and pulled.

"I thought you worked out?" He complained. "Come on, I need serious and fast help here," he demanded.

"Hey, you are easily twice my size. I am trying."

"I am not fat and you're not trying hard enough."

"Is that your actual proposal?" She snapped and yanked as hard as she could. He staggered. They teetered together and fell. Her nightgown and robe flew up in the air as Brian landed on top of her. His hand rested near her chest. She was in an oven and he grinned.

"Thanks, this worked out better than I could have imagined."

She pushed at him but to no avail.

"Get up!"

"Not on your life!" He tried to scoot forward to kiss her. She twisted away. "Are you this grumpy every evening? I thought you weren't a morning person? " Shifting his weight, he managed to move closer to her face.

"You barge in here acting as if we are a real couple and trick me with injury stories." She squirmed, feeling the faucet about to turn on in her eyes. "Do you recall a kidnapping and drug-forcing just a few days ago? You still haven't gotten any answers out of Jazz have you?"

"No, but you can't hold that against me! Did you hear what I said? I love you Penny and I want to marry you! Forget this whole plan of Jazz's and our screwed up pasts. None of that matters except that it brought us together for a reason. We have so much in common. This was meant to be, sweetheart." He slid his body along hers and brought his mouth down on her clenched lips. She turned her head away and he unleashed tender kisses all along her neck and collarbone. She brought her head back and he found her mouth instantly.

"Brian," she mumbled.

"Wil was right," Brian murmured. He kissed her again and again. "You can't deny your feelings for me!" He released her and she scooted away, lowering her nightgown.

"It's not love Brian."

"Help me." He sunk to the floor each time he tried to stand up. She looked at his outstretched hand for a long moment, gripped the warmth and pulled. He laughed and collapsed against her.

"Tickles," he said. Brian laughed harder. She tugged. They stood close together.

"We have fun together and possess an amazing chemistry and we share a lot in common and," his island sea colored eyes caressed her. "Admit it. You like me?" His grin blinded her.

"Brian," she said. He touched her hair like it was fine china and scooped her into a tight embrace.

"Thanks for helping me tonight," he murmured. He ran his fingers along the top edge of her nightgown. She rested her face against his soft blond hair and slight beard.

"That first day in the supermarket I knew I could love you Penny Patrick soon to be O'Mackery! I need your promise." He tightened his grip around her waist and inhaled sharply, "That you won't leave me once you get what it is you're after." His sea gray eyes were like a deep ocean oil rig digging a well.

"I can't do that," she said.

"I'm scared too Penny. Who isn't when they're making a lifelong commitment? Promise me, Penny, please! We can take it slower but just don't cut me out of your life!" His eyes raced back and forth with hers. He wanted to win. Why? Did he really care about her that much? Did he actually love her?

Despite everything her heart was singing.

She twirled the emerald cut diamond ring around her finger, eying the sapphires around the diamond. "Forever, Love, Brian," read the inscription. Henry liked and trusted him.

"Hey, are you thinking what I am thinkin'?" Brian broke into her thoughts as he twirled her across the engagement party dance floor. She put a hand to her cheek. She must resemble a tomato.

"Thought so." He wrapped his arm around her waist holding her tightly against him, teasing her lips apart. He swept her out onto the dance floor as a slow love song enveloped her.

"That color matches your emerald eyes." He indicated her dress. "And this," he said. Brian fingered the bit of lace near her breasts. "Is very sexy," he purred. Brian burrowed into her neck and left rows of kisses. "Almost as much as your nightgown," he said. He rubbed his sweet caramel lips across her chest. Penny was in a warm bubble bath until Sam threw in ice cubes the size of glaciers!

"What the hell are you doing?" Sam hissed. He took a long slurp of some foul smelling dark liquid.

"What is that stuff Sam?" Penny held her nose and turned away.

"Don't worry about it." He pushed Penny. "You have a lot more important things to deal with," he slurred. "Like how to ditch this louse."

"Hey, no shoving your sister and my fiancé! How are you doin' Sam?" Brian countered with the exuberance of an eight year old boy. Sam's clenched fist rose up.

"Sam you're drunk," she accused. "Please don't make a scene!"

"Ha! Too late for that," Sam shouted. "Ever heard of not

counting your chicks until they have hatched?" Sam spit at Brian, pushing Penny away from him again.

Brian rubbed his arm after Sam let go. "Hey, whether you choose to accept it. I am happy and in love like I said the other night remember, Penny?" He winked at her. She blushed and Sam looked from one to the other.

"Uh oh," he said.

"No, not yet, although I admit it has crossed my mind more than once." Brian smiled at Penny. "And your sister's too," he said. "I had to go over to make an improvement."

"What the hell are you talking about?" Sam took another long swallow.

"Sam, stop it, please." She moved toward him and reached out to take his drink away.

"Over the last time I asked for her hand in marriage," Brian explained.

"There isn't going to be any marriage! This is all crap!" Sam gestured around the room and took another long swallow and handed the cup to Penny. "Thanks, I'll take another please."

"No way, you are done Sam. Where's Greg?" Penny asked.

"How should I know? Am I my brother's keeper?" Sam snapped.

"Your sister's is more like it!" Brian blurted.

"If you're going to quote the Bible, then grow up and act civil at least." Penny hissed at her brother.

"I love her and we are going to be brothers, Sam."

"Brian." Penny warned while Sam stuck his index finger in his mouth. Brian shrugged but Penny felt a wave of nausea especially when out of the corner of her eye she could see Jazz, staring at them with a huge satisfied grin. A slithering snake of hot shame wound around her.

"Excuse me for a minute," Brian said. He touched her back before striding over to where his brother, John stood awkwardly with Jazz and their father, Milman.

"Do you see my point?" Sam words rubbed salt into her wounded heart. Sam made a face at Brian's back and staggered back to the bar where he apparently wished to continue feeding his ire.

Penny looked at the various arrangements of people, food and flowers. It was a cornucopia of beauty as far as the eye could see. Her eyes filled up. She looked out toward the big long wall of windows and folded her arms around her waist. She had had another disturbing call this morning, warning her to be prepared for a shock, coming soon, maybe at this party. She spun around. She sure didn't need another surprise! A sledgehammer was beginning to beat its familiar rhythm into the back of her head. She had to make her way across this monstrosity of a room.

"You're afraid of your feelings for me." Brian accused before finally leaving her alone last night. The idea hung before her like a forked path.

"Mommy, help me!" Penny glanced up at the cathedral ceiling. Wrapping her arms around her waist she pushed through the crowd.

"Ouch! You stepped on my toe and in those things." He pointed to her long skinny heels. "That hurt!" He grabbed his foot.

"Sorry." She moved away from the stranger, vowing to be more careful. The room seemed to be filled with people she didn't know. She walked quickly. People touched her forearm, telling her it was a lovely party and asking to admire her emerald shaped diamond with the tiny sapphires, she obliged while fear and sadness leaked from her eyes. She pinned a smile across her mouth and nodded though her head spun like an amusement park ride that went on way too long.

"Excuse me!" she said. A colleague of Jazz's nodded at her. "I need to find the bathroom." She put a hand to her mouth.

"Sure, this is nerve racking stuff. You have more courage than I do," he said.

"More like stupidity," she mumbled. She reached the restroom door to see her brother slide up behind Brian and she hesitated.

"Hey," Sam said. He stuck his finger into Brian's chest. "You don't fool me," Sam said. He took a slurp of his thick dark drink.

"Not trying to," Brian said.

"Liar," Sam declared.

Remi saddled up to her, "Hey girl, how ya holdin' up?" Penny smeared her tears across her cheeks but brought a finger up to her lips and nodded toward the men. "Oh honey," Remi said. She caught her up in her arms, and Penny felt swaddled like an infant might in a fuzzy blanket. "Uh oh, want me to strike up interference?" Penny shook her head, no.

"Sam," Kenneth put a hand on Sam's upper arm. He flung it off with disgust etched on his drunken face. Sam angled his body in close to Brian and wagged his index finger in Brian's face.

"If you hurt my sister in any form, shape, or way," he said, "I'll hunt you down, and run you over until you are nothing. Make that worse than NOTHING!" Sam raged and rammed his finger back at Brian's chest. "Understand?"

Brian stood very still. Penny held her breath. Remi cursed.

"Who will throw the first punch? Care to cast your wager?" Remi whispered. Penny gripped Remi's arm and squeezed hard.

"I think he gets your point Sam!" Kenneth joined them and laughed. Remi cursed again and Penny couldn't help giggling.

"I understand that you care very deeply for your only sister. We share that in common, Sam," Brian held up a hand to quiet Sam. "You need to respect that she is a grown woman making her own choices and she is wearing the engagement ring I gave her last night of her own free will!"

"That's a load of crap and you know it!" Sam said. His fist rose. Kenneth put a hand out to stop his son. Penny ran over and Remi followed.

"Now boys," Remi offered.

"SAM!" Penny shouted.

"Don't you think you're going a little overboard in this protective brother stuff?" Remi exclaimed at Sam.

"Stay out of this girls!" Sam snarled the word girls.

"Sam!" Greg joined them.

"What?"

"Shake it off man! You're going to blow it." He grabbed his drink, and sniffed it. "Whew, no wonder," he said. Greg tossed it into a nearby fake plant arrangement. "It'll be over soon. Meanwhile you need to show some restraint in public."

"How about respect," Brian added.

"You have to earn it," Kenneth said.

"No offense sir, but the same could be said of you!" Brian said.

"Okay, okay, look maybe it is a big mistake, and maybe she'll live to regret it. But I don't think so, and besides it's her life," Greg said. Sam opened his mouth. "Don't encourage this behavior!" Greg directed to Kenneth.

"Oh I am scared." Sam clutched his chest. Looking at his brother, a grin flickered and threatened to surface. Greg smiled at his brother with relief. Brian shook his head.

"This is stupid!" Penny said. She ran back toward the bathroom.

"Like I said twenty minutes ago, boys!" Remi added. "I'll meet you by the cake Pens!"

Penny was about to open the bathroom door when Dana came rushing over.

"Hey," Dana said. Penny took in her floral print bright purple and pink short sleeved dress that matched her softer, sunnier nature.

"I love that dress on you Dana!"

"Thanks. How are you?" Dana asked. "Having doubts about your sanity?"

"Yes and Sam has actually lost his sanity," Penny whined.

"That's to be expected! What can I do to help Pens?" Dana looped an arm through Penny's and kissed her cheek.

"I'll be okay. I'm going to take a break for a few minutes in the ladies room and I'll be fine, thanks," She had an overwhelming urge to be alone. She pushed open the door to the ladies room. Someone tapped her on the shoulder and broke her reverie.

"Hey sweetie, Greg is settling Sam down, don't worry. How are you holding up?"

Penny hugged her sister-in-law tight. Then Nancy pulled back.

"Hmm, I see fear, worry, and anger."

"No reading my face right now! I am not up for one of your soul searching's. I admit I am having my problems. At least I am not as bad off as Sam," Penny wailed. "He's embarrassing me Nance! I love him and I do appreciate his protectiveness, but he's drunk and trying to pick a fist fight with Brian!" Nancy rubbed her hand in a slow circular motion around Penny's back. "What am I doing?" Penny shoved her ringed hand out toward Nancy.

"Oooo, pretty, but listen you can back out anytime." Nancy held onto her ringed hand. Penny rested her head on her sister-in-law's shoulder. Nancy fingered Penny's French braided hair. "What do you feel for him Penny? Are you even close to loving him?" she whispered. Penny nodded.

"I can't believe it! Am I crazy or what?" she cried. Nancy hugged her tight and they rocked back and forth as Penny cried. Nancy handed her a tissue and they laughed and cried.

"Pregnancy," Nancy wailed. "I hang out by bathrooms wherever I go and cry when I notice someone's shoelaces are untied!" That set them alternately crying and laughing again. "See what you have to look forward to!" Nancy blurted. Penny cried harder.

"I already do that and I'm not even pregnant yet! Though Jazz accused me of it the other night," Penny said.

"Don't let him bully you Penny! We'll be here for you no matter what happens okay?" Penny hugged her sister-in-law close and tried not to lose the rest of her make-up.

"You and Greggie are the best!" Penny wailed. "And Remi and Dana too," She added.

"Sam loves you too Pen," Nance said.

"I know." Penny made her way into the bathroom and sighed. She looked at herself in the mirror and wiped at her eyes. She reached into her purse for some tissues and make-up.

"I am handling it! Remember that." She told her reflection as she leaned in close. "Got to keep my sense of humor." She leaned closer and fingered the dark circles under her eyes that the make-up hadn't been able to conceal. A few guests entered and eyed her. She nodded and moved away from the mirror, her face flushing the color of a red delicious apple. She ducked into a stall.

Jazz gasped and swayed. Kenneth watched the color drain out of Jazz's face.

"What's wrong? Having another attack, how convenient, I suppose?" Kenneth prompted.

"She's here Kenny, my plan worked," Jazz hissed.

"What are you talking about?" Kenneth demanded. His head swiveled around the room and he caught sight of a woman with thick auburn-colored hair, skirting between groups, making her way into the ladies room. She leaned back against the door and a smile spread across her beautiful face. Kenneth gasped and turned to catch Jazz's eye.

"You saw her too," Jazz murmured.

"It isn't possible," Kenneth whispered. "She can't." Kenneth was interrupted by Brian.

"Who is she?" Brian asked, looking from Jazz to Kenneth and back out to around the room. Jazz's mouth opened and closed. He put a hand to his heart. His lips moved but no sound emerged.

"Uncle," Brian said. Jazz started choking. Brian watched him clutch his head and then paw at his neck. "You need to lie down. Have you taken your pills today?" Brian escorted him out of the room. Jazz's lips were moving rapidly but no sound came out.

"I am going to call 911. We need to get you to a hospital, for real this time. Do you have your emergency pills? Where are they?" Jazz swung his head back and forth motioning a no as Brian spoke. "I am trying to help. You need real medical attention not Marty Mapman's experimental stuff." They had found a vinyl chair down one hallway. A few people had noticed and come out to inquire if there was anything they could do.

Jazz swiped at his nephew, taking big gulps of air while loosening his tie and unbuttoning his shirt midway down his chest. His voice came out unevenly. "Could – cou – could you – poss-ibly shut up for a min – minute!" Brian stepped back, as if he had been slapped.

"She – she's he—here Bri. It—it worked! Just ask Kenneth!" Jazz was attempting to stand up. "Don't you understand who that was, boy? I have to find her. We—we have a lot to discuss," Jazz said. Brian's eyebrows drew together. Greg interrupted.

"What's wrong?" Greg asked him.

"I'm fine. I had a bit of surprise," Jazz explained. He tried to push Greg and Brian away. "Come on Kenny, let's go."

Greg held Jazz's wrist. "Your pulse is rapid. Let me take a listen and check your blood pressure."

"No need, like I said it was a scare and I am." Jazz attempted to stand but fell back down as his legs wobbled. Greg removed a stethoscope and blood pressure cuff from his ever-present black medicine bag. Brian put a hand out to help his Uncle settle back into the chair.

"Mmmm, Mr. Martin you need to take it easy. Your blood pressure is quite high. How does your head feel?"

"I am fine. I already took a few extra pills."

"Let him decide," Kenneth intervened. Let the man die!

"Who is that woman?" Brian demanded.

"Shush Bri, look I will explain everything if you two would let me get to the restroom and splash some water on my face and maybe take a little rest." Jazz stood up slowly.

"What kind of pills?" Greg asked.

"I am old and sick. I need pills. You two will too when you're my age. Now go back in there and dance with your bride!" Jazz pulled his arm free and stumbled his way toward the restrooms. Brian turned and he met Greg's eyes.

"What's going on?" Greg demanded; then he turned to Kenneth and said the same thing again.

"I'll be back in a minute, let me help Jazz get over to the restroom," Kenneth said. A slow naughty smile inched across his face, like the Grinch Who Stole Christmas.

Brian and Greg walked back into the party. Remi and Dana danced with several male friends of Sam's. Milman and Ruth sat, immersed in a lively discussion about travels with some older friends of Sam's. Work friends of each side hung together and ate and danced and drank. Medical friends of Nancy's and Greg's and work colleagues of Jazz's did the same. Wil was still catching up with John, Brian's brother.

Back in the bathroom stall, Penny pulled her stockings up and smoothed her dress before leaving. It was indeed a lovely party, with gourmet foods and a fun mixture of music by a live band. There were probably close to a hundred guests and plenty of laughter and gaiety as toasts were raised. She had only a few more hours at most to endure, and that included opening gifts and hanging around as the last guests lingered. Despite Sam's rudeness and Brian's unnerving declarations it was good to see so many friends and family together. Everyone except mom was here!

She opened the stall door, just as a woman entered the one next to hers. Penny caught a glimpse of a tall, older, auburn-haired woman. In the distance, a love song played. The lyrics reverberated, 'Never Wanting to Leave.' Penny stared once again at her reflection, took a deep breath and gave a thumbs-up sign. She opened the door, shook her head and turned around. She had forgotten her purse. A stall door opened and a woman emerged. They collided.

Penny gasped. No! It isn't possible. The woman pushed past Penny who was a block of ice, her mind though was a hail storm.

Jazz's voice suddenly boomed. Penny jumped. How long had she stood frozen? Penny crashed through the door past Jazz, stumbling right into Brian's sturdy chest.

"Hey, you look like you have seen a ghost." She pushed and Brian acquiesced. Penny ran to the elevator.

"What's all the commotion?" Sam shouted. The extreme desire to escape made it hard to think about anything except that she had to get away. The threatening call came back to her. 'Expect a shock at the engagement party'.

People were streaming out of the party room.

"Uncle, calm down," Brian shouted.

"Ladies, excuse my impassioned conduct. I lost my cool! I do enjoy being right...on occasion!" he laughed. One young woman stepped forward.

"I can help," she said to Jazz. "My boyfriend and I disagree a lot at these kinds of things. The make-up part is fun later, though."

She winked at Jazz. Jazz offered a dazzling smile and a warm grip of his hand. Penny couldn't tear her eyes away from the scene.

"Brian. Deal with all of them, will you?" He moved toward the young woman who was emerging from the bathroom apparently alone. She shook her head, no.

Sam and Greg caught up to Penny just as the elevator doors finally opened and the three stepped in just as Brian shouted.

"Hey wait! Where are you all going in such a hurry?"

"Brian, the guests; do your job NOW!" Jazz yelled at him.

Brian looked from the closing elevator door to Penny's chalky, crumpling face to all the people filing out of the party room.

"Come on, we'll do this together," Kenneth was suddenly by his side. Remi, Wil, and Dana told them to pull everyone back into the ballroom. He made a quick announcement with Remi's help, bless her bold creative ways. And the party came to a swift end with Remi promising to take care of getting the gifts to them. He and Kenneth made their rounds thanking everyone, and then they swiftly exited down to his car.

"I need to find Penny," Brian said. Kenneth nodded. "That woman was June, Penny's mother, wasn't she?" Brian asked. Kenneth said nothing as Brian drove out of the parking garage of the hotel.

"Answer me!" Brian shouted as he drove too fast down the narrow, busy city streets.

"Slow down, I am far from impressed with your driving skills, young man."

"Was that June?" Brian repeated. Kenneth shrugged and took his time answering.

"Not likely. However, somebody sure wants everyone to believe June is back." Kenneth stared at Brian.

CHAPTER TWENTY TWO

Brian sat on Penny's front step the morning after the engagement party while Kenneth wandered around her yard. Image and reality rarely match, Kenneth mused as he looked at the neighboring homes. As mama would have said, 'speak your heart's truth to the world and be prepared to repeat it!' What lies beneath these manicured lawns? Fault lines, beauty or more fakery? Kenneth watched Brian rest his head against his folded arms as he waited for Penny to return home. Why was he so loyal to his Uncle Jazz? Did he really love Penny?

Kenneth plucked a rose petal off of the rosebush on the side of Penny's house and brought it up to his nose. A car pulled into her driveway and he moved to where he could watch and listen.

"Where were you?" Brian asked.

"What are you doing here?"

"I need to talk to you!" He stood up and stretched his arms above his head. She moved to the front.

"Where are my keys?" Penny's right foot caught on an uneven part of the cement and she stumbled while backing away from the door. Kenneth watched Brian dance along side of her erratic movements. He was like a circus performer.

"Stop it!" she said.

"What?" he said.

"Hovering over me like a puppy!" she said.

"I am not a monster, no matter what Sam claims!" Brian said.

"That's your opinion," she hissed.

"Penny, listen, *to me!*" He reached out to grab her arm. She leaned away from him. Brian lost his footing then she did. They tumbled. Penny landed on top of Brian who smacked sideways into the uneven edge of the sidewalk. Brian groaned as he managed to buffer her fall. He caught her against his side and put a hand on his right rib cage. He pulled her around to face him.

"Let GO!" He rolled over pinning her down.

"I love you and I am going to marry you. Uncle is messed up like your mom. I am not him just like you are not your mother!"

"I don't believe you!" Penny was breathing hard.

"Okay, we have now established that you are a forgiving, compassionate person," Brian said. Sarcasm framed his words. "Oh and let's not forget a promise-breaker!"

"Stop twisting things, Brian." Penny huffed and puffed. "You are incredibly loyal to Jazz."

"I am always there to catch you Penny, and if you notice, that is quite often."

"I wasn't falling down until you arrived on the scene!"

"This just proves what I have said all along. We don't have to let the past define us. A lot of couples have to work their whole lives on that one."

Penny pushed at him. He shifted, but still wouldn't free her.

"You are marrying me." He insisted. "A promise is a promise," he said.

"I lied in order to follow Jazz's plan. It was made under false pretenses!" she said. His sea blue eyes flowed over her forest green ones. She was flooded with longing, but for what? She wanted to laugh out loud but she couldn't breathe that well.

"Brian you're heavy," she said. Brian moved and she sprang up, coughing. Kenneth sunk into the bushes on the side of the house. He didn't want to be discovered eavesdropping.

"I hate lies. That is all my childhood was about!" She turned back to where Brian stood gripping his side. "I have choices today. I am an adult now! I can't believe I ever said yes to this – this – this stupid, dumb, idiotic, crazy, scheme! I one hundred percent change my mind. I quit!" With a burst of speed she ran around to the small back yard. She could hear Henry barking inside the house. Her heart seized with fear. She had to get inside! Why didn't she have her keys? Did she leave them at Sam's? His neighbor had been kind enough to drop her at home. Maybe they were in his car?

Kenneth scrunched further into the large row of bushes. His heart was like a ton of bricks. Penny was right. There had been so much deceit. He could only change things today. He had to locate Genieve and stop Tom.

"Penny," Brian said. He limped, holding onto his side and hip area. He grimaced with each step. "Penny!" He reached the back of her house. "Penny! Come on babe. I apologize."

A door opened and Din, the neighbor peered out. "Is there a problem?"

Brian turned toward the man. "Just a squabble," he said. He smiled and tilted his head. "Thanks Din for your concern."

"Are you sure?" Din asked. "Maybe you need to give Penny some space?"

"Can't," Brian said. A grin spread across his face like jam on a piece of toast. "I have to apologize first."

"Apologies are overrated. Actions speak much louder," Din said.

Penny smiled. Din loved to dispense words of wisdom but she had a feeling he was giving her the space she needed! Thank-you Din! Her fingers roamed around in a plant pot out back but couldn't seem to find a house key. Maybe she didn't have the right pot. She could ask Din to let her in but then Brian would surely force his way inside too.

"Things aren't always as they appear," Brian said. Penny heard the irritation in his voice.

"True," Din said. Penny watched as Brian strode toward the edge of the yard where several clumps of trees existed.

"Penny," he whispered. "Penny?" he called a little louder this time. He swiveled his head back and forth. "Penny! Come on, we are both tired. Let's go inside and I'll make you some of your favorite tea, okay? Penny?" He sighed. "Penny honey, this is ridiculous!"

Kenneth stood up and peered tentatively around to the front of the house as he listened to Brian's pathetic pleading. Penny was running, already far down the street. Probably headed to Sam or Greg's, he thought. Probably where she had been last night but he wasn't about to help Brian. He was sticking like glue to him so he could keep track of Jazz and this mystery woman who was posing as June. Kenneth glanced back at Brian and his eyes widened.

"Hey, look I have decided you are hassling Penny and quite possibly you are the one who broke into her house! It was you or that loony uncle of yours." Din warned. He swung the baseball bat at Brian's head, missed slightly as Brian managed to duck, but he connected with part of his neck and shoulder. Brian winced and crumpled to the ground. Din hovered over Brian for a minute and Kenneth decided it would be best to make a quick exit.

The next morning, Penny said goodbye to her sister-in-law Nancy, after waking up in one of her guest bedrooms. Penny stood on her front stoop, checking the bushes just in case Brian or any of the myriad of attacker's who had her as their target, were ready to spring out at her. The key dug into her palm. Confusing thoughts trekked across her brain. What should she do about Brian? She inserted the key into the lock.

"Hey," he said. Penny gasped. She put her hand over her heart.

"You scared the daylights out of me!" She exhaled like a whale with its blow hole.

"I did it for you and JJ! He is creepy. I don't think you should marry him. He's pressuring you honey into something you don't want and that's never a good thing, except of course in my case when I had to coerce JJ into buying this house with me." Din laughed.

"You cannot give into that sort of blackmail. That's growing up 101." Din walked into the house with her. Henry wagged his tail and jumped with exuberance. "I know I am going on and on." Din explained further why he had smacked Brian with the baseball bat.

"He was stalking you! You know he and your father busted

into your house the other night. Luckily I was inside looking after Henry." Henry wagged his tail and Din spoke lovingly to her mutt who only wagged his tail harder.

"I think they believed I was the intruder but truth be told Brian may be covering his own dirty tracks!"

"I wish I knew what his true motives are." Her lips quivered and her eyes burned.

"Oh honey that's obvious," Din said. His chocolate brown eyes were sympathetic as she looked up at him. "He wants to get in your pants!" Din had been a minor league baseball player. He was tall and thick. He worked as a security guard for a hotel chain. It was nice he cared so much.

"Din," she said. Penny laughed.

"It's true honey. I can tell. But I am sorry I hit him so hard. I only meant to slow him down for a bit. But when he turned around I thought he might attack me. You know, you said his uncle is twisted."

"Where is Brian now? Did you get my keys back by any chance?"

"Uh... here's the thing, sweetie. After I whacked him, I heard someone take off running. I think he may have been hiding in the bushes on the side of the house. I freaked. They may have been working together. I heard JJ holler for me. I ran back to the house. You know how JJ's a little on the possessive side. When I came back out, I brought my phone. I was going to call 911." Penny rubbed her grainy eyes and yawned. "You don't look so hot my dear. Was it another long evening?" he asked. They had settled themselves in the living room. He removed her shoes and began massaging her feet.

She sighed. "Yes. Thanks." She set her relaxed feet onto the coffee table and laid back further into the couch.

"Anyhow, when I came back to the spot where I hit him." He put a hand to his chest. "He was gone!"

"I thought you said you knocked him out?"

"I did, but I guess not for long, or else his accomplice came back and helped him escape," he said, putting a hand up to his broad chest. She thanked Din and after he left she dozed on the couch, only to bolt upright an hour later when the phone rang.

"Hello."

"Did you enjoy the surprise?"

"What?" Penny sat up. Her heart slammed against her chest. "Mom?" she asked.

"You have a few more *tests* to make it through, my dear, any cravings yet? Oh and are you having any mood swings, crying jags or extreme fatigue yet? Those are the early signs the addiction process is setting in, my dear." Penny's mouth open and closed but she couldn't form any words.

"Your brain is growing more befuddled, but don't worry, we'll be taking you away again soon for another round of treatments that'll fix you right up!"

Laughter and the line went dead. Henry stood up and wagged his tail. He stretched, his front legs way out in front of him and put his rear up in the air. Penny curled up into the fetal position on the couch. She had reached her limit. Seeing a woman resembling her mother at a pretend engagement party, crazy phone calls, being kidnapped, having her home violated, Brian with his declarations of love, Sam being overboard with protectiveness and where did all her friends disappear to? Though to be fair she had decided to hole up at Sam's and ignore the world. She had checked in with Dana and would see her the next day at work. She needed to phone Remi. She knew she had flown back home. Her job was demanding.

I need to let you go mom. I am becoming someone I don't recognize! Isn't this what Jazz, Kenneth and Tom did to you?

Henry sniffed and licked her face. He rested his big head on the couch near her belly. His brown eyes flitted to her face and he wagged the tip of his tail. His ears were plastered against his head.

"It's okay boy. I'll snap out of it. I hope, as soon as I figure out my life." She burrowed her wet face into her brown velour pillow.

CHAPTER TWENTY THREE

Kenneth left Sam's while he was in the shower. He didn't have the answers Sam wanted. He couldn't believe the woman at the engagement party was June. He didn't know if Brian was genuine in his feelings and intentions with Penny. Penny's neighbor Din obviously didn't trust him! That had been funny to watch. He imagined Brian had quite an ache in his shoulder and neck.

He had walked for a long time last night after leaving Din standing over a passed out Brian, trying to chase thoughts of the local bar away. As well as figure out what he must do to stop Tom. When he had finally reached Genieve she was remote and cagey for a change. Why was she still playing these games with him? He knew the answer. It was simple. She was with Tom. It was who she was! And yet this morning she did an about face and this kept his hope alive.

Genieve had informed him that Tom was going to one of his client's cellar warehouses in order to re-stock his supply of addictive substances. He was planning another round with Penny! Kenneth watched Tom as he took the keys from inside the small, red velvet box. It hadn't been difficult to locate Tom. Genieve's directions were good. Kenneth spotted Tom's car at the house Genieve had mentioned and parked down the road. He was pleasantly surprised to find a side door unlocked. He waited. Tom went to the bathroom and Kenneth hid inside the house.

She admitted to Kenneth she was angry with Tom for using Penny. Why did he want to destroy Penny? Why target her for his revenge against June?

Tom unlocked the door. Kenneth waited a few minutes before he crept down the small dark stairwell. It was cool and musty. He hid behind some tall shelving. Tom was intent on finding something. Shelves were filled with vials and Tom picked up one after the other of the small glass containers, each filled with brown or reddish colored substances.

Genieve said it was personal. That Penny represented a huge lie. But then suddenly Genieve had to go and Kenneth hadn't been able to figure out what she had meant. What lie could she mean? There were so very many as Penny had shouted to Brian in frustration yesterday.

"Time to play," Tom announced. He was talking to the vials, handling them as if they were newborn babies. A wide, slow grin filled Tom's dark face. He pushed his thin gray-black hair out of his piercing blue eyes.

"I will adjust the dopamine levels." Kenneth knew he was talking about the neurotransmitters, the chemical messengers of the brain which controlled the pleasure center of the brain. "It is time to addict, or renew the addiction." Tom laughed, narrowing his eyes as he glanced around the room for a moment. Kenneth flinched and grew very warm. He loosened the collar of his shirt from around his neck. He had helped determine the part of the brain involved in addiction remained connected to memory, thought, and emotion. Chronic pain, he knew, had very strong emotional and memory components to it. Tom had learned to use that in order to hook people into the experiments.

It looks like a wine cellar. He knew Jazz had created several of these in the basements of client's homes and in some of the scientist's homes who worked for him. Kenneth also was aware that only some of the vials contained any real drugs. The remainder of which were bogus. But how did Tom or Jazz tell the difference? That was the million dollar question.

"One of just six active ones left." Tom handled one container lovingly. "You are a clever one in how you mimic the drugs that create cravings, mood swings, impulsive urges and emotional vulnerability." Tom stroked the glass. The brown liquid seemed to glow in the lone harsh light bulb that hung from the ceiling directly above where Tom stood across the room from where Kenneth hid.

Tom stooped down to put the vial in a box and then a sealed bag. Kenneth made his way back up the stairs and outdoors. These substances did look amazing through a microscope, prisms of remarkable geometric beauty. Inside the body, it could be a different story. Never knowing the exact effects became the fun part, Jazz explained one afternoon many years ago. The specific subject's body chemistry could make or break the effects. So much had depended upon the host's physical, emotional, and mental state. He hoped Penny's system was as combative as she could become sometimes. He ran to his car, not wanting to risk a confrontation with Tom. This was neither the time nor the place. He was not going to become Tom's subject!

Greg had convinced Penny to come into his office for a check-up that afternoon. She sat on his office couch talking to him about her continued symptoms.

"My legs feel heavy a lot. I have headaches." Penny clenched and unclenched her fists as her brother examined her.

"Relax Pen." He put a hand over hers. "What else?" Greg asked.

"I have this memory." Tears trickled down, stinging her cheeks that felt like stretchy hot rubber. "It is about that day mommy left." She coughed. Greg nodded. "Dad spewed out a book."

"About his work?" he asked. She nodded and looked down at her clasped hands for a moment then back up into Greg's dark pools of sympathy. She cried harder.

"Yes but more about mom's problems and he confided to me that mom had wanted to kill herself many times!"

Kenneth drove over to Jazz's rental house after being a voyeur to Tom's plan. He thought about letting Sam, Greg and Penny know about what Tom was up to but he wanted more information and he figured Jazz might know.

His mama had said, 'it's never wise to put off the callings of your heart.' His heart was yammering at him to confront Jazz and Tom! He pulled into the driveway. It was empty. He slammed a fist against the steering wheel just as his cell phone rang. It was Jazz!

"Meet me downtown." Jazz gave him the address of a motel. Jazz explained that it wasn't a good idea to convene at his rental home while Tom was in town.

"Why?" Kenneth pressed, not yet agreeing to this meeting Jazz was ordering.

"Do you want him to discover us working together?" Jazz demanded with impatience.

Kenneth arrived at the seedy motel almost an hour later. The manager, a man named Al, directed him to a room. Kenneth sat in a ripped brown vinyl chair, trying not to notice the enormous bottles of scotch or whiskey that dotted the bar directly across the room from where he sat. The hairs on his neck stood up like antennae. Don't be paranoid, he thought.

The curtains were drawn, crumbs dotted the carpet and the bed looked like it had been made in a hurry. He hadn't sat there for more than a few minutes when he heard Jazz's booming voice.

"Best of luck with your surgery, Al," Jazz said. He made his usual grand and loud entrance. He should have been a stage actor.

"Hello Kenny. Are you ready to bring down Tom Mott?" Jazz pressed a hand on his shoulder. "You do know that he plans on poisoning your daughter past the point of no return?"

Kenneth blanched and stuttered. "Yo—you, ho—how do you know?"

"Have you had your nip today? Some of these bottles you know are special." Jazz opened a bottle of scotch and sniffed.

Kenneth shrank back into the broken vinyl chair. Control, remember. He narrowed his eyes. Why was Jazz doing this to him? A stab of fear went through his heart. He shouldn't have met him here or he should have left as soon as he saw the bottles. He had to reach Sam. It would be his only hope now. He opened his phone in his pocket and hoped fervently he was pressing the number three.

"You'll have to have a sip from them all just to enhance your immunity before taking on Tom. It will prevent you from falling prey to his manipulations, Kenny," Jazz explained. He handed the open bottle to Kenneth.

"NO!" Kenneth shouted. "Hardly the case and you know it. You want to take care of things yourself without my interference or Sam's, Greg's and so forth. It's not going to work Jazz. You are dying Jazz. It's time you let me take control!"

"Ha, ha, ha, oh Kenny," Jazz said. He stroked his chin. "Trying to work it from both sides again? Didn't that backfire in rather ugly ways when June disappeared?" Kenneth rose from the dilapidated chair and began to pace.

"Who was that woman at the engagement party? Some actress you paid to spook the kids? Why does Tom want to destroy Penny?" Kenneth stepped around Jazz who stood in the middle of the room waving the open bottle of scotch at him.

"No I didn't hire an actress. Tom is creating something here and he must be stopped before it's too late. Genieve appears to be very loyal to Tom but she will help Penny. Penny must marry Brian to stay under my family's protection and that can't happen if she's kidnapped again!"

Sam knocked on the door as Penny finished dressing. He came into the examining room and Greg joined them.

"Hey," Sam said. He looped an arm around Penny. She sunk her head into the curve of his shoulder. "I texted Kenneth and set up a family meeting at the hotel where the engagement party was held. We need to figure out who that woman was and why she's pretending to be mom."

"You think he knows the answers?" Greg asked. Sam nodded. Sam drove them to the hotel. While he was driving his phone rang. Greg answered for Sam.

"Hello? Hello? Is anybody there?" Greg asked. "Dad," Greg said. He held the phone away from his ear. "He's not speaking but I hear voices, his and Jazz's I think but everything's muffled."

Penny kept thinking about why her mother might have wanted to fake a suicide. She needed to talk to Kenneth. She hoped he would be forthright. It was like one part of him tried but another couldn't. In a way Brian was like that too.

"Here let me." Sam pulled into a parking space in the garage next to the hotel. "Dad," Sam shouted. "Dad, are you there?" Sam shook his head and closed the phone. "Nothing," he said. They walked inside the lobby of the grand hotel.

"What was that about?" Greg asked.

"Who knows with him? He's terrible with technology. Or he's with Jazz somewhere and needs our help?"

"If that's who I heard," Greg said.

"You think there are some clues here, Sam?" Penny asked. She wanted to know about her mother not Jazz and Kenneth!

"Yes. Jazz rented several rooms here." The brothers approached the front desk. Penny sat down in one of the beautiful shiny red upholstered high-backed chairs in the lobby. Her stamina was still on the low side.

"Hey, we hosted an engagement party here recently," Sam explained, "For my sister," he said. He pointed to Penny. She waved and the concierge nodded.

"The party was interrupted by a ghost." Greg threw in. "Supposedly our mother." Greg snorted.

"Yes." Sam narrowed his dark eyes at Greg. "The groom's uncle Jazz rented several rooms here and,"

"Temporarily, he has a rental house but he may have staged this,"

"Ghostly apparition?" the concierge added.

"Haha, funny," Sam said.

"Interruption which has upset our sister and her fiancé," Greg clarified. Sam scowled at him. The concierge's head mimicked a tennis match.

"We would like to take a look at the rooms Jazz rented," Sam continued. Greg raised a curious eyebrow at him. Sam brought his foot down hard.

"Aaaaaa," Greg yelped. He gripped his shoe. "That was unnecessary!" Greg elbowed Sam in the ribs. The concierge raised his eyebrows and then settled them into a frown on his well-groomed face. Penny grimaced and smiled as she watched her stooge brothers perform badly.

Sam grabbed his side and moaned. A slight smile played on the corners of the concierge's features.

"We believe Jazz Martin may have valuable information and we are trying to help our sister get to the bottom of this mystery so she can feel all right about marrying her fiancé." Greg swatted Sam's hand away from poking his neck.

"You want a key? You wish to locate clues to this Jazz's plan?" The concierge smiled widely.

"Yes thanks." Sam unleashed his devilish grin. Penny rolled her eyes.

Greg turned and smiled at the concierge. "The groom who is also very upset, asked us to find his uncle because he's very sick."

"In more ways than one," Penny said. Everyone turned to look at her.

"No such folks have entered our premises." The smile left the concierge's face as though an eraser had whipped across it. He lowered his head to the papers spread out before him.

"How can you be sure?" Sam spread his palm out across the concierge's papers. The man punched the button on top of his ball point pen and raised it. Sam snatched his hand away from the papers.

"I mean, it's obvious you are a very busy man with much more important things to do than watch out for the comings and goings of one Jazz Martin."

"Or ghosts and sick Uncles or was it the groom who is dying?"

"No it's only the uncle." Greg corrected in a soft contrite voice.

"Let's not forget your three stooges live performance." The concierge did not look up as he raised his arm and flicked a finger. Hotel security approached immediately. "All of our guests are given the utmost of privacy. Now if you'll excuse me, as you said, I am quite busy and your silly attempt at farce bores me." He raised an eyebrow and twitched his lips before he turned and walked in the opposite direction.

"Wait," Greg called. "What if we tell you the truth? I mean, aren't you the least bit interested to learn how there may be a major brawl in your nice hotel?" Greg yelled even as his upper arms were grabbed by two burly security men. They pulled him backward, toward the huge revolving doors in the front lobby of the hotel. The concierge was barely visible as he made his way to the back end of the lobby.

"Well, I guess trouble runs in your family then?" One hotel security man barked as he grinned at his colleague. They shoved the two brothers outside and escorted Penny out, holding onto her elbow. The three of them stood on the front sidewalk. Greg slumped down to the curb. He rubbed the back of his neck and rolled his head from side to side.

"That was only plan A, and not a very good one at that," Sam declared.

"I am done. I need to check in at the hospital and then with Nancy, remember I have a wife, a pregnant one that I need to be with on occasion!" Greg said.

"You blew it in there. If only you would have left it to me." Sam paced back and forth, stopping every few minutes to nod at security. They stood just inside the revolving doors staring at them.

"Guys," Penny interrupted. But to no avail.

"Sam you were lame. I thought we were back in elementary school! We don't even know for sure that the rooms hold any clues from the party!" Greg rolled his shoulders. "We need to find dad."

"No we need to find out who that woman was and about mom!" Penny snapped.

"Maybe he's hanging out with Jazz in one of the hotel rooms right now and needs our assistance?"

"Your imagination is on overdrive, Sam," Penny said. Sam shook his head.

"I don't think so. I am good at my job for a reason. I trust my gut. You should do that more Penny!" Sam snapped. She grew hot with anger.

"I do more than you ever give me credit for Sam! What about mom?"

"It wasn't her, okay?" Sam said. "That guy was a jerk. Dad is close by I can feel it."

"Good, great so go to your plan B. I am out of here," Greg said. Sam tipped a fake hat at security. They walked back to Sam's car.

They drove to the hospital and dropped Greg off. Sam waved and pulled away. "Let's go see Brian," Sam said. "He will know where Jazz is, who that woman was Jazz paid off to act like mom and maybe where Kenneth is too."

"I guess." Penny agreed, but she had mixed feelings about seeing Brian.

"You need to call this whole marriage thing off, once and for all, Penny," Sam instructed. "You can do that too when we catch up with Brian."

"I already told him I quit but he won't listen. He claims I made him some unbreakable promise." Penny shot her arms up in the air, hitting one hand against the ceiling of the car. She brought the hurt hand to her mouth.

"He's been in on everything that has happened from the beginning and he's using this promise thing to keep you hooked." Sam hit the gas pedal hard as they cut across town back to Brian's house that was over near the water. Penny gripped the edge of the car seat. Sam pressed the gas pedal harder, squealing around the next corner like they were in a race.

Jazz held up a bottle of scotch to the dim light and shook it slightly. Kenneth felt his mouth salivating like a dog's.

"One small sip Kenny, you'll be able to think clearer about what to do concerning Tom and Genieve's plan to addict June's kids." Jazz waved the glistening bottle of scotch. The pungent smell reached Kenneth and his knees buckled. He sank to the floor.

"Our kids you mean," Kenneth whispered.

"Only Sam," Jazz reminded. Kenneth was on fire with desire. He clamped his mouth shut. Jazz grinned.

"You're wound tight, Kenny." Jazz patted his arm. "Let me take over for a while. Brian and I will watch out for Penny," Jazz poured a glass. The sound of the liquid hitting the glass roared through Kenneth's brain.

"Mama always said. 'Patience, perseverance and planning, the three P's Kenneth, they will get you far!'" Kenneth licked his lips. "Help me mother, please." He pressed his face against the stained cheap carpet.

"I'll join you." He put the glass beside Kenneth's hand. Kenneth sat up. Jazz turned back to the bar and took an unopened bottle, shielding Kenneth's view of the bar with his body. He poured, turning back slightly.

"Go ahead you don't have to wait for me." Jazz pushed. Kenneth was hypnotized. His eyes glued to the liquid in the glass. He barely registered Jazz's presence.

"Cheers!" Jazz kneeled down beside Kenneth.

"One sip or even two won't addict you Kenneth," Jazz said. "You're stronger than that just like Penny will resist the effects of Tom's ministering as well." Jazz curled a hand over Kenneth's shoulder. Kenneth stared at his glass. Jazz moved it toward his face. The edge of the glass touched his lips, he inhaled and gulped. Two, three, four, he lost track as he grabbed it from Jazz and slurped the drink down. Jazz grinned and reached for the bottle. He filled Kenneth's glass again and sat down on the bed.

"So thirsty," Kenneth murmured. He poured more into his glass. He ran his tongue over his lips and then his teeth. He hovered over the bar, feeling the familiar warmth and numbness seep into him, closing his eyes, he tipped the bottle to his lips. After a while he burped and his mother's words reentered his brain, 'A person's strength is measured not by all he accomplishes but more by what he is able to resist!' He plopped into the nearby oversized chair and let his face fall into his hands. A lovely warm, floating feeling seeped into his brain and he sat back, closing his eyes.

"Later mama," he said. A small smile played on his lips and he dozed. A sudden whoosh of cold air rushed over him and he heard the familiar voice.

"I'll leave you to your indulgences and be back soon for your next assignment! Great job," Jazz said. He chuckled.

"No using the kids or Junie." Kenneth felt like his tongue was swollen. "Protect them."

Jazz fingered the vial in his pocket. "Of course Kenny boy, and regarding Genieve," Jazz said. Kenneth slurped from the bottle he held tightly against him. "You will have to fight Tom and win her back when you are stronger, all right?"

"Yes!" Kenneth rallied. He saw Jazz smile and walk over to the table. There was a loud click. "What's that?"

"I enjoy keeping track of my subjects Kenny." Jazz chuckled. "Surely you remember that!" Jazz threw back his head and laughed.

CHAPTER TWENTY FOUR

Brian opened the door and Penny gasped. Brian looked like he'd been living on the street for a few months. His clothes were rumpled. His hair was unwashed and in disarray. He propped himself up against the door but it looked to Penny as if he might topple over at any moment.

"What the hell happened to you?" Sam asked.

"Slammed by a baseball bat," Brian mumbled. Sam laughed.

"Looks like you are getting what you deserve," Sam said. Brian moaned and stumbled his way to the couch. He teetered and Penny rushed over and helped him lay down.

"My neighbor Din thought you and your partner were stalking me," Penny explained. "Brian," she said. His glazed eyes blinked up at her. "Call Greg," she said to Sam.

Brian didn't put up a fight when Greg instructed them to bring Brian right in for an examination.

"He might have a concussion Penny. That's very serious if left untreated." Greg told them.

"He has a moderate concussion." Greg reported after examining him.

"That's what you get for stalking my sister yet again," Sam admonished. "Tell us who your partner was," he added. Brian pressed the ice pack Greg had supplied him to the back of his head.

"Thanks for the shot and pain medication," Brian said to Greg. Then Brian raised his red, pain-filled eyes to Penny. "If he means by my partner, that Kenneth was with me, then I guess I can answer his question."

"Why would dad have been with you when you were stalking Penny?" Sam asked.

"I wasn't stalking her!" Brian snapped. "We drove over together. We wanted to see if you were okay after the party and you weren't answering your cell phone. I hoped to talk with you. Kenneth was walking around looking at your plants while I sat on the front stoop waiting."

"I never saw dad." Penny focused her eyes on the tiled floor.

"He must have gone for a walk or something after you arrived home and we were fighting."

"Din, my neighbor thought he saw someone running away from the house after he struck you with his baseball bat," Penny explained.

"I am not in cahoots with criminals," Brian said. His voice sounded like a child's. Sam snorted. Penny blushed. "Kenneth was with me!"

"Go home and take care of that lump on your noggin," Greg said.

"Did you guys ever figure out who that woman was who showed up at the engagement party? Was it your mom?" Brian grimaced as he spoke slowly and softly.

"No, we aren't sure. What have you heard?" Greg asked him. Sam glared at Brian. Penny held her breath as she watched Brian's face closely for a sign that would tell her what to believe. He looked so vulnerable and sad. She felt pangs of sympathy but quickly wiped them away as if sponging her heart clean but it made her heart ache all the same.

"Nothing so far, but what's new about that?" Brian sounded bitter and that surprised Penny. She had never heard that tone from him.

"You ought to get some rest Brian. Can anyone keep an eye on you these next twenty-four to forty-eight hours?" Greg asked. Brian nodded and his eyes strayed to Penny. She stared at the tiled floor even harder.

"Sorry, I can't tell you more." He moved slowly toward a

phone. Greg caught up to him with quick strides. He handed him his cell phone. Penny watched, but was unable to rouse herself to go to Brian. He glanced back at her several times. His eyes were sad and seemed full of questions. She looked away.

"Here use this," Greg offered his phone to Brian. Brian nodded thanks and proceeded to call Wil.

After Brian had left with Wil, Greg caught some charts up to date while Sam tried calling Jazz but did not have any luck reaching him. Penny remained standing in a thick pool of guilt and indecision. She felt such an urge to go to Brian and apologize and care for him. But she had to remind herself he worked for Jazz. They set up the appearance of that woman who resembled her mother. The elaborate party was the stage in order to play on her emotions and bring them closer?

The three siblings grabbed a light lunch together and Greg checked in with Nancy who was working at the clinic. Sam dropped Penny off for her shift at the crisis center.

Kenneth woke up. He gripped his pounding head and squinted. Who turned out all the lights? Maybe it was for the best. He rolled over. A wave of nausea made him lay flat on his back on the threadbare carpet. Kenneth squeezed his eyes shut. He lay like that for a while. His mouth grew dry. He rolled slowly this time onto his side and he saw them. So many bottles, all neatly lined up for him. The invitation was clear. Kenneth scooted then crawled. The bottles beckoned.

"Just one last nip to help me think straight and feel better." He toasted and raised himself up slowly and put his mouth to the top and tipped it a little. Warmth filled his throat. He took another bigger swallow and another till he felt pleasant again. He sat up now and examined his new surroundings. His stomach rumbled. He was alone. There was a bed, one chair and a small table. A sink and toilet were in one corner of the room with a mirror hanging above the sink.

He remembered Jazz taunting him but this room didn't feel

familiar. Had he been taken somewhere else, more run down while he was passed out? Kenneth's stomach clenched. He had allowed Jazz to manipulate him again! He fell back against the carpet and banged his fists into the floor. He screamed and writhed like a dying animal in agony.

After a while he took a long slow breath and sat up. He searched the room for a phone and took a few more sips. His eyes grew heavy. He lay down and slept. A few hours later he awoke cold and hungrier. He stumbled over to the phone. Dizzy, he tripped and knocked the phone off its base. It made a dinging noise. He laughed and picked it up. It felt light and portable. He took a few more gulps from the bottle of scotch and frowned, trying to remember who he was going to call. He staggered back to the bed but then realized he had to go to the bathroom.

"Ooops," he said. The phone crashed to the floor and parts scattered and rolled across the floor. Kenneth stepped on some as he struggled to the toilet. Purposefully avoiding the mirror, he scratched his head until all his thick gray curls stood straight up. Once finished, he decided it was time to leave. Jazz couldn't keep him here. He tried turning the knob of the door, but nothing happened. He tugged and tugged.

"Cheap hotel, should grease your doors!" He gave one enormous pull and fell backward with the knob in his hand. Kenneth heaved the knob across the room. It clattered and rolled along the floor with strewn phone parts.

"My life," he muttered. Kenneth let out with a string of curses at Jazz.

Penny yawned and stretched, and sat on the edge of her bed the next morning, convincing herself to start the day. She should exercise. It had been a while. Her body felt as though old pieces of gum held it together. But today she would force herself. She headed downstairs in her oldest sweats. The knees were ripped out and she had on her softest tee shirt that was as thin as paper. She made toast and had some water. She read the paper, forced herself to do some stretches, leashed up Henry and headed out for a run. She was scared so she kept to busier streets and held her cell phone in her hand. She had to live a normal life. She wouldn't cower in her house. When she returned an hour or so later, she headed to the fridge for her tall glass of soymilk, a morning ritual. She was proud of herself! Facing fear was empowering. She headed upstairs to shower and the doorbell rang. Henry barked, his hunch was up and his tail was not wagging. Penny tensed and hesitated as one foot hovered in the air above the stair. Her surge of confidence was spinning down the drain of fear! Wait, remember, facing fear is the way to go! The doorbell rang for the fourth time, she glanced at Henry who stood like a fierce lion by her side and pulled open the front door.

"Oh," she gasped. Penny nearly dropped her soymilk. The woman grabbed the glass from her shaking hand and pushed her way inside Penny's house.

"I am thirsty, thanks and I do love a good iced coffee with cream and sugar every now and again." Penny shook her head, no. "Come sit." The woman patted a spot on Penny's couch next to her. Penny followed like an obedient child, leaving the front door wide open. Henry for all his fierceness trotted alongside of her, tail up and wagging.

The woman wrinkled her nose after she took another sip then placed the soymilk back down on the coffee table. "Must be a new fangled health drink? Hey doggie," she said. The woman smoothed back the fur on Henry's head and back.

"Soymilk," Penny whispered.

"Ah," she said. She scanned the room. "Nice place. I understand you are a full-fledged writer and counselor now. I always thought you'd be good with people—both as a listener and observer."

"You're not my mother," Penny stated. The woman laughed. "Aunt Genieve?"

The woman walked to the window. "Appearances, what does it all mean anyhow? We see what we want to see, true?" She faced Penny and a chill slithered down Penny's spine. They stared at one another. Penny stood up. She had an urge to touch her.

"Have you been calling me?" Penny asked. Her voice was soft, tentative. Facing fear, yet again, she thought!

"Marry Brian."

"Why?" Penny asked.

"Let all these un-answer-ables go. It isn't worth it, trust me." She headed toward the front door. "Things have a way of working themselves out, if you are patient and trusting."

"Trusting?" Penny blurted the word out like she was coughing up something stuck inside her throat.

"It isn't always a bad thing to copy some family traits, just make sure you improve upon them. Each generation should progress, you know? And well Brian is a good guy. He loves you so why not? You know it is just as important in life to ask the 'why not' question!" She slipped through Penny's open door and walked quickly down the porch steps. Her high heels clicked on the cement like a metronome.

"Wait!" Penny ran down the front steps, putting a hand on her chest to try and still her heart that was racing far past the regular tapping of the woman's shoes. "Is, is mommy alive, and if so where is she?"

"Let it go, Penny. Answers that big always come with a price! One that I believe is too large to pay in this life time. Hey, regards to your brothers. My how they've grown up so handsome, so different. Of course that's to be expected what with their very different paternity," she called out as she hurried down the driveway. Penny leaped toward her, making a grab for her arm. She missed and had to run to keep up with her, but then suddenly the woman turned and smiled.

"Okay, I'll give you this sweetheart. I am someone you thought you knew but never really did. I didn't. But none of that really matters now. Do what you have to do Penny. I had to. It will not turn out as bad as you may think. It never really does if you have the right attitude. I have learned that the hard way." Then in one swift motion she spun and ran to a waiting car. Penny's legs turned to cement. The spunk leaked out of her like a pin to a balloon. She was stuck again in the vortex of doubt. There was only so much fear a girl could face in one afternoon!

She slunk back to the house like a team that hadn't won a game all season. But her mind was on fire. Why would Aunt Genieve be playing games with her? Why did this woman show up only for her to see, in the restroom at the party and now at her home? Giving her advice in riddles, answering none of her questions, oh this was frustrating!

A man drove her away. He looked tall and had dark hair. It wasn't Jazz, or Kenneth. She wasn't sure what Tom or Marty looked like. Or it could be someone who worked for Jazz?

She ignored the ringing phone and sat for a long time on her couch staring out the window.

Jazz stood in the lobby of the run down hotel. "That's good stuff, Tricky Sam Nunton." Kenneth listened closely from his hiding spot. He had thrown a fit for hours, smashing bottles, screaming and kicking at the door until finally an old, old homeless looking woman rescued him. She listened to his story and he gave her the remaining bottles and a wad of cash. But the manager intervened before he could escape and now Jazz was here.

"Huh," the long-haired, thin manager said. He was confused.

"The trombone – the music," Jazz indicated. The big band music filled the stale air.

The manager smiled showing his crooked yellow teeth. He was not a handsome man with his pock-marked skin and heavily whiskered face. "You have to do something. He's making demands and it is disturbing my customers!"

"Ignore him. I have paid you well enough haven't I?"

"He repeats your name over and over," the manager said. "He talks about how you have kidnapped him and that he'll pay handsomely to whoever frees him. And with that lock on the door, it does seem suspicious. Customers are comin' to me and askin.' Then leavin' and quite frankly I can't afford this no matter how much you pay. In fact I caught Mary listening to him."

"Well he's supposed to be inebriated, twenty-four-seven!" Jazz snapped and rubbed his chest. Jazz answered his ringing phone, walked around the makeshift lobby and eventually went outside.

The hotel manager tried to follow. "I am not his nursemaid. Listen Mary got the door."

"Not now!" Jazz shouted and waved him away.

"Mary got the door open and he's about to escape for good," he mumbled. Kenneth smiled. Jazz had his cell phone pressed to his ear, a hand on his heart and he was shouting into the phone.

"This is as good a time as any to take that mini vacation – I'm outta here!" The manager walked angrily back inside his hotel. He quickly instructed his staff, one mangy looking middle-aged man to take care of things. The guy nodded. Kenneth slouched further into the sweatshirt jacket the old woman who he had convinced to grab the keys and free him, had given him. He made his way across the small lobby just as Jazz strode back into the hotel. He nodded to the new man at the desk, grabbed the key and opened the door to Kenneth's room. Jazz called out.

"Kenny?"

"Ken? Sleepin' it off?" He approached the bed where he could make out a large lump. Jazz reached out a hand to awaken Kenneth then jumped back. He ripped the sheets back to show four pillows and no Kenneth!

Kenneth grinned as he watched from the lobby. This was too fun to leave quite yet.

"Hey?" Jazz called louder this time as he went to the bathroom and shoved the shower curtain back; then he checked all the corners of the dingy room. Sighing he pulled out his cell phone.

After yelling out his orders, Jazz seemed to scan the room once more. He was checking the bottles. There were several empty ones. Jazz sat down on the bed. He appeared to have trouble taking a deep breath. He took his pulse and put a hand to his chest. He reached into his pants pocket and popped pills. He extracted a vial from a small rectangular box.

"This'll help," Jazz told himself. "Thanks to Marty, I can't seem to live without it these past few months." He swallowed the contents, making a face at the bitter taste. He stood for a few moments and then started yelling for the hotel staff. No one answered.

Kenneth scooted outside, ducking into an alleyway next to the old motel. Jazz never turned around as he stormed his way to his car.

"What happened here? How did Kenneth escape?" Jazz barked into the phone to one of his men. "His kid may have found him? What kid, what?" he yelled. Then he was in his car and Kenneth could no longer hear him from where he stood pressed back against a slight alcove between two buildings. He observed Jazz throw the cell phone against the passenger door. It bounced against the handle and flew back at his head. Jazz ducked and then hit his fist into the steering wheel as his phone bounced and landed on the back seat floor. He pushed down on the accelerator and peeled away from the curb into oncoming traffic. Maybe he would die in a traffic accident? Kenneth laughed with pleasure at the thought.

The next morning was a beautiful, sunny, crisp day. Blue skies and early moderate winter temperatures made Penny stretch her arms wide and high above her head. She called Sam and they agreed to meet for a long run. She was getting back into the swing of things with exercise now at least.

"Feeling better?" Sam asked. It was the fourth time he asked the question as they ran another lap through the park and near the ocean. She nodded and sniffed the air. She could taste the salt and moisture. She stopped suddenly.

"What?" Sam asked.

"That woman who resembles mom paid me a visit yesterday at my house." She squinted at Sam in the bright sunshine.

"What happened?" Sam grabbed her arm and they jogged in place.

"I did nothing, because I froze up like a block of ice." Disgust lined each word. "She came and went, spouting philosophies and skirting all my questions," Penny said. Sam picked up the pace near the end of their six-mile run, like usual. They pushed their bodies hard, neither of them spoke. Some distance away, three men watched, running parallel, but they took care not to be noticed.

"Whew, I need to stop." She bent over and grabbed her rib cage on the right side.

"Cramp?" he asked.

"Mmm, yes I'm sorry."

"Nah, we've done our six miles. This last part was gravy. Let's walk it off and head toward the ocean. I am glad you are getting back into shape." Penny nodded, still breathing hard.

"I ran yesterday too," she said.

"Good," he said. Sam glanced around.

"You keep doing that, Sam. You think someone is following us again?"

Sam shrugged. She watched his face.

"You think someone is trying to pull me in for more experimenting?"

"Of course," he said. "You are obviously a target of all sorts of people." Sam put a hand to her back, indicating they should keep moving. He sped up his stride and she had to jog to keep up with his long legs.

"I spoke with Dana and Rem last night," she huffed. He said nothing but increased his pace.

"Sam, I thought we were cooling down," she complained.

"Yeah, okay sorry." They reached the surf and they each took off their running shoes and waded in.

"Whew that's cold!" Penny exclaimed and hopped from one foot to the next. Sam laughed.

"Feels good." He laughed more as he watched his sister do a silly dance among the small waves lapping at her feet. He slung an arm around her as she finished dancing. "What did your girlfriends say? I am assuming you have filled them in on everything?"

"Pretty much," Penny said. "They think I should follow my heart and go with the flow. That it probably isn't mom but maybe Aunt Genieve or some old colleague of dad's or Jazz's bent on revenge through me! And," Penny swallowed hard, "Mom is never going to return like I want. She left for good one way or another and I need to accept that and make peace with it and stop trying to understand everything or trying to change things." Penny felt like a blob of Jell-o. The woman who visited her had provided the exact same advice!

Sam laughed. "Yes! I hope that doesn't mean they think you should marry Brian."

"Maybe, maybe not, honestly I have no idea what following my heart means anymore! Or who anybody really is anymore?" Penny wailed. "Or how to let go and not get the answers I've longed for all of my life!"

"Other than that, you're fine and dandy!" Sam threw back his head and laughed. Eventually Penny found herself laughing through the tears, feeling crazy as she splashed in the icy water.

CHAPTER TWENTY FIVE

Kenneth sat in the small downtown bar known as "Casey's", celebrating his escape and keeping an eye on Brian who was babbling to the poor slob next to him about Jazz. Kenneth watched as the bartender smiled and nodded to some guys in the back of the bar.

"She's never going to marry me now," Brian said. The drunk next to him slurped his drink and slid over to a darker corner of the bar.

Brian signaled for a refill and unbuttoned the top few buttons on his shirt. The bartender nodded again to someone in the back.

"Don' worry I'm not driving." Brian flipped his pockets inside out. "No keys."

"I ain't anyone's mama," the bartender snapped. Brian let out with a large belch, "I ain't a janitor either!" Brian grinned at him, "Girl trouble?" the bartender prodded.

"A lil piece of the massive' mountain I can' get off no matter how I hard I try," Brian slurred. "I have a crazy, sick uncle."

"What family doesn't?" The bartender wiped a glass dry. "I've heard it all, and I can say for sure, no one has the normal family buddy."

"He tricks people, studies them, and makes them do things. Like me. Not sure he's sick, well not the way he says. He manipulates," his voice dropped, "hurts, really love her." Brian sniffed.

"Be a man or walk away," the bartender advised.

Kenneth swiveled around to see who the bartender kept

glancing at in the back of the bar. Why did he do this every time Brian slugged down another drink? The bartender kept the drinks coming to Brian too. It was dark in here but he could make out a couple of guys on their cell phones in the back. He sighed. Something was up and it probably wasn't good for Brian. He should stop drinking soon so he could be helpful.

Kenneth had bribed an old street woman near the hotel with the tainted liquor to help him make his way through the town. Though he had ended up walking for miles anyways and it had been difficult with so many bars beckoning to him. He finally gave in and had since spent many hours in "Casey's" thinking, and of course drinking. He knew Sam and Greg were hunting for him but so were Jazz and Tom. This had proved to be a reasonable hiding place, until for some reason Brian had appeared. Kenneth didn't think Brian ever drank much. So what was he doing here?

"Can't," Brian said. He shook his head.

"Women!" said a man. He was sitting at the other end of the bar.

Brian looked at the man. Kenneth noticed the heavy-set and balding man raise his lips slightly. He looked so grim. Brian looked away.

"Cheers," the man said. He looked solemn.

Kenneth did a double take. The woman who had helped him escape earlier walked into the bar. Was the whole world following him? Next Sam, Greg and Penny would show up! He should leave and go back to trying to locate his rental car. Jazz had laughingly mentioned that he'd left it in town somewhere for Kenneth to find, like one of many missing pieces to a puzzle. Kenneth frowned as he recalled Jazz's taunting face. He looked up to see the old woman approaching him. She resembled a witch, with her gray-streaked black hair and prune-like skin.

"Hey, long time no see," she threw back her head and cackled. "What's wrong? You look worse than me." Kenneth didn't answer her. He kept his head down, and stared into the brown liquid in his glass. The woman watched him for a minute.

"He has it worse than me. I don't understand how folks live

such complicated lives." She cackled as she hoisted her lumpy body up onto the barstool. She heaved a sigh. "Maybe I shoulda been a teacher." She stuck a finger up for the bartender.

"What'll be, Mary?" The bartender wiped down the counter with a damp rag.

"Don't trouble yourself. I am good for it today!" She slapped a twenty on the bar. "Scotch, the good stuff Lars." She grinned.

"I never worry about you honey." The bartender smiled. "It's comin' right up!"

Mary's sunken eyes held a sparkle as she canvassed the room. Kenneth watched as she sidled over to Brian.

"Nothin' can be that bad," she offered. Brian's sea-green eyes were full of misery. He shrugged and returned to staring into what was left of his drink.

"Well I already did one good deed today." She scooted away.

The bartender pushed a shot glass toward her as he leaned over the bar and whispered, "Girl and family trouble," he explained.

"Join the club!" Mary cackled and threw back her head as she poured the whiskey down her throat.

"Where are we going?" Penny asked while Jazz sat back in the limousine. After her morning run with Sam she had showered and settled in at her computer for a bit of writing before she had to go to work later that afternoon. Jazz had shown up at her doorstep.

He reached into his pocket and took out a pill bottle and shook a couple of purple, oblong pills into his palm and then threw them down his throat. They looked like the ones mom had kept in her tin Sucrets lozenge box by her bed. Penny frowned. She felt not one iota of compassion for this man. Why should she? Serves him right if he is an addict like her parents!

Jazz leaned forward. "Turn down Third Street." He switched the CD and turned up the volume. "That was Dizzy Gillespie, now it's time for Ella Fitzgerald's scat sounds."

"Jazz, you came by my house and talked me into taking this

ride with you, with the promise you would explain what is happening. I want to know who that woman really is and where this is leading," Penny demanded. That was the only reason she had agreed to go anywhere right now with him, was for answers! "Remember I need to be at work in a few hours."

Jazz closed his eyes and took a long inhale, paused and then released his breath as though he were a whale. "Pick it up a notch, Bert." Jazz called out to the front seat.

"Sure thing Mr. Martin," the man replied. "But don't call me Bert!" Trees and buildings were blurs as they whizzed by.

"Jazz, answer me," Penny commanded. "And slow this car down, I didn't mean we had to become speed demons!" What is wrong with this hate-to-be-called Bert guy?

"Take it easy, Bert," Jazz said. He was thrown against the right side of the car as they squealed around a car. They swerved around construction then zoomed down a side street. Penny held onto the car door ledge.

"Don't call him Bert. I think it makes him mad," she said. "Tell me where are we going and who was that woman and why I am really supposed to marry Brian!"

"This isn't Third. Where the hell are you going?" Jazz clutched the inside door handle as they raced down the city streets. He put a hand across his left breast and gasped. "I," he said. He tried to lean forward and fell. "Need to find your father. He's drunk and wandering around the city!" Jazz huffed.

Penny gripped the seat. "Who is that woman?" She knocked into the window and a sudden pain in her shoulder made her gasp.

"Probably your Aunt Genieve, she's working with Tom Mott you know to wipe out all who associated with your mother!" Jazz said. His voice was soft, like an overly ripe piece of fruit.

Penny clutched the seat. They careened down one street and up another. This is my life right now, crazy, out of control and unpredictable. Why aren't I home, getting ready for work, taking a walk with Henry right now?

"You needed to know who your father really is my dear."

"There are a lot of things I wish I knew but I am beginning to think it is better to let things be no matter how maddening it is not to understand," she murmured. "I should never have trusted you! And why would Aunt Genieve pretend to be mom and so she could destroy us?" she asked. Penny eyed the pill bottle he held tightly in one palm. Maybe she should encourage him to overdose?

"She was extremely jealous of June and would stop at nothing to eradicate her and anyone she cared about." Jazz said. They careened around another corner and the car spun out. Penny held her breath. The driver frantically turned the wheel. The car moaned or was it her own terrified voice?

"Ho-ho-sp-ital," Jazz grimaced. His shoulder hit the door and he slumped over.

"Jazz!" She shook him. The driver laughed and accelerated hard.

Penny screamed. This whole thing is another set up to kill her! She scooted forward toward the driver but her seat belt locked up. She saw the red traffic light and knew. Her mouth froze in the shape of an 'o'. He wasn't going to stop! She turned back to Jazz. He hadn't budged but his eyes were wide open. He was scared.

Penny felt sick. "I am never getting into a car again with anyone from mom's past!" She vowed and crouched low. She covered her face with her hands and prayed.

Kenneth watched as Brian return from the bathroom. Kenneth wiped the cobwebs that had formed in his brain off of his face.

"I jus' want to figure her out."

"You got under her at all?" A fellow drinker asked Brian. He laughed. "That just might be the problem."

Kenneth shook his head in disgust as he listened to their conversation about his daughter.

"You sound like Wil," Brian said.

"Uh oh, competition," a man with dark sunglasses said.

"Even more reason to sleep with her." Another with an old

yellow fishing hat, announced. The bar had filled up with more folks in the last few hours.

"What's the problem? Is she playing hard to get?" A silence seemed to permeate the bar. All heads turned in his direction.

"Boys, boys, this ain't a soap opera!" the bartender scolded.

"We had a bad start and there are other people that are in the way," Brian answered.

"Family issues are the worst." A man in a suit and tie argued.

"They think they got the right to butt into everything," the yellow hat said.

"Yeah, too many chickens in the fire, ruins the pot of soup!" An elderly man who had been slumped over his drink suddenly sat up and shouted.

Some of them raised an eyebrow and the suit said, "yeah whatever Jas."

"You got to get away from those other influences they're never healthy. I remember once, back when I was married and my wife's family well, they used to visit a lot." The dark sunglasses man began. "They got her riled up, and she lost her perspective, listening to their ideas. I had to win her trust all over again. This was back when I still wanted to and I still had a chance. I got down on my knees and professed my love, set up the romancin' and I asked for her help. It worked like a charm I must admit."

They laughed and Brian sipped his drink. "Yea I have done tha' and was interrupted," he pushed his index finger into the bar.

"You got to keep on trying with women if you want 'em. You can't give up!" Several of the men chorused.

"They require A LOT of effort," yellow hat said. He tugged on his long beard.

"That's for sure." Jas perked up again.

Brian put a hand to his stomach. "I need some air." Brian wobbled off of the stool. Kenneth stood up. Good idea, he thought. He could use a dose of fresh air.

"I'm goin' to find a way," Brian said. "To have the picket fence marriage and babies." He swayed. The bartender nodded to Brian or to the two men in the back of the bar? Kenneth felt a chill swerve through his body.

"Take care." There was an echo of good wishes from the night's friends.

"Thanks," Brian said. His smile wavered as he turned to leave. Two men in the back followed. One murmured into his cell phone as he kept an eye on Brian who stumbled out into the dark night.

"Hope that guy's guardian angels are on the job tonight," the bartender murmured. "He's gonna need 'em." The elderly man lurched up in his seat.

"Life's full of risks, ain't it?" He hit his palm into the wooden bar. Everyone laughed and ordered up another round of drinks.

Brian stumbled on the uneven sidewalk as he made his way. He scratched his head. He breathed hard, but kept moving. He crossed through an alley, leaned over and threw up, then closed his eyes. Brian made his way out of the alley and back out onto the sidewalk.

He walked a few blocks away from where Kenneth sat hunched over. Kenneth wanted to catch up to him and warn him but of what exactly? He couldn't remember. Kenneth sat down on the curb and closed his eyes. The spinning was bad and he leaned over to throw up, trying to unload the toxins from his body like Brian had done.

Suddenly, a car pulled up in front of him. Two men jumped out and grabbed him. They shoved him into the car, into the driver's seat. One man sat in the back and put a gun right up to his head. The other one in the passenger seat Kenneth recognized even in his alcohol haze. Their eyes locked and Kenneth grimaced. This was bad, very bad.

"Drive, Kenneth!" Tom Mott commanded from the front seat.

"We made it!" Jazz said, his eyes widening in amazement as they sped through the red light unharmed.

"Get this Bert-hater to stop this car!" Penny ordered.

Jazz agreed and hoisted his troubled body forward. "Oh my God," he muttered.

"What?" Penny shifted forward to take a look.

"Someone's in the road." Jazz's words became tangled up in the squeal of the brakes on the asphalt road. A loud thump and the car spun. Pain shot through Penny's head. Someone had been crossing the street. We hit a person! This banged in her head like a drum. Jazz clutched at his chest before slumping onto the back floor of the limousine.

The banging in her head grew to cymbals clanging between her ears. She heard a voice, a female.

"I could have been a stunt driver! Payback is seriously delicious," she said. Penny sucked in her breath. The woman, the one who came to her house, yesterday, Jazz had said who it was. Her vision was blurry. The dark figure of a woman yanking off a black baseball cap, like the one their driver had been wearing, formed in front of her. Penny glanced at Jazz's crumpled body. He looked frail, useless. The woman stretched, rolled her shoulders. Penny swallowed hard. Pain pierced her heart as the banging in her head became unbearable. It was her. She knew it. It was the same woman who had come to her home, pretending to be mom. The world as she knew it was fading away. The woman was being swallowed up in darkness.

"Aunt Genieve," Penny whispered.

CHAPTER TWENTY SIX

Kenneth held the steering wheel as if he were on the edge of a cliff. He pumped his right foot up and down on the brakes. The car zoomed down the city streets. Tom laughed and Kenneth jumped. He saw a black ski mask in the rear view mirror. A gun wagged back and forth and Kenneth abruptly turned around. A foot slammed on top of his, and the car jolted forward even faster.

"There are much easier ways of killing me." Kenneth turned to face Tom. The car swerved.

"Focus Kenneth," Tom growled. A cold piece of metal was pushed back against Kenneth's neck by Mr. Ski Mask.

"If you ever want to see your kids again, drive exactly the way we tell you too!" Ski Mask said.

Kenneth felt a gush of wetness between his legs and his face grew as hot as a broiler. He shifted his weight but it didn't help. He was sitting in a puddle of his own making and driving like a bat out of hell on a suicide mission.

But he knew there would be an upside to all this. He just had to find it. The fog in his brain from the last few days of drinking was beginning to clear. He vowed to not lose control again. He couldn't be any worse off than Brian. He looked over at Tom who laughed and kicked his leg out and over top of Kenneth's, against the accelerator. Kenneth tightened his fists around the wheel. He blinked. There was something up ahead. It was a dark blur in the middle of the road? He tried lifting his foot off of the accelerator but Tom kept up the pressure of his foot. They struggled. Kenneth turned the steering wheel away from the middle of the road. Tom swung it back. Kenneth shut his eyes and held his breath. They were going to hit it! A loud thump and a scream, more screaming and the car careened out of control. Fishtailing to the right and spinning while his hands and arms tangled with Tom's.

Lights were flashing when he came to and he heard moaning and soft screams echoed in the darkness like howling wolves from distant woods. His skin prickled and he touched sharp pieces of hard things all over his arm and face. Glass splintered. He shifted his weight and pain shot through his ribs and leg. His fingers felt a thick sticky wetness splattered on his face and arms and hands.

Air, I need air, please give me some air, he gasped and panic swept through him like a fire in a dry field. Sweating and shaking he pushed at the door. He couldn't open one eye very well. He was stuck. The door wouldn't budge. Wait, Tom and ski mask, where were they? He pushed against the seat to sit up and take a look but cried out as his cut hands met more shards of glass. Nobody was there. He was alone. What had happened? An accident, was he dead?

He floated back to his seat and above the car, spinning, so dizzy until he heard voices yelling. Quiet. He pursed his lips, forming the word. He whispered.

"June." Voices loud and soft came and went.

"Say goodbye." A deep voice whispered beside him.

"Tom," Kenneth murmured.

"Your time has come, the walrus said." Tom laughed.

Darkness closed in, only a faint pinpoint of light, guided him. What? What walrus said, what did you do to me?

"Hush. The ambulance is on its way. Hang in there. Try and relax," a man's voice soothed. It wasn't Tom. Was it ski-mask? No. He had waved a gun in my face.

"Can't say the same for the man he hit." Another voice sounded worried.

"Well he took care of the marriage issue, like Jazz requested. Better check on how Genieve faired with Penny and Jazz." Tom laughed.

"Help," Kenneth cried. Though it came out like a squeak from a mouse. "Wha-what did you do to Penny?"

"Take it easy," he said. Urgency framed his words. "Hey I need help. This guy is in shock. He's shaking like a leaf on a tree in a hurricane!"

"June!" he cried. He saw her stretched out by the dresser in their old bedroom, the phone tangled around her and the blood stain near her head. "Why, why, June," Kenneth sobbed.

"That your wife? Where does it hurt?" A paramedic asked him.

"Jazz," Kenneth choked. "Tom, they took her from me." Kenneth shivered violently as they loaded him into the ambulance.

"Hospital," the paramedic's lips moved.

"Witnesses," a voice shouted.

"Is he going to make it? No, not him I mean the guy he hit?" the voice asked.

"Doesn't look good," the paramedic replied. "There was another car involved. They can't locate the driver of the limousine. The two passengers, an older man and a young woman were taken to a clinic, on the outskirts of town."

"Why?"

"It was a specific request by the older one."

Someone gripped his arm. Numbness and a fiery feeling settled into his abdomen and spread to his chest and head.

Voices faded. Desperation washed over him like a tsunami as Tom sang along with Jazz, Genieve and June, *'say goodbye, say goodbye, say goodbye!'*

"Is he—he going to make it?" Penny asked the doctor who lifted his head for a moment and nodded then he returned his attention to the paperwork in front of him.

"Where am I?" Jazz groaned. "What happened? Why was Bert driving like a maniac? Did we hit something?"

"We are at some clinic, the Janimore clinic I think," Penny said. "I couldn't get a hold of Dr. Mapman," she added. "You kept ordering me to call him over and over and yes we crashed or hit something. I think. I'm not sure. I passed out too and when I woke up the driver was gone and we were sideways on a downtown street."

"Bert," Jazz closed his eyes. A nurse hooked him up to an IV, took his pulse and listened to his heart.

"It wasn't Bert, driving. It was that same woman from the engagement party. The one who looks like June," she said. Penny stood on the other side of the bed, not too close. She yawned. It was dawn. She had been up most of the night, though passed out for some of it. That didn't count as sleep did it?

"Not June, Genieve," Jazz mumbled. "Where's Kenneth?"

"Aunt Genieve? Are you sure? I am beginning to have my doubts, Jazz. I don't think she would try and kill me and use me like this woman is doing." she said. She shook her head. "We never found Kenneth. The driver went berserk remember?" She should be asking the questions and she would have been had they not been on a wild ride about town. Why did things with Jazz always end up more convoluted?

"Someone tried to kill me, us. Focus Penny. Get Dr. Marty Mapman! I don't need this." He pointed to the IV and glared at the nurse. "I need more meds and Kenneth – find him!" Jazz squeaked. His eyes fluttered closed. Penny's face felt tight with anger as though some old relative was pinching her cheeks so hard that her whole face resembled a lemon.

"I don't take orders from you Jazz. I want answers!" Penny hissed. "I agreed to that crazy ride so you would tell me what I signed up months ago to learn and instead have been tricked, kidnapped, used and abused. I missed work again! Lucky for me they are flexible and understanding because I am responsible or at least I can be when I am not hanging around with the likes of you and your stupid family!"

"You are in love with my adopted nephew and you have me to thank for it, missy!"

"Shut up! I am sick of your twisted logic. I trailed along to this clinic at your request too! After I was checked out and slept I have been by your side so you owe me mister and you have from day one when I called you for answers not the other way around! And you have done nothing but play games with me and my family and for what, for what? Your own sick satisfaction, so it serves you right if you lay there dying!"

"That's enough!" the tall, stern nurse reprimanded. "You need to rest Mr. Martin." The nurse gripped Penny's upper arm and began to escort her out of the room just as the doctor walked in and went over to Jazz's bed.

"Yes, visiting hours are over for now. He'll be out for a while with all the sedatives we gave him," the doctor added.

"But I need to ask him," Penny said.

"Not anytime soon, missy," the nurse said. "You had a blow to the head. You should rest, but not sleep, and calm down," the nurse scolded.

"You're not my mother!" Penny snapped and she touched her hand to the bandage across her forehead.

"Apparently you need one!" The nurse slammed the ball back to her. Penny reddened and her eyes filled up like a swollen river after a storm. She glanced back at Jazz.

"He is maddening but it sure appears as if he may not be the one calling the shots anymore!" she murmured, wiping her damp cheeks.

"Okay then, time for you to take care of yourself, hmmmm?" the nurse instructed. Penny nodded, still eyeing Jazz. Was it all an act? He appeared to be asleep.

She shuffled to the door of the clinic. The nurse released her. Penny thanked her and stepped outside into the glaring sunshine and cool fresh air. She stood very still. Her head ached. Her stomach burned with questions. What am I supposed to do now?

The next morning, Kenneth checked himself out of the hospital against doctor's advice. He was banged up pretty good, with bruises and cuts all over his legs, arms and face. He looked like the walking wounded from a war zone but he had things to do before it became too late. Luckily he was drunk when they crashed so his body had been loose. It could have been much worse for him.

Had they hit someone? He thought he would head back to Sam's and rest for a while, but first he called the rental company and explained that his original rental car had been stolen and he needed a new car. They were nice about it, and told him they would report it to the police. He would need to file a report. Sure, he said but he had some errands to run first. Another car was waiting for him at the hospital. Of course it didn't hurt that he was willing to pay quite a lot of money.

Jazz sounded groggy. He said he was at the Janimore clinic due to an automobile accident! Did Tom force him to run over Jazz? Kenneth's thoughts took all sorts of turns as he drove. Who was in charge Tom or Jazz? What was their ultimate goal, to wipe each other out?

Kenneth walked into the Janimore clinic and stopped short. There was a tall blonde woman leaning over Jazz. Jazz smiled but even from a distance Kenneth thought he looked as white as a stick of glue. The woman turned and Kenneth's heart dropped to the floor. He leaned against the wall because his legs were suddenly made of Jell-o.

"Are you okay, sir?" A nurse was by his side, guiding him to a chair. "You were in the accident?" She nodded toward Jazz. He nodded. She brought him a glass of water and he took a small sip and stood up, leaning heavily against the chair. Words floated over and he tensed.

"You are dying," the tall blonde woman said. Jazz snorted. The clinic phone rang and the nurse ran to answer it.

"Your body will continue to serve." She touched Jazz's cheek.

"Need to see Marty, everything's blurry." Jazz whined and she threw back her head and laughed. That's when Kenneth was sure.

"My job here is done," she said.

Kenneth forced his wobbly legs to move as the woman strode toward a back door on the other side of the room. Jazz flailed his arms and reached over and grabbed paper and a pencil from the table next to him.

"Kenneth, wait!" he said. Jazz wrote.

"I can't!" Kenneth said. Jazz kept writing. "Genieve," Kenneth called. The woman didn't turn around.

"Go after her!" Jazz shouted and kept writing. Kenneth ran toward the woman. Why is Jazz writing a book?

"Genieve," Kenneth yelled. His thoughts twirled and tumbled like an overfull dryer. He willed his tired achy body to hurry.

"Hey Kenny, Tom's waiting and I have to deal with Marty." She smiled and walked backwards, facing him. Kenneth felt weak.

"What are you doing here? Why didn't you let me know you were in town?" he pleaded. She grew farther away from him.

"I'm busy Kenny but don't worry, everything is going to work out in a way you will approve of." She smiled as she reached a car.

"What do you mean?" he said. He stopped to catch his breath which seemed to have left him an hour ago!

"It is time to say goodbye to Jazz!" She did a little dance with her feet and laughed. She opened the car door. "Who will be next?" She sang out as she sat down in the driver's seat.

"Genieve," he said. She waved goodbye! Was that even Genieve? A gust of doubts blew through him. The woman did resemble June.

He stood outside the clinic battling with his thoughts. A nearby bench beckoned and he lay down and slept. When he awoke, he noticed a van parked by the entrance fifteen or so feet away. He stretched and walked closer to it. Jazz was being loaded into it! He hurried over.

"Hey where are you taking him?" Kenneth asked the attendants.

"Dr. Marty Mapman's clinic in Maine," the driver told him.

"Want a ride?" The other, shorter burly-looking man teased.

"No thanks," Kenneth said. He made his way back to his rental car, wondering if he should follow them or head back to town and check on Penny and her brothers. Uncertainty circled him again like a dark cloud of dust.

–

Penny awoke with a start. The nurse had helped her call a cab. After her long, expensive ride home, luckily taxi cabs took credit cards these days she fell into a long deep sleep. Her moose beanie-baby named, Bull Winkle, lay on her chest as she groggily reached for the jangling phone.

"Hello?"

"Hey sweetie," her friend said.

"Hey Rem," Penny said. She exhaled the breath she had been holding for days and rubbed at her sleep-filled eyes.

"Did I wake you?"

"Yup but that's okay. I need to get up and do some things before I check in with work to see if I still have a job." Penny eyed the clock by her bedside.

"They love you there. So take it easy okay? You don't sound too good." Concern etched her words.

"Yeah I know but I have hours to make up still." Penny yawned and she proceeded to fill Remi in on the crazy car ride and accident with Jazz. "Do you think he's dying and the woman is Aunt Genieve?"

"Who knows sweetie? You sure you have to go to work?"

"It would only be about a five hour stint, but I should take a shower," Penny said.

"Okay I'll let you go in a minute," Remi said.

"Rem, I miss Brian." Penny sighed and began gathering clean clothes to change into after her shower, "I shouldn't even like the guy!"

"You are in love with him," Remi stated. "And as for all the other questions and problems Pens, mostly it isn't about you. You have to remember that. This whole scheme of Jazz's or Tom's or Marty Mapface's is about old vendettas. They are people who like to play games with other people's lives. Maybe for you it was about meeting Brian, and about really seeing how crazy these people your mother let herself become involved with are."

Henry ran toward the stairs, looked back at Penny and

barked. "Okay, okay," Penny said. She followed him to the back door and let him out; then she headed for the bathroom.

Remi was chattering the whole time. "Remember when I prayed endlessly for my mother to start her life over after my parent's divorce when I was eleven years old? And then,"

"Yeah, then she met ratfink!" Penny interrupted.

"Yeah," Remi said. She laughed. They had come up with the horrible nickname one night when Remi was at a very low point when they were both in the throes of middle school woes and major family disappointments.

"Listen, I know it's not the same. I wouldn't begin to compare. However, pain and confusion over love and over trying to find the truth, your truth, and then all the disappointment that comes with it, is a part of life. You'll get through all this mess. You'll find your own way, not your mother's, but in time you'll come to accept her choices, maybe not agree with them but you'll accept her life, however screwy it became, probably because she was searching for love in all the wrong places!"

"Maybe I have been seeking answers from the wrong avenues, Rem."

"Maybe, but remember the old hindsight rule?"

"Yes, you can't know until it's over and you look back and everything's as plain as day only you couldn't see it through the thick mess of being in the middle of things!"

Remi laughed. "You do have a way with words, being a writer and all."

"Yeah, yeah, thanks."

"Anytime, well honey, I better let you get going, me too. I have some heavy duty meetings tomorrow morning at the hospital, wish me luck!"

"Luck and thanks again Rem."

"Rock on, and call me with the wedding date and any other news, okay?"

Penny hung up and finished getting Henry's dinner. She checked in with Din who was all set to take care of Henry for the evening. The phone rang and she ignored it. She did a few yoga poses and stretches and showered.

She checked in at work and ended up staying for a make-up five hour shift. It was tiring but felt good to be back. Her headache improved and she went to bed as soon as she arrived home.

She awoke early, ate some toast and tea, did a Jane Fonda exercise tape and showered. She was proud of herself. She was putting one foot in front of the other. She hummed as she dressed and listened to a book on tape, one about a man named Greg Mortenson who was building schools in Afghanistan! It made her feel good. There were lots of good people in the world, doing wonderful things for others. It was so very important to remember that.

She emerged from the bathroom with a towel wrapped in a turban over her hair. She had her jeans on was barefoot and was buttoning up a blouse. Her bedroom door flew open and Penny screamed.

"Have you ever heard of knocking?"

"I did, and I called from my cell phone on the way over and had to go to the neighbor for a key because you didn't answer!"
"I was in the shower."

"Who was in there with you?" He strode toward the bathroom. His face was as dark as a storm cloud.

"What are you talking about, Sam?" She followed him into the bathroom.

"Where'd they go?" Sam threw back the shower curtain, spraying water all over them.

"Hey watch it!" she snapped.

"I heard a man's voice Penny!"

"Try this!" She shoved the tape recorder into his belly.

"You still listen to books on tape when you're in there?" He chuckled but he did look sheepish. She whacked his stomach and shook her hand. He was muscular.

"That hurt." He rubbed his tight abdomen.

"Not quite," she said. She scowled at him and held her own injured hand. "What are you doing here, Sam?" He dropped down onto her bed. "Has something happened? Tell me!" Her voice was shrill. Sam wouldn't make eye contact.

"I am composing myself Pen." He looked upset. She lowered her own body to the bed and breathed slow, long breaths.

"It's bad?" She asked. He rubbed his forehead. She popped up and grabbed her brush and ran it through her long thick hair in rapid strokes. The phone rang, Sam bolted upright and she dropped her brush.

"I am learning to hate that thing," she cried.

"Get it," Sam commanded.

"You answer it or tell me first what's wrong!"

"It's your friggin' house!" The ringing went on.

Penny held her stomach. "I have a really bad feeling." Sam nodded. The line went dead as soon as she picked it up. "They are seeing if I am home so they can kidnap me again." Penny shivered.

"Not with me here they won't!" Sam stood up and began wearing a hole in her rug. Penny flopped down on the floor crossed legged. Sam flung out a hand to raise her up and then hugged her hard against his firm chest.

"Be scared, it's okay, though you are the one who dragged us all into this mess!" He pulled her close for another bear hug, but she pushed away from this one. She sighed and sat down on her bed. Sam resumed pacing. She popped up.

"Tell me why you're here, Sam." She indicated he should follow her downstairs. "Do you want anything?" He hovered around her in the kitchen as she put foods for her meals together in a bag.

"You might not want to go work," his voice was soft. She stopped moving. The phone rang, interrupting them again. They stared at one another and then Penny reached for it. It was Greg and she heaved a big sigh of relief.

"Is Sam there?"

"I'm here, what's up?"

"I should talk to Sam first."

"Why?"

"Okay, look I don't have much time. I am at the hospital." Greg hesitated.

"What's wrong? Is it Nancy? Oh no did, did she lose the baby? Is that why Sam broke into my house?" She scowled at him.

"I didn't break in." Sam held up the borrowed key. She shushed him.

"No, no Nance is fine, honey. Look it's about Brian. There was an accident." Greg sucked in his breath and then sounded like a whale as he exhaled his words. "He was hurt pretty bad."

Sam strode over. "What is it? Give me the phone!" He wrapped his long fingers around the receiver just above hers.

"No." She hit his hand, turned away and held the phone close against her ear.

Greg was speaking. "I am sorry Penny, I know you liked him." She pushed at Sam who kept trying to wrestle the phone away from her.

"You sound like he might not – like he's – not going to---make it."

"He might not, Penny. He was in a hit and run accident and he was the pedestrian hit by a moving car."

"Oh," she said. All the blood in her body drained down to her feet, boulders in her shoes, while the rest of her floated. "What's wrong with him?" Her heart turned into a gymnast and the lump in her throat made her unable to swallow.

"Did someone try to kill him?" She thought about her car ride with Jazz. We hit Brian? Her head reeled. She spun. Sam's face was red. His fists were clenched as he leaned on the counter near her.

"We don't know a whole lot, but I overheard a few witnesses talking to the police. It looks like it might have been deliberate. I was hoping Sam knew something."

She sunk down into a kitchen chair, staring at Sam. He met her gaze for only a second. He thinks I am guilty!

"Somebody urged him to cross the street while coordinating with the driver of the car. I don't know. It sounds farfetched," Greg said in her ear.

"Give me the damn phone!" Sam yanked the receiver out of her limp hand.

"Brian was in a hit and run car accident," she told him in a monotone voice.

"What did he hit?" Sam shouted. Penny glared at him and her hand shot out and slapped him on the arm.

"NO you stupid idiot, he was HIT by some madman trying to kill him! Didn't you know already? Isn't that why you came to see me?" Penny screamed at Sam. Sam shrugged and held the phone out so she could hear Greg.

"He's in really bad shape. Listen, Sam, find out what you can from your detective friends. I have to work for a while, okay, so I'll have to meet up with you both later in regards to dad's rescue mission. Is Penny going with you or coming here to see Brian?"

"I don't know yet but I think I am the one that's going to need medical attention." He rubbed his arm where Penny kept a steady stream of slugs. "I have a feeling we'll be at the hospital very shortly."

Penny suddenly leaned into Sam's shoulder and sobbed. He softened and he threw an arm around her. "Don't worry, I forgive you," he whispered, "Even if you are found guilty of a hit and run on your phony fiancé!" She leaned into him and sobbed louder.

"I never wanted Brian to die. I never meant for all these bad things to happen. Am I just like mommy in all the awful destructive ways?" She sobbed harder into his shirt.

"Okay. Yes. Okay. Check in later, right." He hung up. "Penny I was working up to telling you. I just couldn't get it out." He lowered his head to rest on the top of her head. "No one thinks you planned any of this and no you're nothing like mom. You don't sleep around and you don't do drugs do you? And you couldn't have been driving the car that hit Brian, could you?"

"No I was with Jazz and some guy who hates the name Bert. No wait it wasn't a guy it was Aunt Genieve or someone who looks like her or mom or I don't know," she cried. "The woman at the party and the one who came to my house." She knew she sounded crazy yet again and that only made her cry harder. "How am I going to go to work now?"

"Call in sick, it's not like you haven't done that before." He grabbed her arm as she went to gather up her purse and keys in the hallway near the front door. "Listen I need you to tell me everything in that crazy story you just spun all over my shirt." He wiped at the stain of wetness on his shoulder. "But first I need to let you know something else too."

"I can't miss more work again." She fiddled with a button on her blouse. "But I have to get to the hospital to see Brian before I go in." She sniffled and hiccuped.

Sam rubbed the hair on top of her head. "Try the other shoulder." He made a show of offering it to her.

"Before he dies!" she cried.

"Whatever. You need to listen to me so I can tell you something else!" He sighed. "The police are going to pay you a visit."

"About the accident?" she asked.

Henry came over to him wagging his tail and with a hopeful look. Sam petted him. Penny barely noticed Henry.

"They'll have questions about your relationship and break-up and where you were when it occurred." Her mouth fell open and the tears seemed to freeze on her face. "So let's sort out this Jazz drive by thing, okay?"

"It was a car ride to find Kenneth, Sam." She corrected, wiping the rainstorm off of her cheeks. "Do they really think I am a suspect?" she asked. Her stomach tightened. He shrugged. She squeezed her eyes shut.

"You have motive," Sam reminded.

"Because I was mad at Brian for setting me up?" she asked.

"This whole scheme lends itself to motive Penny. What did you say earlier about dad being Jazz's target?" Sam asked.

"I don't know. It was insane. I agreed to the ride so I could get answers out of Jazz. I thought it would give me the chance I've been looking for to ask a lot of questions but instead the driver sped up and Jazz took pills and passed out and then we spun and crashed. We, we might have hit something or maybe it was just the curb or something in the street. I blacked out for a few minutes. I hit my head on something and when I woke up, some medical people convinced me to go along to this clinic Jazz goes to and I rested a while. I tried to ask him questions once again but a nurse shooed me away. She bandaged my head and I spoke with Jazz for a few minutes. He kept ordering me to call Marty and find Kenneth. He seemed sick but as usual one dimensional and unyielding. I was tired. The nurse called a taxi and I made it home and slept and worked and slept again."

"Wow, you should have called me, Penny," Sam scolded. "It probably wasn't the best idea to sleep that much and be alone with a head injury. Not to mention follow Jazz around like that. He might have put you in a lab to do more of those experiments."

"I don't think that was him," Penny said.

"How do you know that?"

"That's not part of his plan. He wants me married to Brian."

"That doesn't make sense."

"None of this makes sense. Who is that woman Sam?"

"I don't know but we will find out believe me! Listen though call me next time Pens, please! You don't have to be so self-reliant all the time!" He looped an arm around her shoulders and held her close. "Be careful, I love you, sis!"

"I love you too," she whispered against his hard chest. "Drive me to the hospital?" He nodded. "Help me find out who did this to Brian?"

"Of course," he said. Her stomach felt like an angry swarm of bees. "How's your head feeling?"

"Okay," she said. "Am I really in trouble with the police?" her voice trembled.

"Maybe but it helps to have connections." He smiled down at her and kissed her forehead. She nodded and her leaky faucet turned on once again.

CHAPTER TWENTY SEVEN

"We haven't been able to locate dad." Sam told her as they drove to the hospital to see Brian. Her stomach was doing flip flops and her face was a puddle. She couldn't get the image of Brian in a coffin out of her mind. Why would Jazz want to run him down like he was a piece of trash? Did he suspect Brian wanted to partner with her in order to defy him once and for all? She had questioned Brian's intentions thinking he was loyal to Jazz. Had she been wrong all along? A sob tore through her at the thought.

"I mean it is entirely possible Dad is in a bar somewhere downtown. Or doing some job for Jazz," Sam speculated. Penny realized he had been talking the whole time. It was like when she was reading and discovered she had gotten to the end of the page and had no idea what she had just read because her mind was elsewhere!

"I'd rather not think the worst of dad," Sam said. "The question is who does he most want to help? Us, I think," Sam said. As they sped along the winding roads Sam grew quiet.

While they walked toward the entrance of the hospital though Penny couldn't stop her thoughts from pouring out of her mouth like an overflowing pitcher, "Why would Jazz set up our marriage and then kill him?"

Sam took her arm and they went through the large double doors. He whispered, "Maybe Jazz has been setting you up to take the fall." She faced Sam as the shock of what he said sent an earthquake rumbling inside of her.

"He wanted us to fall in love? He wanted to addict me and kill

Brian?" Incredulity lined each word. Sam gripped her arm harder and nodded to the woman behind the desk. They checked in at the desk and were told to go to ICU but that only family could visit. Penny informed the receptionist that she was Brian's fiancée. The receptionist nodded and told them the procedures they'd need to follow. First they were instructed to wait in a special area.

"Jazz is a sadist, Penny, haven't you realized that by now?" Sam was exasperated with her. They didn't speak for a while. She sighed.

"Can you do me a huge favor?"

"What?" he asked. Sam kissed the top of her head.

"Can you call work for me and tell them, a really good story?"

"I can do that, sure. However maybe the truth would work? Your fiancée is near death from a horrible hit-and-run accident?"

"Yeah, I guess that is a pretty good story especially if you mention the part about me being the one who ran him over!" Penny paced until she was breathless.

"Technically you weren't driving."

"Great yeah, thanks for that," Penny said. She flopped down onto the slippery torn vinyl couch.

"We do not have any proof Penny so you need to relax." He held up his hand. "Okay, okay, an impossible task obviously but if you wear yourself out within the hour, what good will that accomplish for your beloved fiancé?" He walked away to make the call. She took slow even breaths until Sam returned a short while later.

"Did you get through to Angela?" she asked.

"Yup, she said they'll be fine for a few days without you, but to call her and keep her posted and to take care. I made a few other calls as well."

"Thanks." One less thing to worry about, she thought, except not really!

Sam cleared his throat. "Penny I need to find out what happened to dad even if you don't seem to care much so put the police off as best as you can."

"You're deserting me right now?"

Sam opened his mouth to reply just as Greg came rushing down the hall toward them. Penny grabbed Sam's hand and hung on for dear life while she said numerous prayers for Brian.

Greg's features were grim. Sam unlocked her fingers from his and slung his arm around her shoulders. Slivers of ice swam through her bloodstream, like the day she learned her mother was 'gone'. They sat down to wait and hours seemed to pass. Sam put off finding Kenneth and brought them two tall coffees. She wrinkled her nose at the strong odor and sat hers down on the table in front of her. Sam slugged his coffee down in one swallow! He strode back and forth across the small room while sending text messages.

"Sam!"

"What?"

"Go, please!" She yawned. "Greg is in the hospital and he'll check on me."

Penny awoke to a ringing sound. She looked around, feeling stiff and disoriented. The cream in her coffee looked like pieces of a button mushroom. She pushed the Styrofoam cup away from her. A page was sent out and phones rang in the distance. A well choreographed dance of people and machines swirled around her.

"Hello," she croaked. My voice must sound like a frog adding to the night's rhythm, she thought.

"Two down, a few more to go, including you," the mechanical voice proclaimed. Penny puffed up like a defensive bearded dragon lizard.

"Who is down?" she whispered.

"June has many debts. It's time to take responsibility." The line went dead. Penny dropped her head into her waiting hands. She massaged her temples. She propelled her shaky legs in the direction of the nurse's station. Her feet were cold. She blushed and ran back to the couch and retrieved her shoes. People looked away as soon as she made eye contact as if they could feel her shame. She stood at the desk while the two nurses were busy talking on the phone.

Why should she continue to pay for her mother's choices?

Wasn't it enough to be deprived of a real mother for years? Penny clenched her fists against her thighs. Her mother had abandoned her over and over again, seeking something that didn't exist. Why couldn't she escape her mother's life? It had become so entangled in hers, inside of her. It was time to separate.

A man walked up and stood beside her. Penny thought he looked familiar. He was tall and thick, but not fat. He was older, probably around her father's age. His hair was thinning in places and blond with grey streaks. He had a small beard. He closed his eyes and took a long slow deep breath. Penny felt sorry for him and thought he must be waiting for someone who was hurt badly or undergoing surgery or very sick.

"Yes, may I help you dear?" The woman behind the desk asked Penny and she jumped. The man opened his eyes and they stared at one another. All of a sudden it dawned on her who he was, and she could feel his tension.

"I, I am checking to see how Brian O'Mackery is doing and if I can see him now?" she said.

"Yes and I'm his father, Milman O'Mackery. I drove over eleven hours to be here. I'd appreciate seeing my son as soon as possible!" he said. He turned and gave Penny a hard stare.

"Hello Mr. O'Mackery, of course you should see Brian first, sir," Penny stammered. She had been about to say more when the nurse interrupted.

"Yes, Mr. O'Mackery your son is back from surgery. You may go and see him. Mary will take you." She nodded to a nurse who stood by smiling at both of them. Milman nodded but his steps faltered. He wiped at the tears that ran down his lined face. Penny thought he'd aged in the few weeks since she had met him at the engagement party. He put a hand over his heart. Mary, the nurse, paused. She squeezed his arm.

"Are you okay, sir?"

"Hardly," Milman retorted. The nurse nodded and led him to where Brian was recovering. Penny followed. She would stop when someone told her she had to, but for now she couldn't stop her legs from moving toward Brian.

Mary pointed to where Brian was and Milman slowly made his way toward the unrecognizable figure of his youngest son. "Oh God," he said. Penny's heart stopped beating as she inched forward. Another nurse was examining Brian by taking his vitals, checking the machines that were keeping him alive, and she pushed a button on the screens and examined the IV. The nurse nodded at Milman as he wiped an errant tear.

"He can hear you," she murmured. Then she indicated for him to move closer and take Brian's bandaged, cut hand in his and speak to him.

Milman took a step toward the bed. The nurse moved away. He took another step forward. Penny stood close to the end of Brian's bed. No one was telling her she had to go. She looked down at the floor tiles. They were large brown squares with a sprinkling of white sugar. Milman's hand shook. He touched Brian on a small exposed part of his skin near his pinky finger and he collapsed, leaning over his son, kneeling by the bed he put his head against Brian's arm and wept.

Penny wanted to touch his back and offer comfort, but she wasn't sure if she should. He was angry, probably blaming her for everything. Maybe he was right. She had started this whole thing with her incessant need to understand. Perhaps her brothers had been right to keep her questions squelched all these years. It was a bad can of worms to open. She could see that now. She backed out of the room on her tiptoes and returned to the waiting room couch, praying like there was no tomorrow which there might not be for Brian! It was her fault!

A while later Penny decided to make her way back to Brian and was relieved when she didn't catch sight of his father. He must be down in the cafeteria. The nurse informed her Brian's mother couldn't come for a few days since she was stricken with a bad case of the flu and his brother was due in soon. He was delayed for some reason. They didn't know why, when Penny inquired. She sat with Brian for a short while but kept tensing every time she heard a noise. She didn't relish a confrontation with Milman. It wouldn't be a good idea to have a fight with him in front of Brian and so she went back to the waiting room. She was restless and so she took to walking down the long corridors of the hospital, half hoping she'd spot Greg or Nancy at some point. She didn't. Instead she came across Milman with a foot braced up against the hallway wall. Penny was hungry and tired but Milman looked worse. She stopped. His eyes were closed. The line of muscles near his jaw twitched. The gymnast inside of her chest made her hyperventilate slightly.

An orderly walked by, his eyes lingered on Milman who suddenly pushed off from the hospital wall with one foot, blinked and swerved his blue piercing gaze to Penny. Penny froze like a deer caught in the headlights of a car.

"How dare you," Milman growled. Penny flinched. "Is this why you agreed to marry my son? It would be the ultimate revenge!" He was bitter. "You make my brother and son out to be the bad guys." Milman stabbed the air with his index finger. "You wormed your way into our lives with your need for the truth and look what happened? Was it worth it? Don't you know about letting sleeping dogs lie?" Penny nodded yes, then no and cried.

"I'm so sorry," she gulped. "I never meant for any of this to happen." She swallowed hard and coughed. "I lo--love Brian. He is amazing. I should." She broke off.

"Shut up!" Milman shouted. "You should have thought of that before you ran him over!"

"You shut the hell up." Sam seemed to leap up out of nowhere. He pushed his face up close to Milman's. Greg stood next to Penny. She looked from one to the other. Where had they come from? She had been so focused on Milman that she hadn't noticed anything else.

"You're Brian's father? I'm Dr. Greg Patrick. We met at the engagement party." Greg shoved his brother aside. Greg extended his hand but Milman ignored him. Instead, he opened his mouth just as Sam maneuvered in front of Greg so that his face was once again inches from Milman's.

"Where do you get off blaming my sister for any of this?" He swept a hand around the room. "Your precious brother kidnapped and drugged her. Brian of course knew all about it. They continue to stalk and threaten her." Sam stabbed his index finger into Milman's chest. He swung around for a moment and hissed at Penny. "I told you to stay in the waiting room!"

"I, I couldn't Sammy. I had, had to see Brian." She swiped at her cascading waterfall.

"Look," Greg interrupted. He pushed the side of his body against Sam's but his brother did not budge this time. So he snaked an arm in between the two men. He tried again to push his brother back but succeeded in moving him only about an inch.

"What's the use in pointing fingers right now? We need more facts. Let's agree to work together, help each other cope with all the tragedies that keep piling up." Greg cleared his throat. "Besides, we should keep it down. People are trying to heal, and all this tension can't be good for Brian or any of the other patients or their families."

Milman O'Mackery scowled at Penny and one second later a low moan escaped his throat. "My son, my son," he said. Milman put a hand to his mouth. Tears slipped down his aged cheeks. Penny cried harder. She moved as if she were learning a new dance, toward Milman.

"I'm so very sorry Mr. O'Mackery, sir!" Penny touched his shoulder. Milman flinched. She jerked her hand back as if burned. Sam stepped up close to her and Greg rubbed her back.

"Brian loves her for a reason and I'm not talking about your adopted brother's sick plan of revenge or control or whatever it was meant to be," Greg said.

"Jazz obviously has you wrapped around his little finger if you can't see his twisted ways for what they are. Your son chose to work for him, knowing the risks and it has cost him dearly!" They gasped at Sam's frankness. "Not that I care much for Brian and his manipulating my sister for Jazz's benefit."

Milman was slow to form his words. "I realize Jazz is far from angelic," he said. His teeth were clenched.

"Perhaps, Mr. O'Mackery, your time would be better spent in the ICU," Greg said. Milman slumped into the nearest chair, like a balloon that had lost all of its air in one big whoosh. He rested his head in his hands. His body began to shake. Penny wiped her face and spoke in a soft, compassionate voice.

"Milman, I care about your son. I do." Her voice cracked and she looked up at the ceiling. "I am praying every second that – that he's – that he'll be all right." Steady streams of tears ran down her face. "And you are correct. I did make the phone call to Jazz. I did want answers, so I started this whole mess! But my goal was not for anyone to get hurt, including me!" She hiccupped. "I wanted to understand my mother better and try and make peace with her decisions and also with my father leaving and living like a recluse in Canada afterwards. I thought if I could make sense of them, I would be happier and could move forward better. I made a mistake. I should have let the sleeping dogs lie, you're right, all of you." She swung an arm around.

"It's a little too late for that epiphany Pens," Sam said.

"I need to accept that there are things in this world that I will never understand," she whispered. "I need to accept."

Milman raised his face. It was as wet and red as hers. He exhaled loudly. "No, I," his voice equaled her whisper. "I, it's Jazz." He cleared his throat. His chin quavered. New tears formed. He stared up at the ceiling for a moment. "My adopted brother is manipulative, controlling and warped."

"How about evil," Sam added. Milman and Sam locked eyes and slowly Milman nodded.

"My wife and other son would agree with you. I'm afraid I let this go on." His voice broke. "His schemes, his sucking in my boys with promises of money, fun," he said. "I have never broken totally free of it. He has a way of involving me and my boys in things. The money helped, and it was exciting at times, but I never thought what he did was right or good and now look," his voice broke. "What he has done to my family and I allowed it to happen! Ruth is so sick right now. She can't even come to see Brian. She blames me. John isn't here either. Neither of them can face what we've no I, let happen!"

"We don't know that it was Jazz who did this," Penny added.

Her hand still rested on Milman's arm and he now covered it with one of his.

"It was bad with John, but never," Milman said. He rubbed his features, looked down at the table and brushed an imaginary crumb off.

"What is Jazz doing at the moment? Is he in some clinic? Why isn't he concerned about Brian?" Sam asked.

Milman shrugged. "He tried to phone me but he didn't leave a message. It appears he is being treated at one of the clinics he has utilized over the years. I don't know why he isn't worried about Brian. But it doesn't surprise me. He always takes care of numero uno first and foremost!" Sarcasm filled each word.

"I'd like to ask him about Kenneth. He's missing and was last known to be with your brother." Sam raised his voice.

"That won't be possible. I don't believe any of us will be talking to Jazz again," Milman said. He stood up and blotted his face with a handkerchief.

"Oh yeah why is that?" Sam looked amused.

"Is he?" Penny asked. She saw him at the clinic, pasty and weak when she left in the taxicab only yesterday or was it the day before? Penny couldn't remember.

"Is he dead?" Sam said it.

CHAPTER TWENTY EIGHT

The phone woke Kenneth up and since it could be one of his kids, he answered it.

"Brian's in a coma," Tom announced.

"Brian?" he asked. Kenneth rubbed the sleep out of his eyes. Kenneth had watched Jazz being loaded into a van the day before yesterday. Supposedly Jazz was headed to Maine and Dr. Marty Mapman. Kenneth meant to call Sam or Penny but somehow he had not gotten around to it. He drove for hours and until his bruised and battered body cried out for sleep. He found a hotel room, showered and collapsed.

"Yeah remember the guy your daughter is supposed to marry soon?" Tom said.

"What happened?" Kenneth sat on the edge of the bed. This wasn't going to be good news. He wished he hadn't answered the phone. He wasn't expecting a call from Tom.

"He was the victim of a 'planned' hit and run accident," Tom said. Kenneth felt his smirk through the telephone lines.

"That's what we hit?"

"Yeah, only the-what is a-whom and it wasn't we it was you!" Tom chuckled. Cold liquid fire spread through Kenneth's veins.

"You fat, greedy pig," Kenneth shouted.

"Oh that really hurts Kenny!"

"You and ski mask planned every turn I took, putting a gun to my head, stabbing the accelerator every time I tried to stop the car." Kenneth felt like a giant hole was sucking him down and under. He looked heavenward. Mama would tell him to, 'face the down and dirty truth of your life'. Ha! A drink was better. It would obliterate reality.

"Witnesses recall you as the driver Kenny."

"What witnesses? You and ski mask," Kenneth asked. "It was two am!"

"Your prints are all over the steering wheel. Oh and by the way Genieve and I took care of Jazz. Genieve said her goodbyes to Jazz and Penny. I'll take care of Genieve soon enough, along with Penny, don't you worry, Kenneth." Tom cut him off. "Oh and let me know if you need a ride up to Maine! I'll be in touch, happy drinking!"

He hadn't been able to get a word in edgewise and yes he wanted a drink. He was an addict after all. He admitted it but right now he couldn't let Tom destroy Penny. He had to warn her and Genieve. He scooped up his keys and walked outside. It was dark again. Another day had gone by. He reached in his pocket for his cell phone and instead found a crumpled twenty dollar bill, some fuzz and a quarter.

"I saw Jazz at the Janimore clinic when, I mean after," Penny faltered. She didn't want to tell Milman she was in the limo with Jazz when it hit Brian!

"You went to get answers from him," Sam interjected.

"How did you know he was there?" Milman asked.

"Jazz called," Sam said. Milman nodded.

"Brian loves you Penny and I believed you were his ticket out from under Jazz's thumb."

Sam interjected. "Did you and John turn down Jazz's offers?"

"Sometimes," Milman admitted. "I know, I know, hypocrite, don't say it."

"The police are questioning everyone." Sam spoke after an uncomfortable silence. Penny shot her brother a wary look. "I just want to warn everybody."

"He has a lot of internal injuries." Greg patted Milman on the back. "But there is always hope. Brian is in excellent physical condition and that is always a plus."

"Are you his doctor?" Milman was incredulous. They walked toward the elevator doors.

Greg shook his head. "No I am a general practitioner and he needs a variety of specialists right now. I found out what I could for Penny." The elevator doors opened and Penny walked in. Greg said he needed to make his rounds on the second floor. Sam told her he was still looking for Kenneth, so he followed Penny outside and made some calls as she inhaled the fresh air. It was dark. Stars were like specks of glimmering sand across the black sky.

She was losing track of her life. Marrying for answers to questions about another person's choices, how insane is that when she really considered it in the moonlight! Her job might be taken away and her writing was going nowhere fast. She was on a monstrous mountain, endlessly climbing upward.

She swung her face upward toward the mystery and promises of miracles, and she prayed for Brian's full recovery and another chance to see what they had without all sorts of interference from their pasts. Sam hung up and they went back inside. Penny wrinkled her nose at the sterile, medicinal smells.

Milman told them he wanted to sit with Brian for the night, alone in order to make amends. Penny hated to leave Brian. So she wandered back to the waiting room and curled up on a corner of the couch and closed her eyes.

The next morning Penny walked slowly over to the area of the ICU where Brian was recovering. Milman was slumped over a chair. Machines that worked with Brian's body bleeped and the bumps moved up and down rhythmically. A nurse nodded to Penny and put a hand gently on her shoulder and Milman's eyes fluttered open.

"Huh, is everything okay?" He was instantly alert. She nodded and smiled at him then patted his shoulder.

"We need to work on him a bit, so maybe you could take a break for a while?"

"What do you mean?" He rubbed his crusty eyes.

"Oh don't worry, it is just routine stuff. We like to keep the muscles active, do a bit of wash-up and adjust his fluids." She looked compassionately at both of them. "He is hanging in there so far. How's your wife feeling?"

"O-okay, I think I better give her a call, thanks," Milman said.

"Don't forget to grab some breakfast Mr. O'Mackery. You need to keep your strength up and you too Penny."

"Yes, but I am not hungry. I am not even sure what time it is." Milman rolled his neck. Then he massaged the muscles behind his head.

"It is just after seven in the morning." She smiled and began touching Brian, checking his pulse and then listening to his heart.

Penny grimaced as if she were the one bandaged and in pain. Milman yawned and stretched. He looked miserable.

"I—I better call my wife," he said. He gathered up his book and jacket. Penny followed him not able to stay with Brian yet. It was too painful but she didn't care to be alone either.

They made their way down the corridor and to the elevator without speaking. As he reached his rental car, he paused, stretched and told her to hold on while he checked in with his wife. He sat in the car and tried Ruth. They spoke briefly while Penny breathed in the fresh air again. Bright morning sunshine greeted her this time. Blue cloudless skies and chilly air lifted up her spirits at least for a moment or two and then the image of Brian laying in a coma returned and the ton of bricks settled back down onto her shoulders.

Milman informed Penny that John was due in late the next day. Ruth wanted both her boys to stay with Brian. She didn't want Brian to feel alone. Penny took Milman's arm.

"We should try and eat something. There's a diner two blocks from here. Let's walk," she said.

Penny ordered a cup of tea and an English muffin. Milman quickly ate eggs, toast and drank two cups of coffee while Penny took small bites and sips, chewing for long intervals.

"Did you know my mother, June?" Penny asked him as they waited for the bill. Milman nodded. "What can you tell me about her?"

"She was beautiful, mesmerizing with her poise and grace." Penny reddened. "She loved hard, deep I guess I mean, but not always well." His smile was sad and Penny looked down at the table. She folded her napkin a few times.

"She was smart and funny but lacked confidence, a lot." He emphasized the last word. "Because of that I think she agreed to things that were not safe or in her or her children's best interests." Penny looked up at him.

"You have her smile and strength, grace and determination I think," Milman commented.

"How can you tell all that?" Penny blushed.

"I have been around the block a few times. Do you really care for my son?" He waved away her offer to pay her share. "He's not like Jazz. Brian is honorable and decent."

"It's hard through this mess to be sure." She was uncertain of his reaction.

"I can imagine, but you can trust his word." Milman was firm in his conviction. Penny lowered her gaze and resumed playing with her napkin.

"He loves you Penny and he needs you now more than ever. Will you help him?"

"Of course," she said.

"Are you ready?" Milman asked. She wasn't sure in the least that she was ready for anything let alone what he was asking but she nodded. He stood up and stretched his arms above his head and rolled his shoulders. They walked back to the hospital.

"Thanks for talking about my mother." She was floating a few feet above the ground. "I forget sometimes how she was a person."

"Oh Penny, we all are full of glaring imperfections, foibles and extreme beauty! Most of what we see depends upon our attitude each day." He turned to her. Tears formed in the corners of his worn eyes. "I forget too. I think we all do."

Penny couldn't say anything. Her throat was full of emotion, mostly gratitude in this moment for Brian and his family. Wow, life is strange!

After arriving back at the hospital, Greg updated Brian's progress for them. "His spine is fractured along with several ribs. He has a concussion, a broken ankle and wrist and he's hemorrhaging somewhere. His pressure keeps falling and he's losing blood," Greg explained to the faces lined up in front of him. Penny thought her brother looked unkempt like he hadn't slept much in days. He rubbed his head, making his hair stand up funny. Penny felt a stab of love for him. It always endeared people to her when she glimpsed their underbellies. Then she thought of Brian and felt a deep stab of guilt. Milman's face drained of all color and he lowered his head slowly until he sat with his face down.

Penny walked away. It was too much. Alone in the bathroom, she began to sob. She wanted to confide to her brothers about the threatening phone call she had received a few days ago, but the timing never seemed right. Her sniffles punctuated the otherwise silent room. Suddenly the door opened with a swish of outside air and there was a knock on her stall door. Penny tensed, remembering the bathroom scene from her engagement party where the woman who looked like June fluttered in and out, like a butterfly.

"Pen you in there?" Nancy called. Penny stood up and opened the door wiping her eyes.

"I can't believe it," she sobbed. "I told him to go away. Those were my last words to him. I thought we shouldn't be together. I didn't trust him!" Penny wailed.

"Shh shh," Nancy soothed. "It's okay honey. Let it out. But let's get one thing straight." She pulled Penny's head back to look straight into her sister-in-law's red-rimmed eyes. "It is NOT your fault. Not any of it, not because of your search for your mother or your saying yes to Brian's proposition. You are not responsible!"Nancy implored her, still holding the sides of Penny's head and stroking her hair while staring deeply into her eyes. Penny squirmed and half nodded then continued.

"I was in the car when it crashed. Ja—Jazz's driver, a woman, maybe the one from the party sped around town and then we hit something or someone and, and," Penny babbled. Nancy interrupted.

"It wasn't your fault. You weren't driving or deciding where to go!" Nancy responded. She wasn't even showing shock at what Penny was saying.

"I lo care for him and Milman, Brian's father claims Brian truly loves me so what if he di-dies," she hiccupped. She gulped air. "I'll never know—I'll never." The ocean seemed to gush out of her. "It'll be just like with mom!"

"Aw Honey," Nancy said. She held her tight.

"He was drinking. They said his blood alcohol level was way high. He never drinks. Never! Do you think he was infused with stuff like I was in that warehouse experiment place? Or, or was he in despair over our breaking up?" Penny had diarrhea of the mouth. Nancy had that effect on her. Everyone should have a 'Nancy' in their lives!

"Hon, listen, anything is possible with Jazz. Brian was responsible for his actions. He chose to go to a bar and not look where he was going as he crossed a downtown street in the middle of the night. He hooked up with his sick twisted Uncle for years and perhaps it was Jazz who decided to wipe him out with you in the car for added twisted revenge?"

"Yes but," Penny said.

"The facts will all come out soon enough," Nancy interrupted. "So there's no point in speculation or throwing around the blame."

Penny sniffled. "I'm scared." She looked at her sister-in-law's kind face. "What if I am next?" A fresh wave of tears flowed down her cheeks as she voiced this thought aloud for the first time.

"Don't let your imagination run away with you," Nancy said. "Stay close to Sam and Greg and visit Brian, talk to him, help him come back, help him heal. It'll help you too, okay, sweetie? Now give me a big hug, and then let's go back out there and face this mess together, all right?" Penny wiped her nose on some toilet tissue. She took a deep breath and her hand shot out to stop Nancy's movement toward the door.

"I—I got another one of those phone calls. This time it was on my cell phone here in the hospital." Penny blurted. She might as well get it all off of her chest, every last speck. Nancy hugged her tight.

"Do you know who it is? What did they say? Did you tell Sam and Greg?" Nancy peppered her with questions.

"I think they want me to know they are watching my every move and are close by wherever I am." Penny wiped her face. They eventually rejoined the group with Nancy begging Penny to give a full disclosure to her brothers.

"The toxicology report shows strange amounts of substances mimicking some of the brain chemicals – neurotransmitters like epinephrine, dopamine, and serotonin."

"Talk normal Greg." Sam was irritated.

"The experiments, they got to him whoever they are. I guess he's not immune to their manipulation." Greg was agitated. Nancy came to stand near her husband and leaned her head against his shoulder. He, in turn, hugged her.

"So he's a pawn in this just like us?" Sam exclaimed. "I don't buy it!"

"He's been under my brother's thumb too long. He's wanted out even longer," Milman responded.

"I was supposed to be his ticket out." Penny wore her vulnerability on her sleeve.

"There'll be proof soon enough." Sam whipped his head around to glare at Milman.

"Haven't you heard when you point a finger there are always three more pointing back at you!" Milman was angry.

"Cute," Sam quipped. Penny winced.

"It is not a competition!" Greg snorted.

"I think we should be praying for Brian's recovery. We can at least be united on that front." Nancy reached for Penny's hand and held on tight. "And you are still his ticket out more than you think?" She squeezed Penny's hand. Milman went down the hall. Sam followed him.

Two men waited in a dark corner. They jumped back into the shadows when Milman and Sam appeared and emerged again after the two men left.

"Nice threads," one commented. They looked at each other's scrubs and nodded.

"We are off schedule. We need to grab her pronto."

"Yeah, we've got to quit wastin' time."

"Let's do it!" He checked the needle he had been hiding and held the vial tight. His colleague fingered the gun shoved in the side of his scrubs and underwear. Jeans worked much better, he thought and shifted as the weapon dug into his skin. Suddenly she came hurdling around the corner and almost bumped into them. They flinched then glanced at one another.

"Penny Rose Patrick?" She whirled around.

"Yes?"

"We need a word with you."

"Why – is it about Brian?"

"Yes. Could we speak with you in private?"

"O-okay I guess." They sidled up next to her. One smiled.

"Let's go outside. I imagine it's been a while since you've had any fresh air?"

Electricity traveled up Penny's spine and neck. She eyed the corridor behind her. It was dark and empty.

"Is it really bad news?"

"You'll have to be the judge of that," the taller one said.

CHAPTER TWENTY NINE

Kenneth waited in the hospital parking lot for Sam. When he had found his phone in the glove compartment of his rental car there were numerous messages from Sam. They agreed to meet at the hospital. Kenneth wasn't ready to see Brian or rather face up to what he had done to him so he told Sam he'd wait outside for him.

"Hey," a tall man said. He touched his arm and Kenneth jumped up. "Are you waiting for Sam?"

"Are you Brian's father?" Kenneth asked. He was a handsome man like his son, blond, fit and trim, but broad and his smile was warm and inviting despite what he must be going through.

"Milman O'Mackery, we met at the engagement party." He extended his hand.

"Yes, where's Sam?" Kenneth shook his hand. "Sorry, how is Brian doing?" Milman looked down at the curb and back up into Kenneth's eyes. They were full of pain.

"He is holding his own for the time being." Milman sighed. "That's about as good as it gets right now." Kenneth nodded. "Sam is busy with some police matters but if you are up to the task, I am determined to find Jazz or at least discover what is happening with him."

"Sure, let's go," Kenneth said. He could put off seeing his kids for a little longer. They located Milman's rental car and set off for the Janimore clinic, the first place Jazz was taken when he fell ill. Though they both had heard Jazz was most likely up in Maine where Marty Mapman ran things, Milman wanted to re-trace his brother's footsteps, to learn what he could.

Kenneth was not about to talk with Milman about Tom and Genieve and he hadn't confessed much in his brief exchange with Sam. Though he had mentioned he had been thrown into a car with Tom and that they had hit something or someone a few days ago, maybe the same night Brian was run over.

Kenneth looked out the window at the passing cars and the trees that were gradually losing their colorful leaves. He sucked in his breath and rubbed the waves of thick hair on the sides of his head. Something had to help him out of this awful mess. How did he tumble head first into these predicaments? Drinking was the culprit. It was a weakness used by others to control him.

They entered the facility. Kenneth glanced around at the sea blue walls framed with photos of ocean scenes. He heard Milman. He was asking a nurse a question.

"Do you know where my brother, Jazz Martin was taken for further treatment after he left here?" Milman asked.

"No offense Milman, but this could be another one of Jazz's tricks," Kenneth said. They waited for the nurse while she answered the phone.

"I know, no offense taken," Milman responded. "I am done taking offense about Jazz. I ask myself why I keep caring a hundred times a day but that's nothing new."

"He has a peculiar effect on people, luring them in with such charming force and then frustrating them to the point of considering blind murder!" Kenneth blurted. Milman turned to stare at him and then a slow, handsome grin spread across his tense features.

The nurse didn't know much, so they headed for the administrative offices.

"Listen, I believe that my brother's life is in imminent danger." Milman plunged in as he stepped inside the office of one administrator who appeared none too happy to have to deal with them.

"Records are strictly confidential, one of the hallmarks of this facility. No one is more special than the next," the white-haired, stern-looking man replied.

"Yes, we are well versed in Jazz Martin's twisted logic, thank-you."

"He is the boss!" The man pointed out.

"Perhaps he was but my daughter, and two sons, his two sons," Kenneth said. He pointed to Milman. "My missing wife and her sister among others are in danger because of Jazz Martin! So it is a matter of life and death which is far more important than any stupid protocol you feel so compelled to follow!"

"While I can appreciate a good drama, our policy stands." The man looked down at his desk and shuffled his long fingers through a stack of papers.

"Did Jazz teach you that trick too?" Kenneth sneered.

"What's that?" the administrator asked.

"The rude art of dismissal," Kenneth answered.

"Look while we do appreciate your rules sir you must be able to bend a smidge." Milman countered with a large toothy politician-seeking-election grin.

"Look for most if not all of our patients it is a matter of life and death. They qualify for space here when the coma has deepened to such an extent that there is little hope of recovery but usually their loved ones aren't ready to give up."

"So my brother slipped into a deep coma?"

"I have already explained." The man sighed and returned to shuffling papers, keeping his eyes glued to his desk.

"Jazz Martin set this clinic up originally and financed a great deal of its years!" Milman was exasperated.

"Yes, he was an important man and he deeply valued the confidentiality policy and privacy of all our clients."

"Clients," Milman snorted.

"Sirs, I need to ask you to leave. I have told you all I can at this time. I am very sorry about your brother, about Jazz. He was certainly a great man. Now if you please," Kenneth interrupted.

"Does this change your game?" Kenneth grabbed a framed photo off of the man's desk. It showed him with three children and an attractive woman. Kenneth was sick and tired of being pushed around. His mother would say, 'feel your oats son and pour them out onto the world!'

"His son," Kenneth said. He pointed again to Milman. "His son is recovering from a serious hit and run accident." He shook the photo in front of the man. "My daughter was kidnapped and forced to participate in some of Jazz's experimental work! We need to learn where Jazz is, so he can help us help our children!"

"He was taken to Dr. Marty Mapman's newest facility in Maine. It didn't look good. He's failing fast and there are many who feel it cannot come fast enough!" The administrator exploded.

"Like who?" Milman and Kenneth asked at the same time.

"I've already said too much." The man opened his office door. Kenneth handed him back the family photo.

"Nice family," he said. The man held tight to the photo and glared at them. They walked out, thanking him for his time and help. The door slammed behind them.

"Do you want to return later in the evening, perhaps bribe technicians and see what more we can learn?" Kenneth asked Milman as they walked out into the bright sunshine. Milman nodded and they back-tracked to a diner they had seen on the way over.

Penny followed the men toward the exit of the hospital. As they rounded the last corner of hallway and could see the front exit they put their hands on her elbows and pushed her forward.

"I think we should talk inside." She swung around to face them. They each gripped her arms. Penny looked around frantically and suddenly a nurse appeared. Penny cried out and doubled over.

"Are you okay ma'am?" The nurse leaned over Penny. Then she straightened and looked the men over.

"She's fine, just upset nurse, thanks. The man she's marrying is dying."

"You don't look so good," the nurse interrupted. "Come here." She proceeded to lead Penny back to her ward and sit her down in a chair by the nurse's station. She took her vitals.

"I think she just needs some fresh air," the one explained.

"Yeah, that's what we were about to give her," the other added.

"I don't want to go outside with either of you," Penny said. She breathed as if she had just run a marathon.

"Give her some space guys. She looks as though she's going to pass out. What's the rush? Let her sit a while. I think she needs that more than fresh air." She rubbed Penny's back. "Relax," she murmured. Her brown eyes were warm with sympathy.

Penny sighed. "They told me they had news about Brian O'Mackery, my fiancé. He was in a hit and run accident," Penny told the nurse. "But for some reason they wanted to talk to me outside." The nurse's brown eyes were like sparklers on the fourth of July. She glared up at the men.

"What floor do you work on? Better yet, tell me your names and what you were going to let her know?" The men backed away. Excuses flew out of their mouths one on top of the other. The taller one stuck his hand in his pocket and a beeper went off. They mumbled apologies, walking backwards and then they turned and fled.

"What in the world was that about?" the nurse asked aloud.

"That was weird," another nurse replied. She came up to them. "Want me to call security?"

"I think they meant to kidnap me *again*!" Penny blurted. Both nurses stared at her.

The two men ran toward the front of the hospital.

"What now? Do you want to wait and try again?"

"We blew it again!"

"Nah, momentary set-back, we'll get another chance."

"Maybe, maybe not, we should have injected her right away."

"Then how would we have gotten her out of here unnoticed?"

"We could have found a laundry cart!"

"Yeah I guess so. We can't have no more mess ups. So that means taking our time." They slipped into the nearest men's room and discarded their scrubs.

"Let's move the van closer." They walked a few blocks away

from the hospital.

"Yeah and I want a hot dog." He nodded at the stand nearby.

"Forget about food, we need to focus on kidnapping the girl."

"I need food so that I can focus on kidnapping!"

"Fine, I'll buy you three hot dogs! Then we nab her, stick her with the stuff and transport her up there before Marty puts us in the bed next to her!"

Greg rushed over. "You shouldn't be alone Penny." Greg cupped her chin. "It's all going to be okay." Penny dried her face. "Breathe okay, and no running off without an escort. Brian's exam is over. You can go ahead and visit him if you still want."

"What did they say?" she asked. Before Greg could answer she turned to the nurses who had helped her. "Thanks."

"Sure no problem hon, be careful okay?"

"Get some rest." The younger one added and smiled at her. Her eyes overflowed with kindness and Penny's felt as though she had been warmed by the sun. Greg gave the two nurses a thumbs up and then he took Penny's hand.

"According to what I could discern from just the neurologist and internist." He eyed her closely. "The damage is extensive." Greg squeezed her shoulder as they walked side by side. "He is holding on, but the next 2-3 days are critical; especially the next 24 hours. There's internal hemorrhaging around the duodenum area and near the liver and a kidney but they can't go in *yet*."

"So they just let him bleed?" Penny exclaimed.

"They'll have to hold off for a little while. His condition needs to stabilize further before they can risk opening him up. They are monitoring him closely and trying various medicines too." Greg rubbed his tired eyes. "His spine is cracked too."

"Will he be paralyzed?" Penny sniffled. "He was so athletic."

"There's no way to know Pen, he has to live first. It IS that bad." Greg paused. "Most of his vertebrae are severely bruised and a few are fractured. Several ribs are broken with one on his left side—pieces of bone are," he said. He stopped and pulled her around to face him. "Are protruding, so that that may be the cause of some of the internal bleeding," he sighed. "Look, it is amazing the guy is here with us as far as I can see, probably in part because he keeps himself in such top condition." Penny swiped at new tears. "They are also doing some detoxification on him due to the alcohol poisoning and other chemicals that may have been added to his drinks."

"Experiments," she said. Lumps of coal sat in her stomach. She gripped Greg's forearm.

"Maybe," he said. "He wasn't tensed up at the time of the accident though, that might have helped too."

"What are they doing for the protruding bones?" Penny demanded. "Won't it puncture something if they don't fix them?"

"They are doing all they can. Trust them Pen, these guys are the best." He paused. "He also has a severe concussion both in the frontal lobe area and in the cerebral cortex. He has multiple contusions and bruises on his legs and a severe sprain of his upper left thigh."

Penny put her hands to her ears. "Okay, enough! What isn't wrong with him?"

"Hey I am sorry, I was trying to let you know everything," he said.

Barely any of Brian was visible through the massive bandages and the parts of him that were, made her want to turn away in horror. He wasn't recognizable. She yearned to double over and sob or scream for hours.

Greg held her tight. "He needs to hear your voice." She turned back to Brian. Her whole body shook and her heart thumped wildly in her chest. Tears spilled down her cheeks and she wiped them with her fingers. Then raising her chin a notch, as June used to do, she steeled herself. She moved close to his bed. One nurse made a beeline for her.

"Are you Penny by any chance?" she asked. Penny nodded. Her throat was choking with grief.

"He said your name over and over when he was brought in." Penny nodded and stared at the apparatus that was keeping Brian alive.

"It was amazing he was conscious. It was as though he had something urgent he felt he must tell you," she said. Penny needed a plumber. She sat down with a thump in the chair the nurse had pushed over to her. She was a bucket of water about to tip over.

"Well I'll leave you, just thought you'd want to know that."

Penny reached out her hand tentatively to touch Brian's bandaged and bruised one. An IV was in the center of the back of his hand so she merely touched her fingers to his long lean ones or at least to the two that were visible. The nurse put a hand on Penny's shoulder.

"You can only stay a few minutes this time hon, he has just been through so many tests, and he needs rest and quiet." She squeezed Penny's shoulder and then walked away. Penny took a deep breath. A fleet of wild bumper cars tore through her mind. She brushed her cheek against his fingers and her long blond-brown tresses stuck to her damp face.

"Oh Brian I am so sorry, so very sorry, so very, very sorry." After a few minutes she raised her tear streaked face and whispered to him. "You are good. We had fun. I love you," she said. There she told him! Okay it was cowardly to wait until he couldn't hear her. But she said it and she had no way of knowing this is how things would turn out.

She stroked two of his long fingers. "You – you can't leave me with this mess. We are in this together, remember? That was the deal. You promised!" Her voice cracked and her lips quivered. "You promised and I bailed over and over again! I was always making you prove yourself, so what's new for me? I have to stop that I know. You were sincere weren't you?" She laid her head gently across his abdomen. She willed her love and forgiveness to flow through her and into him.

She could hear Wil and Greg's voices drift in from the waiting area as she sat with Brian.

"How is Brian O'Mackery doing?" Wil choked out.

"Hanging in there," the nurse said.

"When can I sit with him?"

"He has a visitor right now. I have to check to see if he requires a rest period first, okay?" she said.

"Not good," Greg said.

"Has he been awake at all?"

"He was conscious briefly when they first brought him in."

"Is he going to pull through?" Wil asked.

"I don't know. These next hours and days are critical. He's unconscious and they've already had him under the knife once to try and stop the hemorrhaging but could only do so much. They had to stop and now they are waiting until he's more stable. All sorts of specialists have been examining and working on him, so he has the best care possible," Greg explained. "The body possesses an amazing capacity to heal itself. He's in top physical condition, which is a huge plus, and he has lots to live for, which is another big advantage."

"What are his odds?" Wil pressed.

"The car hit him *deliberately.*"

"You mean it was attempted murder?" Wil was puzzled.

"Sam thinks he was followed and that maybe there was a set up at the bar. His drinks were tampered with. Traces of drugs similar to what they gave Penny were in his blood," Greg explained

"Is his uncle responsible?" Wil's eyes darkened and he clenched his fists.

"Maybe, but Jazz is in bad shape too," Greg said.

"Rumor, or do you have proof?" Wil questioned.

"I don't know, it comes from one of my brother's sources, I think. Milman and Kenneth are out investigating. There could be someone involved we haven't thought of," Greg said. Penny thought, yeah me, I was in the limo with Jazz!

"Like who?" Wil asked. Penny couldn't hear Greg's answer. He must have whispered it.

"What about the mystery woman from the engagement party who showed up at Penny's?" Wil asked. Yeah, Penny thought she was driving the limo and didn't want to be called Bert!

"She is not our mother, it just isn't possible. It is probably somebody with a nasty vendetta against Jazz," Greg said.

"Who doesn't have that?" Wil was sarcastic. "I hate not being able to do anything to help him!" Wil said.

"I need to see my brother," Greg said.

"Let me know if you find out anything. Do you think I can see Bri when Penny's out?" Wil asked.

"Yes, though they may make you wait a while first. They'll probably want to check him for a bit before allowing another visitor. Giving him quiet rest time is important but so is talking to him to bring him around."

"Okay thanks, man," Wil said. His voice sounded like how her heart felt right now. A raw wound that someone was rubbing buckets of salt into.

CHAPTER THIRTY

A nurse tapped Penny's shoulder and told her it was time to go. Brian needed to rest.

"How's he doing?" Wil asked. He set his coffee down on a table next to the couch where he had been sitting and waiting. She lifted her shoulders in response. She was afraid of saying much. She might lose it. He nodded.

"I need to find Sam." She put a hand to her mouth and ran out of the waiting room. Her legs felt like bricks she was dragging ten feet behind her. She craved fresh air. She touched her cell phone in her pocket and headed for the stairs, increasing her speed until she was racing down the steps.

She heard noises behind her. A prickly feeling went up and down her spine. She gripped her cell phone and pushed open the heavy stairs door, emerging onto the first floor. Out of the corner of her eye she watched a colorful display of balloons bobbing up and down. The lady at the gift shop spoke animatedly to a customer. A faint scent from the flowers in buckets lined up in the corridor near the shop followed her for a brief moment then the fresh, cool air splashed Penny's face as though she had just stepped under a shower. A little breeze blew her hair back from her face where it had hung as a shield. She inhaled, trying to throw off the stale chemical hospital aromas. She looked up at the blue sky filled with puffy white clouds. Penny absorbed the sunshine and let it thaw her.

She wondered if Brian was floating somewhere in that in-between world. She tried to imagine his handsome face grinning and telling her he was fine and would be back soon. She crossed the street to the park and found a spot under a huge, very old oak tree and sat. She leaned back against the massive gnarly trunk and closed her eyes. She heard the leaves rustling in the trees and the squeals of the few young kids playing nearby. She opened her eyes and touched the number on her phone.

"Hey it's me!"

"Hey, me, how are you? Where are you? I have been wondering about you."

"Near the hospital," Penny explained.

"Hospital, who's in the hospital now?" Remi asked.

"Brian had a terrible accident *on purpose!*" Penny shouted. The park noises suddenly seemed to evaporate. Penny felt like she was drifting away on one of those balloons she had seen on her way out of the hospital. Brian, Brian where are you?

"Oh my God, tell me what happened sweetie?"

"Oh Rem," Penny said. Her cheeks were wet as if she'd stepped under a shower.

"In case I have to go. I never know with this silly job and all the damn meetings and interruptions. Don't take it personal okay? I'll call you right back as soon as I can, okay? What's your cell number again? I want it right in front of me!" As a hospital administrator at a mid-size hospital in Arizona, Remi's schedule was often full. Penny gave it to her before she launched into what she knew about Brian's hit and run and Jazz's ills.

"Oh Rem, it's my fault Brian is dying," she confessed.

"That is a load of crap and you know it!" Remi said sharply. "Come on honey, I don't mean to be rude. But don't go down that God-complex road. It has never suited you, or anyone else for that matter." Remi advised. "And you don't know he is dying!"

"You're right." Penny inhaled deeply. "Someone's after me again Rem."

"Right now, as we speak?"

"Yeah, I don't know, maybe. I'm scared."

"Are you safe at this moment?"

"Yeah I think so." She looked around the park.

"Well, don't be alone. When you hang up, call Sam or Greg or Nance to be with you," Remi said.

"Okay."

"Let me just say a few things because I'm getting flagged. Listen, someone has to get you to quit blaming yourself for other people's lives. That's a non-negotiable issue Pen. Then I'd say spend as much time as you can with Brian. You could be the one responsible for bringing him around! Let the boys search for your mom or that mystery woman whoever she turns out to be, and let the boys deal with Kenneth, Jazz and whoever else is mixed up in this thing. And get help, okay? Don't be alone!"

Penny sat for a moment, soaking in Remi's words of wisdom. She thought about calling Dana, but then she'd have to deal with work. She left messages for both her brothers and Nance. She called her neighbor, Din and asked how Henry was doing. She missed cuddling with him and their walks. Din gushed that Henry was fine but pining away for his mistress! She'd have to pick Din up a small gift to thank him for all his care of Henry. Henry needed a large chew toy too!

She leaned back against the sturdy trunk and closed her eyes. She rubbed her temples and took deep breaths. She felt the strength of the rough tree trunk against her back and knew what it felt like to hold up a host of heavy branches all day long!

She prayed for more strength and for Brian's recovery and sighed. The tension left her body a little bit and a soft breeze caressed her skin like a soft feather.

Then an awful but familiar smell assaulted her nose as a cloth was shoved up against her mouth and nostrils. NO! The two men from the hospital, one grasped her arm, holding a long needle and the other pinned her body against the tree trunk. She squirmed and yelled. A sharp sting in her upper arm, she stopped moving and within a few minutes her limbs felt like cooked spaghetti. It was funny! She was floating, for real, up, up and away! She hummed. They escorted her to a van.

"Hey, where we goin'?" She giggled, feeling loose like soft silly putty! Penny laughed harder.

"For a ride, sweetheart, don't you want to see your Mama finally?" The man said. He pushed her into the back seat of the van and hopped in front.

"Yes," she said. The other man spoke into a phone.

"We're on our way."

"Can I talk to her?" Penny asked.

"Soon, baby, soon," he said. His craggy face split into a wide mischievous grin.

"Okay," Penny said. She stretched out in the backseat. One way or another here I come mom, she thought.

Milman and Kenneth drove back to the hospital late that evening. They were not able to glean any information from any of the evening clinic employees. One nurse caught up with them as they left and handed Milman a note. It was from Jazz. Milman glanced down at the paper as Kenneth drove.

"Tell me what it says," Kenneth demanded.

"I need to call Ruth and John and see when they'll be able to visit Brian. I promised Ruth he wouldn't be alone." Kenneth nodded. He couldn't argue with that. So he waited through the long drawn out calls.

He should have grabbed the note from Jazz. He had seen him scribbling furiously before he passed out. Genieve distracted him. Plus he was banged up from the accident! What did Jazz write? It couldn't be good for him or his family.

Milman rubbed his eyes as he hung up from his call with Ruth. "I will read the note to you soon but first tell me why our past ends up defining us and in the most unexpected ways? How can we stop the familial patterns and finally learn? So we are not held back or propelled into relationships that perpetuate all that needs to change?"

"Philosophizing is pointless, Milman. I would know because I have spent a decade mired in it and look where it's taken me!" Milman cocked his head. He listened and waited. "Nowhere," Kenneth blew the word out of his mouth like it was a pit.

"You, he and others were seeking cures? But you didn't manage to do that?" Milman sighed and his voice took on a low disgusted edge, a hiss. "You tricked people, made them into addicts of all kinds and then discarded them! You don't even allow them to die, just so you can keep experimenting on them!"

Kenneth's hands tightened on the wheel and he sucked in his breath but before he could say anything Milman went on.

"Jazz was convinced of the connections between immune function and emotional states and how memory, interpretation and perception could be manipulated with the right drugs and conditions."

"No. For Jazz, it was all about psychological conditioning, with drugs and sex," Kenneth stated. His hands were turning white from gripping the steering wheel so hard. Milman put a hand to his throat. A choking sound escaped.

"My son," he cried. He bent his head down into the crook of his arm as it rested on the car door and sobbed with anguish.

They arrived at the hospital and Milman went to see Brian. They learned there had been no change in Brian's condition. Kenneth saw the crumpled white sheet of paper half sticking out of Milman's pocket. It was like a deep splinter in his hand. It was probably nothing and would work its way out eventually.

Kenneth went in search of his family. He was told Greg was home with his wife, though still on call and Sam and Penny were out searching for him! He decided to head back to Sam's. He explained to Sam how Jazz had tried to wipe him out with tainted liquor but he had managed to escape and now it appeared Jazz was at a clinic in Maine where Marty Mapman may be trying anything at his disposal to revive Jazz. He told him about his trip with Milman and even about the note left by Jazz that was stuck unread in Milman's pocket.

"What do you think it says?" Sam asked.

"Nothing good," Kenneth said. Sam told him he had spent much of the afternoon and evening with his police friends.

"Did you run over Brian?" Sam asked.

"I don't know," Kenneth said. "It's the truth, Sam."

Sam shook him awake early the next morning so they could go over to Greg's house and fill him in.

"Is Penny joining us for breakfast?" Kenneth asked.

"I jogged by her house before getting you up but she wasn't home nor is she at the hospital or at work!" Sam said. "I am worried she is missing again." Sam slammed his fist into the steering wheel as they pulled up into Greg's driveway.

"You think she's been kidnapped?" Kenneth asked. They stood

in Greg's kitchen. The early morning sunshine streamed in through the windows. Greg yawned. Sam briefly filled Greg in on Kenneth's mishaps when he ran upstairs a few minutes ago and woke him up.

"Pipe down Sam. I could have slept another several hours. But now that I'm up – and it's not the hospital because that's what I thought this early emergency call was – tell me what's wrong with Penny. Keep it down though, Nance is trying to go back to sleep or at least rest, and I don't want to worry her needlessly," Greg said.

"Okay, okay, if you'd shut up for a second I could tell you about Penny!" Sam hissed. Kenneth opened his mouth to intervene but Greg spoke first.

"When was the last time you saw her?" Greg asked.

"Yesterday, she was visiting with Brian and then she went outside to talk to Remi. I called Remi this morning when I was searching for Penny. She told Rem she was scared she was being followed again," Sam said. He ran his long fingers through his black hair.

"Why does she keep going places alone?" Greg asked. Sam groaned.

"Stubborn like her mother," Kenneth murmured.

"You think she's been kidnapped again for the experiments don't you?" Greg dumped the rest of his coffee into the sink and rinsed out his green mug.

"Probably by Tom," Kenneth said. He kept his voice low and flat, devoid of emotion. Greg stood still and no one spoke for a few minutes.

"It's about revenge." Kenneth held up his right palm. "Tom is still angry that he didn't win June."

"Penny has become June for him?" Sam's phone rang. "Hang on," Sam barked.

"That's sick," Greg said. He went up to check on his wife. After a while he came back into the kitchen.

"What's up?" Greg asked. He was relieved that Nancy was sleeping.

"Penny IS in trouble man. The gift shop lady and a few nurses outside having a smoke saw her run across the street to the park and sit under a tree. She was on the phone and then left with two large men. She seemed drunk, laughing, and acting silly, at least that's what the witness told Bernie. They all got into a grey van."

"Dear God," Greg said. He rubbed the back of his head as it began to tighten.

"Let's go!" Kenneth shouted. "They must be taking her up to the clinic in Maine where Jazz and Marty are waiting."

"I need to put in some hours at the hospital and then at my office. Call me when you find out anything!" Greg ran upstairs.

Penny couldn't see a thing with the blindfold on. She could feel her hands and feet bound up. She felt lightheaded yet in the pit of her stomach a sense of foreboding swirled. She cleared her scratchy throat.

"Thirsty," she said.

"You'll be plenty hydrated soon enough, sweetheart." The man laughed.

"Where going," she said. Penny licked her dry, cracked lips. Silence greeted her for some time until finally one man turned in her direction from the front seat.

"To a place you'll never forget, though you won't remember much either," he said.

"Who are you? The Riddler," she asked.

"What's the guy on the radio call it Pete?"

"Hey don't say my name!"

"The north country," he laughed, "Yeah that's it."

Penny was on the tilt-a-whirl at an amusement park and sleepy at the same time but as the van sped through the remainder of the day she gave in, allowing herself to be lulled to sleep. What else could she possibly do at the moment?

It was late afternoon when Sam and Kenneth drove north. Kenneth kept speed dialing Genieve.

"She's avoiding you dad," Sam said. Irritation oozed as he

judged Kenneth as stupid.

"Genieve helped me. I will always owe her." Kenneth said.

"She's involved in kidnapping Penny," Sam growled.

"She is probably looking out for Penny in whatever ways she can," Kenneth said. He wanted to believe his own words.

"How do you explain her alliance with Tom then?" Sam pressed.

"She's drawn to danger and I would bet she's playing many sides of this game right now. She always has." Kenneth exhaled and gripped the seat as Sam drove fast on the highway running up through New Hampshire. "And I am sure he's running experiments on her and has been for some time. She must be too addicted to leave. She's vulnerable like June. They lived crazy lives before I knew them just in different ways. Genieve had such a need to have all that her sister desired. It was a sick kind of admiration, but it dominated her life; it still does."

"So many people wanted June," Sam murmured. Kenneth felt a wave of sympathy.

"She was a very compelling woman between her strength and extreme vulnerability. She possessed a kind of mysterious allure." Sam passed another car and accelerated again.

Kenneth studied his son's profile. He was handsome, determined, aggressive and smart. He was intrigued by danger, hence the work he did. But he didn't want to know about June or the past, not like Penny did. Sam kept his eyes straight ahead.

"Tom is probably the one making the secret calls to Penny."

"How do you know this?" Sam asked. Kenneth heard the annoyance framing each word.

"He's the one running the experiments on her. I saw him at the warehouse where she was kept last time!" Kenneth admitted.

"What? Why didn't you tell me or try to stop him dad?" Sam shouted. Kenneth lowered his head.

"I tried but I don't control the man just like I couldn't influence Jazz or your mother much."

"Obviously, but you could have informed me, the police, Greg, Penny, just to name a few, dad!"

"I know I just wanted to understand and then fix things

myself for once!"

"Bad mistake," Sam said. "You just admitted you have never succeeded!"

"Tom considers himself an expert on the concept of 'wanting'. He's caught me up in it more than I care to admit."

"What?"

"He examines it from a biological, psychological, and any other angle. He discovers the best way to own a person's body and mind," Kenneth explained. "Genieve is fascinated by this concept as well though she lives it too, always wanting June's life, the men, and materialism. It's sad the two sisters were messed up by their mother's wanting and so it goes.

"That's weird," Sam said. "And now you think Penny has caught this bug so to speak?" Kenneth nodded. "So who would this other woman be? It can't be mom!"

"It may well be Genieve at times but other occasions it could be a stranger who is paid by Tom or I was thinking about Kathy, the wife of the plastic surgeon who lived near us just before June left for good." Kenneth paused for a moment. "Also Sammy I believe Tom may be Penny's father." Kenneth exhaled the words from a deeply painful place inside of his heart. Sam spun his face around to glare at Kenneth. The car swerved to the right.

"Keep your eyes on the road, son!" Kenneth exclaimed.

"Sorry," Sam righted the wheel.

"He and June were together plenty. She told me she was pregnant after we returned from our Asia stint. It all fits I just didn't want to acknowledge the truth to anyone."

"Poor Penny," Sam said.

"How can you fight or escape people like this Sammy?" Kenneth whispered. Sam's jaw muscle twitched.

"We can and we will dad but one thing is very clear. None of us should try to go it alone!" Sam pushed down on the accelerator and they sped along through the darkening sky on the highway heading up into the North Country.

CHAPTER THIRTY ONE

Penny slid herself up onto her elbows. Something pinched her. She blinked, trying to erase the heavy sleep out of her eyes. Only a small bit of light came in from a far window. Her heart sank to the floor. Both her arms had IV's in them. She pulled slowly at the one in her left arm, when it wouldn't give, she pulled harder. She twisted her arm back and forth until the IV came loose and fell to the floor. Her arm throbbed and she groaned. A wet spray shot out and up at her and she flinched in disgust and fear. The IV tube was like a snake that had been hit by a car. A loud noise like an alarm went off. Penny tried to slide off the table. Stickiness everywhere, yuck, she twisted her other arm but that IV didn't budge. A loud beeping noise from a blinking machine echoed throughout the small room. Shouting voices, oh no, she wiggled and writhed on the table. She had to hide. Footsteps running, they grew closer and the room spun. She flailed her arms and legs, black dots lined her vision. The voices and footsteps grew louder. She strained to lift her head, a sharp pain in her neck brought her head down with a thud and the blackness dissolved her into a million pieces.

Kenneth's phone vibrated in his pocket while Sam drove through New Hampshire on their way to the clinic in Maine. They hadn't stopped much except to switch drivers or spoken since Kenneth announced his suspicions that Tom was Penny's father. Except Sam reported after a round of phone calls from his various detective friends, that they believed Penny was being taken to

Marty's clinic in Maine.

Kenneth rolled his shoulders and bowed his head to stretch his neck. Then he answered his phone.

"Hello," Kenneth said. "It's Milman," he told Sam. "How's Brian doing?"

"He's hanging in there and the nurse said that is a good sign. Any luck locating Penny?" Milman asked.

"We are getting closer to Marty's clinic in Maine," Kenneth said.

"You think she's there with Jazz?" Milman asked.

"Most likely, listen Milman, about that note that Jazz left you," Kenneth said.

"I haven't read it yet," Milman retorted. "I've been a little busy. You know, son in a coma and all? Let me know when you find Jazz and Penny."

Kenneth turned to Sam after the call ended. "Milman is keeping it to himself."

They drove in silence, stopping for more coffee at a roadside stand. They walked around the small park area before getting back in the car. Kenneth knew it was time to talk to Sam about the accident. He had to break the tension and face the fact that it was his fault that Brian was in a coma.

"Sam," he paused. Sam had insisted on driving again since he had to be doing something at all times! Kenneth gladly let him take the wheel.

"I was the one who hit Brian," Kenneth exhaled. "I mean Tom forced me to do it!" He tied is hands in a knot on his lap and dared not glance over at Sam.

"It might have been the limo Penny was in with Jazz and Genieve!" Sam was hoarse.

Kenneth sat back in his seat and unclenched his hands, "Wow."

"Yeah what a mess," Sam agreed.

"Brian *was* set up," Kenneth said. "I was at the bar. I watched the whole thing unfold." He stopped but Sam didn't interrupt. "I left and sat on the curb. Brian stumbled around. It's obvious someone tainted his drinks, which explains why as a non-drinker, he kept drinking so much. I saw two guys following him and I heard them talking on their cell phones about where he was headed. Then before I could do anything, I was forced into a car with Tom and Mr. Ski Mask with a gun. Tom pressed his foot over mine on the accelerator. I couldn't focus. I panicked!"

Kenneth stuck another piece of the chewing gum he was living on into his mouth. It helped with the terrible dryness. The gum was an invention of Marty's wasn't it? He couldn't remember. It was loaded with vitamins and a few substances that soothed the areas of the brain involved with addiction. He would probably grow to need the gum. That's always how these things worked. Sam continued to say nothing and Kenneth was exhausted. He shut his eyes and leaned back against the seat.

Penny held her breath. It was dark now. She felt like someone was nearby. A door opened. Her leg itched! Footsteps, clicks and tapping noises, and then sounds receded and she heard a door close. Taking a deep breath, she scooted off of the makeshift table and stood on wobbly legs, letting her eyes adjust. She had to escape! She yanked out the last IV. Oh that hurt! She held a hand over the crease in her arm and the pain subsided. She steeled herself for the alarm but the machines were quiet. Eyeing the door and the medical apparatus surrounding her, she made her way to the one window. The room tilted sideways and she gripped the sides of beds walking as if she were recovering from a stroke. She pushed the window. Her head throbbed. She had to stop and lean against the wall. Breathe, Penny. Breathe! You can do this.

She faced the window and tried again and again and again. What was I expecting? Nothing is easy. She scanned the room. There were portable stretchers and machines and one massive door that of course was locked or led to her captors! She leaned against the wall, shut her eyes and slid to the floor. What was she going to do? Stupid, stupid me, what was I thinking going outside by myself! My brothers are probably disgusted with my idiocy.

She hugged herself and clenched her teeth together to stop from sounding like a wind-up plastic toy. Henry, where was poor Henry? At home with Din, of course while she was stuck in some science lab again! It was all her mother's fault. All of it, every last problem in her life was June's fault!

Sam's phone rang. "It's Greg. Brian made it through surgery to repair the internal bleeding. He is moving his fingers and his eyes are moving as if he's dreaming. The family and the nurses want Penny to visit. They think she could bring him out of the coma. What?"

"What?" Kenneth echoed with concern.

"Marty Mapman is trying to intervene. One of the nurse's believes he's attempting to prolong Brian's coma or worse!"

"Keep him away from Brian!" Kenneth shouted. Sam nodded.

"Greg heard you." Sam went on to talk a few more minutes to Greg, filling him in on their conversation about the *accident*. "We are nearing Portland, Maine right now, so we are getting close." He thanked Greg and hung up.

Kenneth sat very still. Sam drove with his foot pressed hard to the accelerator. Traffic had been light. They were making good time.

They drove through Portland, Maine and Kenneth did something he had not done in a long while. He prayed. He must have slept for a short time because Sam was shaking him. Kenneth rubbed his bleary eyes and looked around. The nondescript brick building was surrounded by a few tall pines and several old oak trees. It was late fall, but some of the leaves were still red.

"Manomly clinic," he read. The small brown sign with gold lettering stood to the left of him and Sam as they walked through the front doors. A large dark haired woman behind the counter looked up and smiled at him.

"Can I help you?"

"Yes, thank-you, I am looking for Dr. Marty Mapman. We have a meeting set up for late today but I was hoping to make it earlier,"

Kenneth said.

"Okay and you are doctor?" she asked.

"Dr. Westsymer and this is my assistant James." He smiled at her.

She looked down at some papers. "I don't have you listed on his schedule." She glanced back up at them, shifting her eyes back and forth. "However, Dr. Mapman keeps his own set of hours. We do expect him to check in soon." She glanced at the clock on the wall.

"He likes that diner out on route seven A." A nurse sauntered over to them.

"Yes, that's true. You could try there, or we could page him for you." The large woman offered.

"Let me try the diner. That actually sounds pretty good right about now, can you give me the directions? If I don't have any luck I will return and wait for him."

The two women laughed. Kenneth headed back to the car as Sam used the bathroom. He had wanted an excuse to quickly check out the clinic just to make sure Penny wasn't there. Kenneth stood under a tree by their car. They planned to head to the diner, assuming Penny wasn't here. It was close to six am. The sun was awakening across the sky, in a bright yellow splash. He closed his eyes and imagined himself back in Canada, having a nice cup of tea, overlooking the rocky coast.

His phone danced inside of his pocket and he jumped. His heart performed a belly flop. It was Genieve.

"Where are you?" he asked.

"I'm escaping!" She whispered into the phone. "Penny's in trouble," she said.

"Yes we know. Where's Tom?"

"In the car sleeping and I am in the bushes near the overlook where we stopped. I called a cab."

"You sound a little crazy Gen." Fear stabbed at Kenneth.

"I am but haven't I always been? But don't worry, I have my gun," she whispered. "Oh here it is, hang on!" He could hear rustling and a car door slamming. A man's voice and the line went dead.

"Genieve, Genieve!" He looked up. Pink, orange and bright yellow ribbons filled the horizon. A blanket of sadness fell on him while the birds sang, good morning. His phone was like a jackhammer. He jumped.

"Sorry my phone cut out. Kenneth it's bad. Tom's horrible vengeance toward Jazz and June includes destroying his own daughter and Brian."

"Penny will be okay. Sam will see to it." Kenneth ached with the heaviness in each pore. "Gen is it you who is showing up all over town, at the party, at Penny's house, and crashing limos into Brian?" Kenneth pressed.

"I did it for Tom," she murmured.

"Tom's using you. He's running experiments on you right now."

"I suffer from debilitating headaches," she admitted. "I needed his help."

"No he caused the headaches so he could addict you!" Kenneth thought of Greg. He knew headaches could be the start toward addiction. It was how Jazz and Tom brought the body toward needing, wanting the substances, the dependence. It could be very convincing. Sometimes it never progressed. This used to fascinate him. How some bodies fought through it and others succumbed. Greg fought it didn't he? He made a mental note to discuss this with Greg when he saw him.

"The headaches can be intricately intertwined in the addiction process, Gen, you know that?" Kenneth was losing patience with each word he uttered.

"Whatever it is it's too late now! Listen, I made promises about Penny and so I will stop Tom once and for all and if I have to I will expose Marty! I'll see you soon, Kenny, honey. I have to go."

"Wait! Where are you going? Let me help you. This is more than a one person job!" Kenneth implored remembering Sam's words earlier of not going at any of this alone.

"I am meeting Marty and then I'll have to have it out with Tom, I am sure." A quiet conviction was obvious in her tone. "Will you save me if I need you to?" A cold gust of wind blew into the center of his heart.

"Yes. Tell me exactly where you are and where you are going to meet both of them," he pressed.

"I'll be in touch if I need your help, but I have to try this on my own first, you know me!" She laughed and hung up.

Kenneth sat down in the car as Sam abruptly slammed the door. "She's not in there!" he said. His frustration made Kenneth want to hit something.

"Okay, so we head to the diner," Kenneth said.

"Is there another clinic in Maine where they could be?" Sam shouted.

"Yes of course but let's first meet up with Marty." Kenneth tried to keep his voice level as the long icy fingers of fear squeezed tightly around his chest. Was that even Genieve on the phone? Is he being set up again by Tom?

Sam put the keys in the ignition. "Who were you on the phone with?" Kenneth stared into Sam's coal black eyes. "Dad," Sam commanded.

"Genieve is planning on exposing Marty and eliminating Tom."

Penny floated up from the bottom of a pool, slowly while a woman whispered in her ear.

"A bit longer, okay to sleep. Change in plans."

Penny felt a sharp pain in her arm. Bubbles escaped her pursed lips.

"Anti-viral compounds, immune boosters, very addictive; they are viruses themselves and many were only placebos, we have tests. See what the body was capable of doing," she whispered. We tried to manipulate emotional states using drugs, addiction studies, how the body and brain responded. So many became addicts either physically, emotionally or both."

Mommy, Penny said. Only no sound emerged from her lips.

"Jazz manipulated personalities with drugs and then experimented on how to undo addictions, like I am trying with you right now."

Penny drifted down, down, down to the bottom of the pool as the woman injected her twice more.

"I have more unfinished business yet today but Jazz won't bother you any longer, nor will Tom Mott. Brian will come around and you need to be with him. Cut Kenneth some slack and your brothers too." She touched Penny's arm as she bobbed up and down like a bird sitting on the ocean's surface.

"It is better if you relax. It'll kick in faster and you'll feel better sooner." A bell rang. "Remember, no one is quite what they seem." Penny felt a whoosh of coolness.

Penny slept. Clicking noises repeated and this annoyed her. It appeared to be coming from the bed next to her. She grabbed a hold of the railing and slid out of bed.

"Hello my dear," the voice boomed. Jazz!

"How is life treating you? Have you seen your mother yet?"

"Jazz," Penny stammered. Another click sounded and she backed away from the bed. Was she awake? Penny pinched herself. Nothing happened.

"Ah, you are about to make some very interesting discoveries, my dear," Jazz said. "Enjoy," he chuckled. She backed up, bumped into her bed and ran to the next one. She gasped at the woman in it. Her hair was long and auburn. Penny doubled over and clutched the bed railing.

"Mom," Penny said. Panic flooded her like an intense rain storm. "I am dreaming," she repeated this a few times.

"Keep going, you are doing so well," Jazz said.

"Shut up!" she said. "Mommy," she whispered. Her mother's cheek warmed Penny's icicle fingers. Her mother looked alive? But she didn't move nor did Jazz! She ran up to another bed.

"Aunt Genieve? Wait, but you were just helping me?" Her aunt's face was disfigured, maybe it wasn't her?

Penny ran to other beds. Many faces she did not recognize. However there were some she knew from her parent's work parties! What was this place? She pinched herself over and over. A sob bubbled up as if she were a burping volcano. Wake up she shouted inside of her head. But she didn't.

She ran back to where Jazz Martin lay. His eyes were closed. He looked happy. She ran back to her mother.

"Mom," she said. Choking as the sobs grew from deep inside. Hot lava of fear and long buried pain wanted to erupt. She shook the bed and yelled louder. Her mother slept. Peace emanated.

"Mommy, what happened to you? Why are you here? What is this place? Talk! Tell me! I have waiting so long to know, to find you!" Penny sobbed. She ran around the long room, to bed after bed. She was breathing hard. Fire swept through her bloodstream.

"NO!" she screamed. Her mother wanted this? Was this to be her fate? To become a vegetable or a permanent science experiment?

Penny screamed and crumpled to the ground like a used parachute. A horror movie, she was stuck in purgatory! She lay on the hard, cold linoleum floor. This is what I wanted to know. This is the truth. Why? She sobbed until her stomach hurt and her eyes felt like a puffed up blowfish.

"Help me mommy!"

CHAPTER THIRTY TWO

"Say it!" the tension was thick as fog.

"What?" Sam snapped back as he pulled into the diner parking lot.

"You think I am in cahoots with Genieve," Kenneth said.

"If the shoe fits," Sam said. His sarcasm irritated Kenneth further.

"Well I am not!"

Sam flipped open his cell phone. "It's Greg." Sam put his phone on speaker.

"Brian is moving his fingers and toes upon request and he is responding to touch."

"He's coming out of the coma," Kenneth asked.

"He hasn't opened his eyes yet," Greg said. "Early toxicology reports came back. There were definitely drugs in his system. Plus Marty Mapman was calling in more meds for him."

"So Jazz was behind Brian's so called accident?" Sam said.

"I guess," Greg said. "Brian is under the care of a new doctor and we are all closely monitoring his recovery."

Sam waved for him to go check out the diner. Kenneth stepped out of the car and stretched his back. He walked with a stiff gait toward the diner. He wasn't as young as he used to be. He missed his long walks by his Canadian home. He glanced back and saw Sam gesturing angrily. Kenneth knew he was talking to Greg about Genieve. What a father he had turned out to be! Though he could console himself with the fact that he was a better one than Jazz or Tom!

–

Penny lay next to her mother, trying to ignore stomach cramps. She dozed with one hand touching her mother's. She dreamed. Brian, her mother, and her aunt blended together, like in a kaleidoscope.

"Pe—ee—nn—yyy," he said. His voice was low and raspy.

"Brian," she whispered. Brian's little finger beckoned to her.

Kenneth scanned the diner. He spotted a man with a blue baseball cap on, seated at a booth with a woman. Their heads were close, as they leaned across the table talking. Her pink baseball cap was low, over her face. It was hard to tell. He stepped over to the counter as close as he dared and ordered coffee and a Danish.

"You should not have gone," the man said. Was it Marty?

"I have everything under control," she said.

"Hardly," he admonished. Kenneth sipped his coffee. What is she doing with Marty? He missed what she said.

"Wait for me. It's almost over," Marty said. Kenneth strangled the mug of coffee he was holding.

"I can't make any promises," she said.

"You are still holding a torch for Kenneth?" Kenneth felt feverish. "I have meetings at the Manomly clinic." Marty was abrupt.

"Marty, wait!" she said. Kenneth watched them hurry out of the diner. He momentarily felt super-glued to the stool. She still wanted me? Tires squealed. Marty peeled out of the parking lot. Kenneth slapped some bills on the counter and nodded to the waitress. He quickened his pace. Sam was still on the phone but he saw him glance up and watch Marty speed down the road away from them. Genieve was crossing the large adjoining parking lot. Kenneth kept his eyes on her as he made his way to Sam's car. She stood outside a small motel, talking on her cell phone. Tom, he thought. He leaned into the driver's side window watching Genieve gesturing with passion.

"Was that Marty who blew out of here?" Sam asked.

"Yup and I am going to stay here, Sam," he said. "He met with Genieve who is now over there, probably on the phone with Tom. I think he will end up meeting her here and I want to be here for that. You go and find Penny." Sam nodded and relayed to Greg what was happening.

Sam told Greg he'd be in touch and hung up. "Greg said he, Dana, Wil, and Remi were questioned intently by the police because of a note that fingered Penny."

"The note Milman's been carrying around." Kenneth turned to look at Sam. "The one I suspect Jazz wrote to frame her," he added. "What exactly did it say?"

Sam looked down at the pad of paper in his lap and read, "Penny set whole thing up. She's guilty. Brian, she couldn't go through with wedding and took drastic measures. Ask her about June look alike and Kenneth's fate. Faked kidnappings and if you acquire this note, she killed me, was her plan all along. She blames me for her mother... for Kenneth's addictions and reclusive neglect...for everything." Sam glanced up at Kenneth. Kenneth gripped the side of the car. He felt bloodless, as though the words Sam just read were a needle draining his body of all life force. A grim tense silence soaked the space between them, making it dense with emotion. They each spoke at once.

"It's crazy," Sam said.

"Jazz," Kenneth said. Anger radiated from every pore. "He lives on. Find her Sam, and bring her home, please." Sam nodded fiercely and for once Kenneth applauded Sam's swift exit out of the parking lot.

Kenneth felt more determined than ever to end whatever Jazz had put into motion and he didn't have to wait long in the lobby before Tom pounded into the foyer, grabbed the key from the motel clerk, confirmed the room number three-eleven and headed for the stairs. Kenneth secured Sam's black and orange baseball cap low over his face and followed.

'Let it unfold,' one of his mother's most simple sayings. Maybe he should revise it to, 'may the best screwball win!'

He waited and then found the room. He heard Tom laugh and glasses clinking. He held his ear to the cheap door. A mattress squeaked, and a woman yelped in surprise? Tom laughed and the mattress moaned. She shouted.

"Tommy, I – I changed my mind about some things."

"Mmm, like about my daughter becoming a vegetable?" Tom yelled back. Kenneth couldn't hear what Genieve said. He flattened himself on the floor to try and listen through the crack between the bottom of the door and the floor. Silence for a while then he heard footsteps. Icy fingers of panic hugged him like a boa constrictor. What was happening? Should he try and break in?

A moment later the door swung open. Tom stuck out a hand as Kenneth scrambled to stand up.

"Come on in Kenny, I was expecting you! Join the party." Tom's grin was ugly like a madman with distorted features. He shoved Kenneth through the door and over toward the bed where she lay, looking disoriented and vulnerable. Or was it an act? Had she planned this with Tom all along?

"Describe June's last day to me," Tom demanded. He flung himself half on top of her.

"I'm th-thirts—thirsty," she slurred her words

"Drink," he said. Tom put a vial up to her lips. She automatically opened her mouth.

"NO!" Kenneth propelled his body like a missile, toward her. Tom laughed and kicked Kenneth's shin. Kenneth moaned and rolled onto the floor.

"The June story, come on," Tom said.

"June left you! And I have stayed with you for years, for years I have, have tried to become her to make up for the loss, haven't I?"

"You enjoyed every minute, yet it wasn't enough was it? You were cheating on me with both of them, Marty and Kenny! Isn't that so, Kenny?" Tom turned his hateful look onto Kenneth.

"Stop this! Get off of her!" Kenneth came around to the other side of the bed.

"So who is your final choice honey?" Tom ignored Kenneth.

"Poor geeky Kenny," he chuckled, "always on the losing side or Marty, though not in my league, a mastermind." He slapped her across the face. She put a hand to her burning face and laughed. Kenneth tried to grab Tom's arm. Tom easily spun off the bed and punched him in the jaw. Kenneth reeled back, putting a hand to his aching mouth. Tom slapped her again, harder this time. Kenneth stumbled forward. Tom kicked him again. Kenneth doubled over.

"About June," he growled.

"She wanted an escape because as usual she couldn't stick with anyone person for long! I was so sick of her clawing needs and the way men fell on top of her like sauce on a sundae." She giggled. "Kenneth never could have done those final experiments on her. He said he wanted to be the one, but I knew he required my assistance like he had all along, with the kids, the house. Do you know how many times I stepped in and pretended to be her, long before I actually became her?"

"So you gave her enough to put her into a coma?"

"Hey, I gave her what she wanted – as always, just never the exact way she envisioned but that's life, isn't it?" She laughed, to Kenneth it sounded both bitter and weak.

"She gave me the opportunity I have always wanted. I wasn't about to let it pass me by." She huffed. "She tried to change her mind. Kenneth saw the blood. I'm sorry Kenneth that you were banished to Canada, and blamed. It wasn't your fault. None of us could save her from herself." Kenneth sat on the thin motel carpet. What it must have felt like to have a mother and sister want you gone forever and then men who wanted you for their own purposes! What did you want June? His heart thumped, *to be loved.*

"She was weak, an addict, an emotional wreck all of her life," she said.

"I wonder why?" Kenneth let his words drip with sarcasm. "And if so, why in the hell was your whole life dedicated to having everything she had, to becoming her for God's sake!"

"I tried to love her Kenneth. I tried to help her get well. I helped raise her kids! I had to try out her life to understand her," she explained. Kenneth shook his head.

"Enough with the phony drama," Tom said. He fingered her face. "Nice work with the cosmetic surgery. Was that Kathy's husband, Jerry?" he asked.

"Yes," she said. "That was what some of Jazz's more edgy experiments were about, trying to alter personality. Why did Penny have to call and get everything stirred up? You put her up to it didn't you Kenny? You couldn't stand not really knowing about June's last few hours!"

"I do not control other people's lives," Kenneth retorted.

"When did you hook up with Marty?" Tom asked.

"A while back," she said evasively.

"How long," he demanded. "And I am guessing you have always kept in some sort of touch with him." Tom pointed to Kenneth. She shrugged.

"Yes, and what a fool I have been." Kenneth said.

"No surprises there," Tom smirked.

"Years Tom, years, I kept up with both of them!" Genieve raised herself up onto her elbows and shouted at Tom. Disgust surged through Kenneth. It was time to go. Let them kill each other for all he cared. He should have stayed with Sam and searched for Penny!

"You weren't faithful to me either Tommy! You want June! You made me become her and still you never really ever had her, did you?" Genieve was panting. She was gloating, goading Tom.

"She loved Jazz and made a home with Kenneth no matter what you tried to do to win her!" Genieve added. Kenneth stood by the door.

Tom withdrew a needle from a bag he grabbed off of the table. He held it over her while he stretched himself across her. She flailed with a strength he must not have expected, knocking the needle from his hand. It dropped from the bed to the floor and rolled. Kenneth ran over, caught it and stumbled toward them. Their bodies shot forward then back. They rolled around on the floor. Her fingers drew close to Kenneth and the needle. He scooted away, staring wildly at the two of them. Which one?

Tom's hand shot out. He knocked the needle out of Kenneth's hand. It spun and rolled. She bit Tom, stretched her arm way out and grabbed the needle.

CHAPTER THIRTY THREE

Penny's eyes fluttered open. "Hey sleepy-head, how are you feeling?"

"Sammy?" she murmured. Penny rubbed her eyes. He ruffled her hair and she smiled. "You look so good." He laughed.

"Can't say the same about you sis," Sam said. "You really need to end this kidnapping hobby of yours." The door flew open and Marty Mapman walked up to her.

"How are you feeling dear?"

"Better," she said.

"Your guardian angel paid you an important visit. You'll need to proceed with a regimen. A couple shots now and then onto the pills."

"I am in charge of her care," Sam said. Sam stepped in front of Penny's bed, blocking Marty's access to her. Penny cleared her throat and touched Sam's arm.

"I need to use the restroom," Penny whispered. Sam waved the nurse away and helped her off the bed.

"I've got it under control!" Sam used his body to shield her from everyone.

"Fine," the nurse said. She threw her hands up in the air and backed away. Dr. Mapman and the nurse argued as Sam and Penny rounded the corner. She spotted the familiar sign for female and entered. Sam followed.

"Uh Sam," she said. Penny gave him a stern look.

"Nope," he said. Sam stared hard at her. "There is no way I am leaving you alone in this place or anywhere else in this country for at least the next century!"

"Sam, please!" Penny pleaded.

"Okay I'll put in a quick call to Greg but I am standing right outside the door." Penny eavesdropped as she took her time.

"How can Penny be responsible for everything?" Sam spoke, irritation distinctly framing each of his words. "Okay, yes, she was the one who contacted Jazz. So she agreed to marry Brian only to maim him? And why would she endanger her own health? Hang on hang on, Penny you okay in there?"

"Yes, I'll be out in a minute," she said. She washed her hands and face. Keeping her eyes on the sink as much as possible, to avoid her pale, sick features!

"They're blaming me?" she whispered. "Is it true, mommy? Because I wanted to know why you chose Jazz and Tom, and did those experiments." She sucked in her breath. "Why did you marry Kenneth? Did you love him or was it to spite Jazz?" She could hear Sam murmuring into the phone to Greg. She stared hard at her features. She looked like her mother in small ways, her wide, infectious smile, her almond-shaped eyes that narrowed when she was mad and the way her chin tilted up when she set her mind to something.

"You let yourself become lost," she whispered to her mother. "Help me!"

Genieve touched the needle but as her fingers tried to close around the fat part, it rolled a few inches away, out of her reach. Tom leaned his full weight into her midsection, grabbed the errant needle and put it up against her neck. She went limp.

"What's in that?" she whispered.

"You'll soon find out," Tom said.

"Kenneth, help me, please," she pleaded. Five feet away from them, Kenneth was like a block of ice.

"It's all about mind control." Tom laughed as though she were stupid.

"No it's about using potent, addictive drugs," she argued. "My headaches," she accused.

"It was your choice." Tom said. Her eyes fluttered closed.

"I was in pain," she murmured. "Kenneth." Tom poised the sharp tip of the needle against her neck. Kenneth trembled. He knelt on both knees and began to slowly inch his way toward them

"Tommy," she panted.

"June should have been mine." He hissed like a threatened snake. "All of you interfered, influencing her, taking her away from me. I had plans. You stepped in that day and put her in a coma!"

"She wanted it!" she cried.

"Maybe I would have had a chance with my daughter, Penny. I didn't even know about her until years later. June finally told me over the phone when she was drunk as a skunk! She was so very unhappy in her life with you Kenny and Jazz only made her feel worse."

"I tried to help her." Kenneth rasped, on his knees close to where they lay.

"You wouldn't allow her to leave and Jazz, with his charm kept June hooked to him like an appendage." Tom said.

"She was afraid of you! I tried to be a better her for you!" Genieve whispered with passion.

Tom laughed. "You despised her and yet you spent your whole life trying to become her!" He laughed harder, a wicked sound. "You killed her that day. You tricked her into thinking she could escape Kenneth and be with Jazz forever! You gave her all the narcotics you could lay your hands on for months and months. She was a mess and I couldn't fix her after you all were done with her!" A groan of pain seemed to explode from Tom's chest. He slammed one fist onto the floor and his face was screwed up with the agony of defeat or regret? Kenneth couldn't tell.

"We all killed her," Kenneth moaned aloud.

"She wanted notoriety! She begged me for more," Genieve said in a whisper. Her eyes closed as if they felt too heavy to remain open.

"Did you kill Kathy too?" Kenneth asked her, ignoring Tom.

Maybe he should let him kill her now. She was the one who had been in the house that night with him when he found June. He sat back on his heels as the revelations flowed through him like a dam that had burst.

She took June away before he had the chance. She framed him. She was at the lab just before the police came and questioned him. She insinuated herself into their lives when June was weak or gone, encouraging confusion and turning those feelings to her favor.

"Was Kathy there with you that night I came home to find June bleeding and unconscious?"

"Yes, we were supposed to finish her off. However, Kathy was angry because June was rethinking things after her conversation with you Kenneth. She kept mumbling how she had let you and the kids down, that maybe it was time to face her mistakes." Kenneth interrupted.

"Why then," he said. His voice was hoarse with unshed tears.

"Kathy argued with June. June made a grab for the phone but she was so drunk. The cord tangled around her. She fell and hit her head hit on the corner of the long dresser. I panicked." Tom snorted.

"I ran out then I heard you come in. We fought then hid in the closet. We decided to get her out of there. Tom tried to bring her around but after all we had given her I guess it didn't matter." Tom grimaced.

"She called me or was that you?" Kenneth asked. Tom must have loved June, in his own way. He had used Genieve to fill a need and to punish her for June's permanent disappearance.

"Me. I wanted you to wonder what had happened. There was hope. She wasn't in a coma quite yet!" Genieve said.

"You squashed all chances of that Gen," Tom accused. Kenneth had to agree.

"I didn't touch the kids and I've tried to help Penny through this whole revenge scheme."

"You blew it over and over again!" Tom's angry countenance was ugly. Kenneth forced his legs into a squat. He would have to act fast. He leaned forward but Tom surprised him. He lowered his mouth to Genieve's. Their kissing grew frenzied. Kenneth fell to the floor on all fours, horrified.

Genieve pressed her body into Tom's, knocking the needle out of his grasp. It rolled under a table. She watched it then looked with pleading hopeful eyes at Kenneth. Kenneth was careful to keep his look neutral. His heart pounded, making his shirt appear to house a live critter. Tom seemed engrossed in having his way with Genieve one last time, right in front of him!

Sam looped an arm around Penny as they walked back into the main part of the clinic together.

"Greg said Brian is really coming around. He's speaking words."

"I dreamed he was calling to me," Penny said.

"Cool, Wil is with him every day and he tells the doctors that Brian squeezes his hand whenever he talks about you," Sam added. "He told him we found you and that you'll be back to sit with him soon." Penny sank into a chair in the waiting room, touching Sam's arm, she smiled up at him.

"Are you a fan of Brian's now, Sammy?"

"Not exactly but I wouldn't wish this kind of nightmare he's going through on anyone."

"When can we head back?" she asked.

"I need to check a few things out first, okay? It won't be long, I promise."

"Sam," her voice wavered. "Mom's here." Sam stared at her.

"Penny," he said. He put a hand to her forehead but she swatted it away.

"I saw her and Jazz and he spoke in a mechanical voice. Kathy and other colleagues of dad's are all inside a room in this building in beds." She pointed toward the back of the clinic. Sam's black eyes widened like a sink hole.

"Sam, Mom was warm. I tried to talk to her." Penny studied her shoe.

"You were dreaming."

"NO it was real!"

"You said Brian spoke to you." Sam squeezed her shoulder.

"Go look before Marty hides them!"

"Show me!" he commanded. Tears made it hard to see as they walked down the long corridor. Sam slipped an arm around her waist. She stiffened for a moment then she leaned against his solid strength.

"There were beeping noises and bells. This woman helped me. I dropped my cell phone and I noticed other beds and I heard Jazz's voice," she said.

"What woman," he asked.

"Aunt Genieve who I believe visited me, came to the engagement party and pretended to be mom. She saved me because of a promise she made to mom." Sam interrupted.

"Or because of the guilt she carries around about what she did to mom," he said.

They reached big double doors. Penny started to shake.

"I can do this myself." Sam turned to hug her.

"None of them were dead exactly. They were in a limbo state." She pulled away.

"You mean they're in comas like Brian? You think that was supposed to be your fate?" He rasped. She nodded. He hugged her tight.

Footsteps pounded down the hallway. Penny jumped. Sam shoved her behind him and kept one arm touching her waist.

"You can't go in there, not without my permission," Dr. Marty Mapman said. "It is for authorized personnel only!" Marty ran up toward them. "I have been looking for the two of you."

"Hey," Milman said from behind Marty. A nurse came to stand next to Penny.

"You should come with me dear and rest." She tried to take Penny's arm.

"Get your hands off of my sister. You have done all the damage you are ever going to do to my family!"

"You two are trespassing!" Marty said.

"You mean you don't wish for us to discover the warehouse of victims of your work!" Penny snapped.

Tom rolled onto his side. Kenneth felt a waterfall of relief cascade over him. He was not a sex voyeur! Tom sprung up and jabbed the needle into her arm, grinning with triumph as Kenneth's mouth fell open.

"Bath time," Tom said. He scooped Genieve up into his arms. Kenneth stood up. He needed to go but what about Tom?

Tom dropped Genieve into the tub with a thud.

"Ow," she said. He turned on the water.

"Nice and warm, like the place you are headed to." Tom's laugh was ugly.

"What if I really am June?" She smiled up at them as the warm water sloshed against her half-clothed body.

"Monster," Kenneth mumbled. He was unable to tear his eyes away from the scene.

"Helped," she mumbled.

"Debatable honey," Tom said. The water nearly covered her whole body. He touched his lips to hers. Her eyes were open. Kenneth watched them widened to the size of the Gulf of Mexico. Tom spun around on his knees.

"You haven't the nerve!" Tom spat as he yanked another needle from his pocket. He looked ready to launch himself.

"Sorry," Genieve said. She gurgled as bubbles popped from her mouth and water overflowed out onto the bathroom floor. Tom shot his body forward with the needle extended out in front of him and slipped. He smacked his head on the side of the tub. A sickening thud that made Kenneth throw back his head and guffaw.

"Payback bites," Kenneth said. He chuckled. Tom's body twitched and jerked. His head rested at an odd angle. His eyes registered shock. The needle he had been holding bobbed in the water. Kenneth searched Tom's pockets, extracted a vial and another needle and tossed them into the water.

"You came well prepared. I am impressed Tom." He kicked Tom in the ribs. "Thanks for everything." Kenneth couldn't seem to stop his legs as he relived the horror of June's addiction at their hands.

The water sloshed over the sides of the tub and turned red upon meeting Tom's body. He stepped back. Water was beginning to snake its way to outside the bathroom perimeters.

'There are times to turn around and show your backside and there are times to plant it somewhere!' His mama's words reverberated.

He slipped his shoes off at the edge of the last puddle and holding them in one hand jogged around the room. He erased himself, for once enjoying becoming invisible. Satisfied he turned and ran to the door, yanked his sleeves down over his hands before making his way out.

CHAPTER THIRTY FOUR

"Where is he?" Milman shouted as he catapulted himself around Marty.

"How did you get here? Is Brian okay?" Penny asked.

"Yes, Ruth and John are with him. I flew up here with Sam's friends to see Jazz as soon as I learned about this place. Now let me through!"

"Can't you people read the sign?" Marty pointed to the red letters. "Authorized Personnel only," he said. Marty was interrupted by two policemen.

"Move aside, sir. They have a right to enter. They have relatives in there." One detective showed his badge and nodded at Sam.

"They don't have rights! I am the director of this clinic and without a search warrant," Marty said. He was shoved aside by Milman, Sam and the two detectives.

"I am calling my lawyer!" Marty made an about face turn.

Whatever, Penny thought. All she wanted was to go home but she couldn't leave until Sam saw mom. Penny hugged herself and stayed in the back of the room. Milman and Sam searched the beds.

"Jazz," Milman said. He bent over close to his brother's face. "It's Mil." Milman paused then he leaned closer. "Are you here like this because of Marty? Squeeze my hand, blink, anything to let me know you heard me!" he implored.

"Where is she Penny?" Sam looked back at her and Penny pointed to another row of beds. Penny knew what he saw. They looked like they were sleeping. Sam caught Milman's eye and gestured with his finger his intention to search the room further. Milman nodded then turned back to his brother. Jazz still hadn't moved or responded. Milman sighed and rested against the side of the bed. He rubbed his forehead and then stared down again at Jazz.

Sam's phone rang. "Yes? Okay. Good. Let us know about Brian. We've seen Jazz. I am looking for mom. Yup, be in touch."

"Greg?" Milman asked.

"Yes. Your son continues to improve, don't worry." Sam continued to scan the room. Penny watched him hesitate. His steps slowed and he ran a shaking hand through his thick black hair. Milman must have noticed too because he made his way over to Sam.

"Is it her?" he asked. Sam didn't answer but moved up close and Penny couldn't help herself. She joined them.

"Mom," Sam said. His voice was so soft that Penny barely heard him. They leaned forward and examined her. Sam touched her hair then her cheek. She didn't move, though her skin was warm.

"She's alive." Sam turned to look at Penny and Milman. His eyes were full. Hope, confusion, pain and more filled them. Penny knew, because she felt it all too and she nodded. Milman put a hand on Sam and Penny's backs. They looked at June. Her eyes remained closed. Despite everything, Penny was suddenly clear about one thing. A surge of a myriad of intense feelings flooded Penny.

"I love you mom." Sam echoed her.

The door opened. Marty appeared. Penny thought he seemed very sure of himself despite the fact that he would soon be exposed, for all the mistakes he had made. He checked his watch and pulled a cell phone out of his white coat. Sam and Milman roamed from bed to bed.

"Yes, who is this?" Marty was surprised. Penny tried to catch Sam's attention, but he was too engrossed in what he was doing.

"Well yes, but I was trying to reach my lawyer and then my—

my girlfriend. She hasn't answered her phone. What do you mean? And to whom am I speaking please?"

Penny watched his face grow tense and angry.

"Genieve Endence," he said. Marty seemed unsure. "She might be using the last name, Mott, or Mapman. What? Because I don't know if she married him!" He sounded like he was speaking into a megaphone.

Penny backed up as she listened, taking small steps in Sam's direction. Something had happened to her aunt. Penny glanced over to a bed where she thought her Aunt Genieve was housed but she recalled the woman's face hadn't really resembled her aunt when she had closely inspected it.

"It's complicated," Marty said. His face was the color of a fire engine. He fidgeted with a blanket on one of the beds and exhaled loudly. "Dr. Marty Mapman, now please tell me what happened officer."

Penny touched Sam and Milman's arms and nodded toward Marty, putting a finger to her lips.

"Plumbing problems? What are you saying? What happened?" Marty snapped. "No I have rounds. Camden, Maine, please sir is Genieve okay?"

Sam whispered, "Dad stayed behind to confront Genieve."

"I think she was the one who helped me when I was laying on one of these beds." Penny said. Milman put his index finger to his mouth.

"Bl-blood, there was a fight?" Marty ran a hand over his balding head like he was smoothing out dough for a pie. "Dead, a man and a woman," Marty squeaked. He spun around, stared at all three of them with venom in his black eyes.

"It was Kenneth Patrick!" Marty stabbed the air with his index finger. "He is a murderer!"

"What?" Sam strode over to Marty. His two detective friends were by his side.

"Sam," One detective said.

"Don't do anything you will regret. He's not worth it," the other detective said.

"Needles in the tub," Marty said into the phone. I am at the Forward Thinking clinic in Camden Maine. It's near the Manomly clinic off of Interstate 95."

"One last thing officer," Marty pleaded. "Are you sure that she is dead? Sometimes heavy doses of certain drug-like substances mimic a death-like state, such as a coma." Marty wiped his forehead and glared at Sam, Penny and Milman.

Kenneth sat in the corner of the hospital room after deciding his best defense would be to hurry back to Brian's bedside. Only Sam knew he had gone to the motel where Genieve was meeting Tom but he could claim he never found her. Or it wasn't her. Or Tom never showed up. It could be a long time before they were discovered.

The good news was Brian had been moved out of ICU and he was steadily improving. The trick will be to not allow the blame for Brian's accident or Gen and Tom's deaths or whatever has happened to Jazz, to be placed on him! Furthermore he could not let Penny take the fall either.

"Brian honey, you're okay. You are coming back to us now. Take your time. Are you having nightmares about the accident? Are you in pain?" Brian's mother fussed. Kenneth ached for his mother who would have been his greatest ally! Despite all the trouble he stumbled into time and time again.

"Pe—penny," Brian said. He was hoarse and a deep frown etched his bruised features.

"Brian, it's Kenneth, she'll be here soon." Kenneth stood by Brian's bed.

"Okay, thanks," Brian said. He nodded off to sleep within a few moments.

"Kenneth is responsible!" Marty raced past them to the bed where Jazz Martin lay.

"You involved Tom and Kenneth! Look at the messes they

created!"

Sam and Milman ran over. Penny backed up toward the big double doors. Her head throbbed. She longed to see Brian and her beloved mutt Henry and have her brother Greg and his wife Nancy fuss over her. She wanted to bake a wild concoction for Sam and watch him wolf it down and ask for more. She jumped as the doors flew open and two nurses walked in with two more detectives. Marty stood by her mother's bed and pointed at Sam.

"I hope you're satisfied." He looked desperate, panicked, Penny thought. "Your aunt is dead! Your – your father and Tom killed her and now I'll probably take the rap for it and all of this!" Marty swung his arms around the room like he was fighting for his life.

"Dr. Marty Mapman," One detective said. He held up a hand. "Nathan Beats, the officer who you spoke with earlier on the phone, needs you to identify the two bodies discovered in the Motel 6 off route one."

"Wow that was fast! But listen I told him I am busy right now. I have patients to take care of! Can't all of you people see that?" Marty waved a hand around the room. He ran his tongue over his lips and Penny wondered if he tasted poison. The kind he seemed so adept at injecting into others in the name of science.

The detectives moved forward, one saying, "Sir, you need to calm down. There are plenty of nurses on duty right now who can tend to these," he hesitated.

"Victims," Sam supplied.

Mapman laughed. "Yes and make sure you tell the police that your dear father, Kenneth is the perpetrator once again!"

"Sir," the tall meaty detective said. "Let's go identify the bodies."

"Why don't you ask Kenneth to do it? Too busy I presume, running over his son," he said. He pointed to Milman. "As well as interfering in the experiments on Penny and arranging a vengeful marriage scheme, killing Gen and Tom and, did I leave anything out? Yes, I did, how about the on-going affair with the deceased Tom Mott's wife, Genieve?"

"Your girlfriend," the meaty detective said. He looked down briefly at his small white notebook.

"Can't confirm anything yet Sam." The detective standing next to Sam threw the reassurance softly over his shoulder.

"We were supposed to finally be together. She was leaving Tom. She wanted one last goodbye, to settle the score 'her way' she said." Marty's shell was cracking.

"You have some explaining to do," Milman piped up. "What exactly did you do to my brother, June and all these others here?" He pointed around the room.

"That's supposed to be my line," one officer joked.

"They *willingly* made contributions to the study of addiction." He smiled at his live audience. "Lots of people paid big money. Jazz hooked me with his games of addiction through emotional mind control and drugs. We created chemical mixtures with drugs and we used placeboes to create 'dependencies' of all types. We played with adaptogens, a handful of herbs that increase cellular energy production and counteract the effects of stress. We called them immune enhancers. And then Jazz allowed his personal feelings to ruin the work. He became obsessed with June." Sam moved toward where his mother lay still as Marty explained and paced around the room. Penny sat down on one of the chairs near a wall by one of the beds.

"The triangles of love, and need—addiction grew. It was no longer experiments it was our lives! June for him, Genieve for me, Tom and June, Kenneth and Genieve, you name it, the combinations grew complex. He wanted this! Jazz was like the director of an orchestra."

Sam interrupted, "Are they dead?"

"Their bodies eventually give out, but in the mean time, a host of experimentation can continue."

"Don't worry," one detective said to Sam. "This place will be shut down. And legitimate *professionals* will see what can be done for these folks! Meanwhile sir, you'll be answering questions downtown," the heavy-set detective said.

"Genieve put your mother here," Mapman blurted.

"What," Sam asked. He spun around to stare at him.

The detective spoke up, "with a little extra help from you I assume?"

Mapman snorted, "Try Tom and Kenneth!"

"My father did NOT kill my mother nor did my aunt! It was you!" Sam strode over to Marty. "You talk, talk, and talk." Sam gestured with his fingers. "Entertaining is all it is to you." Sam gestured to all of the people in the room. "You did this! YOU!" He aimed his index finger like a dagger thrusting into Marty's chest. Two officers stepped next to Sam and Marty.

"Okay, okay, let's go!" One read Marty his rights as he handcuffed him.

"Oh there's so much you don't know," Mapman taunted.

"And you will be enlightening us all down at the station after you identify the bodies of your beloved colleagues."

The bulky officer stepped forward and took hold of Marty's left upper arm. When he struggled to twist free a second and third officer stepped closer. Marty jerked his body to the left and toward the door. The officers gripped his upper arms tight and twisted, Marty howled in pain and they left.

"Where is my father?" Sam hurled the question at Marty's retreating back.

"He is traveling to faraway lands, escaping his many crimes! After all running away is what he does best!" Marty grinned.

"We'll get to the bottom of things Sam. Don't take this crazy guy's babbling seriously," the detective assured Sam.

"He might be visiting Brian," the other detective said. "We haven't had time to call back to confirm this information."

Sam pulled out his phone. "There are two missed calls, both from Kenneth," he said to Penny.

"Can we go home, please?" she cried.

Before they left one detective who stayed behind to begin the investigation of the clinic and its inhabitants informed them that Marty would be taken into custody and the clinic closed off for a full investigation. All patients would be transferred and examined closely.

"Please be gentle with our mother, June," Sam pleaded.

"Of course," Sam's friend said.

Penny let out the breath she had been holding for the last number of hours. Sam drove for a few hours and then stopped for gas and coffee. Penny didn't want anything. She rested her head against the back window and watched the tall pines and black-eyed Susan's while Milman called Greg.

Kenneth was visiting Brian and Brian was asking for her. What was Brian thinking? Did he realize Jazz or Tom through Kenneth tried to kill him? Would Brian recover?

She leaned her head into cool smooth glass and a puddle formed, like in a sudden rainstorm. She prayed there would be a rainbow at the end of it all.

CHAPTER THIRTY FIVE

She was driving out of a long dark tunnel. Someone was yelling.

"It's locked! Is she alone?"

Her eyes flickered open and a man with a surgical mask leaned over her. "Penny," he said. He pressed a hand on her shoulder. Alarm shot through her like a bolt of lightning.

"It's me, dad." Kenneth lowered the mask. Her body was like a shelf of books. There was loud knocking at her door and voices calling her name.

"You're in the same hospital as Brian. You were sleeping when they brought you in. You're supposed to rest. Don't answer them for now Penny, please. I wanted a few minutes alone with you, okay?"

"Okay but why are you wearing scrubs and a mask, dad?"

"Henry's fine. You're neighbor Din, is taking care of him," Kenneth said.

"Okay. Are you about to run away again?"

"I have to head back up to Canada. I need to take care of June and a few other things before I do some necessary traveling. I will be back for your wedding though," a small tentative smile relaxed his features.

"Dad, don't." A stick was in her throat, she coughed but it was stuck. The knocking on her door had stopped. It was quiet except for the thundering of her heart.

"Penny, I know it hasn't been an easy road with us." His eyes were sad and she interrupted.

"You're the only dad I have." She wiped a tear away.

Cindy Simon

"Thank-you and you are a wonderful daughter with all of your mother's good qualities, Penny. Give Brian a chance. She would want that." Penny thought for a moment of Genieve's similar advice. "I think he is a decent young man, nothing like his uncle," Kenneth said.

"I thought you didn't approve?"

"I didn't want Jazz orchestrating our lives anymore," he said.

"Is Mom in a coma? Is that why she never came back?" she pushed a few long thick strands of her hair out of her face and reached for the cup of water on her bed side stand. Kenneth helped her and she drank a whole cup.

"Yes," he stroked her hair. She lay back against the pillows and sighed. Her eyes were suddenly very heavy. Her bones were made of concrete.

"Rest, okay? Take care of yourself and help Brian recover and I'll be in touch. We'll talk." He kissed the top of her head. Footsteps outside her door and the knocking began.

"Goodbye for now, sweetheart," Kenneth said. Keys jangled in the door to Penny's room. Kenneth climbed out the window and jumped the short distance to the ground and limped to the waiting cab. He instructed the driver to take him to the airport. He bent to massage his old legs.

"You okay?" the driver asked, eyeing his scrubs.

"Sure and you," Kenneth asked.

"Never better," the taxi cab driver smiled back. Kenneth pulled his cell phone out of his pocket.

"Hey," he said. "Is everything okay?"

"Not really."

"What's been going on?"

"Marty was frantic while Milman and Sam were discovering all the *mistakes.*" The loyal nurse reported. Kenneth sighed. "The police have him now, questioning him about Genieve and Tom's deaths and the drugs they found there."

Kenneth rubbed the curls on his head.

"Hard to do?" she asked. He didn't respond, "Didn't end up as you hoped? Plus it must be difficult to leave your children, again?"

"Things rarely end up like we expect. I explained to Penny and I am sure Sam will be in touch. My leaving is necessary," he said.

"Listen thanks, Marguerite for everything." He hung up before she could ask any more questions. There were hidden parts to the experiments that needed to remain so, sealed in the ones that were gone!

'The mystery of another's soul cannot be found by anyone else', Mama would say. He leaned into the ripped vinyl seat. Relief poured over him like a cool shower after a hot day spent in the sun. Tom deserved his fate, as Jazz did.

His cravings had ended. Genieve had slipped him the necessary antidotes, helped Penny, kept Tom at bay and taken ultimate care of Jazz with Tom but she was a true double-edged sword. Life was indeed complicated. Time to simplify again in Canada, he sighed. A lot more was now right. He could relax.

"Penny!" She awoke this time to Greg stroking her hair. "You okay? Who was in here? Why was your door locked?"

"Daddy was here. He wanted to see me before he left for Canada," she yawned. She must have been asleep five minutes. Why did it feel like hours? Her eyes fluttered like the tides.

"Let her sleep, you can see she's fine, Greg." Wil said.

"Yeah okay, glad you're safe sis," Greg said. "I still don't get why dad had to be so secretive and lock the door. Do you think he gave her stuff?"

"No Greggie, I'm fine." She murmured before drifting off.

Hours later Penny opened her eyes and stretched. Penny rolled onto her side and noticed the covers on the other bed in the room were rumpled and pulled back as though someone had just been there. She glanced at the bedside clock. It was nine o'clock and through the blinds she could see the sun shining and needles of a pine tree swaying in the breeze. There was a tap on her door.

"Well hello Ms. Penny," the nurse said. "You've been out for quite a while, how do you feel? I'm Karen by the way."

"Better thanks."

"He should be back soon." She winked at Penny, indicating the empty rumpled bed next to Penny's.

"He," Penny asked with a frown. Did they allow male and female patients in the same room?

"Oh honey, you don't remember?" Penny swung her head back and forth. "Let me check a few of your vitals okay?" She took Penny's pulse, blood pressure and temperature.

Is Brian rooming with me?" Penny asked.

"Yes dear and he is getting better every hour that goes by and it is helping him immensely knowing you are here beside him. It was my idea." She winked as she tightened the blood pressure cuff on her arm.

Tears trickled down the sides of her face. "I could fill an ocean up by now." Penny laughed and the nurse smiled at her and patted her arm.

"Hey, are you okay?" Greg walked in and seeing her distress was by her side in one second flat.

"I feel." She paused. "Lost," she whispered. Greg glanced at the nurse.

"Can you give us a minute?" Greg asked them. The nurse nodded.

"Sure hon, take your time."

"So," Greg said. "You've had quite a time of it lately, hmmm?" There was a knock on the door before it swung open and Penny cried out.

"Oh Nance," she moaned. Her arms swung open like a revolving door. Nancy gave her a watery hug. "I want to go home. I miss Henry. Is he okay?"

"He's great. Din is fussy but wonderful and I just stopped by and walked him a little while ago." Greg smiled.

"Look who is up and about." Dana popped her head inside the open door. "Can I join the party?" They hugged tightly. Penny wiped her messy face.

"I bathe myself," she said, laughing about her ever present tears. "How's work?" Penny was anxious about Angela's patience with her. "Do I still have a job?" She tucked a strand of hair behind one ear over and over again.

"You are irreplaceable Penny! Besides we've been covering

for you."

"Thanks," Penny said. She breathed out like a whale as she sat back in bed. "I want to go home," she said.

"Probably tomorrow Pens, you need to rest and continue to help Brian," Greg said.

"How, if I wasn't even conscious," she wailed. "Was he in here when dad visited me last night, I guess?"

"I don't know when he was moved into your room but honey, I do know your presence is tremendously healing to him," Nance said. Greg rubbed Penny's back as he and Nancy answered her myriad of questions about what had gone on since she had been sleeping.

"What will happen to mom?" Her heart slipped up into her throat.

"Sam and dad are working on it. Relax okay. You've had quite an ordeal. Let us figure it out." Greg said.

"You'll tell me everything?"

"Of course," Greg assured her.

"Why don't I believe you?" Penny asked.

"Trust issues," Dana murmured.

"You're one to talk," Penny said, smiling.

Dana smiled back. "Work is not the same without you Pen. I miss our chats and meals together," Dana said.

"I do too, believe me! I want to hear about your life." She dropped her voice and smiled at her friend. "I swear on a stack of bibles to let things go more!" She looked to Greg then Nance.

"No guilt allowed," Nance said. "Or crying," Nancy said. Her blue eyes became swimming pools to match her own.

"Or self-flagellation," Greg added. Penny leaned back against the pillows, sniffling and wiping her cheeks. Until one by one they left and sleep took her away again.

A few days later Kenneth sat in the airport. He forced himself to listen to Sam's harsh reprimands.

"Look, I did not run over Brian."

"I need to know the truth so Penny will stop blaming herself, dad."

"Okay. Technically speaking I was in the car and I may have been driving, but I was drunk! "

"You hit Brian?"

"Yes."

"You're saying none of this is your fault because you were drunk!" Sam hollered. "Does that truth hold for all your other mistakes? Like mom's addiction and coma, your affair with Genieve and alliance with Tom Mott, your work with Marty," Kenneth interrupted.

"Enough! I know what I did but I was also set up for a lot of that," Kenneth said.

"Old news," Sam spat.

"I have to go." Kenneth stood in line to board his foreign flight. "Welcome Brian into the family okay?"

"You're running away again? Penny was right. Is it permanent this time?" Sam sounded shocked.

"I told her I'd be back for the wedding."

"Why disappear again like before, need I remind you, when you claim or claimed then innocence to the vast array of crimes before you? And I am not just talking about Brian's *accident*. There is the probable fact that you were involved in Tom and Genieve's deaths and the multitude of folks in comas in the Maine clinic, and there are other clinics aren't there? I know there are a few in the Northeast, Canada and abroad, aren't there?"

"You did your research," Kenneth replied. "I am not running away. I need to take care of a few things. I'll be back and I'll stay in touch like I have always done to some degree. You three, didn't want to hear from me much last time, remember? I need to get well too again, Sam."

"Are you're responsible for mom becoming a vegetable?" Sam punched him.

"Absolutely not," Kenneth said. His tone was like a sharp knife. "She made her own choices and mostly she acted on Jazz and Tom's ideas, not mine. Genieve only added to the volatile cocktail, so to speak. I tried to talk June into other solutions but she wouldn't listen. I pleaded with her Sam, to go into rehab with me on numerous occasions. Together we could have recovered from these addictions we both indulged in for the sake of the work. It took over our lives. She wouldn't give up what Jazz and Genieve promised."

"She chose Jazz and to remain an addict," Sam confirmed.

"Yes, though she never saw it that way. Look, I will work to help June and the others too. There are excellent facilities to attend to their needs but I won't apologize for the fates of Tom and Genieve or Jazz. They deserved what they got!" Kenneth added in a low voice. "I have never proclaimed innocence. I did what I had to do, much of the time and still do."

"Yeah, looking out for number one," Sam grumbled.

"Not always true. I tried to help Penny and Genieve, June many times. I tried to follow Jazz's demands. Nothing is as it seems, Sam."

"With liars, no," Sam said. He used a nasty tone.

"Look, it's over finally. Can't you be satisfied with the truths you did find out at least for the time being? I need to rehab a bit more to fully regain my health once and for all. Then I will be in touch and I can try and explain more of what I know."

"Wait, at least answer this with the truth! Why should Brian and Penny marry?"

"It's a good thing that came out of all of this Sammy."

"How is it real? How do we know we can trust Brian and that he's right for Penny?"

"Or that I don't have some hidden agenda? Is that what you're alluding to Sam?"

"Yeah, maybe," Sam admitted.

"Trust is illusive, Sam. For the record I think Genieve helped Penny recover and she acted as a buffer between Tom and us when she could."

"Yeah, she has had more than a soft spot for you over the years."

"Brian is a decent man, look at Milman, John and Ruth, they're a good family. You have severe trust issues, Sam and it is not healthy."

"Thanks for the gifts that keep on giving dad!"

"I am sorry Sam." Kenneth exhaled loudly into the phone. "I loved your mother," Kenneth replied, wearing his deepest feelings on his sleeve as best he could. He wanted Sam to feel it with him.

"I have to go. I am boarding the plane in a few minutes."

"Thanks at least for checking on us, especially Penny," Sam acknowledged. His voice was softer. He had heard Kenneth.

"Sure thing, I will be in touch soon. Please help your sister. You do know that Tom was her father, you're mine and Greg's father is Jazz? At least from a biological perspective, but I love each of you as if you were mine."

Kenneth sat back and looked out the window of the plane. They were about to take off. He smiled. The first thing he would do when he eventually arrived home in Canada was to burn all those files! 'Time to let the past slumber' one of his mother's sayings, and he planned to finally listen.

CHAPTER THIRTY SIX

Penny wobbled out of bed. It was very dark. She groped her way to the bathroom and back to bed. A folded piece of paper lay half under her pillow, in Kenneth's handwriting and she went back to the bathroom to read it.

Perhaps it all had been worth it, for a fresh start with him and in a way her mother. She couldn't change what they had done or how they had chosen to live but she could alter her perspective. It wasn't her fault. They loved her and had tried to do their best.

She re-read his apology and his declaration of love for her, her mother, and her brothers. He wrote about how much her mother had treasured having a daughter. She rolled over and closed her eyes, clutching the note against her chest.

She opened her eyes to a glorious sunny day. She blinked and stretched. A nurse knocked gently on the door. The bed next to her was empty again. The covers were all scrunched, so Brian must have slept there. She should have talked to him when she was up in the middle of the night.

"You can go home today!" Penny smiled at the nurse. She set down her breakfast and Penny did her best to eat the cold cereal, fruit and juice.

Sam pushed her in the hospital required wheelchair and they made their way to see Brian who was in the physical therapy room. As they waited at the elevator, Nance, Dana, Wil, Sam, and Greg stood beside Penny.

The elevator doors opened. Penny eagerly leaned forward to try and peer in the rectangular window as they came over to where Brian was working his body. She could see Milman, Ruth and John. She angled her body further and then she saw him, sweat poured down his face and stained his t-shirt. Her heart felt like it would burst out of her chest. Then she jumped as Greg spoke behind her.

"We all wanted the truth for years Pen. You just had the guts to confront it head on," Greg said.

"Yeah and look where it got me?" Penny cried. She put a hand to her chest as she watched Brian struggle.

"Some of the answers at least," Dana spoke up.

"It's all going to work out in the end," Wil added.

"No one ever believed I was responsible for Brian's *accident* did they?" She shivered.

"No," everyone said.

"We didn't believe you were responsible," Dana said.

"You are not responsible for any of this mess Pen," Wil added.

"Brian doesn't believe?" Penny whispered.

"No," Wil said. He was firm.

"Was Kenneth the one who ran over Brian?" Dana blurted.

Penny felt a bolt of electricity race through her body. She turned to Sam.

"I, I heard someone talking," Dana stammered.

Sam cleared his throat, hesitated then cleared it again. All eyes were on him. "I spoke with dad."

"He left me a note after he visited yesterday. He never mentioned trying to ki—kill Brian!" The words rushed out of Penny's mouth like a swollen river on a mountainside. Her eyes followed Brian walking albeit slowly but relief flooded her. She wasn't in the car that hit him!

"Why didn't you mention this earlier to me?" Greg said.

"What did he say?" Nancy asked.

"Let the guy talk," Wil said.

"Is he responsible—did he admit it?" Dana interrupted.

"Okay, okay," Sam said. He held up a hand. "It was yesterday, I think, or the day before. I don't know." He ran a hand roughly through his black hair. "He confirmed a few things. One, mom has been in the clinic where Penny was taken and another one before that, that was located in Nova Scotia. She and Jazz are being transferred and the police are conducting full investigations. Dad said he will make sure everyone is thoroughly examined."

"So it was like Penny said." As soon as the words came out Dana blushed.

"It's okay." Penny jumped in. "I wasn't sure."

"She's been in this odd coma-like-frozen state for many years and Dad visited her at a clinic in Nova Scotia for years without our knowledge?" Greg was angry. Nance squeezed his hand.

"He claims he was protecting us," Sam answered.

"Bull crap," said Greg.

"Probably," said Sam. "Anyhow, Jazz is a more recent addition and is being used for experimentation quite frequently."

"There is some justice," Greg said. "I don't care if he is my biological father." Nancy squeezed his arm and Penny reached out to him. Greg hugged her.

"Dad admitted he drove the car that hit Brian." Sam's voice was like an icy feather going up and down Penny's spine. "He told me he was set up by Tom and that he was under the influence." Sam glanced at Greg. "And he confided to me, Tom and Genieve killed each other with injections just as he broke into their hotel room. He attempted to intervene but it was too late!" Penny felt a lump in her throat the size of Texas.

"I knew he wasn't innocent. He worked for Jazz for years and he had to have collaborated with Tom and of course he was intimate with Aunt Genieve." Greg rubbed a hand across the back of his neck. "I didn't think him capable of murder or attempted murder."

"And that's only what we know for sure," Sam said.

"Yeah, right," Greg said. "I hope I am a better father."

"No doubts honey," Nancy said.

"He always makes it seem like he's a victim." Penny hung her head. She wanted to tear up the ridiculous note. She was clutching it like it was a golden ticket.

"So did mom," Sam reminded her.

"She was more than dad," Penny defended.

"Maybe," Sam said.

"Aunt Genieve," Greg said. Sam interrupted.

"Aunt Genieve was responsible for mom's demise. She played around with all the men mom showed interest in. She became a huge part of Tom's revenge."

"She helped me." Penny felt like a small child.

"Wow," Wil said. "Somebody should write a book about all this!"

"Could Kenneth be protecting someone?" Nance asked.

"Like who?" Greg demanded. "There isn't anyone left to accuse, is there?"

"One of us I guess." Wil's sarcasm was like molasses.

"Jazz already did that," Dana said. "Did Kenneth fly back to Canada?"

"He's going to oversee mom's care and keep residing in Canada. First though, he's going for more rehab while traveling."

"On the run to avoid his guilt," Greg asked. Sam nodded.

"I can't believe they're all dead. Mom, Aunt Genieve, Tom, Jazz might as well be," Penny said.

"Good riddance," Sam and Greg announced.

A door opened in front of them and Milman, Ruth and John emerged from the physical therapy room. Penny grabbed a hold of Sam's arm.

"Later tell me more about how Tom and Aunt Genny died and dad's involvement, okay?" He nodded. "How is he?" she asked Milman. He grasped her hand and smiled.

"Good, good, he wants to see you."

"How are you dear?" Ruth asked her.

"Better, thanks." She smiled though her eyes were focused on Brian. She could see him through the glass, pulling on the huge rings. His arms then his whole body shook.

"He's worried about you," John said.

"He loves you," Ruth said.

"He will make a full recovery. It is a miracle. Experimental treatments have worked wonders. Ironic isn't it?" Milman commented.

Penny nodded and wrung her hands. She tucked strands of her thick hair behind one ear over and over again.

"You look lovely," Ruth said to her. Penny gave her a quivery smile.

"I need to finish my rounds. I'll stop by with some groceries later Penny. Take it easy okay?" Greg said. "I love you, little sister."

"I will and thanks. I love you too Greg." Penny said.

"Hey that goes for me too," Sam said.

"I need to call Remi," Penny said to Dana.

"We've been keeping her up to date." Dana rubbed Penny's back. "I'll call work and figure out your schedule and be in touch Penny."

"Thanks," Penny said. Gratitude filled her up like a hot soup on a cold wintery day.

"My wife thinks I have forgotten I am married," Wil joked. He left to call her. Nancy kissed Penny's cheek.

"Call me for anything, any time, all right?" She grabbed Greg's hand in the hallway where he had waited for her. They kissed and then went their separate ways. Sam hung back. Penny glanced over at him and smiled.

"I'll be okay," her voice cracked. "You need a good long run and a shower," she said.

"Oh I see how it goes. You feel a little better and you're back to giving me orders and the boot?" Sam looped an arm around her shoulders. She leaned in for a brief hug then pulled away.

"Okay, okay I am going. Be careful." He kissed the top of her head. Penny waved and walked to where Brian was waiting. She heard Sam's loud sigh and felt his eyes burning a hole into her back. She turned back and their eyes met. Sam gave a salute and a small grin. He was trying.

"Hey you okay," Brian whispered. His eyes were as bright as a full harvest moon. His voice was raspy.

"Sort of," she said. Brian's cracked lips moved upward into a crooked grin.

"You're working hard." Despite the bruises and cuts he looked amazing. "You look handsome," she murmured. He laughed.

"Ow that hurts," he said. Brian put a hand to his side.

"Sorry," she said. Penny touched a crease in the sheet on the bed, smoothing it out with her fingers a number of times.

"You're still afraid of me," he said. She laughed and shrugged. He pointed to his cheek with his good arm.

"My hugging skills are impaired." He reached out for her hand. His arm shook. Her eyes welled up. She moved toward him.

"I'm so sorry, Brian." Penny's voice quavered.

"You didn't run me over," he said.

"I might as well have. I—I started this whole thing in motion!" A dam burst inside of her. She shivered and wound her arms tightly around her body, trying to hold it together.

Brian patted the bed. Tears rolled down her cheeks. She sat on the very edge.

"You are not responsible for other people's actions!" he reprimanded. "You led us to the clinic and the discoveries there and got this all out into the open." He cleared his throat. "I drank like a fool and crossed a street in the middle of the night without paying attention."

"We were supposed to beat them at their games and we ended stuck as their pawns!"

"They're dead. We are not! I'd say we won." He pointed to his shoulder. She leaned closer. He touched her arm. She laid her head on his shoulder very gently and he stroked her hair and sighed.

"Feels good to touch you," he murmured. "Life is a lot of stumbling and happenstance. Discoveries of the gems that are sprinkled in, is up to us, some come with pain," he grimaced.

"Why does it have to be so hard?" She exhaled a deep breath. "I am sorry I didn't trust you more, that I pushed you away and said you were like Jazz."

"He tried to make me his puppet," Brian said. "I let him succeed way too much and it cost me."

"I know it's stupid, but I wanted mom to be alive and Aunt Genieve to have changed into someone nice and for Tom to not be my real father and,"

"Penny," Brian said.

"And Kenneth," she sighed. "I know he did some good things but, he was heavily involved in the addictions that ruined mom, he had a long affair with Genieve, and he ran you over! He probably killed Tom and Genieve and he knew mom's whereabouts and condition all these years, but never told any of us." Her voice grew louder and full of passion, Brian put a finger to his lips.

"Wow, he ran me over, why? And he killed them and was involved with Genieve and knew about your mom? Jazz was right about him!"

"Well, he was under the influence and Tom really made him run you down. And I don't know all the details about Tom and Genieve's deaths."

"He needs help, but I bet he loves you. It is hard to accept your family's foibles. I am learning though that someone else's mistakes need not define us, unless we allow it."

"How is it you're not bitter?" Penny marveled.

"I am making that choice Penny for my own health and well being. When you almost die and have to re-learn a lot of the basics; it puts a lot of things into perspective, like the need to accept the families we are given despite their warts! It'll be a part of our journey together, like we planned?" he asked. She nodded into his chest.

"Hey, we already got through the hardest part in any relationship. We saw the flaws, made mistakes, met the severely dysfunctional family members. Now it's time for the fun. We have earned some time to coast, maybe years of it! We have some physical recovery work, probably some emotional work too. Who doesn't?" His eyes fluttered.

"I need to let you rest." She tried to pull away. He held onto her, surprising her with his strength. Her legs wobbled and she leaned against the bed. He let go. Kissing his forehead she let her lips linger.

"Sorry for everything," she added.

"Hey, you're not leaving me again and I'm not—sorry that is. It was all meant to be, you know?" He opened his sleepy eyes as he lay back down further to rest.

"Yes," she answered. Suddenly, she felt that he was right.

"Do you have to go? Can't you lay here with me?" he asked.

"Well, I guess for a few minutes anyhow."

"Hey, don't sound so excited," he teased. She kissed his forehead and then poked her head out the door to tell his family. Sam was back and she smiled. She told them everything was fine and that she would stay with Brian for a while longer. Sam started to protest but Milman and his family dragged him away. Finally, Sam laughed and waved for her to go back in to Brian.

Penny snuggled up close to Brian. She thought he had dropped off to sleep but as she cuddled he sighed and touched her hair.

"I love you Penny Patrick, soon to be O'Mackery!" Penny had been settling herself into a comfortable position in what was relatively little space when she bolted upright at his words.

Brian grinned, with his eyes half shut then made smooching noises with his lips. Penny brought her lips to his and they kissed.

"Sealed on a kiss," he murmured. She kissed him again and again. She'd deal with her doubts later.

Penny made it home hours later and fell into bed. Henry curled up half against her and half on top of her. He had been so glad to see her that she had a hard time getting him to settle down. They slept a long while.

Her days became filled with a pleasant routine of naps and being with Brian whereby they talked and shared endlessly laughing and planning. She was able to slowly voice her fears and concerns about marriage. Brian listened and revealed some of his own and they agreed it would be a while anyhow due to his long recovery process. Penny returned to writing and to her counseling job at the crisis center. The weeks went by.

Her brothers grew happy for her, though Sam still had a need to find out all he could about what had happened in that hotel room with Tom and Genieve and at the clinics all these years. He had a feeling his father was more a part of things then he'd thus far admitted. He was determined to learn more details about the exact nature of Jazz's work. Milman promised to help him, since he also craved more specifics about his brother's life.

Jazz Martin died a few months after Penny was found at the clinic. His body gave out. Many of the others housed in the clinic and a few other facilities scattered around the country lived, but only in permanent coma-like states, completely unresponsive.

Over a hundred people from all over attended Jazz Martin's funeral. Milman had decided to honor his brother and the fact that some of his cutting edge ideas were useful, though filled with a multitude of risks and consequences. He had been a charmer. Larger than life for many and so they came to pay their respects. Milman grieved for his brother as did Brian and the rest of the family but they also felt relief.

Kenneth traveled, working on ideas he, Jazz, and Tom had brainstormed years and years earlier before the twisted tangents began. Some of it after all had helped Brian's remarkable recovery.

He took to caring for June and the others he had helped put in the clinics, those that refused to let go for one reason or another. Thus affording further experimentation despite the edgy legalities involved. Perhaps it was as it was supposed to be. June wanted such notoriety!

One night, nearly six months after Penny had discovered her mother in the permanent coma state at the clinic, she had a powerful dream.

"Penny – Pen – Penny," a voice called. From far across a field Penny squinted to make out the lovely figure in a green flowing chiffon-like gown. It was the color of trees in the spring.

"MOM!" she said. Penny ran but no matter how fast she pushed her legs Penny could not grow closer. Bent over, breathless, her legs aching and her arms like bricks; she fell to the ground onto her knees.

"Mommy," she cried.

"Stop trying so hard!" Penny's chest heaved. She gasped and then finally she nodded.

"I did die that day, at least the few parts of me that I tried to have for you, your brothers, and our family. I am grateful I affected a lot of people, just as you seem to be doing too and you're doing it in a much more positive way, honey." She drew closer to where Penny was on her knees, immobile, listening intently.

"The wanting never ends, and that's a good thing dear. It leads you through life, let it do so, but learn to let go sometimes. That's so important though difficult to know when. I never learned! Don't resist what life is. You'll be left like me, in pieces, never satisfied." She smiled and Penny felt warmth and peace. It was as if her mother's words came from inside of her.

"I am okay. I am never alone. Courage is mysterious and comes in all shapes. The power is in the love, both the giving of it and the receiving. Love," the voice said. It was an echo from deep within Penny.

The images faded and Penny slept. She awoke hours later. Bouncing out of bed, she laughed as Henry stuck his rear in the air and wagged his tail. Play time! She heard her mother's infectious laugh. Joy!

Penny knew her mother was always inside of her, guiding her, and helping her whenever she needed it. All she had to learn how to do was ask and let go!

CPSIA information can be obtained at www.ICGtesting.com

228648LV00006B/69/P

9 781612 960210